SMART

Joel Mentmore

SMART

prolibris

SMART

For D, A & M.

Here, at last, is the word I wrote.

Saturday

HI!My name is Werner Brandes.http://goo.gl/eUSkMi

The message was a string of data streamed across the rooftops from the Tea Building base-station on Shoreditch High Street. The data said, I am a text message, I am 49 bytes in total, I am using the normal character set, I am sent today at 2:47 Universal Coordinated Time, I am sent to your number, I am sent from number unknown, and this is my payload:

HI!My name is Werner Brandes.http://goo.gl/eUSkMi

But the message was not from Werner Brandes. Skull knew that. Staring at the words of the message on the screen, Skull knew it was not from Werner Brandes. And Skull knew more. He knew the author — the real author — was Jon Fast; old friend, ex-friend, fool. And he knew he should delete the message, erase it without a second thought, but he'd been out, come home, carried on drinking.

Skull was not a natural drunk (something else he knew). There was no joy in drinking scotch, even very good scotch, at nearly three o'clock in the morning; but while there was no pleasure in the drink itself there was pleasure in the prospect of oblivion, and there was a comfort in the company of pity to be found in the bottle of single malt, as well as the satisfaction in seeking it.

In a better state he had ignored the earlier messages — all of them, deleted. Four yesterday, four the day before, one the day before that. Now new day same message, same link.

And yet a link — any link — in any message, is an invitation to someone's hell. This of all things Skull knew; it was a topic on which he held strong views and could offer pertinent advice: never follow links. Never follow links in messages. Never follow links in messages from friends or friends of friends or family because these are all in the set of Other People, and Other People are promiscuous web-whores walking the Internet for thrills and pleasures lured by the come-on of folksy communities and the promise of free stuff, waving their country bumpkin flag ...

But Jon was his oldest friend, even if now unfriendly because of the argument about money. Jon had said, It's just business — you're a bad risk; and Skull had asked, So our friendship means nothing?

It means nothing; it means nothing. Skull thumbed the blue link on the smartphone screen: *http://goo.gl/eUSkMi*. The smartphone shivered briefly, obediently fetching the web page which streamed a short, unwanted video.

Jon says, Help me. In the video his face is a pixelated orange, a sickly yellow against the grey shadows behind him. As he speaks, he turns towards the figure sitting beside him darkly. The movement is jerky. This other, on the edge of the video, is part neck, part shoulder only.

I cannot, the voice of the other says. The voice is subdued, the voice is flavoured, pitched low, neither old nor young. I told you, it says, there is nothing I can do for you.

I'll pay you, Jon adds but the other quickly says, It won't help. You cannot stop it.

Jon asks, What are my options? There's a note of frustration in his voice, just a ding.

The dark shoulder rises a little, falls suddenly in a shrug, the muffled voice saying, Disappear.

Disappear? Jon glances sharply at the other again, but the voice continues: If it was me, I would disappear until it is completed.

Or I could take the chance, Jon says, but his tone is flat and without conviction. He goes on, Perhaps nothing will happen.

There is a pause, a heartbeat in which a finger of cold white light flicks over Jon. The voice says simply, Perhaps.

Then Jon asks, What would my chances be?

There is merely the hint of a shrug from the other.

The clip ends.

Skull stared dumbly at the small screen, unsure of what he had just watched, unsure of what it meant, unsure whether he cared, decided he did not. The clip had run barely half a minute. The visual quality was poor, shot from a low angle in the dark except for the occasional lick of light as from a distant lighthouse, and a random, pulsing, orange-red glow. Sound was not good either — two flat voices reaching above a scratchy background of chatter and canned music.

Now that he knew he didn't care, he re-ran the clip, hitting pause-play, pause-play, and leering closely at the smartphone to see if he could make out more detail, extract more context. Finally he cast the whole thing onto the large screen on the living room wall hoping for the clarity that comes with scale. All he got was bigger pixel blocks. He shut the browser, deleted the message, and continued sipping his single malt until sleep came.

*

Old people sometimes forget that not everybody wakes at five each morning, has dressed, breakfasted and walked the dogs by seven. Maybe they do remember; maybe they simply can't forgive the world its easy sleep. Professor Fast, in any case, did not own a dog but he did call early, allowing the phone to ring through to the answering machine each time he called. By the time Skull rose from his uneasy sleep to prepare, slowly and with reverence, a multi-shot coffee, the old-fashioned recorder showed twenty four messages waiting for his attention. Five of the messages were from the Professor, all saying the same thing.

"Have you heard from Jon?"

Skull was wary. Professor Fast had never liked him as a boy, was openly hostile now he was a man. "Should I have?" he asked, when finally he returned the calls.

"Should you? It's hardly for me to say whether you should or should not," the Professor responded tightly. "I asked whether you had."

"Indeed," Skull parried.

"Well have you?"

"I haven't." The lie came easily enough although Skull felt it wasn't strictly a lie. The texts and the video clip weren't exactly hearing from Jon. All the same he added some clarity: "We haven't spoken to each other for quite a while now." In fact they hadn't spoken in months.

"Indeed," riposted the Professor, and then after a pause, "Never mind. Worth a try."

A second lengthy pause passed beyond the perimeters of Skull's social comfort zone. Luckily a thought occurred: "Has he asked you to phone me?"

"Who?" barked the Professor.

"Jon."

"Jon? Don't be so absurd. Why would he do that? If I had heard from him I should hardly be calling you. We can't get hold of him. Surely that's the point."

"Indeed." It wasn't impeccable logic that distinguished the Fast family, it was their disdain, Skull recalled. In the Professor's world everyone else was a fool. Skull considered ending the call there but something jarred, something the Professor had said, so he asked, "When was the last time you heard from him?"

"From Jon? Well ..." the Professor dithered professorially. "Let's see: we got the letter early this week but I last actually spoke to him on — on the eleventh day of last month," he said with the sudden precision of a court witness. "That was — that was a Tuesday." Skull actually heard the big index finger tapping at the calendar above the telephone table.

"We?" That had been the jar factor. The Professor lived alone, but he'd said "we".

Now the Professor said, "What?"

"We," insisted Skull.

"We?"

"Yes. You said 'we'."

"Did I? Oh. We. Yes. I said 'we'. Jacqui's with me. She's come to help, so she says. She's right here. She's standing right next to me," he said, hanging out the expectation. Skull let it hang so the Professor continued, "Would you like to speak to her? Speak to her."

Before Skull could say "No" the old man's voice was fading in his ear and distantly he heard: "Here, talk to Matthew. He's speaking French or something. Can't understand a damn word he's saying." There followed a hissy exchange on the other end, voices muffled behind the scraping and knocking as the old fashioned handset changed hands.

"Hello, Skull."

Her voice was low, pitched flat with disinterest, with dismissal. Hearing it again returned to Skull an unexpected wave of recollection: her unfathomable brown eyes, his ancient adolescent longings, the smell of fresh cut grass and old boiled rice.

"I'm afraid I've not been much help," Skull said quickly. "Jon and I haven't really spoken for a while."

She had been beautiful, sophisticated, poised and unreach-able while he and Jon were still sniggering youths saturated with unwelcome hormones and unwanted feelings. She was assured and haughty, Skull recalled, but when she walked by, disturbing scents trailed like stardust from a comet.

Now she was silent, saying nothing. It seemed she had inherited her father's disposition for the awkward pause.

"Are you staying long?" he asked eventually.

"Daddy's worried about Jon," she said.

"Indeed."

It was Jacqueline who had first called him Skull, labelling him for his hollow looks, his thin smile drawn back on rows of small white teeth. But there was more to it than that. There was, he always thought, the sense of being something exhumed, a curiosity dug up by Jon, a relic providing evidence of something descended, of something evolved from. It was a Fast family joke, he felt, with him as the butt of it.

Back then no gawping adolescent like Skull made it far inside Jacqueline's circle of interest, although she had noticed him briefly one summer's afternoon when they talked of books and reading. He knew nothing of literature in those days (knew nothing now — a few lines of popular verse, some names). She mistook his passion and interest for literary ardour and lent him a sad novel in which nothing happened to a group of loquacious friends over a very long and very miserable time. He never finished the book, never returned it. His literary repertoire had not expanded over the years.

"Daddy's had a letter from Jon," Jac said. "Jon seems to be in some kind of trouble. And he mentions you."

"Daddy?" Skull sneered.

"Jon."

Skull recalled her reluctant smile, a rare, wide lascivious grin, lopsided, enticing, revealing the tips of her even white teeth. Same mouth as her father only fuller, less acerbic.

"He implies you know something about it," she said.

"About what?"

"About why he's had to go away."

"He's gone away? I didn't know." Skull tried to sound bored.

"He implies you do," she persisted.

"He implies wrong, then. I know nothing about it. What does he say?"

"Daddy had a call last week from Jon's work. It seems he took a fortnight's holiday which ended three weeks ago. Coming on top of the letter, it is a bit of a worry."

"Surely Anka knows where he is," Skull said, adding snidely, "Or is she also missing?"

"She's not missing," said Jac.

"Then she must know where he is."

"She left Jon."

"She left him?"

"God."

"I didn't know." He wanted to laugh. They had seemed such an unlikely couple, Jon and Anka. That's why he thought it might work. Even so, he was surprised at the satisfaction that came from the knowledge of their broken marriage. "He'll turn up," he said soberly.

After a short pause she went on, "You don't know anything, then."

"Nothing."

"Can you think of anyone else we could contact?" she asked. "Perhaps someone Jon may actually still be talking to. A mutual friend, perhaps?"

"I'll have a think," Skull volunteered, motivated entirely by the desire to end the conversation.

"A think?" She didn't mask the antipathy now. "Yes. Have a think, Skull. Please do have a think. I'm up in London tomorrow," she went on. "It would be useful if you could have your think before then."

She gave him her mobile number and carefully he tapped it into his contacts list without the intention of ever using it. The conversation ended. Later, he thought, he might have a look at Jon's Facebook page although he knew there had been no public updates for quite a while; he and Jon had long since un-friended and un-followed and un-liked everything about each other everywhere. At least he could say he had tried.

*

The voice Skull most hoped to find on his answering machine was absent. Emily had extracted herself from his life, scrupulously taking only what was truly hers, since when she had not called, texted nor messaged him using any of the numerous services and mechanisms that they held in common. He ached for her voice, he told himself.

The next most frequent message depositor (after Professor Fast) was Simon Betterson, formerly Director of Business Development at Smartor PLC.

"You cunt," Simon had recorded.

If smart is the ability to understand complexity, then genius is the compulsion to reduce it to a simple pattern, a singular concept, a formula. Skull had not always been a genius. Before Smartor most of the smart people he knew would have classed him as merely averagely intelligent, rating him at best, he suspected, an over-achiever. He was conscientious though; he put in the hours, learnt his craft, mixed with the right sort of people. When the opportunity came he recognised it for what it was and made the most of it. Now everything had fallen apart.

Back in the good days, through a friend of a contact who knew some people, Skull had landed work with an over-funded technology startup launched to the public as Know Your Motor. KYM, as they liked to call themselves, provided simple web-based diagnostic information for motor cars. It wasn't a new idea: customers bought a cheap device (the KYM-a-Tron, in this case) which they could plug into the vehicle's On Board Diagnostic port (usually called simply the OBD port).

The point, of course, was that you could monitor the health of your vehicle, get early warnings of potential trouble, even give your local mechanic access so he could pre-order replacement parts for you. In the folksy world of the social media startup there seemed no end to the clever and useful things you could do with the data once you started augmenting it with social information: compare your mileage with the mileage your friends were making, compare your repair bills with your neighbours' bills, check that your mechanic was not cheating you on parts or labour.

The data pummelling, the sexy visuals and brand persistence, was the preserve of company founders Rich and Neha because big data, informatics, visualisation was their thing. That, and raising funding. This was their fourth startup and, according to them, they'd pretty much nailed it.

Skull had been happy to get the gig even if initially it was only a casual, short-term hire. Car tech was interesting, it might be the Next Big Thing, so adding it to his list of skills was somewhat optimal, he told himself. Since he was a competent programmer, Rich and Neha always found new things for him to do. One of his first jobs was to clean up the incoming data, make it nice, before piping it into a large database.

"The diagnostic data are only a small subset of the traffic on the CAN bus," explained Keith, the hardware man, when Skull went to see him for an overview.

"The CAN bus?" Skull asked.

Keith rapidly expanded: with all the sensors, actuators and processing units running on modern cars manufacturers have opted for an internal car network, called the CAN bus. With a suitable device like the KYM-a-Tron plugged into it, you can look inside this network, and since cars nowadays are almost all run by electronics there is potentially a huge amount of data you can read.

But, Keith confided, with the right hardware and the right knowledge you could also send data and instructions onto the network.

"Indeed," Skull observed. "Dangerous?"

"Oh yes," Keith said.

But it was a lot more complex than that. Keith explained it, but Keith compressed knowledge. He spoke in bullet points, his speech emblazoned with promiscuous use of technical jargon. He delivered the information raw, without body language or gesture, illustrating his key themes with greasy printouts and fast, impenetrable demonstrations using test rigs mounted on his workbenches. He was a man with a rack of solutions looking for worthwhile problems. Skull was impressed.

"There's a lot more data on the CAN bus than we're using," Skull told Rich, the founder.

"Yeah, well," Rich shrugged. "Undocumented. Proprietary. What you gonna do, eh?"

Rich was right. The structure of much of the data running over the network was known only to the car manufacturers, and they weren't sharing that information voluntarily with anyone.

Skull set himself to learn everything there was to learn about the CAN bus and Keith was a willing teacher. Keith was also a master in the design and construction of electronic boards laced with capacitors, resistors, processing modules, all stitched together with tiny silvered beads of solder. These circuits did subtle things that only Keith seemed to understand. He had a quiver of finely crafted instruments and with these he was able to probe the hidden sensors for information, prod the stubborn controllers until they emitted screens of inscrutable code.

That was Keith's gift; also his limitation, for he had neither the interest nor the ability to interpret the meaning of the data sets that were returned.

"It's like squeezing the balls of a pig," Keith admitted. "I can make it squeal loud, or I can make it squeal soft, but I really don't know if it's squealing for pleasure, or pain." Keith was all value and no essence. He was the most self-contained technician Skull had ever met. Skull really liked him.

There were other interested parties on the Internet however — technologists, enthusiasts, idealists — slowly hacking away at the CAN bus, reverse-engineering the data formats, byte by byte, discovering their payload and posting their breathless adventures on the forums. Delighted at first to discover these communities Skull gradually grew despondent: there seemed to be at least one group for every model of car, each bounded by their own agenda. It was all so piecemeal, the victories over silent sensors and secretive processors so tiny. Progress was painstakingly slow.

"There's sensors and actuators and processors of all sorts producing a ton of data we could use," he enthused to Neha one day as she sat on her Swiss ball squinting myopically at a bank of screens.

"Sounds like a bandwidth headache to me," she eventually replied.

"We could even write to the CAN bus, you know. We could let the users control some of the actuators using their smartphones."

"Ooh, that sounds dangerous," she sniffed. "So I think the diagnostic data is enough for us. Tell me, grey button with Garamond? Or aqua with Futura? I like Futura. It's modern. Whatcha think?"

Rich and Neha's vision seemed so small. It lacked ambition. This was the age of the motor car; vehicle technology was rapidly accelerating, the driver-less car was just around the corner and this was no time to be sitting in the slow lane. Here was a system generating megabytes of valuable, usable, marketable data every second, and all Neha and Rich could do was worry about fonts and pie charts. The opportunities were immense, but progress was painstakingly slow.

Skull studied the data, did some calculations and concluded that at the current rate of discovery, by the time most of the data had been exposed by enthusiasts the next generation of vehicles would be on the streets and they'd all have to start all over again.

True, there were technical problems. Huge volumes of data needed fat data pipes to move it about and large reservoirs to store it all, but these were physical limitations that were solvable by almost anyone. Understanding and liberating the proprietary information was challenging, but the rewards were waiting for whoever could get there first.

There was a moral dimension too. Skull had read the forums. "Everyone gets screwed," he told Keith. "As long as the data formats are proprietary your data is owned by the manufacturers. You might buy and own the car but they own the data. If we open it up, everyone benefits. It's a level playing field."

Keith smiled benignly, nodded earnestly, wiped slowly the oil from his hands before typing with two fingers onto a keyboard the numbers he had been holding in his head.

"Even the manufacturers will benefit in the long run," Skull continued, "because eventually they'll just have to settle on an open standard. Then they can focus on what they do best."

Over the following weeks Keith willingly bent his skills to building prototypes for Skull. Together they designed a pluggable box encompassing a collection of network probes, sniffers, prodders and pokers. They called it the CANCan and they plugged it into every vehicle they could get their hands on, recording all the outputs that were produced whenever a switch was flicked, a button pressed, a lever pulled. Reluctantly the sensors and actuators revealed themselves. Progress was painstakingly slow.

When Skull thought about it, the approach seemed all wrong. It had to be simpler, so he looked at the simplicity of the problem rather than its complexity. He decided that a car is simply a box which carries people and things from a known A to a known B without bumping into other cars and things.

After that it was easy. Skull didn't start with the function, he started with the data. He looked for the regularities in the data and found them: vehicles start and stop, they go fast and they slow down, they turn left, they turn right, they try to keep their passengers safe and warm and dry and happy. Instead of the dot-and-carry-one approach he applied heuristics, deploying a range of techniques which gradually, iteratively, built a model of the data starting with small measurements, then sampling, testing, growing.

He bolted together a framework of programming libraries and routines that responded not to the information itself but to the flow of information, de-constructing the patterns of messages rather than their payloads, inferring their meanings, sampling, testing, growing the data model.

His genius was that he continued reducing, refining the pattern definitions to the irreducible minimum. These he wrapped in a set of algorithms that mapped the data model to an abstracted layer and allowed a relatively simple device to learn how to get information out of, and into, almost any vehicle's internal network.

These mapping algorithms were the key to the whole thing so he patented them, encrypted the source and incorporated them into a new device he and Keith called the TwoCAN.

That's when he approached Simon, at that time Head of Sales for KYM.

"What if we could grab nearly all the data off the CAN bus and process it?" he asked.

"Don't we have enough of that crap already?" Simon sneered.

Skull was serious. "If we had more we could do more. We could see what music our customers are listening to, what days they drive the most, what times of the day they drive best; we could let them know where and when their partner drives the car or how fast their kids are driving. And we can do that for any make or model of car. The possibilities are limitless."

"Happy days," said Simon without much enthusiasm. "All that fucking data? Just imagine that."

Skull was not swayed from his pitch. He said, "And what if we could also let the customer configure his car with his own smartphone?"

"Oh fuck. That sounds dangerous," Simon grinned, piqued now by the destructive possibilities.

"We design simple controls," Skull went on. "A slider so you could, say, set your drive for either more power or better economy; or maybe you want a softer more comfortable ride rather than a more edgy performance. Simple, menu-driven configuration of your own car."

"Can you do that?"

"Indeed," said Skull.

"That would be so cool," laughed Simon. "That would be so fucking awesomely fucking cool. On your fucking phone? Jesus. Even a cunt like me could sell shit like that."

"Not at KYM you couldn't," Skull deadpanned. "Apparently here we only like diagnostics. To do more we'd have to go on our own."

"Well OK," Simon had enthused evangelically, way back then.

Now he was leaving venomous messages for Skull because he wanted the mapping algorithms: 'You're not fucking getting away with it, you skinny fat fuck. You better fucking call me or we'll all just fucking have to pay the fucking lawyers to fucking sort it out. You cunt."

But Skull had already had that conversation with Simon and saw no profit in repeating it. If Simon wanted the algorithms he could find them and download them from half a dozen project sites where Skull had checked in the unencrypted source along with wiring diagrams for the TwoCAN, gifting the world what the world seemed not to want. The algorithms were no longer a secret.

Let the lawyers pick over the bones of that cadaver, Skull thought. They would have to queue behind the legal team from KYM who were still aggrieved at what they saw as his theft of both staff and ideas. Then, when all the lawyers had finished deciding who owed what to whom, they could fight over who was going to pay them how much with what monies, because it wouldn't be Skull. Skull was broke. Skull was bankrupt. Skull was finished.

*

He made a second coffee to greet the afternoon. The doorbell rang. He ignored it.

Browsing the hollow fridge Skull weighed the narrow options available to him, briefly pondering the simple joy of a round of toast, but his stomach said no-not-yet so he sat at the breakfast bar and thumbed his smartphone, ignoring the persistent ringing at the front door, while taking new comfort from the coffee.

There were a hundred unread emails, a hundred chat requests, texts, tweets, status updates: Richard had re-tweeted some motor industry news along with an arrogant comment while Philippa Miller liked a link to an article on spaghetti that Jamie Wood had posted on LinkedIn; Dom was overly grateful to a technical forum for a series of poor solutions to an obscure problem, and Razzi Amett had downloaded some MP3s from Amazon. The Twydle twins confirmed their meeting tonight. There was nothing from Emily — no chats, no texts, no missed calls.

HI!My name is Werner Brandes...

There it was again. Just the short link with the line from the film, the line he and Jon as schoolboys had made their own — a sort of buddy catch-phrase. That's why he knew it was from Jon, making a claim on their friendship; but they were no longer friends. Not after the argument.

"You're a bad risk, Skull," Jon had told him straight. "Can't do it. If it was just me, you know I would lend you the money."

"It's short term, it's just short term. Anka doesn't understand how these things work," Skull had reasoned.

"It's not Anka."

"Our friendship means nothing?"

"It's a lot of money, Skull." It was a splash in the river of hard cash Skull needed to keep control of Smartor and would have held off the vultures barely a week. "Sell your house," Jon advised.

"Fuck you."

"Fuck you too."

We carry our schooldays like old sandwiches squashed and mouldering at the bottom of a satchel, Skull decided. Every now and then you open the bag with the hope of something fresh, something palatable, but finding the same stale whiff you quickly shut it up again.

On the phone earlier he had promised Jac he would have a think, try and remember if there were other friends but really there was no need to think about it because he no longer knew many of Jon's friends, and those he did — old school friends, college friends — he didn't care to know, had long since lost touch.

He had a think about Jacqueline though, sitting with his phone cupped in hand, sipping his coffee, remembering his wonder at how her ivory neck hid amid the dark curls of hair like a swan among the weeds, recalling the thrill of her smile bestowed one summer's afternoon; even after all this time her subtle smell caught him, her delicate perfume a breath of promises.

The doorbell rang again, a lingering, angry ring that surely bore the fingerprint of Simon. Skull made the mistake of peering out the window. There he was: Simon, with the cocky, stiff-legged gait of a dog that just took a shit on the carpet and got away with it. Not now, though. Now he was just the peeved, balding salesman, hunched against the cold and unexpected rottenness of his life. He looked up suddenly. Skull stepped back. The doorbell rang accusingly.

Skull knew what Simon wanted, knew how the conversation would go. It would go something like this:

"Listen, you cunt. Do the right thing. Give them the fucking code. Just give it to them. When you give them the fucking code, we get the fucking money."

They didn't buy the code, Skull would say. They stole the company. The code is mine.

"They don't want the fucking company. They just want the fucking code. Fucksake, Matt, what is your problem? You fucking lied to them, you wanker. Now you're bust, I'm bust, we're all fucking dead here. The code is useless; to you, to me, to Keith who doesn't even give a shit. No one else fucking wants it — no one would fucking touch it. It's fucking dangerous. Come on, man. We gave it a shot, we lost, they won. Boo fucking hoo. They won't release the money till you give them the fucking code. Give them the fucking code. Do the right thing."

But I did the right thing, Skull thought. I patented the code and licensed the use to the company. I retained the Intellectual Property. That's what the lawyers advised. The code is mine, mine to keep, or mine to give away.

"Don't be such a pedantic, fucking, anal, fuck. So you have the fucking IP — well-done-you-cunt. Now what you do is you fucking give it to the fucks at BläsHög and they will wipe our sins clean away with a great big fucking cheque. Fuck-sake Matt I have children. Fucking children. Do the right thing."

What was the right thing? Skull swallowed the cold muddy slug of coffee at the bottom of the mug and pushed up the lid on his laptop which beeped in sleepy protest and flickered on.

He was sure he had done the right thing, although maybe not the right thing by Simon. He had in any case done the smart thing, and in most cases the smart thing is the right thing. BläsHög wanted the code so they could extort money from rival manufacturers, or license it to governments. Or bury it. What did it matter why they wanted it? They'd lied and cheated to get it, now everyone could have it. It was worthless.

Manually he typed the link from Jon's text into a browser and watched, again, the video: "Help me."

It felt all wrong somehow, the low angle, the sweeping lights, the basey music. In the browser, the short, inscrutable link had resolved to a full web address which showed that the video was served from a media sharing site calling itself rewindr.com. There was only one publicly shared video for the account.

"Roadrunner has shared this media with you. Join rewindr free today," flashed below the embedded video window. There were links inviting visitors to "Find Out More", "Compare Subscriptions", "Signup Free", or "Login".

Roadrunner. Jon Fast. Jon liked connections, no matter how thin. He had probably used the name on a hundred different web accounts.

Skull clicked "Login", then in the dialogue box which popped onto the screen he typed roadrunner into the field labelled "Username".

Other People are trusting and believe things will always work out for the best and that bad things only happen to other Other People which of course, Skull reflected, was probably true. Other People know that the Internet is huge and that they are but a small, shrill voice in a vast arena filled with the dark howlings of beasts and monsters; but in the infinite crowd of all the other Other People, Other People feel safe. They feel they are too insignificant, too obscure, too other, to be a target for malicious intent, and so they use the same password over and over and over again — words like "password", or "secret", or worse, a lover's name or an obscenity.

Into the password field Skull typed limpet, a password Jon had repeatedly used all through college for its reference to his name: stuck fast, like a limpet.

He clicked "OK" and a red-rimmed dialogue box popped open on the screen with a big red cross and the words: "!Oop fat finger! Try again!"

He tried again, using password variations around stuck, sticky, tight, hold, glue; then abstain, diet, forgo; easy, loose, lewd. After that he tried *beepbeep*, *meepmeep*, and *wileecoyote*.

After each few dozen failed attempts a new dialogue box would appear: "Sorry! To many trys!" There was a limit on the number of password attempts. He needed to pause before trying again.

He moved over to the window, cautiously peering down to the street below. The ringing at the door had stopped a while back and now the street was empty.

Emily had left abruptly taking all the soft things — the scatter cushions, the nice duvet, the sofa. There had been a polite note:

To Matthew Morrell.
I took only what is mine and also what I know you did not like of ours. If you disagree I will be at my parents' house.
Emily Parks.

She had planned it quietly, executing it without fuss — a friend, a van, a morning's work. Now the flat felt empty and, well, flat; it was just the place he lived in now, lacking the features and arrangements that had made it whole, made it a living space. He could never make it nice again and besides, what was the point in trying? Soon he would have to leave.

He clicked Login again, typed *roadrunner*, then started on password variations around Jon's family names and the names of all the old girlfriends. After that he worked through school related words: friends, enemies, teachers, hated prefects and pets.

"Sorry! To many trys!"

Skull had called Mrs Parks straight away. "It's too late, Matthew. You can't go around treating people like, like computers, with an on-off switch which you switch on and off. Like a computer." Emily refused to speak with him. "Do you want to leave a message, Matthew? I can give her a message," Mrs Parks prompted gently.

"No," he had said. "There's no message."

In a new login box he typed in words based on holiday destinations, Jon's favourite foods, wines, beers, drugs and cars. Books and films yielded a rich seam of significant words as did actresses, singers, bands, music styles, albums, songs and lyrics.

He typed in the names of employers, restaurants, pubs and clubs, significant street names.

"!Oop, fat finger!"

At the end of an hour Skull was impressed with how much he knew of Jon's life and just how useless all that information was. He also knew that if he was to succeed he would need a more robust approach, an industrial method that could lay bare the secret of Jon's video account. Cyber security wasn't his area of expertise but he knew that password cracking was moderately trivial for those who knew their business.

He found Josh where you always find Josh, on one of his private Internet Relay Chat channels. Josh had done some security consultancy for Smartor, best white hat in the business. Anyone who needed something bad done for a good reason usually went to Josh, although Skull didn't know anyone who had actually met Josh in person. Contact was always made through the IRC channel, payment via wire transfer, eCache, Bitcoin.

```
<Skull>       hey
<hawsehole69>   yo
<Skull>       hows things
<hawsehole69>   meh
<Skull>       you should get out more
<hawsehole69>   dint like it
<hawsehole69>   how u holdn up ?
<Skull>       ok
<hawsehole69>   wot u doin now?
<Skull>       sulking
<hawsehole69>   haha cum work for me
<hawsehole69>   pays shit but prns good
<Skull>       haha best offer yet
<Skull>       defo think about it
<hawsehole69>   serious
<Skull>       I need to get inside a web service account
<Skull>       cant pay much
```

```
<hawsehole69>  legit?
<Skull>  mate lost her password
<hawsehole69>  go thru site admins to get pwd reset
<Skull>  its scumbag x bf account
<Skull>  she thinks he's got sum pics and vids of her
<hawsehole69>  bad pics? :-P
<Skull>  very
<hawsehole69>  link?
```

Skull gave Josh the details but left out the thirty years of friendship he'd shared with Jon.

*

For Skull the ambush was a shock. He was to meet the Twydle twins for drinks later that evening but his fractured thoughts, his hunger and restlessness drove him from the flat even before the winter sun went down. He wasn't to know that lower down the street, in his car, Simon sat with his three children, his resentment, and a baseball bat.

Skull had already shut the front door, a glossy royal blue with matching new old-brass letter box and knocker, and which opened directly onto the pavement, when the anxious shriek of a young child caused him to look up. He was surprised to see Simon, coatless, cantering towards him, a wooden bat raised awkwardly overhead ready to strike, his face contorted horribly in a worried frown. At the same time there came from Simon a thin howl: "Oah!"

The attack was badly planned and poorly executed. In the congested one way system Simon had failed to find parking sufficiently close to the flat and so he miscalculated how far and how fast he could run holding the baseball bat aloft. Skull had time to pull his keys from his pocket, re-open the front door and slip quickly inside long before Simon reached striking distance.

Seeing his victim disappear behind the closing door, Simon lunged too soon. Swinging from an oblique angle, the wooden bat glanced off the glossy blue door and slammed into the brick post around the door frame. The bat, rotten from too many summers left out in the garden, splintered wetly.

"Fuck you Morrell you fucking fuck." Simon continued to pound the door with kicks and punches, wringing much venom from the narrow range of expletives in his vocabulary. Skull stood immobile in the small communal hall inside the house. His hand shook a little. He hoped his neighbour Mr Beavis was out and not witness to this display.

In that part of Shoreditch the streets were mostly residential, seldom busy, an awkward mix of new-trendy and old-social housing, with large red brick apartment blocks alongside the Victorian terraces and modern council houses, now mostly all private. An odd one-way system constrained the traffic and made the area a peaceable island dividing the restless throb of the High Street from the steady thrum of Bethnal Green Road.

Buying the flat had been a fatal expression of optimism when optimism was both possible and necessary. He had bought the upper floors in the converted Victorian terraced cottage. On the first floor, the merged living-dining space was divided from the kitchen area by a grotesque breakfast bar — Skull's favourite feature. Above, in the renovated loft accessed by another set of steep, narrow stairs which pressed against the back wall, was the bathroom, the bedroom he and Emily had shared, and a smaller room they called The Stuffroom for obvious reasons.

Below lived Mr Beavis, who shared the front door. The two households hardly ever encountered each other and when they did it was, thankfully, brief and cordial. Mr Beavis left for work early and returned soon after lunch. He may have been a milkman or an FX trader.

Soon the energy ebbed from Simon's assault, the ferocity sucked out as suddenly as it had descended leaving a filthy trickle of weeps and sobs. Skull shouted through the closed door, "I'll call the police, Simon."

"I'll fucking kill you, you cunt," was returned with a final surge against the door.

Through the fish-eye lens of the peep-hole viewer Skull saw the distorted figure slouch away. After a short while he opened the front door cautiously, peering out. Across the road an elderly couple stared back, observing the drama impassively, their shopping drooping in round bags from round shoulders. Further through the gap in the door he watched Simon step mechanically into his car, start it and pull into the street. Slowly the car passed the open door where Skull stood openly now looking out. Simon stared ahead but from the back seats three small pale disks swivelled to look at him as they drove past. Simon's children.

Skull was therefore already quite drunk by the time he made the appointment with the Twydle twins in a traditional English pub just off the Farringdon Road.

"Dude. You are such a legend, man," said Tom across a limp handshake.

Sam agreed, "Seriously ledge, man."

"If we," Tom waggled a bony finger, "if we can disrupt half what you disrupted with Smartor we'd be ... like ..."

"Disraptors?" Skull slurred.

"Yeah — like awesome raptors, man. Like disraptors."

The twins looked like they'd be more at home disrupting a cocktail at the trendy bar across the street, and perhaps they already had for they were equally drunk. All the same they gave him their "elevator pitch" from which he misunderstood that they were looking for angel funding for a startup providing a free service to low income users of a third party application on a declining social network platform. He encouraged them to pursue their dreams.

They, in turn, flattered him into relating what went wrong with Smartor so that they could enjoy the dancing flames and smell the burning flesh of failure. Skull stepped easily into the role of Hardened Veteran bearing Honourable Scars and Fight Forged Enlightenments, for in the quixotic world of technology startups the narrative of defeat has the power of parable. He hoped they'd offer him a job so he could have the pleasure of turning them down. Both parties despised each other instinctively; consequently they drank more heartily, swearing lasting friendship and successful future partnerships.

Sunday Morning

The combination of telephone and doorbell woke him. It wasn't early but he could have done with more sleep. Taking the easier option, he answered his phone.

"I'm ringing your doorbell," she said, ringing the bell again. "Are you home?"

At the front door, Jacqueline was dressed for Sunday out, him for Sunday in, bare feet, shorts and tee.

"Your text," she said by way of explanation. "I did phone earlier."

"Text?" he managed, his mouth thick with sleep, breath foul with old alcohol.

"The video from Jon," she added.

"Video?"

"This may flow better, Skull, if you do not repeat everything I say. You sent me the message. Remember?"

"Indeed." He thought he did not remember but was pleased to have uttered at least his own word. Aware that he was now staring at her, he regretted that this was not a classic reunion in the great tradition. Far from being pleased to see him she seemed annoyed, her eyebrows arcing over her eyes like an albatross turning on the wing, the set of her neck (tanned dark now by the Mediterranean sun) said simply, "Disappointed".

"Invite me in, Skull," she prompted him. There was going to be no apology for disturbing his Sunday morning.

The front door closed behind her just as the door to the ground floor flat opened sufficient to allow Mr Beavis to pop out his curly head.

"Matthew. How are you? Have you seen all these take-away leaflets? Pizza and chicken-poop, it's a total mess, all this paper. I'm thinking they must be for you 'coz I've seen you eating the take-aways. I don't eat that crap so can you tidy it up? That would be great. How are you, missus," Mr Beavis nodded briefly at Jac without making eye-contact. "And that feller that was here yesterday — was he like some kind of a mate of yours? Haha, Jesus, 'coz he was loodering the door like a hod carrier on a Friday night. It needs a proper job, I had a look. Rub down, filler, base coat, everything. A proper job, Matthew. Alright? Proper job, no cowboys. Oh, and there was this other feller here looking for you Friday, said he was about the electric, said you hadn't paid, that's what he said. I'm just telling you what he said, Matthew, I'm not even joking, and I'm not judging or nothing, but you have to pay the bills, Matthew. You have to pay the bills or they cut you off and that's just the start of it."

Mr Beavis nodded curtly. The door closed with the quiet plop of a frog entering water.

They climbed the narrow, noisy stairs in silence to the flat above. Nothing was said as she followed him into the living room where they paused, standing briefly side by side, surveying the detritus of his life, the clothes, the books, the boxes of old kit, empty bottles scattered about obscuring the clean geometric surfaces of the open plan space which had once harboured ambitions of functional minimalism. Nothing was said but he heard the comment on his life.

"Sorry," he grunted, waving a disconsolate arm at the mess having decided there was no excuse for it. "Shower." He gestured upstairs. Finally he pointed towards the kitchen area, managing, "Coffee. Breakfast." It seemed like a lot of talking and arm waving, so he took himself upstairs.

He showered slowly, recollection returning like a bad meal in burps of sour memory. He recalled drinking the last of the scotch from the bottle. He recalled swearing mournfully at a late night film on TV and worrying too late if he'd over-tipped the cab driver who'd brought him home. He recalled receiving a cryptic message from Josh just before leaving the pub: *dic atak bomd sugest bf wanna up 4 net? 10ph mates gotta lng pwd*

It had taken the entire cab drive back to Hoxton to figure out that "bf" meant "brute-force" and "net" meant a "botnet". The gist of it was that Josh had tried a dictionary attack which had failed and was now proposing Skull pay for the hire of a botnet, an illegal network of zombie computers working in concert to break Jon's password using a brute-force attack. He was certainly not going to stump up for that at £10 per hour. He was broke.

Back home and awash with beer and self-loathing, he had managed to key his response: *Tnx will let you know o u 1.*

Now, as he stood bowed in the shower, the water beating the soap from his head and frothing over his face in streams of fat bubbles, he remembered all the rest. He remembered sucking at the last drops in the whisky bottle, he remembered swearing at the TV and then his phone had buzzed on the breakfast bar in front of him. He remembered the surge of hope: Emily. He had lifted the phone, flicked the screen to check.

HI!My name is Werner Brandes.

He remembered now.

Skull stepped from the warm pleasure of the shower, drying himself thoroughly and thoughtfully before replacing his glasses, picking up his phone to check if he had remembered correctly. There, under Sent Messages, just as he had forwarded it to her: *Hijack. Got this yestrday.*

He dressed slowly, reluctant to return down the stairs to the living room.

She was waiting in the kitchen, a hip against the counter top, gazing out the window, her coat and scarf draped over the breakfast bar alongside a small leather handbag. She had grown thicker than he remembered her, adding curves, gravity. Kids do that, he thought, but he couldn't now remember if she'd had one or many, if she'd married the Italian or subsequently divorced him. In Jon's intermittent news of her she was always unhappy.

"So you've seen the clip," he said.

She turned, surveying him briefly before she replied, "I didn't understand it." She sipped tentatively from her coffee mug while she observed him over the rim. She nodded at a mug on the counter next to her. She had made him coffee.

"Is he being threatened by this Werner Brandes?" she asked.

"No," Skull laughed. "Family joke. It's a quote. From a film we saw. Robert Redford, and that guy who did Ghandi ... What's his name? Anyway. It's a good film," he tailed off, lifting the mug she had indicated. She continued looking at him without expression so he expanded: "Werner Brandes is a character in the film. Long story."

"Who's he talking to then? On the clip."

"Don't know," Skull shrugged, sniffing the coffee. She had made instant coffee which annoyed him immensely because prominent on the counter was his beautiful, retro-style, cream-coloured coffee maker along with the matching, un-missable, and utterly gorgeous, ceramic burr coffee mill.

"Well whoever he is," Jac noted irritably, "he says Jon should disappear until it's over. Until what's over?"

"Don't know."

The instant coffee was intended only for the cleaning lady who no longer cleaned, and the occasional painter or plumber who would never call again.

"He says Jon will not be able to stop it. Do we know what it is he can't stop?" she asked.

"No idea." Skull couldn't remember the last time he drank instant coffee. It smelled odd.

"Is there some sort of extortion going on d'you think?" she asked, her voice clipped, her brows mashed together.

"I don't know."

"Do you have anything of any value to add to this discussion, Skull?"

Skull shrugged again, eyeing the coffee suspiciously. He wondered if coffee had a use-by date, if it could go off. "Probably not," he said at last.

She looked away, staring out the window. He sipped tentatively at the coffee. It was foul. He made a face.

"I gather he sent that message to you last night?" Jac asked.

"This morning, actually."

"This morning?"

"Early. He always sends at that time."

"Always? I thought you weren't friends." She compressed her lips, suppressing a smile or a sneer.

"We're not."

"But you still exchange little text messages at regular times." She turned again to face him directly over her coffee mug. She shared Jon's high forehead but her lips, Skull noted, seemed harder than his, her eyes a deeper brown, more steady.

"No exchange," said Skull. "He sends that same message. Always just after one in the morning."

"That same message?" she asked.

He said, "This conversation might flow better if you didn't repeat everything I say."

It didn't sound as clever as he thought it would, but she looked away then and he had the satisfaction of receiving the flicker of annoyance. He couldn't decide if she was annoyed with him, or with herself.

"So how long have you been getting this same message?" Now her articulation was careful and pedantic, intended to make him feel stupid. Mostly he just felt ill though. What he really wanted was to lie down, spend the day feeling sorry for himself, although he knew he probably needed something for his stomach. The instant coffee, he felt, was not going to do it for him.

"Couple of days. I've been getting them for a couple of days. Look," he put his coffee on the counter and pulled across a tall stool from the breakfast bar, perching on the edge of it. "It's really simple: Jon and I aren't speaking. We had an argument so he's winding me up. He did that. Quite a lot, actually. That's all it is. It's a wind-up."

"When did you see him last?"

"About five, maybe six months ago." He reached for his coffee mug. Some of the undiluted granules had gathered with bubbles in a brown slurry ring, slowly dispersing to the edge of his mug. He wondered at the physics of this effect.

"Six months?" she said slowly as if she didn't quite believe him. "Do you think he waited all this time just to wind you up? Is that really likely?"

Skull sipped at the coffee again. Sometimes a first sip can clear the palate to make the second tasting more palatable. Sadly not in this case. The coffee remained stubbornly offensive.

"You don't think it might be a genuine call for help?" she persisted.

"No, I don't think it's a genuine call for help," Skull said. "If you're going to ask for help, genuinely ask for help, why send a link to a video clip of yourself talking to someone else in a nightclub?"

"His letter said he was in trouble," Jac said quickly.

"What letter?"

"He sent Daddy a letter. I told you about it."

"Oh, that letter."

"I told you about it," she said again.

"Yes." Skull nodded. He had forgotten about the letter.

Jac bent towards him, saying, "Jon said he needed to sort out some kind of trouble. He said you knew about it."

"Really?"

"Apparently you might have helped him."

"Really?"

"So why didn't you help him?"

"Do you have the letter?" Skull asked. "Can I see it?"

"Answer my question, Skull."

"It sounds more like an accusation," he countered. "I don't know what you're accusing me of. Can I see the letter please?"

She reached into her handbag, extracting a folded note.

"It's a copy," she said.

"A very wise precaution," Skull noted, but she ignored the irony.

"In case we need to take the original to the police," she explained.

She had written it out in long hand on a sheet of A4 ruled.

Dear Daddy
You may be wondering why you haven't heard from me in a while but I've had to go away for reasons I can't go into now. I asked Skull but we're still not talking. There's nothing to worry about. I will be back after Christmas.
I thought things were really starting to improve but something has come up which I need to sort out but once this trouble is over everything will get back to normal. Please don't worry. Call Anka if you can.
As ever, your son,
Jon

Skull read the letter twice and handed it back. It seemed oddly formal; he had forgotten Jon still called the Professor "Daddy". Behind his back it was always "the Prof".

"Well?" she demanded sharply when he didn't respond.

"Well what? He says not to worry."

"He mentions you."

"He mentions me but I don't know what he means by it. He says we're still not talking, which is entirely correct: we are still not talking."

"What did he ask you, Skull?" Her voice had risen, harrying him.

"What did he ask me? I don't remember. I really don't remember. That was six months ago." He gestured out at the room, the boxes, the books, the bottles. "I was having a bit of trouble of my own."

"You turned him away." Her voice was low, disappointed, accusing. "He asked you for help, and you turned him away."

"In fact," Skull said, "the opposite. I asked him for help and he turned me away." She said nothing, returning just the level stare, the compressed lips. Skull continued. "He's a grown man, Jac. Perhaps he really does need to be left alone." She shook her head, but another thought had occurred to Skull. "Was there a postmark on the envelope?"

"London," she said. "It doesn't help. We couldn't make out the area. But the address on the envelope was in a different handwriting. Someone else addressed it." She scanned the letter again before folding it thoughtfully and replacing it in her bag. She said, looking up at him, "I think it's so sad. You were such good friends."

"Not any more. I'm sorry, I can't drink this," Skull said suddenly angry, tipping the contents of his coffee mug into the filthy sink. The drain gurgled then burped in quiet gratitude. "I need a serious coffee, a real coffee. Want one?"

"This is fine for me," she said primly, holding her mug closely with two hands. "Your kitchen is — complicated."

His kitchen was squalid with unwashed pots and plates filling the sink, the surfaces crowded with mugs, tumblers, empty bottles, tins.

"You like your little gadgets," she added. It was an insult, of course. A put down.

"I like good coffee," he retorted. They were both surprised at the edge in his voice so he smiled to smooth it over. "I really do need a substantial caffeine stimulant and I can't make myself one if you don't have one too."

Reluctantly she surrendered her mug.

"Sorry about the mess," he said as he rinsed both mugs under a stream of hot water. "I've been a bit busy and the cleaner's away on holiday." The cleaner had stopped cleaning when he stopped paying her. It seemed an equitable arrangement. "I'm trying to do the right thing, Jac."

"Really? Why now?"

"Oh, come on," he protested, shaking the water off the wet mugs and placing them on the counter top.

Jac shrugged. "You didn't think to tell me about the text message when we spoke on the phone the other day. Or about the video?"

"I forgot," Skull said.

"Ah," she smiled without warmth. "What else did you forget to tell me?"

He moved across to the fridge, reaching in for a tightly rolled brown paper package. "I've been getting that message several times a day," he said, opening the package and carefully pouring coffee beans into the coffee mill. He didn't look at her. "I always deleted them. It was only when you said he was missing that I took a look."

"So you agree he's missing."

"He's not missing." He flipped the switch on the coffee mill and watched the grounds piling magically into a small hill in the glass catcher, the elusive essence of fresh grounds lingering momentarily on the air. "He said he's gone away", Skull added when the whine of the burr grinders stopped. "Espresso? Latte? Cappuccino?"

"However it comes," she said.

"It comes however you want it to come. I thought you Italians were fussy about your coffee."

Jac shrugged. "I'm not Italian."

"Americano?"

"Why not."

"With milk?"

"A little milk."

"One shot? Two Shots."

"Surprise me. Did you watch the video?"

"Of course."

"Didn't it worry you?"

"Well I didn't take Jon for a strip club kind of guy. But he's changed recently. A lot."

"It wasn't a strip club."

"No? Night club, then. Late bar..."

"He's in a car."

"A car? No. How'd you get that?"

"You can hear traffic. And also by the way that he's sitting." She used her hands to demonstrate. "He's in the driver's seat talking to someone in the passenger seat. The camera's on the dashboard."

Skull couldn't recall the sound of traffic, but realised he hadn't really listened to the video, just watched the image. A strip club would be preferable, he thought, but her interpretation was more likely.

"What about the light? The flashing red light?" he asked, unwilling to concede yet.

"Brake lights, perhaps. Maybe he parked near a junction. Does it matter?"

"Maybe not, but — fatal flaw: Jon doesn't own a car." He tamped the grounds down into the filter holder before locking it firmly into the machine.

Jac shrugged. "Hire car? Anyway, I'd like to know who he's talking to," she said.

"Well you seem to have interpreted the hell out of some slim evidence," Skull said, pressing the start button on the machine.

"Professional hazard," she laughed.

The machine refused to work. There was no friendly click or burr, no humming, no dark flow of vital juices. Skull swallowed hard and pressed the button again. Nothing. It was dead, something else that had abandoned him, shut down, given up.

"As a palaeontologist," she went on, "I can infer a whole new species around the imprint of a sliver of bone." Her short laugh hung in the air like an odd smell.

Skull checked the plug, confirming it was pushed in, switched on. He reseated the basket holder, ensuring it locked securely into place. Click.

In silence Jac observed him, his frantic labours. Skull focused on the machine, the necessity of animating it, giving it the attention, the understanding it needed so that it delivered up the coffee he deserved, craved. Resisting, at this early stage, the temptation to percussive intervention (a sharp bash is a proven fix for any indolent engine), he pulled open the water tank drawer in the side.

"Ah, water," he quavered with relief. Skull felt sure she would not have noticed the tremor in his hands as he filled the reservoir with fresh water before slamming the drawer shut once again. When he fingered the rocker switch this time, the machine purred gently, rewardingly, before at last a gush of golden liquid slid into the cup below, the rich Arabica filling the kitchen with heady, earthen aromas.

"The coffee ritual of Hoxton man," he could joke now. "I can see the paper in Anthropology Today —" he turned, smiling towards her but she had moved on, standing by the window in the sitting area, gazing down onto to the street below.

"Sorry?" she called.

"Nothing." Skull bent his head to the task of making another two shots of coffee, frothing up the milk, easing it slowly into the mugs.

*

They sat in a formal silence, him on the rumpled armchair, her on a straight-backed dining chair, neither knowing how to restart.

"Coffee's good," she said after her first polite sip. She leaned forward then, placing her mug down carefully on the table. "Skull," she began, frowning, "I understand that you and Jon had an argument; I understand that you're perhaps angry and you probably —"

The speakers for the sound system gave a low double-bleep, a polite a-hem, the large wall screen flickered on, a small dark panel opening over the top of other windows and panels. In Skull's flat everything was connected. His communications followed him through the house like a faithful dog.

Jac paused, glancing at the screen, disturbed by the interruption. Skull nodded at her to continue but she had lost her thread, the intensity of her appeal was spent. "Daddy's so impractical," she said at last. "My life is ... complicated, to say the least. I live far away, I don't know anyone anymore — no one who might be able to help. Would it be at all possible —?"

The speakers warbled again, the panel on the screen flashed, and some text appeared:

<hawsehole69>   hey

Skull picked up a keyboard. "Sorry," he said to Jac. He typed: *hey*

Jac subsided in her chair. She glanced at the screen, compressed her lips at Skull, defeated. "If not for Jon," she concluded, "at least for me."

Skull said, using bluntness as a form of resistance: "Jon thinks a phone app is trying to kill him. He's running away from his phone." He nodded at her astonishment. "Yes. That's what all this is about, I think."

"Is that even possible?" she asked.

Skull smiled, raised a sceptical brow. "No," he said. "How would it? How could it? Excuse me, I need to ..." He pointed at the screen. She pursed her lips again, turning to watch the conversation unfold.

```
<hawsehole69>  can get a cheap net
<hawsehole69>  7 ph for 48hrs
<hawsehole69>  ?
<Skull>  no thanks, no need
<hawsehole69>  ?
<Skull>  got password from boyfriend
```

During the pause, Skull sipped a little coffee; Jac was right, it was good.

```
<hawsehole69>  np
<Skull>  I O U
<hawsehole69>  get the vids? :P
<Skull>  yep
<hawsehole69>  any good?
<Skull>  disgusting
<hawsehole69>  ??
<Skull>  deleted them
```

Another pause. He glanced at Jac who deadpanned him back. "Long story," he told her.

```
<Skull>  o u bigtime.
<hawsehole69>  np bye
```

Skull tossed the keyboard aside. "Josh did some work for us. Security stuff."

Jac nodded. "What's NP?" she asked.

"NP? No Problem," Skull said. "He's not too chuffed with me."

"Chuffed? I'm not surprised. You deleted his vids." She said 'vids' with the same distaste she might have said 'poo'.

"There weren't any vids," Skull laughed. "Not in the way he thought. I sort of tricked him into attempting something a bit — well, a bit dodgy. The very best intentions, of course." Skull grinned.

She viewed him archly, feigning mild shock. "You used your friend's good nature?" she asked.

"No, that would be wrong," Skull said with equal seriousness. "I used his bad nature."

"Intriguing," she said, glancing with renewed interest at the busy noise on the screen, the residue of the brief chat with Josh. "How does your boyfriend feel about it?" she asked at last.

"Boyfriend?"

"With the password," she said nodding at the screen.

"Ah," Skull laughed again. "There's no boyfriend. I asked Josh to break into Jon's media store — where the video clip came from," he explained. "There are probably more clips. So you see, I have been trying to help."

"More clips like the other one?"

"Probably."

"Can you show me?"

He reached for the keyboard, resting it across his knees while his fingers played quick chord-sequences, popping open a new browser window on the large screen and opening once again Jon's media streaming website. The familiar video clip ran automatically and this time as he listened he heard the traffic noise, saw the brake lights, accepted Jac's interpretation.

"But we've already seen this," she said. "Where are these others?"

"That's the point. I don't know his password. That's what I asked Josh to get."

"Josh? Haws- I can't say it. Your friend's real name is Josh?

"Indeed. Not a friend, as such. A supplier."

"But he is an expert?"

"One of the best."

"Well, clearly not," she said.

"Despite what you see in the movies it's not always that simple. Josh is good, but so far he's only run a dictionary attack." She raised an eyebrow so Skull expanded: "A dictionary attack the simplest password cracking method. It's a list of common words which a computer tries one after the other. It's very simple and very fast and that's usually all you need since most people use a word they can remember: aardvark, secret, Janet, that sort of thing. What he's proposing is what's called a brute-force, which is to try every possible combination of letter, lower case, uppercase, symbols, everything. Brute force. It needs significant computing power to achieve. I said no."

They both stared at the screen where it had frozen on the final frame of Jon leering to camera.

"Beepbeep?" she said, unexpectedly loud. Skull laughed. "It's Roadrunner," she said, unable to hide the tinge of annoyance. "Did you try that?"

"Plus all the variations in between: beep dash beep, Wiley Coyote, Disney, 31st July 1977, King's High, Sienna. Everything I could think of."

"Julie — what was her name?"

"And all the other girlfriends," Skull nodded.

"Matt Morrell?" she asked. "Skull?"

It hadn't occurred to him. He tried a range of combinations on his own name without success. After a few more suggestions she conceded the impossibility of it.

"I should go," she said, standing. "I promised Anka I would call in at her sandwich shop. It seemed terribly important to her. She's — she seems a bit bewildered by all of this. Have you spoken with her recently?"

Skull shook his head and helped Jac with her jacket.

"Well. Thank you for the coffee, Skull" she said. "It was very nice."

Skull said, "If you'll agree to pay, I can ask Josh to run the brute-force attack."

"Why?" She looked back at the screen then added, "What will more of these videos tell us?"

"He wanted me to see this one," Skull said. "It must have some significance."

"Maybe." She looked down then let her gaze travel over the boxes stacked, the space where the sofa went, the naked windows, the gaps on the wall. "I'm sorry for taking your time, Skull," she said. "You have your own difficulties. I was hoping it would all be much simpler than this."

You were hoping to blame me, Skull thought as she turned towards the door above the stairs. Nothing would be simpler than that: a friendship betrayed, trust broken, bad blood. Human failings.

"If he is trying to get your attention," she paused, her hand on the door handle, "why not just ask for it? Why send this video link? And why all the stuff about this Werner Brandes?"

"Oh that's so I knew it was from him and not some random spam," Skull explained. "It was a regular joke. Only I would know that."

"How is it a joke?" she asked. "It's not particularly funny."

"You have to be sixteen, and say it in a funny voice."

"Family joke," she said. "You told me."

"Indeed." Somehow she had managed to make him feel the gauche schoolboy again. "In the film," he said by way of explanation, "there's a group of hackers who record this Werner Brandes character saying different words in different contexts. Then they splice it all together to make up the sentence required for a voice authentication system. Jon and I saw the film a couple of times when it came out. We thought it was the smartest, funniest thing we'd ever seen. Anyway, when they play the finished version of the tape it sounds funny, you know, disjointed — a collage of words: Hi. My-name. Is. Werner? Brandes," Skull said in a funny, disjointed voice which visibly surprised her, so he continued. "My voice? Is. My passport. Verify —"

Skull paused, frowned, then continued slowly, "Verify me. Verify me. It's the password, isn't it? He sent the password. Josh said it was a long password."

Skull sat down again quickly and typed the password, *myvoiceismypassport.*

"!Oop! Fat finger!"

HI!MynameisWernerBrandes.

"Are you typing it exactly as it is in the text?" she asked, now standing over his shoulder.

He typed, *HI!My name is Werner Brandes.*

The banner flashed across the top of the screen: "Hi roadrunner Welcome Back to rewindr". Underneath it said: "Rewind Your Awesome Lifestream".

An information panel titled "Your Life" showed there were 2736 private video clips and over ten thousand photos stored on the account. The storage allowance was impressive.

Along a horizontal date line, strung like bunting, were tiny images taken from the videos and photos. Mostly they showed Jon's face from different angles. The images were tightly packed, overlapping, and shouldering each other for attention. A slider on the side allowed you to zoom onto particular dates, or you could grab the line with a little grasping-hand icon, and drag it forwards and backwards over time. Hovering over an image popped up a little information box with title, tags and comments, and indicating if it was public, shared or private. The titles and comments were empty, there were no tags and all were marked Private, the standard setting. Jon had spent no time maintaining his Awesome Lifestream.

The "Help-me" clip was easy to find, right near the end of the collection, mid-November, around the time Jon disappeared. It was the only item marked Public.

"My God," breathed Jac staring up at the screen on the wall. "What is this?" she asked, removing her jacket and arranging it over the back of the dining chair. She sat. "When does it start?"

Skull slid the time-line left, tracking back to the first entry. The beginning of time was around two years earlier with close-up images of Jon's face peering suspiciously towards the camera. There was at least one video clip for each day, usually many more, and numerous still images.

"What is this?" Jac asked again, her face pinched with bafflement and faint disgust. "He must have been taking pictures of himself all day."

"It's automated. I think it's automated," said Skull. "It's a life log; or a life caste some people call it. It's supposedly an automated visual record of your day."

"Why in heaven would anyone ever want to do that?"

"Quite," said Skull.

He picked an arbitrary clip and screened some footage of an ear in close-up, while the voice of Jon told a portion of an elaborate and expletive filled anecdote. It lasted about half a minute. A second random selection, of a similar duration, filmed a naked leg dangling over the arm of a chair with a can of lager popping in and out of shot, all to the accompaniment of a dull sports commentary. Skull deduced that the camera may have been sitting on a cradle above a television set.

"It must be his phone," Skull said. "It's taking a random photo or a bit of video throughout the day and storing it here. Perhaps whenever he switches it on, or when it hits some sound or movement threshold. He doesn't seem to be aware it's happening."

That was a puzzle. Over the last year, at least before their bust-up, Jon had assiduously recorded the minutiae of his life in intricate and obsessive detail using every new tool or gadget that would count, measure or record him. Yet here was a bizarre visual record, a stream of candid selfies, of which he seemed entirely unaware.

"Go back," Jac said suddenly, pointing at the screen. He pulled the time line back towards the beginning. "Further," she said. "Further. There. Is that you?"

A group of images huddled around a date point over eighteen months back: Skull driving, Skull walking through a field, Jon in front of what looked like a building site, Jon in a car, Skull and Jon in a car, a pub, an empty packet of crisps.

"Oh," Skull said, remembering the day. "Godwin Hill. I'd forgotten."

"Godwin Hill? You mean *the* Godwin Hill? On the South Downs? The flint mines?"

"Indeed. We took a day trip. Me and Jon. Memorable for all the wrong reasons."

"What were you doing there?"

Skull shrugged. "It was a day trip. Jon's idea."

He flicked through the images. They told an odd story. Jon looked cross; Skull looked miserable.

"Looks like a nice day out," she said, apparently without irony. "Why don't you tell me about it?" So he told her.

Godwin Hill

The outing to Godwin Hill was Jon's idea and, as usual, I fell in with it.

Mud and muffin, he said. Young women in shorts and damp t-shirts kneeling hopefully in low trenches. The smell of dirt and sweaty girls, the sound of trowel on stone, the rhythmic hammering of marker pegs going in, the trill of young women laughing, the wanton looks across the open top of the wet-sieving barrel.

"I lost my virginity to Sarah below the trestle tables in the finds tent," he told me. "It was a damp summer's evening in the flower of my youth. Her hands were as rough as a sandstone rock from washing mud off pottery crocks, and she smelt of mud, and of unwashed camp girl, but I loved her lustily because she let me touch her anywhere I wanted to. You really have to experience the joy of The Dig, Skull," he told me. He was being satirical, of course. I knew he hated The Dig.

We've always had meet-ups, Jon and I. But over the years since school and college they've become more erratic, less frequent. Nowadays it's maybe two, three times a year and usually we meet in a pub, or sometimes a restaurant if we're parading a new, current partner. Before the Godwin Hill outing, we hadn't had a get-together for a good while and we'd been bouncing emails and texts, promising each other with a proper outing, trying to arrange a mutual date. I suggested a race driving day or a ballooning flight but Jon insisted on Godwin Hill. "It's the beginning of the digging season," he said. "We've been invited. Un-box your trowel; shake off your anorak."

Jon had his agenda of course — well, you know Jon — and I went along with it as usual. None of it interested me; not the girls, not the ancient relics and specifically not the mud. But I didn't really care where we went; I wanted to test out the new car, show it off a bit, so at least the drive to the South Downs gave a common purpose to our day.

I picked him up outside Greenwich Station just after the morning rush hour — it was a perfect late spring morning with crisp sunlight and whimsical breezes.

"Hi! My name is Werner Brandes!" he sang as he flopped onto the passenger seat. He had a small day sack which he tucked between his feet in the foot well, and his walking jacket he slung onto the back seat. "Whoa," he said, looking at the car's cockpit hemmed with dials and switches and wired-in displays. "There're more boys' toys in here than in a tart's bedside cabinet."

He grins, I grins; it's a lads' day out.

The midweek traffic was light, driving a pure pleasure. As we wiggled onto the South Circular I demonstrated some of the toys — the voice-activated controls, the dashboard screen projection, the component-status monitoring system which came via the on-board diagnostics feed; and, of course the very expensive in-car entertainment system. I was streaming, I think, something classical off the company servers. The music was definitely designed to annoy him, so it would have had violins and singing in it.

He pressed a few buttons and flipped through all the media streaming possibilities on the passenger touch screen. He seemed bored. "Very cool," he said. "Where can I get one?"

"You can't."

"Well, you got one, bruv. Why can't I get one?"

"You can't afford it, for one thing," I told him. "And for another, you don't drive."

"Ah, detail — picky, picky detail." He waved a dismissive hand. "Maybe I don't need the whole car. Maybe I'll buy just the gadgets. I am buying gadgets now, you know. Bought a garlic press the other day, and look at this," he said as he rummaged in the depths of his day sack. "You'll be so proud of me, dad. I'm growing up, see? I have cast off my boyish mantle and have donned the poncho of a real man, adopting the manly bearing of a man wielding manly tools." He flourished a large-screened smart phone in front of my face. In the brief glance I got as I drove, the only distinguishing feature was the cardinal red colour. "See?" he said proudly. "I bought this a couple of weeks ago. It's incredibly cool and — and incredibly red."

"The two are practically synonymous," I said.

"It's a smart phone, you know," he responded with venom, then went on: "One of the tech support wonks at work sold it me, so now I've joined the vanguard of the revolution, bruv. We'll keep the red phone ringing," he said, but he sat with the phone in his hands, holding it as you might hold a toad, something fragile and faintly disgusting.

"Who's it made by?" I asked.

"Ying Lee Po," he said without pause. "And her six year old grandson. He held open the case while she popped in all the little electrical bits."

"What's the brand, idiot?"

"Jesus Christ, Skull. Who cares about brands nowadays? A phone's a phone and this one is a," he turned it over in his hand, "— a Lucy Phone. How's that for you? Any good?"

I'd never heard of a Lucy phone. "4G?" I asked.

There was a significant pause before he said, "A hundred quid is what I paid for it. I don't think I'd want to pay any more than that for something like this. I mean, who pays four grand for a plastic phone?"

For a moment I thought he was joking but he was genuinely angry. I laughed. "Not the cost, fool. Does it support 4G? It's a protocol — like a fast broadband for mobiles. Although it's somewhat academic for a cheapskate like you. I doubt you'd be able to make the most of 4G even if you had it."

For a while he said nothing, long enough to unsettle me. His timing is always perfect, although there are times when he genuinely takes offence at the smallest thing. Eventually he said in a small voice, "The Lucy Phone phones people, Skull. It takes pictures, it sends and receives emails, it twitters, it chatters and farts. I also have it on good authority that it will stream pornographic movies in small but pleasing detail, and I believe it would probably even make the tea if I knew where to put the water in. But it does make phone calls."

"That's progress," I laughed. "So who are you? And what did you do with my old friend Jon?"

You have to realise that this was the man who until a few years back would not even contemplate owning a mobile phone that did anything other than make phone calls. Even his camera was the old fashioned film camera which he loaded with black and white Ilford film stock. As far as I know, he still carries with him a one year diary planner and a lead pencil.

"I've not conceded defeat, my friend," he told me. "Don't think I'm giving in. I am simply rolling with the punches of a particularly brutal and modern reality. I was incredibly disappointed — saddened, actually — to discover that you can no longer buy an ordinary, decent cell phone. Just as you can no longer telegraph your uncle in Australia to tell him granny's dying and he should catch the fast steamer, soonest, from Canberra; nor can you walk into your bank and discuss frankly with your bank manager the delicate state of your investment portfolio. Did you know you can't even buy a paper ticket on the London buses anymore? Which means you have nothing to use as a handy bookmark when you've reached your destination and need to close the paper pages of your paperback novel.

It's your world now, bruv, and I'm merely an honest citizen doing his best to live an honest life inside its revolutions as it spins us all into oblivion. So I bought the smartphone. I bought the smartphone without rancour, and without bitterness; also without the hope or the anticipation that it would make my friends any smarter, or any more inter-esting, or even more attractive. As I look at you now, dear boon companion, surrounded with all the knobs and bobs of your trade, I reflect with sincere regret, that it's hard to be right all the time."

Vintage Jon. I laughed. "Glad to have met your expectations," I said.

"You have exceeded them, Skull. You have exceeded them. Tell you what: if I buy the car, and gather together all the gadgets myself, would you at least fit the gadgets to the car and make sure they all work together?"

"No."

"I'm bringing you business."

"We're not mechanics," I explained.

"Ah," he said. "Disappointing. I see what you did with the name, by the way. Smart-or. That's clever. Smart motor — Smart-or. It's catchy. And very modern, but I'm having some trouble understanding what it is exactly that you do."

"Well, we do a number of things." I'm never sure when he's joking, but I took him seriously now. I said, "We're a smart hub, a sort of portal for making cars social." It was my standard line. Most people were impressed.

"It's beautiful," he cut over me. "This is truly the modern age. You have a thriving business worth maybe millions of pounds but you don't sell any products, and you don't supply any services."

"We provide solutions," I said.

"You're living on fumes."

"Not at all," I insisted. "We're the glue that connects connected cars and their owners."

"Eh-ha, lol," he said. "Glue fumes for glue sniffers." And he actually did laugh out loud as he jabbed at the touch screen in front of him, unleashing *Nine Inch Nails* in a blast of tormented mechanical rhythms.

Success without the admiration of friends is really only doing-quite-well. I concentrated for a while on the enjoyment of driving Betty.

Betty was our latest test car, our beta model, which we bought when Smartor raised a new round of angel funding. Of course none of the car manufacturers would partner with us. None of the main venture capital funds would touch us either. We took that as a good sign. Obviously we were too innovative, too disruptive for their taste, but it did make raising capital a challenge.

Our first car was Alphie (naturally), a second-hand mutt of a vehicle, now mostly in ruins on the workshop floor. Betty was built for phase two of our plans, which was really just to get the website up and demonstrate some very basic functions on the phone app, like controlling the music, managing climate control, navigation, stuff like that. Betty was a top of the line Ford Focus Titanium Navigator. Nothing special, but a good mule for our product, something we could take to roadshows.

We weren't doing anything very advanced at that time, just gathering up and processing data. We were processing about seven percent more of our customer's data from the CAN bus than any of our nearest competitors. But the momentum around the connected car was mostly to do with in-car entertainment and mobile integration at that time; hence the ultra-cool hi-fi system in Betty. We were finding interesting correlations, like music type and the interior temperature of a vehicle, or average speed and distance per day of the week. So for instance we knew that hip-hop devotees tended to average higher engine revs than the fans of traditional RnB, but their mean speeds and mileage were lower. World music lovers enjoyed a higher ambient temperature over the length of their journey than fans of classical music. We were also getting good press coverage for these snippets of information.

For Phase Three we were working on more advance tweaking — for instance allowing a remap of the ECU profile to favour fuel consumption over performance, or adjust the power steering to give a lighter, more racy touch. We'd bought a third car for that, the gamma vehicle, Gabby. Gabby was in the workshop at that time.

So Jon was wrong. We had a product and a service. We were building a business. I was proud of our achievements.

I waited for a pause between tracks and said quickly: "Didn't know we had this album."

"It's crap, isn't it," he said, sliding down the volume and flicking through the catalogue again. "When are you going to get some decent music?"

"Not mine," I told him, "They're demo tracks on the company servers. Everything's streamed from the office." Eventually he found something he liked and sat back to enjoy the drive. "So, Goodwood Hill," I said. "What's so good about Goodwood Hill?"

"Godwin Hill," he corrected me. He'd given me only the nearest town for the GPS. He said he'd navigate the rest of the way with "a proper map".

"Is there a pub?" I asked.

"Doubt it. It's a hill," he said, adding, "with an invisible fort on top and some filled-in old flint mines underneath."

"Cool," I said, but without much joy. "Remind me why we're going there again?"

"Women, of course. Young, women students."

"Cool."

"Although," he added as an aside, "we also need to pay our respects to Uncle Daffy."

I must admit my enthusiasm for the day took a dive right there. I've never shared Jon's affection for Uncle Daffy. I know he's an old family friend and not really related, more like an older brother and all that; and I know he helped Jon at various times over the years, particularly when the Prof wasn't too happy about his degree choices. But Uncle Daffy never liked me, and has always made that as clear as broken glass on the few occasions we've met. I asked Jon, "He's not still your uncle is he?"

"He will always be my lovely Uncle Daffy," Jon said. "Although now risen in the world of men of learning. Professor of something ... can't remember. One of these new-fangled places — University of something incredibly big and totally traditional. Anyway, he's running the dig up at Godwin Hill."

"Ah. Professor of farming then," I suggested.

"That'll be it: School of Artichoke. Beets working for a living."

"Bet he knows his onions," I parried with a flash of inspiration.

"Well he's no rocket scientist but he is the top banana. Honours from Brussels sprout from his chest."

"Not a has bean?" I was struggling. I knew I couldn't compete. Jon is a walking thesaurus.

"Well he barley makes a living. Annual celery is a joke. Doesn't avocado, lettuce not forget."

"Ay?"

"Unlike you, he doesn't have-a-car-though," Jon explained slowly, as if speaking to someone stupid.

Stupidly I said, "Oh, I get it, avocado. But the Greens must love him when he turnips on his bicycle."

"No," he said emphatically. "You can't have turnips. Greens, yes. Turnips, no. You killed it." He held up a half bottle of scotch which he'd excavated from his daysack. "Too early for you?"

"I'm driving," I said lamely. It was barely past ten o'clock.

"Talking of women," he said a little hoarsely after cracking open the lid of the bottle and swigging generously, "How's the lovely — ah, Lillian?"

"Emily."

"Emily? Since when? Are you sure?"

"Fairly sure. We've been living together for a couple of years as Matthew and Emily. And she was Emily when I left her in bed this morning."

"I could swear she was Lillian when I left her in bed last night." He never tired of that joke. "You lucked out there, bruv. Punching way above your weight. Bit of a trophy wife for you, I'd say. Sadly Cin left me. Or rather, requested that I leave her."

"I'm so sorry," I said. I rather liked Cindy.

"It seems I am a man more sinning than Cinned. I have been un-Cinned. I am absolved of Cin. In a stoning situation, for instance, I could well be the first to cast my stone due to the fact that I am, at present, without Cin. Apparently," he took another swig, "apparently I was too free in the use of her cosmetic care products, despite polite requests and a warning, which I don't recall receiving but, in any event, wilfully ignored. There were a few other things of note which I can't repeat for reasons of modesty; and she made a number of hurtful observations on a selection of my personal habits, as well as some surprisingly negative comments regarding my more endearing eccentricities. The main thing however seems to have been the unauthorised use of cosmetics, which may seem to you rather slim grounds for divorce, as it did me, but we must face the fact that these are now perfectly adequate justifications for termination in this new, confusing world we live in."

"It's a mad world," I agreed.

"Your world, bud. Remember that. Your brave new world, not mine."

"Sorry about that, too," I conceded.

I was disappointed because Cindy had seemed so promising: she was heterosexual and in possession of an unexpectedly filthy laugh in addition to her own stylish flat. On the down side she owned a cat, along with all the baggage that goes with it.

Jon was in full flow. "The mud packs," he said, "were rubbish. They did nothing for my complexion, in fact if anything they made things worse. I came out in a rash of the most revolting contusions and pus-filled pimples which left my face pocked and scarred like some kind of ancient orbiting astral body. It was upsetting for all of us, but the bright side was that the shampoo was alright. At least I thought it was shampoo. She said otherwise. She maintained it was an expensive hydrating lotion of some sort. I concede that it didn't lather up very well; on the other hand I got some incredible bounce," he said, rubbing his thinning top before continuing bashfully, "Some of the guys at work observed that my hair looked shinier and had more body, so go figure.

"Sadly, however, I must report that her toothbrush — well her toothbrush was a catastrophe. Far too soft. You'll back me up on this, I know you will, but have I not always maintained that the gums should tingle just a little after a good brushing? We're not talking rubbing back to bare bone, here — we need to be just this side of bleeding — but it's English, it's proper, and the right thing to do. Now my experience with her toothbrush was that it felt no different to rodding your mouth with the end of the cat's tail. I know because I tried 'em both: brush, cat; cat, brush; and really, you couldn't tell the difference. It just didn't feel like you were entirely purged after you brushed, rinsed and spat in the kitchen sink. Seriously, a soft toothbrush is a red marker for moral turpitude; everything that's wrong with our society today can be laid on the bristles of the soft toothbrush. In my view. Bring back the ash-and-twig dental programme, I say, and Britain could be great again. But d'you know what?" he asked with amiable pleasure, "When I explained all that to her — when I laid it all out — there was no gratitude. In fact she looked quite sick about the whole thing."

It was a shame because for a while I thought she might be "the one", although I've made that mistake often enough. I did think she would last longer than eight months, but who would have thought that her replacement would be quite as different, and quite as permanent, as Anka.

Sunday Afternoon

"He says to go away. He tells me: hide Anka. Where must I hide? I have business. London is home. Where must I go?" Anka squinted with unhappiness, flapping her hands in frustration at her inability to find her feelings in English. In the end she simply shook her head, eyes hooded with hurt, lips compressed in a tight diagonal grimace.

"We don't understand it either." Jac reached out to touch her gently, the hand of understanding, the squeeze of compassion. "It's not at all like Jon. To do such a thing."

"He did it," Anka insisted, but then her eyes brimmed suddenly, her vulnerable heart exposed by the unexpected gesture of sympathy.

The two women, wrapped in winter jackets, sat tightly together on a small plain sofa. The sofa itself was squeezed in at the far end of the sandwich making warehouse, up near the office and cold storage room, backed hard against the glossy-white breeze-block walls. Directly in front, commanding the centre of the narrow room like a mortuary table, was a long food preparation surface over which the bare strip lighting threw a clinical white hue. Old fish, old meats and disinfectants made for a noisome palette of smells.

On the table top, above the eye level of Jacqueline and Anka sitting on the sofa, a plate of crumbling oat cakes and broken cookies was provided, offcuts and seconds from the catering business. For Skull, sitting high on a bar-stool alongside the sofa, and also backed up flat against the wall, the cookies were an easy stretch, which was a lucky break for him since, although already mid-afternoon, he had not yet eaten. He munched steadily as he looked down on the two women. Arranged in a line along the wall, the seating added an interesting technical challenge to an already tense social encounter.

"Tempory," Anka had explained earlier as they stood staring through the glass window into the office at the far end of the warehouse. This was the small office they might have conducted the meeting in if it was not now overwhelmed with the contents of Jon and Anka's flat. Through the window Skull spotted Jon's expensive Cherrywood speakers stuffed into a corner on top of the Eames copy lounger; kitchen gadgets in boxes squatted over the hi-fi separates while a large flat television screen balanced dangerously on the edge of a glass coffee table.

"Why?" he had asked. "Are you selling the flat?" Anka had ignored him. She was looking for somewhere bigger, she confided to Jac, somewhere she could store furniture and live and sleep, but at the moment she was staying with Ruza. Here she had waved towards the two women, round-backed and aproned, working noisily in the sink area on the other side of the warehouse. From time to time Ruza, or her companion, would trudge the length of the warehouse to the cold storage room next to the office, self-consciously bearing bags of chopped salad, returning with tubs of gherkins or vats of cold meats.

"We must prepare fillings," Anka informed Jac. "For Monday always there are big orders. We must have rocket, lettuce, tomato ..." she listed all the necessary salad ingredients, tapping them off her fingers. The sandwiches were made, cut and packaged over-night for delivery first thing in the morning, she explained.

"Do you make the deliveries yourself?" Skull had asked. Anka ignored him.

"I have delivery van," she told Jac. "Monday is very busy day."

Now Skull sat sullenly, feeling isolated on his perch. He regretted his earlier curiosity. He had been trapped by the casual enquiry Jac had made on the point of leaving his flat: What's the best way to get to Greenwich from here? she had asked.

It was a fatal question for Skull. There is no target so tempting to the average metropolitan as the clueless visitor; nothing is more likely to produce the neck of condescension than an opportunity to unpick a seemingly simple cross-town journey and lay bare the country-cousin naivety of the enquiring traveller with a blizzard of alternatives. This reflexive impulse to provide routing information is the exact inverse of the city native's heart-stopping horror of the map-waving tourist's request for local directions: few Londoners know the name of the street behind the house where they live. But route-planning for a destination that lies in the heartland of a distant neighbourhood is a welcome platform to parade worldly knowledge and flex the urban navigational muscle.

Like a general in his war room Skull quickly raised maps and timetables onto his vast wall screen, reviewing bus routes, rail and underground stops. It all worked against him. The more options he paraded, reviewed and dismissed, the less certain Jac became; as Skull chipped and polished the journey to create the quickest, most efficient transit, Jac's confidence diminished.

The maps had shown Anka's address close to a railway line; the street view revealed a light industrial park.

"You must come with me," Jac insisted. Skull resisted, but Jac reasoned that since she had not yet met Anka, Anka would be wary and distrustful of her, whereas she already knew Skull and so would be more at ease; his warm presence would be reassuring, Jac said. Skull knew otherwise, but he allowed himself to be persuaded nevertheless. He had a sudden curiosity about how Anka was coping without Jon.

Anka, he confided to Jac on the drive to Greenwich, had come as a complete surprise to him when he first met her. She did not fit the archetype, had not been pulled from the same mould that shaped all Jon's previous girlfriends, nor had she been fabricated from the same materials. Since his time at university, Jon had attached to delicate brunettes with doe-brown eyes and sad family histories, or fey redheads with ballet-dancer necks and eating disorders, whereas Anka was a big boned blond who moved with purpose when she moved at all. Jon's past partners were fragile, slightly damaged young women in need of gentle coaxing and tender attention; invariably they were smart, over-educated girls, intellectual, opinionated and sulky, demanding care and comfort, requiring regular placation for subtle infringements, always accompanied by expensive proofs of devotion. Anka, by contrast, was plainly self-reliant, taciturn, competent, robust and, according to Jon, kind and loyal. For that reason Skull had really tried to like her and hoped that she would like him in return.

Jac had listened to Skull's assessment without comment. In her turn she described the aftermath of the wedding when Jon had taken his new wife down to Churnwell House to meet the Professor. The meeting had not gone well. The Professor was suspicious at the haste of the marriage, scandalised by the lack of observance, upset at the honours due but not paid. Anka was respectful and demure which the old man chose to read as contrived and designing. Anka tried hard to please, to make herself likable, worthy; the Professor decided that he had difficulty in understanding her English and so spoke only to Jon, as if she wasn't there. According to Jac he now referred to Anka simply as "the Polish carthorse" or "that Russian sex trade worker".

"Are there any friends that Jon may be staying with?" Skull asked, reaching out for another scalene triangle of oat flapjack.

"Is he staying with you? No," she sneered, refusing to look at Skull directly. "You are not good friend."

"I think what Skull means," Jac said quickly, "is do you know of any other friends that Jon has, that he may be staying with?"

"Yes. We have many friends," Anka responded to Jac, her voice sweet like Madeira cake, her face soft with the smile of a girl thinking about puppies. They had many, many good friends, she asserted, and she had telephoned them all ("so many"), but none of them had either seen or heard from Jon recently. She had called just about everyone she could think of including the Professor, she admitted, uttering the word "Professor" with all the sibilant reverence of a priest intoning the name of "Jesus".

"But I do not phone him," she jutted her chin at Skull, spitting out her words, still refusing eye contact. "So."

"Anka, was someone threating him?" Jac asked, moving the conversation on. "Did he owe anyone money, for instance?"

"We have money!" Anka objected. "Why would we owe?" Then as if explaining to strangers, she told them that Jon had a fine job, a respectable job, with a desk and a salary that was paid into a bank. They had the flat and investments: "Phone tells him: Sell this, buy this. He does it. It makes money."

She too worked hard. Her business she had built from nothing except the will to succeed and the willingness to work whatever hours were needed. They had money. She had done nothing wrong. Why did this bad thing happen?

Anka slumped on the sofa, her shoulders round in a tableaux of misery, her face a turbid oval behind which, to Skull, it nevertheless seemed possible to read the ripple of internal processes much like the muddy swirls on the surface of a wide, slow river. There were no hidden undercurrents here, no subtle counter flows, only broad streams, the flat wash of wants, of needs, the curl of impulses and sudden anxious eddies, bubble trails of uncertainty borne downstream as the waters flowed naturally to the sea.

It was a momentary insight. Anka has no sides, Jon had once told him, and briefly Skull saw what he meant, saw that her honesty had nothing to do with truth and lies and everything to do with simple purpose. Skull had always wanted Anka to like him.

"He has a friend who killed his wife," Anka announced unexpectedly.

"My God," Jac exclaimed. "Did you know this?" She turned to Skull, leaning forward to glare at him. Skull, mouthful of oatcake, shrugged. Jon may have mentioned it.

"Yes," Anka continued. "Police arrested this man. Then, they let him go." She shrugged. Jon had only found out about Deepak's situation through a mutual acquaintance. At first, Anka told them, he had followed the story "like a joke, funny", but increasingly he had become troubled by what he learnt. After Deepak's release, Jon had telephoned him and they had engaged in a series of lengthy conversations. About what? She would never listen to a private conversation. Had Jon and Deepak met face to face? How could she know? She ran her sandwich business, he went to work. They lived busy lives.

But, Anka said (her small, hurt voice returning), that was the change point in their lives. Soon their happiness went dark, their joy fell silent. Jon became secretive, spending hours on the Internet, obsessively reading websites, forums, mailing lists, messaging people. Anka didn't know what he was looking for, and when she asked he denied there was a problem, but he slept badly, drank more, ate less.

At the far end of the warehouse a food processor began shredding vegetables.

"Was he unhappy at work?" Skull yelled over the grinding, stuttering buzz.

Again Anka would not answer Skull, would not look at him, but her pursed lips said: Of course — who is happy at work? She half rose from the sofa, solemnly selecting a sliver of seed-coated confection which she nibbled at.

The noise of the blades and the engine grind rose and fell as Ruza, or her companion, fed the machine, apparently with concrete ballast. Eventually the engine and its blades spun down. Jac asked, "He didn't own a car, did he?"

"He takes my van. If he needs."

"Did he often take your van? When was the last time, for instance?"

He borrowed the van over a few nights shortly before he disappeared, leaving late and returning in the early hours. She didn't know where he went, didn't ask, but the mileage was not high. Then one morning he told her he had to go away and that she too must leave. "He is frightened? Yes. Nothing bad will happen, he says, but I must hide. He tells me nothing. He says everything will be okay, but he says I must leave flat. Now I am here," she shrugged, the diagonal grimace underlining her sadness. "It's not okay."

"Show her the video, Skull," Jac said. "Show her the video Jon sent you."

Anka wobbled her head at the smartphone screen almost as soon as Skull started the video clip.

"Yes, I have seen," she said dismissively. "It is from his friend."

"You've seen it?"

"Yes. His friend sends me. Text. Willem, I think."

"Werner Brandes?" Skull asked.

"I think so."

"But Werner Brandes —" Jac began.

"How," Skull quickly asked, cutting in, "how did you know it was from Werner Brandes?"

"He said it. In text. Hello, it's Werner Brandes, here is link." Anka was distracted by the activities of Ruza and her companion. The women were arguing over dressings.

"So you've seen this video?" Jac asked.

"Of course. He keeps sending. I clicked the link. Always the same one." She glanced down the room to where voices were being raised in the salad section.

"So do you know who this is in the video?" Jac asked. "Who's the other man?"

"Yes," Anka said. "It is him — Werner Brandes, I think." She paused briefly, her focus hijacked by the increasingly piercing exchange at the far end of the warehouse. Nevertheless, she caught the look that passed between Skull and Jac so she added: "Yes. He is friend of Jon. From work."

"Can you show me the text you received?" Skull asked.

"I deleted it," she said. "Always it's the same. Some stupid joke. I don't understand it. It is men," she said, shaking her head sadly at Jac before abruptly yelling the length of the room, a tongue twisting barrage of consonants that licked the women into temporary silence. "Excuse me," she said sweetly to Jac, as an afterthought.

*

They left Anka in the warehouse, her attention sucked into the gravity of sandwich fillings and the shrill squabbling of her workers.

"I'll run you back to Churnwell, if you like," Skull offered, thinking only of the quiet pleasure of the return journey. Threading a quick car through thick, fast moving traffic can rapidly drive out old stale thoughts, the pure thrill of the road mediated only by a hundred dedicated sensors. He regretted immediately his spontaneity, expecting her anyway to refuse his offer. A train from south London would be simpler for her, leaving her without obligation, without the necessity to make small talk, but she accepted with a warmth that surprised him. She kicked off her shoes as soon as she had settled into the passenger seat, wiggling her toes with relief, the bright, chipped varnish beneath her stockings strangely intimate.

They spoke little as Skull worked his way onto the upper reaches of the A20, joining the thin trickle of cars on the road which would take them out of London. She gazed silently out on the shuttered shops, the muffled peoples of south London going out, going home, going nowhere particular. He focused on his driving, giving close attention to the flow of traffic, enjoying the responsive feel of the wheel under his hands, relishing the chemical mix of car odours, the waxy polish, the breath of fumes, of plastics, upholstery glues, oils, and Jacqueline, her own mysterious smell woven through it.

Take the second exit, instructed the voice of the navigation system. The black Honda Civic, two cars behind, followed.

"D'you think she's got something to do with it?" This, at last, was her blunt opening to the conversation she wanted to have about her sister-in-law.

"No," Skull said.

"No. Unless she's playing a really clever game. She's not that smart though, is she? Is she that smart?"

"No."

"No, but deliciously grasping and avaricious. From one angle. Don't you think? I mean for God's sake, how do we interpret the hoarding of all Jon's things?"

"Their things."

"But why take them from the flat and pile them in her warehouse? Like a squirrel. Or a refugee. That's it, isn't it? The warehouse is her donkey-cart — it's her wheelbarrow — for trudging down the dusty road. Oh my God, I sound like the Prof. That's exactly the analogy he would use, and not in the sympathetic way. But she did seem genuinely upset, I thought? Didn't you?"

The late Sunday afternoon traffic was all in-bound. London was drawing her restless inhabitants homeward along the venous mesh of roads and highways feeding north and south, east and west; a mighty pump, an implacable heart. On Friday night the flow would be reversed but for now, travelling outbound, driving east into Kent, the road was mostly traffic free.

"She doesn't seem to like you very much," Jac said. There was a playfulness in her voice, not mocking, just teasing.

"She likes you," he countered.

"Maybe." Jac seemed pleased.

In the pale blue sky behind them the winter sun, like an angry boil on a sickly face, was sinking early and rapidly. Anyone travelling out of London to anywhere in Kent would follow the same route, Skull reasoned, watching in the mirror as the black Honda Civic pulled out to overtake the van he himself had just passed. In any navigation system, assuming the inputs were reasonably constant, the algorithms for calculating an efficient journey would produce pretty much a standard route, he reasoned, even if the final destinations were a few miles apart.

Skull hadn't found much opportunity to drive his car since Smartor's collapse. Strictly speaking it wasn't really his car. When the end was obvious, when he knew the company was doomed, he had called a meeting of the directors and they had agreed to a fire sale of vehicles and parts, agreed to sell them cheaply to themselves through the agency of close friends and relatives. They thought of it more as a Phoenix sale so that when they could begin again at least they would have a starting point; they would re-emerge through the smouldering remains of the burnt-out Smartor PLC, their assets intact, their resolve hardened by their flame-tempered experience.

During a bad tempered coffee break they drew straws, literally, drinking straws sourced from the local cafe and cut to different lengths. Simon drew the longest and punched the air laughing tears of merriment as he chose Betty. Betty was the obvious choice since, as the beta vehicle, Betty had all the gadgets, all the flashy and expensive kit with every conceivable option for in-car entertainment, navigation and comfort. He persuaded an elderly cousin from Grimsby to put the car in his name, and made a complicated financial arrangement with yet another relative to secure all the funding needed. Keith drew the short straw and got Alphie (the Alpha car), a shell barely worth the scrap value.

But Gabby was Emily's. Loyal Emily, dutiful Emily, foolishly signed the documents, paid the money to own the car although she never drove it, didn't even have a license to drive. Skull was silently thrilled. Gabby was third generation, Smartor's Gamma vehicle, the most advanced of all their cars, both technically as well as conceptually. She (all their vehicles were feminine, even Alphie) was also incomplete.

Gabby sported a suite of powerful on-board systems, integrated devices, sensors, advanced diagnostic hardware, all installed but not all fully configured. Like the third party heads-up display unit which was intended to project important data onto the windscreen in a gentle muted light; or the predictive passenger monitoring system designed to increase the comfort and safety of the vehicle's occupants.

On the other hand the self-parking facility was fully enabled, as was the smart air-bag system; and the auto-pilot module had already demonstrated great promise during early trials. Gabby was also hooked into the Smartor grid for monitoring, which meant that, for now, Skull had fast Internet access while on the go. Nobody, at what was left of Smartor, was monitoring anything as far as he knew, but when someone decided to shut down the grid (and figured out how to do it), the fast connection would go too.

Gabby was greater than her working parts, greater than the compression moulded plastics, the forged metal blocks, the extruded pipes, the laminated glass, the natural woods, leathers, wools, and rubbers; she was more than the complex structured lubricants, greater even than the latent silicon circuits wired into the system, or the complex control software, the living data that coursed through her networks like blood through veins. For Skull, Gabby bound together everything he knew, all he had worked for; she embodied his aspirations. More than that, Gabby encompassed all that was possible, he believed. She was at the very pinnacle of human technological development.

"Say something, Skull."

"Sorry."

"Well?"

"Miles away."

He wondered how long Jac had been studying him. She had been mulling, still, the meeting with Anka, but now he couldn't recall if she had asked him a question. He smiled blandly.

"Have an opinion," she said. "Ask me a question. Anecdote me. It's your turn."

"How do you find family life in Florence?" he asked lightly. "Is it the ideal combination of Mediterranean lifestyle and Italian culture? I imagine leisurely strolls around the galleries followed by long, loud family meals in vine-covered courtyards."

She straightened stiffly in her seat, turning away to look out the passenger window at the passing motorway. Maybe she gazed across the pink-grey landscape of Kent, briefly fragile in the sinking sun; or perhaps she observed the distorted reflection of her face in the window. She said nothing for a long while and then at last, as his smirk faded, she said, "Florence is, really, as grim as any other city."

Skull felt uneasy now about his question. He had meant it lightly, a bit of chat, but somehow now it sounded facetious, maybe insensitive. What did he really know of her? Snippets of news from Jon, mentions in dispatches, casual asides, updates spread in a patchy mosaic of bulletins, streamers and tattered flags from a life lived distantly. In his mind she had always been eighteen and angry; she was angry still it seemed. What did he know of her? She had a husband, he recalled, and a child, but now that he thought about it, there may have been a problem. With the husband? An Italian academic — the marriage was clearly doomed. Or was there a question about the child?

"One city's much like another to the people who live in them, I suppose," she added at last. "Crowded, squalid, expensive — rotten."

The child had a defect (that was it!), an unmentionable blight. Skull hadn't paid attention when Jon stopped speaking of his nephew, when news of Jac's life became muffled, as if a white sheet had been laid over it.

Jac went on: "Perhaps that's just Florence, or Italian cities in general. I find old, historic cities mostly grim. They bring out the worst in the tourists, and the worst in the hosts. The tourists push the prices up and push the locals out, and along the way the history gets lost. We're supposed to like the tourists, because they bring in the money that greases the city gears, but I'm not so sure. They seem to attract the very worst of … well, the very worst of everyone, really." She tailed off, shrugged.

Maybe the child had died.

*

On the London-bound carriageway the traffic was almost stationary, queueing to exit, queueing to enter. The light was fading rapidly now, the bright headlights in front and behind increasing the sense of enveloping darkness. The black Honda was still doggedly present, although slowly dissolving into a pair of disembodied lights in his mirror. Skull noted that when he increased his speed, the black car caught up; when he slowed, it dropped back. He was fairly sure it couldn't be coincidence.

He said, "If Anka also got the text, I wonder who else might have got it?"

Jac was silent a while. "Is it important?" she asked, but in a distant, dismissive way, as if he'd interrupted her thoughts.

It was important to Skull. It was important because the message was not, after all, a private joke with him, Skull, in his usual role as fool, nor was it yet another odd appeal for his personal help. There was nothing personal in the message. It was important because it was not about Skull at all.

"You didn't get it," Skull observed. "And neither did the Prof."

"Well," she ruminated, "Jon and I are intermittent correspondents at best; sometimes an email, sometimes a postcard, maybe a phone call on special occasions. We don't text or tweet, we don't chat, or any of the other things everyone seems to be doing nowadays. He did email me a photograph of Anka though. My new wife, it said. But I think he sent it to everyone."

"Indeed."

"You too?" She glanced sideways at Skull. He nodded, remembering the image of the bride in verdant green clutching a single white rose, smiling bleakly through the camera into the future.

"Clearly we're on the same list for family photos," he said. "But not for texts. The texts I'm getting are not coming from Jon."

"But you said they were. Who are they coming from then?"

Who indeed. The messages were delivered regularly, four a day, on schedule. The originating numbers were always different, or were blank. The source, therefore, was not a mobile phone but a selection of SMS gateway services on the Internet, services designed to send text messages to lists of recipients. It was easy enough to fake an originating number on these services. Perhaps there was even some kind of mechanical process behind it, but who was controlling it? Jon?

"Maybe there are other lists?" he mused. "Other lists of contacts that received a different text message. Or perhaps other messages with different links and different passwords, maybe passwords to some of Jon's other accounts? Social media accounts, perhaps. Why not his email accounts, or even his bank accounts?"

"My God, Skull," she said. He had her full attention now. "Is that possible?"

"Why not?"

It was an exciting idea, suggesting some kind of malware that spewed out personal information to random contacts, but when he thought more about it, it seemed unlikely. Where were the benefits? If you could get hold of bank account details and passwords why would you text them to everyone? Besides, there was no evidence any of that was happening. The link to the *rewindr* site and the password for the site suggested that the source must be the site itself.

"I think it's re-winder," he said, then startled Jac by commanding loudly: "Gabby! Open re-winder dot com."

Opening webpage, Gabby responded, and displayed on the screen a website promoting tourism in Ruanda. Slowly Skull spelt out the full address for Jon's life casting site, then commanded, "Login as roadrunner," when the now familiar web site covered the screen.

Password prompt, said Gabby.

"Shift aitch, eye, exclamation ...," slowly he spelt out the password, letter by letter.

Password incorrect, said the car. *Password prompt.*

"Can you type it in," he asked Jac irritably, adding a grudging, "Please?"

Laboriously, and with lips tightly compressed, she pecked out the string of letters using the on-screen keyboard.

Login successful, said Gabby. *Re wine dhur dot com says: Welcome to your awesome lifestream, roadrunner.*

"Gabby!" he commanded. "Display Settings Menu."

The screen flashed, the web site disappeared and in its place was displayed a comprehensive set of on-screen buttons: Braking System Menu, Powertrain Menu, Steering System Options, Suspension Settings ... It was the base menu options for the vehicle's major subsystems.

Skull was impressed. What was particularly interesting was that the menu was available on a live running system so it was almost certainly a bug. He was momentarily curious as to whether it would accept any in-flight changes, suddenly horrified that it might. He was unsure how to close the menu safely without doing it manually. He felt stupid. They were on the borderline of unsafe driving, but he had one more trick.

"Gabby!" he said. "Engage automatic pilot." Jac laughed; perhaps she snorted.

Confirm automatic pilot, Matthew, Gabby responded.

"Green. Box. Rabbit," he said. He wished he could see the look on Jac's face. Her body became very still.

Driver confirmation accepted. Confirm vehicle challenge: Baker, Larry, Tosca.

It was a lengthy process of challenge and response. He could not now recall exactly why they had made the control handover so unwieldy. It had something to do with an avid attention to security but, on reflection, a button would have been sufficient. Everyone else had a button. He wished they had installed a button.

Finally Gabby said, *Autopilot engaged. Please remove your feet from the pedals. Please remove your hands from the steering wheel.*

Slowly he removed his feet from the pedals. The car maintained a constant speed. Slowly he raised his hands from the wheels. The vehicle maintained its direction.

"Jesus wept, Skull," Jac said, as quiet as a breath.

The on-board systems were now in control, scanning the road in front, to the side, behind, calculating the vehicle's location, its velocity, its distance from other vehicles and objects. The systems would keep the vehicle in its own lane, at the current speed, indefinitely, avoiding the cars in front, avoiding the cars behind, and to the side.

"It's perfectly safe," Skull said with all the conviction of a vicar peering over the edge of a bell tower. He found he was holding his head rigidly forward, his eyes fixed firmly on the road ahead, feet cocked above the pedals, hands like open claws poised over the steering wheel, ready to wrest back control. Nothing he could think, nothing he could do enabled him to override the sense of danger. A voice that was his said, "Entirely illegal of course, but perfectly safe. At least on the motorway."

Only once before (outside of the simulator) had he engaged the automatic pilot and then only briefly on the test track shortly after he had integrated the modules downloaded from an enthusiast site. On the other hand Keith had reported good results when he'd tried it very early one morning on the M11 approach to Cambridge.

Jac whispered, "I don't like it, Skull." He knew she spoke softly not from awe but from a simple instinct not to disrupt, not to disturb, the fine balance of the car. They observed the approaching curve where the road seemed to end as at the edge of a flat earth, dipping away into a monstrous void.

"It's perfectly safe," he said again, and he really meant it, but his hands hovered still near the wheel. The techniques and methods for autonomous, driverless driving were well known and well understood: the fusion of multi-sensor data, the real-time environment modelling, the hierarchical control systems — all understood, all decomposed and encapsulated in algorithms, routines, software modules that had long been verified, proven, tested, published. Skull had considerable confidence in these artefacts, was satisfied that his own implementation, as embodied within Gabby, was state-of-the-art. He trusted the technology.

He lowered his hands. Gabby swept gracefully through the gentle curve, the wheel rotating naturally above his lap, the broad highway ahead resolving, receding into the distant east, in the dark Downs of Kent. Control, he thought, as he observed the trembling fingers in his lap; it's simply that I like to be in control.

"Christ," said Jac. "Can we go back to the ordinary way now please?" Her eyes remained staring ahead.

Skull leaned over to the screen. He said, "I need to check the website." Carefully, and manually, he closed the vehicle's control menu, then re-opened the *rewindr* website and tapped on the icon at the top of the web page that looked like a gear-wheel. A simple menu opened with a few simple options: set a background colour, set the size of the thumbnail images, edit label names, restrict downloads, reset password and so on. There was no list of users, no group shares, no notifications lists or schedules.

He was sure that the messages he was getting were not coming from the *rewindr.com* site.

"Well the list has to be somewhere," he said, gratefully taking hold of the steering wheel once more, allowing his foot to come to rest on the accelerator pedal.

Autopilot disengaged, Gabby intoned evenly.

Jac observed this with approval, saying, "Please don't do that again." After a few deep breaths she went on: "The whole message thing is a dead end. In my view. I think, this Deepak chap is the key."

"Deepak? The murderer?"

"Anka said they let him go," Jac said.

The black Honda was still behind.

"Perhaps he's the other man in the car," Jac continued. "The man on the video. Talking to Jon. Perhaps that's Deepak."

"Gabby! Display rear camera view," Skull called. Jac fell silent again, watching the display. A few hundred yards back, the Honda was clearly visible in the yellow cast of the motorway lights.

They were fast approaching the Maidstone bypass, a monumental civic sculpture in grey concrete, tar and metal. In a twisted homage to motoring it was formed into sweeping curves that threaded an underpass through a flyover and a slip road under an overpass. Two junctions, in close succession, created a frantic flow of local traffic which wound and wove around the stately progress of through-travellers, a to and fro of restless vehicles over several miles of fast highway.

It was always busy here. Skull knew the area. He had paid increasingly difficult and infrequent visits to his mother who, for many years, had lived on the outskirts of Maidstone before moving with her new partner to a grim Welsh resort. Now they would not speak to him: they had entrusted their savings to his venture. He had let them down too.

With a rough mental map of the layout of the Maidstone interchange Skull calculated that anyone unfamiliar with the sequence of the two junctions might easily become confused. It would be a good opportunity to get rid of the black Honda which on balance, he felt, probably was following them. However, the structure and function of a motorway is designed to remove the possibility of surprises. Sudden turns or odd manoeuvres were unlikely to work. Any following vehicle would have plenty of time to react. Confusion, deception, sleight-of-hand was what was needed.

In the long approach to the bypass, the exit lanes for both junctions split from the motorway with one leaving and one continuing to run parallel with it. Skull gave plenty of notice, indicating that he intended leaving the motorway at the first junction. He watched the black car follow him into the exit lane but at the last minute Skull crossed back onto the motorway, joining the second exit lane for the next junction. On the display he watched as the black Honda carried out the same unusual move.

Skull increased his speed slowly as he drove down the long road to the Chatham exit at Junction 6, gradually opening the distance between him and the Honda. He wasn't entirely sure how this would work but as the second exit split from the motorway and climbed gradually to the Cobtree roundabout, he lined up in the right hand lane, indicating right, as if he intended travelling into Maidstone town centre.

Far behind at the bottom of the exit road he could see the black Honda once again adjusting similarly. It was fully dark now but the whole area was flooded with yellow light and he knew the driver in the Honda would easily be able to follow him onto the roundabout. Traffic was moderate but moving freely.

He took the roundabout at speed, slipping quickly between two cars already in circulation, moving into the inside lane, still indicating right. The car behind hooted, flashing lights in silent annoyance.

Thick shrubs and small trees covered the central island obscuring the exits, so while the Honda would see him enter, it could not see where he left it. He passed quickly inside the car ahead, then at the exit onto the slip road which would take him back onto the motorway, he cut back into the outside lane and left the roundabout, killing his lights and flooring the accelerator pedal. A distant honk behind registered the further protests of irate drivers, but Skull was already merging back onto the M20 at high speed.

Over the next few miles he monitored the road behind while maintaining a steady speed over 100mph, but observed no one attempting to catch up.

Jac had said nothing during the entire episode. Now she stirred in her seat. "Having fun?" she asked.

"Somewhat. I thought we were being followed."

"At this speed?"

"Well, they're not there now." He eased his foot from the accelerator, gradually slowing so he could tuck Gabby into the line of vehicles plodding the inner lane.

"Why would anyone want to follow us?" Jac asked. "Or is it just you?"

"Maybe it's just me. Maybe I imagined it."

Sunday Evening

The plan was to drop Jac at the gates of Churnwell House and return indirectly to London, perhaps via a long hook south through Sussex, enjoying some fast, quiet country roads.

"You must come in and say hello. He'll be very hurt if you don't," Jac said, so Skull allowed himself to be blackmailed into paying his respects to the Prof. He eased Gabby between the stone pillar gate posts and up the short un-raked gravel drive.

Churnwell House was the Fast family seat, a puffed up Victorian house set on the edge of the North Downs. Grandpa Fast had bought the house in the 1930s, since when much had been sacrificed to keep it. The views over the Weald were magnificent though.

"You must stay for supper," Professor Fast insisted. "The traffic will be simply awful at this time. It would be ridiculous to go back now."

Skull didn't want to be ridiculous so he sat down with them in the oak panelled dining room and ate re-heated lamb stew supplemented with chunks of stale wholemeal bread to make it stretch to three. Jac was embarrassed by such thin hospitality and consequently the conversation was equally sparse.

Nothing had changed in the twenty-or-so years since he'd last sat in that room. Perhaps the smell of boiled rice had faded a little but much else seemed the same — the waxed wooden floor, the ochre walls, the solid, humourless sideboard pushed against the wall; and here the antique dining table with the weight of family history polished deep into the wood's dark grain.

Skull remembered well the cloth of misery thrown over the table at meal times, for these events brought about the unhappy confluence of father and children. Their mutual proximity produced taut exchanges unfathomable with compressed subtexts. There were sudden betrayals, there were looks charged and cocked with warnings, and there were bulging silences stuffed, like sacks, with odd resentments. Oh, the relief when dinner or lunch or (worse) breakfast was over and all were excused.

Now the Professor opened a bottle of French wine excavated from his cellar. He poured the wine frugally into wine glasses engraved with a spray of fruiting vines. Cautiously they sipped at the thin red liquid, sparring with pleasantries until sufficient collective confidence allowed them to begin the evening's labour: mulling "the Jon situation".

Using the license age grants itself to be blunt or plainly rude, the Professor opened with: "Was it a woman?" His mop of academic-grey hair had thinned, lost its independence, and now lay limp and oily along a receded hairline revealing liver spots on his head that looked like blots of old browned ink. The Professor wanted to blame someone for Jon's disappearance and for the distraction his anxiety was causing him. Skull was an excellent candidate. "This Polish woman," he glared down the table at Skull, keen to scrutinise the causes of the broken friendship. "Did you want her too?"

Jac raised an anguished arm in protest. "Daddy," she said pathetically.

Skull responded lightly, "It wasn't a woman, Professor Fast."

"I'm sure you could have come to some arrangement," the Professor persisted. "One week on, one week off. Or weekend access. That's common enough. She would have accommodated you both, I'm sure of it. You've met her, Jacqui. Wouldn't you say she could accommodate both young men?"

But Jac had regressed to an anguished teenager, chewing her lips with embarrassment, refusing to look at Skull. Pass the salt, Daddy, she mumbled, or words to that effect.

"Jacqui has a theory," the Professor announced, changing direction.

"Daddy."

"No, no. It's a good one," the Professor insisted. "No false modesty here; we must be open to all possibilities, all lines of analysis must be pursued. Jacqui has suggested a mother substitute scenario — with a rather clever sort of oedipal twist to it."

"I didn't say that." Jac's eyes rolled in Skull's direction, appealing for understanding, for rescue.

"I expect it's an Italian sort of theory," the Professor continued. "Well you know how they are about their mothers." Professor Fast was at last beginning to enjoy himself. He leaned forward conspiratorially: "Jon and Jacqui's mother ran off with the milkman, you know. Well you did know — that's not news to you is it? You knew that. Everybody knew that. What a cliché. Wife runs off with the milkman. What a joke. Joke's on me, of course: crusty old Prof, can't keep his woman, can't be much good in bed. My fault, my shame. But then, when all the giggling and whispering fades away, who's the real victim? Well, apparently it's Jon. Who suffers over the long term? Jon does: a young and vulnerable boy, rejected and abandoned by his mother, can't come to terms with it. Consequence? Boy grows into serial womaniser, taking up with one woman after the next because he can't form a proper relationship. And then, hallelujah, (or whatever the Russian equivalent is) along comes this Russian carthorse. Big breasts, wide hips: Mama! Problem solved."

Professor Fast sat back, sipping severally and delicately from his glass, looking from Jac to Skull and back, eyebrows arched in a fake expectation of horrified reaction. When none was expressed he turned to Skull: "Well come on, Matthew. You don't have to spare my blushes. We're men of the world. What's your view? Is he fucking his mother?"

"My God," Jac huffed quietly, rising to clear the table.

"I'm afraid I'm not much of a psychologist," Skull smiled blandly at the Professor. "That's why I think I'll stick to computers."

"Computers? I thought you were selling cars. Didn't it work out?" Skull smiled politely. The Professor sloshed a little more wine into his glass. "Can't persuade you?" he asked, waggling the bottle half-heartedly at Skull.

"D'you want dessert? Daddy?" Jac's voice was clipped, sharp, as she clattered at the dishes. "I'll get dessert," she said, leaving.

The Professor watched her leave the room. "It's Jon," he said confidentially, twisting the stem of his glass between thumb and finger with a practised twirl. "She's worried about Jon. But I suspect she's even more worried about her own boy. Had to leave him with the husband, you know. Did you ever meet the Bert? Nice enough chap but," he tapped the side of his head, "not really her equal. Big Italian family. All very close. Too close maybe, if you know what I mean." The Professor twirled away watching the wine swirl in the glass. "You must give him a job, you know," he said with sudden conviction after they had sat a while in a stiff silence.

"Bert?"

"Jon," the Professor barked. "Jon, not Bert. My God, the Bert's probably the one Italian who actually has a job."

Skull smiled thinly without showing his teeth, hoping to keep this new direction in the conversation light. The Professor had never been so garrulous. Skull was wary.

"Jon has a good job. Why should I give him a job?" Skull asked.

"Why? Because I should think he can sell cars better than he sells mortgages, or whatever it is he does at that bank."

"I don't sell cars, Professor Fast."

"Exactly my point," he said waving his fork at Skull. "That's why you need Jon. Computers are dead. It's all smart this and smart that, so every stupid person can feel a little less dumb. Cars are the thing now. Jon could help you sell cars. Banking's not in his blood, you see. You need a certain thread of dishonesty running through you to be a banker. Like the shiny silver thread in a twenty pound note: you get all the promise of something of genuine value, but it's still merely a piece of paper with a strip of glitter in it; and it'll probably be worth less in a year than it is today. That's a sleight-of-hand dishonesty, you see? Not like the friendly false smile of the used-car salesman which is infinitely more honest because everyone knows it's a fake."

The Professor set the fork down carefully on his plate and with his big gnarled fingers tore a lump of bread from the slice on his side plate, examining it closely. "I know a bit about fakes," he sneered at the crust before wiping it over his plate to mop the gravy. "Trust me."

Skull had heard the story. Thirty years ago, and not yet a professor, Dr Fast had unwittingly staked his reputation on a fragment of thigh bone he had dug from a Norfolk trench along with some potsherds and worked animal bone. The assemblage had seemed propitious. He wrote a number of papers in which he speculated about pre-Bell-Beaker cultures, hinting at mechanisms that were not consistent with the thinking of the time. Outside his circle there were doubts, naturally, professional scepticism, a reluctance to throw out existing models without solid proofs. A relative dating of the key finds proved inconclusive, while a few unhappy members of the dig fouled the trough with whisper and innuendo. Finally someone wrote "Nonsense"; emboldened, another cried "Fake!" Few of the combatants emerged unbloodied from the ensuing rumpus which seeped swiftly through the loose stitching of academia into the media and from there, inevitably, into the courts of law. The matter was never entirely resolved to anyone's satisfaction, and neither was Professor Fast's reputation. Was he a clever cheat, an unfortunate victim, or a gullible fool? When a few years later his wife ran off with the local grocer, many were confirmed in their views.

After a syrupy dessert of tinned peaches with glacé cherries, the Professor stood up abruptly. "Quite," he said distractedly, picking up his wine glass and the half empty bottle. "Good luck with the ... ah ...," he waggled the glass at Skull, then paused at the door on his way out. "If you find my boy, bring him back to me, Matthew. Bring him back."

*

In the kitchen, after dinner, Jac tied a grubby apron around her before rinsing the plates, the bowls, the cutlery, and stacking them beside the sink ready to wash. Skull watched as she ran hot water into the butler sink, added a squirt of detergent.

"He's worried about Jon," she said, cautiously testing the water below the suds in the sink. She ran more cold before dumping the plates in. "I don't know if he sleeps in the library, or works. Both, probably. He only gets to bed around three or four in the morning. The wine makes him sour," she added.

Don't worry, Skull did not say to re-assure her. Nor did he add, I am not offended — your father is your burden. I have other burdens but I thank God this is not one of them. I will go home to my singularly shattered life, but the grey dolour of this home has already saturated everything you are and everything you do, like an odour, like a strong odour ... He said nothing though. It didn't need to be said.

The kitchen, like the dining room, was much as he remembered it: state-of-the-art country kitchen, 1992. Except below the chimney breast the massive Aga, long cold and dead, was browning with rust, while on the counter a utilitarian microwave and work top grill, camouflaged by a thin layer of grease, looked out of place. In a grimy corner the aged fridge wheezed and whined as it re-frosted and defrosted according to its own mutant schedule. A nidor of grilled fat and fried fish clung to the walls.

Head bent, Jac sloshed through the hot water with a dish brush, scrubbing each plate before holding it up to drip, then stacking it upright it in a greasy yellow plastic drainer from where the remaining foam slid off and gathered in little grey heaps on the counter.

"Skull, what are you going to do now?" she asked.

"Dry," he said, picking up a forlorn tea towel, selecting a still dripping plate.

"Dry," she laughed, turning towards him. "You were always so dry, Skull. Dry and serious." She wiped, on the apron, her soapy wet hands, saying: "Thank you, Skull. Thank you for helping me today. I really was not looking forward to it. I was, in fact, dreading it, but you made it easy for me. And you brought me home. That was an incredibly kind thing to do."

"Ah — you're welcome," he muttered, shrugging diffidently, his courage failing him like a schoolboy. He looked away.

"And then to show my gratitude," she continued lightly, "I gave you the host from hell and fed you slops and left-overs."

He got the irony in her voice but missed the joke in her eyes and the lopsided grin as he focused his attention on smearing a glass with the tea towel. "It was fine. It was lovely to see you again," he said stupidly.

The tiny lines etched around her eyes deepened unseen by him, her head cocked a little sideways before she turned back, awkwardly, to the sink, plunging her hands into the soapy depths once more.

He asked, politely, about her plans and she told him she would be staying with Daddy for the rest of the week but needed to leave on Saturday so she could be back with Paolo and Roberto in Florence for Christmas. Paolo loved Christmas. Also she didn't like to leave Roberto too long to cope on his own. "Italian men; Italian families; etcetera, etcetera," she said.

But, on Friday, she would attend a lecture at the British Museum; she didn't care for the topic, she told him, but the lecture was being delivered by an old family friend and, since she was here in England, she felt she ought to go.

"But of course," she pointed out, "you know Daffyd. From Godwin Hill."

"Uncle Daffy. Indeed," said Skull with not much enthusiasm.

"Come with me," she said. "I'm sure he'll be delighted to see you again."

"I don't think so," said Skull.

"Why not?"

"He really doesn't like me."

"Well he can be a bit abrupt at times."

"Indeed. But he actually hates me," Skull winced, adding, "I think he thinks I'm a thief and a liar."

"Oh, good lord. What happened?"

A lith on a stick

If you've ever been to Godwin Hill you'll know that it's all rolling farmland and ploughed fields around there, with the occasional woody copse sprouting from a hilltop like a big, green, mohican haircut. Godwin Hill is just such a hill, an oval promontory rising quite suddenly from the surrounding fields, a wooded valley to one side, and topped with the requisite punk spray of trees.

You arrive along a ragged chalk and flint farm road which deposits you onto the broad saddle at the foot of the hill. Betty, of course, was not designed for bouncing over the rutted dirt roads more suited to big-wheeled tractors and Land Rovers. We bobbed along slowly in first gear, me anxiously surveying the ground ahead of my expensive, high-tech car, and Jon impatiently craning his neck to look up the hill.

Crossing the saddle, the chalk road curves gently right and, just where it descends into the valley, there's a rough track which splits from it and continues on up the hill along the eastern side, edging between the wood and a ploughed field which covers the shoulder like a fleecy brown blanket.

A few cars and a van were parked up at the point where the rough track started, so I drew up alongside them. Jon immediately leapt out, slinging his day sack over a shoulder and striding jauntily along the track in hardy walking boots and jacket. I carefully locked the car and followed in my clean white trainers. I thought he had been joking about the anorak.

Halfway up the hill Jon paused, pretending to admire the view. I knew he was really catching his breath. Let's not kid ourselves, we're both power diving towards middle age with our flaps wide open and our under-carriages hanging out.

"Smashing view, Carruthers," he puffed, pointing back the way we'd come.

"Topping," I replied plodding on, knowing I would struggle to start again once I'd stopped to indulge in bucolic views.

Godwin Hill is deceptively steep. It's one of those climbs where you keep reaching the top only to find there's more to go, so despite the spring nip on the breeze I was sticky with sweat long before we reached the summit.

Actually I don't think we ever did reach the summit. You couldn't see anything from below because of the trees, but once you passed through the tree line, the area inside had been cleared, a tonsure on the dome of the hill. This was the site of the dig.

It wasn't exactly a hive of activity. To me the work seemed random and surreal — easily mistaken for some strange earth-worshipping cult whose members, dressed in dull jackets and baggy shorts, are required to climb inside long shallow graves and bend low for their devotional ritual. These genuflections are then observed by small groups of watchers leaning on picks and shovels in poses of utter boredom.

I remember one stout, bearded fellow marching glumly over the hill pushing a wheelbarrow heaped with dirt. He passed wordlessly within feet of two women gazing sadly and silently into a water trough. An empty L-shaped trench, criss-crossed in a busy matrix of string, was guarded by a lonely theodolite on three yellow legs; and all about were dirty yellow buckets, mucky green barrows, dusty brushes and brooms, soiled planks, a scattering of poles scaled in red and white and muddy stripes, and middens of chalk and grime.

Higher up, alongside the track where the angle of the slope became less acute, were two grey prefabricated huts, levelled up on short stacks of breeze-blocks; behind them, two bright sentry-style box-toilets.

Beyond the huts a small, grubby yellow digger slouched wearily on its mechanical arm. Nearby, a group of men wearing plastic hard hats huddled around a large sheet of paper, a map or a plan, spread over the bonnet of a Land Rover. They looked authoritative, pointing and gesturing, so I headed for the group.

"The path goes round!" someone yelled. A woman emerged from the nearest hut and stood staring at us from the steps. She wore an over-sized lavender jacket and she cuddled a mug of something in both hands, holding it to her chest like a devotional candle.

"What?" I shouted back but she continued to stare at me, making no attempt to repeat her challenge. I changed direction towards her.

"The path's down there," she said as I came within speaking distance, and she lifted her chin fractionally to point down the hill. "There's no right of way through here." Up close, she was younger than her frumpy jacket suggested. Her voice was flat, offhand, and she spoke with a slight sibilance due to two small rings piercing her lower lip. An unruly frond of bright purple hair flapped forward over her eyes and from time to time she would bend her head sideways to let it fall back.

"We're here to visit," I said.

"Who are you?" she demanded, after subjecting me to her sceptical face. When she sipped from the mug her wide black eyes peered over the rim; the nails on her fingers were filed to a blunt point like the tip of a heart icon.

"I'm Doctor Fast," said Jon catching up at last, flushed and panting. "And this is my colleague Matt Morrell from London. Where's Daffy?"

The girl now assessed Jon with a cool sneer. "Daffy?" she asked.

"Professor Daffyd Sayer." Jon grinned back, but I felt his charm was wasted. She raised a pierced eyebrow and nodded at what looked like the top of a blue tent hidden among some scrub a little way off.

"You should sign in at the plans office first," she said, and here she part inclined her head towards the adjacent hut.

"Don't fancy yours," said Jon as we made our way across the lumpy ground towards the part-hidden tent.

It turned out the tent wasn't a tent but a big blue tarpaulin stretched across a framework of scaffolding pipes mounted above a dark hole. We ducked under the tarp and stared down into the chalk pit below. It looked deep, perhaps nearly two stories, and as narrow maybe as a large bedroom. The walls were a rough and crumbly chalk, dark earthy brown at the top fading to a lighter tan as it descended. The narrowness made the shaft look much deeper, and the damp tomb smell that erupted from it made me uneasy.

"I'm not going down there," I said.

A rope on a pulley system dangled from a pipe reaching across the pit not quite centre. Presumably it was used to haul everything from below except living humans, for whom was provided a long ladder which dropped vertically all the way to the bottom and was roped at the top to the scaffolding. Alongside the ladder a yellow hosepipe and a couple of thick orange cables cascaded down, the cables disappearing into one of several side tunnels leading off the main shaft at various levels. At the top, still below the tarpaulin cover, the cables were plugged into a portable generator that chugged throatily. Down below, the shaft was empty.

"Call down," whispered Jon.

"What?"

"Call him." He took a quick swig from his bottle of scotch.

"Me? He's your Uncle Daffy. You call him."

"I can't shout 'Uncle Daffy', can I?" He wouldn't catch my eye. "Sounds silly."

"Shout 'hello', then."

"It's OK for you. You don't know him."

I shrugged. I didn't understand this sudden coyness.

"Uncle Daffy!" I yelled. "Daffy!"

Jon was livid. He glared furiously at me and was about to hiss something abusive when an echoey voice from below called up, "That you Jon?"

We looked down. Slowly a pair of legs waggled out from the side tunnel at the base, followed shortly by their owner's body. Uncle Daffy. He stood flicking his hands over his knees in a futile attempt to brush the chalk dust off his coveralls or wipe it from his hands. Still brushing he looked up.

"Hang on," he called. "Coming up." We stepped out into the sunshine while he made his ascent.

I'd met Uncle Daffy a few of times before, most recently when Jon bought his first flat and threw a little house warming party. I recall that Uncle Daffy and I discussed the relative merits of a variety of savoury snacks, at least I think that was the topic: the music was loud and there was a lot of drinking. We disagreed as to whether pork scratchings were better than peanuts. I can't remember now my position on the matter.

Even back then, as usual, he didn't remember me from any of our previous meetings, although the very first time was at the Professor's book publishing barbecue. That was the summer I seemed to spend entirely with your family at

Churnwell House. If you remember, my father was taking a while to die at home and nobody wanted the dark presence of a teenage boy to add to the gloom. The Professor was kind enough to open your home to me. It was probably the longest sleepover in history.

So, the barbecue I recall because Jon and I were tasked with carrying trays of food and drink around, and later with clearing away empty glasses and beer bottles. We got completely drunk, of course, but then so too did everyone else. I don't think anybody noticed, except Uncle Daffy. He made it clear he blamed me for being a bad influence on Jon, but he seems not ever to have liked me. I don't know why.

Uncle Daffy ascended from the pit quickly, almost leaping from the mine head as he reached the top. A few rapid strides on his short legs brought him over to us. His face was brown and healthy with the sun, his hair more silvery than I remembered, and now worn long to the shoulder, giving him a messianic quality.

"Welcome to Godwin Hill," he beamed as he reached out to hug Jon.

"You remember Skull," said Jon.

"No." He stared me in the face and wrung my hand in that hard, manly way that makes you respond in kind, only too late and too hard. "But you are welcome to my dig, chap." His hand was rough, like builder's hands. "Did you chappies sign in? No? Well let's all go and sign in. Health and safety, isn't it. And as the chappie in charge I have to set the standard, see. We'll get you fixed up with some top hats as well so we can all go down into the pit. You want to go down into the pit, don't you, boys?"

"Yes, please!" said Jon.

As we walked back up the hill to the huts, Uncle Daffy threw broad gestures over the site, pointing at features, describing all the activities and the people involved. And the people involved paused their activities to wave back at him, shouting friendly insults as we walked within hailing distance, which pleased Uncle Daffy enormously.

"So why here?" Jon asked. "What's the big deal about this site?"

Uncle Daffy frowned. "Now that's a very good question with not a simple answer," he said gravely, then flashed a quick smile. "First and foremost, we've got the money, see. That's always the most important thing, isn't it." Then he got serious again. "But it is a virgin site. It's long been known there was an Iron Age hill fortress here, but some fools with a stupid metal-detector found a few Roman coins and a couple of bronze axe-heads a couple of years ago. So when the local archaeological society did a quick survey it looked like there was a bit of a Bronze Age settlement here as well. No big surprises there but what was a surprise were the flint mines. Totally unexpected. We thought we knew where all the Sussex mines were and, well, Sussex hasn't had much archaeological love recently. Hence the funding. So here we have a virgin site with the possibility of a longitudinal excavation from the Neolithic all the way through to the horrible Romans."

"Ah, that's interesting" Jon nodded. "I told the Prof I was coming down here to see you. He sends his regards, by the way. He said most of what's worth knowing about flint mining is already known. That's what he said."

"Did he, indeed? Indeed. Indeed." I thought I detected a slight edge in Uncle Daffy's tone, but he went on smoothly enough. "Well, yes and no, really. Your dad is right, as usual. As usual he's right, but there's always something new to learn. Always something new. Yes, of course a lot of field work has been done on the Sussex flint mines — some of it over a hundred years ago now — so we already know quite a lot from that work. But the techniques change, you know; the methods are different and there's always something new. What's interesting here is that these shafts seem to have been worked rather later than the other mines along the South Downs. What it seems is that they were being worked well into the middle bronze. So more contemporary with the mines at Grimes

Graves, see. And with a possible bronze foundry there's the whole transitional element to look at. Transition is all the rage nowadays. It's bankable." He laughed, apparently surprised at his own astuteness. "It really is bankable."

Jon laughed loudly too. "So, any touchy-feely archaeology? The Prof said you'd probably be indulging in some new-fangled touchy-feely methods. For the money."

"Touchy-feely? What can he mean?" They both laughed a bit more, but it seemed to me without humour. "Well, you know," he said dourly, "we have the opportunity to try out some new-fangled high-tech equipment, but nothing touchy-feely. Archaeologists these days indulge in more naval gazing than nuns on a nudist beach, but we still wash our souls in the mud, don't we? Don't we? Digging the dirt is cleansing, man."

We could all laugh at that.

After signing the visitor's book Uncle Daffy took us to the neighbouring hut, the Finds Hut, the domain of the young woman with the purple hair and lip studs. The hut was stacked with stackable chairs and lines of trestle tables on which were laid out rows of mud-smeared, plastic ice-cream tubs and gardener's seed-trays. The trays held muddy things — pottery sherds, bones, stones, blobs — all labelled with labels in little plastic bags. It looked like a church-bazaar selling all the rubbish the boy-scouts had picked up in the graveyard. Some of the bones were surprisingly big.

Uncle Daffy handed me a bent and knobbly stick with worn points on both ends. It felt heavy.

"Last man to touch that lived around five thousand years ago," he said significantly.

I gave him my wow-face, and examined the stick with some reverence, hoping that an intelligent observation would spring readily from the object itself.

"Red Deer antler," he continued after I said nothing. "Harder than wood, see. And drawn from their own local renewable source, because back then, this whole area would have been thick woodland — none of the nice farmland you see today."

He took it back and, holding it by the hook, he jabbed at an imaginary chalk wall to demonstrate how he thought it might be used to punch holes, or hook out blocks of chalk or nodules of flint. "Fantastic for close up work in the tunnels," he said.

"Don't touch," the woman warned Uncle Daffy when he lifted a grey stone from one of the plastic trays. He laughed, but she didn't.

"Pepper's our chief pot washer," he explained.

"Finds Director," she corrected him.

"I'll put it back where I found it, alright Pepper?" he said tightly, passing the stone to Jon.

"Make sure you do," she huffed, retreating to her desk, a mess of grubby papers and clipboards, her tea mug, her mobile phone.

"Ah," said Jon as he hefted the stone in both hands, stroked his fingers over it, nodded; it was flat and smooth. Even I recognised it as a flint axe. "It's had a bit of a polish. Votive?"

"Yes," Uncle Daffy nodded, pleased. "We think so. Found in gallery three. Arranged along with these." Here he let his fingers walk over a few old bones and a couple of dark black flints, flat and roughly chipped.

"Lovely." Jon passed the stone to me, explaining, "Votive means they were left as a sort of offering to the underground gods."

"I know," I said, and I sort of did.

The axe-head had the same smooth, glassy feel as my smartphone although it was somewhat heavier. The surface was a ghostly smoke finish which veiled a darker interior, giving it a living quality and a depth as if inside the stone lay a thick, black oil. At the broad chopping edge it was about the same length and width as my phone, narrowing to the rounded butt end. The tool seemed almost mint, unused, and I wondered at a people who could invest the effort in making such a tool and then simply bury it.

Uncle Daffy walked on down the line of tables (watched closely by Pepper) pointing out his favourites from the assemblages and artefacts that had been surfaced: a massive auroch shoulder-blade used by the miners for shovelling lumps of chalk; some copper waste from a possible forge; a piece of chalk with a phallic shape. Jon followed asking all the right questions.

There were a series of curling photos pinned to the wall and to which Uncle Daffy drew our attention. They showed a flat crouching skeleton partially embedded in a chalky soil. It had the coy modesty of recently exposed bones, grinning with embarrassment.

"Young woman," Uncle Daffy explained. "From last year's dig in shaft two. It's all gone for analysis but we think that's an axe wound." He pointed to a close-up of the skull with a narrow void cleaved into the side.

"Fuck me. It's like a soap opera," Jon said appreciatively, examining the photos close up. Uncle Daffy glanced towards me, frowning.

At that moment my phone plinked loudly a few times — Emily's tone — so I took it out my pocket for a quick look. She had shared with me a video clip of a cat that barked like a dog and sang like a child. It looped loudly a few times and ended on a cackle of laughter from, presumably, the cat's owners. It was improbable, but somewhat funny.

"I'm so sorry if we're boring you, chap," Uncle Daffy called from across the room. Everyone was staring at me.

"No."

"You might get a better signal from higher up the hill." Behind Uncle Daffy, Jon was making childish faces at me.

"It's fine," I said.

"I know it doesn't look like much here. There's nothing very fancy about this old hut, with the tables and the plastic buckets; but it is a place of learning, of contemplation; a place of respect. Feel free to step out if it doesn't suit you, chap."

"I'm sorry."

"It's not for everyone, of course. I know that. Not everyone can be as passionate as I am about it. Some people look at all this and see only the dirty old stones and the broken pots and the bones, but I see these as priceless human artefacts. These are fragments of humanity that speak to us. I see here the remnants of lives past that are still communicating, that are telling us something important about how people lived and thought and died back then. And maybe they can tell us something about how we live now." He paused angrily before going on, "Not everyone has that passion."

It seemed everyone was glaring at me now.

"What are we doing here?" he demanded. I looked uncertainly across at Jon who pulled another face. "Come on, what are we doing here?

"Finding out about the past?" It felt like school.

"Wrong. We're finding out about ourselves, about who we are, now. And what do you think these Neolithic men and women and children were doing here five thousand years ago?"

I shrugged, swallowed hard, my mouth unexpectedly dry. "Making tools?"

"Wrong again. Making tools is probably the least of what they did here. Here they were winning the stone from other worlds, reaching for their ancestors, working hard to make sense of their own world, to bond within their own communities and the communities living alongside them. Yes, they cut and shaped and polished the axe-heads, but that was a mere by-product of all the work and the striving done here."

"It's a very beautiful stone," I said, holding up my phone-hand by mistake.

"Yes it is," he smiled, appeased for now. "Yes it is. But it's not what you think it is." He looked at Jon then back to me. "Look at him," he laughed, as if I wasn't there. "He has the flint axe in one hand, phone in the other. What separates them, I wonder? And what joins the dots between them?"

"Ooh, I know this one," Pepper said with her bored tone. "Is it the fool that's holding them? Or the fool that's asking the question?"

Uncle Daffy ignored her. According to him there were just four and a half, maybe five thousand years between the production of the axe and my smartphone. A mere blink, he said, of time, when you consider that the first stone tools were made and used over two and half million years ago. Those were our first baby steps with technology, he said. It was a simple pebble chopper then, and he joked, "a small chip for man, a giant chopper for mankind". Here he hacked at the air by way of demonstration, his hand a prehensile claw curled over a crude imaginary pebble. I was the only one who laughed out loud.

It took a million years before the emergence of Stone Tool Two, Uncle Daffy told us. He called it "a real beaut, a leaf forged from stone, a lithic tear drop, a monument to man's nascent intelligence, the Swiss army knife of all Stone Age tooling". He chewed over the observation that while each found axe from this Achulean industry is unique in its execution, the design is uniform, a conceptual template which persists ("more or less, more or less") for another million years until: Stone Tool Three — specialised flakes.

And that was that. Uncle Daffy was adamant: no more real innovation, no more new development, just the sporadic refinement of technique: flakes, blades, blades on sticks, flakes on sticks.

"So you might think that the axe you are holding sits at the pinnacle of Stone Age achievement because it comes at the very end of the longest evolutionary development of a technology ever, but you'd be quite wrong. Evolution does not equal progress, merely adaptation. All the good things with stone had already happened by the time that axe was made."

The axes that came out of Godwin Hill were mostly for trade, Uncle Daffy explained sadly. It was big business. They would pull the flints out of the ground, shape them up, polish them like the one I held in my hand and then they'd be traded for other stuff — pottery, skins, respect, maybe women, who knows.

"So in the lower Neolithic," he grumbled, "they seem to put less effort into producing working tools. All the work goes into these status tools. Now why d'you think that was?"

"Well once you've put a lith on a stick, what else is there?" Pepper remarked.

"Bronze, obviously," said Jon. "They'd invented bronze."

"Yes! Well done, Jon. That's quite right," Uncle Daffy said as he strolled down the aisle, rooting among the finds in the plastic tubs. Jon followed him closely, pleased with the praise, taking sneaky gulps from the half-bottle of whisky when Uncle Daffy wasn't looking. "It's funny," Uncle Daffy mused, "that the stone chopper starts as a universal tool and ends up as a high status item, whereas the mobile phone starts as a high status item and now everybody's bloody got one." Nobody laughed, not even me.

"So aren't you going to tell us?" Pepper asked.

"What, Pepper darling? What do you want to know?" Uncle Daffy was distracted. He was looking for something particular.

"Why the decline in quality controls among the flintknapping folk of the Neolithic?"

"Oh I don't have the answers, Pepper. I just ask the questions. Perhaps innovations around stone technology no longer gave any advantage. They were farming by then, don't forget. It was probably more important to understand the landscape and manage the livestock. Ah, here we go now." He pounced on a seed tray, grabbing a fist sized black stone which he flourished in the air at me. Now he seemed to remember his earlier annoyance. "Talk about your smart tools, chap. Here's your stone age smart tool, see? App store of the Neolithic — and the Mesolithic — see? It's what we in the profession would call a prepared flint core. It's your smart tool and app store all rolled into one."

He held the small rock out closer towards me, turning it over in his hands so I could appreciate the magic of it. Whatever it was prepared for, other than throwing, was not immediately obvious to me. It was more or less cone-shaped and retained a brown chalky carapace on one side while the rest of it was a liquorice black, faceted down its length as if slivers had been scraped from it with a thick butter knife.

"Portable, flexible, dependable. Whatever you needed — a scraper, a blade, an arrow-head, see? You knock one off, retouch it, and you're good to go."

"There will be no knocking-one-off in the Finds Hut please," Pepper said dryly. Jon giggled.

"The mobile phone may be the most ubiquitous personal tool since the days of the flint core," Uncle Daffy informed me with all sincerity. "I recently read that there's a mobile phone for every man, woman and child on the planet now. Can you believe that?" He shook his head at Jon. "That's a lot of chatter."

After that he gave us the tour of the rest of the site. We walked up to the top of the hill and looked at a muddy hole, then we trudged around to the side of the hill and watched some students brush dirt from the rocks buried in a muddy hole, before returning finally to the head of the great muddy hole he called the flint mine.

Pepper intercepted us as we passed by the Finds Hut on the way down.

"Whoever it was took the axe head, can they put it back." She was looking at me. "If you don't mind," she added with a raised brow.

"I don't have it," I said.

"You had it last."

Uncle Daffy looked at me too, frowning. After a pause he said, "Come on, Pepper. We don't have it."

"Well it's not there, and you said you'd put it back where you found it. He had it last." She was still looking at me.

"Well, d'you have it, chap?"

"No," I said. I had put it back in the seed tray.

"Jon?" he asked but Jon was already shaking his head. "We don't have it," he said again.

"Well someone has it because it's not there now." She was an unmovable rock, a human sarsen stone. In the difficult silence I was aware that the attention, once again, was all on me.

"You didn't slip it into a pocket, by accident like, with your phone or anything?" Uncle Daffy asked me. "It can happen. Do it all the time."

"I don't have it," I said, pulling the smartphone from my pocket and raising both hands in submission. I knew they wouldn't touch me, but they looked me over slowly to check if anything heavy was weighing on me. Jon pursed his lips, shaking his head with disappointment. "I put it back," I said. "I swear."

"We don't have it," Uncle Daffy said finally, turning away. "You must have mis-boxed it."

"No."

"Well we don't have it."

"I'll sign it out to you then." Pepper watched us as we walked away. We walked away in silence.

I could hardly refuse to descend into the mine after that. It would have been odd. It would have made me more of an outcast than I already felt, but the joy had truly gone from the day.

Monday

We get the dreams we need. Take the Greeks, for instance. While they slept their Gods brought portents and prophecies of favour or disaster. And ancient man endured millennia of restless nights while his plangorous ancestors harangued him to do-this, and don't-do-that. Nowadays we know from science that our dreaming is threat-response conditioning, a mere function of evolution. It seems we get the dreams our times deserve.

Skull had no dreams, at least none that he remembered. He woke late to the ruin of his morning, unrested and with the sense that his sleep had been besieged by Jac's unhappy voice. Without curtains to hold the darkness in, the winter light easily penetrated his bedroom, exposing him as he lay under a tartan car blanket to the pale grey of a day already half spent.

He rose immediately, made coffee, toast, ignored the flashing light on the answer-phone with the 99 messages. Today was designated tidy-up-day, but first he watched twenty-four hour news while he drank and ate. The news was all pomp and tragedy, speculation and chat. How far, Skull wondered, had we really travelled from skin-clothed flint-knapper to chattering smartphone user? If politics is the oil that lubricates the engine of human endeavour, gossip, he decided, is the thick, brown grease slapped over the cogs.

He watched the news, but watching provided inadequate stimulation, insufficient interaction, so he thumbed on his smartphone in a thoughtless, practised reflex.

Over seven hundred new emails had been delivered since last night, and scores of unread texts. As he flipped through them all a flock of new messages landed: Jamie Wood liked a link that Philippa Miller had posted on LinkedIn; Razzi Amett had downloaded more MP3s from Amazon. A handful of blogs gave notice of articles on the death of Smartor, while a hack from *The Register* invited a comment on information that the Smartor code had been open sourced.

He checked for tweets from Emily, checked her Facebook, checked all the other social networking sites he knew she liked. He realised that he missed her now for all the wrong reasons. He missed her simple joy of kittens, crafts and squirrels, the photo-snaps of morning flowers and greeting cards, the scowling selfies, the pouting selfies, the salacious, teasing, cheery selfies; the weird food treats, happy tears for sad songs, lady-day hair dos, silly presents ("yay!"). He had shared none of that with her, given nothing back but had enjoyed her saccharine pleasures with a sense of prurient superiority, delighting vicariously, like a stalker, in her girly musing.

Mostly he missed her missives. There were no conversations he wanted with anyone else now. He set his smartphone so it would receive calls only from any of Emily's numbers, as well as any calls forwarded from his land-line. He had already muted the land-line phone, first making sure that all calls from Emily would forward instantly to his smartphone. After a bit of thought he added Jac's numbers to the list of calls to accept. That done, he bent his resolve to dismantling and cleaning the coffee machine.

He hoped a practical task would fill his mind with simple, practical thoughts, driving out the dead and dying. Sadly nothing induces sombre reflection more readily than the doing of household chores. His fingers worked the tubes and valves, the spigots, pipes and springs, but his attention, like a fly, chased from corpse to corpse until he forced it to settle on the fragrant puzzle of Jacqueline's departing kiss.

They had finished the washing up and Jac had offered him coffee — one for the road, she'd laughed. He had thought he would leave as soon as he could but she seemed reluctant to see him go and he, surprising himself, readily accepted a cup of tea. Anyway he liked the new warmth in her eyes, and it seemed to him that her problems were more interesting than his.

"So what are you going to do about Jon?" he had asked, and she replied, "I don't know, Skull."

She set the two chipped mugs of tea down on the kitchen table before lowering herself slowly onto a chair. He sat across from her, a corner of the table between them, the steaming mugs cheerful and bright enough for breakfast. "I suppose we have to trust Jon," she said. "After all, if you don't know where he is, and Anka doesn't know where he is, what can I do? I wouldn't know where to start looking."

The police, Skull had suggested, but she interrupted him before he finished: "The police won't do anything because of the note. There's no evidence of a crime, and the note says he's going away. They have no reason to do anything; and perhaps neither do we."

Skull nodded, mashing his tea-bag against the side of the mug with the teaspoon, squeezing out the brown juice.

"Like you said this morning," Jac continued, "he's a grown man and he's probably simply gone away to find himself. And why wouldn't he?" She waved vaguely at the kitchen, the house, the home, beyond. "I often wish I could do the same. I'd run away. Wouldn't that be wonderful?"

"Indeed," Skull said, casting about for somewhere he could deposit the now dead tea-bag. Where would I go, he mused, if I ran away? Florence might be quite tolerable, he reflected, waving the bag irresolutely in a small circle. Jac relieved him of both teaspoon and bag, tossing them blindly over her shoulder at the sink. The bag struck the wall with a moist plop, the spoon tinkling musically on the flagstone floor where it fell. She laughed at his astonishment.

"Indeed," she said.

When they had finished their tea and Skull, on the point of leaving, was telling Jac he could find his own way out, she stepped in close and, reaching up, kissed him softly on one cheek, her hip pressed gently against him, the warmth of her body a brief sensation.

"You're a good friend, Skull," she said, and then, "Thank you. Again." As she stepped back she reached out and touched his cheek where she'd kissed him, as if to press it home, as if to make sure it didn't accidentally fall off. That's what he was thinking about as he re-assembled the coffee maker, driving out the bad thoughts with thoughts about Jac's touch.

After the machine was rebuilt he flushed it with a few empty brews, stacked the dishwasher, made a shopping list, and went out. His first call was to the bank where he withdrew three hundred and forty pounds in cash from the dregs of his joint account with Emily, leaving a balance of seven pounds and 87 pence. He bought coffee beans, milk, bread, a few frozen ready meals, and a duvet.

*

Home again, Skull made coffee. He ate a ready meal, watched more TV. Different men and women reported the same news on different twenty four hour news channels. There were hundreds more email messages on his smartphone; a hundred texts, a hundred notifications. A number of bloggers had noted their astonishment that the Smartor source code was available for download at various sites, which they listed; Razzi Amett had downloaded MP3s from Amazon; Phillipa Miller liked Jamie Wood's new profile photo on LinkedIn.

A quiet week, Jac had said, spending time with Daddy before Christmas since there was now plainly nothing more to be done about Jon, and she was here, and because she and Daddy hadn't really spent much time together because there were always family interruptions, so now was a good time to catch up and re-connect. Thanks, she said, for all your help; good luck.

Along the wall sat the un-sorted-out boxes, overstuffed with knots of dusty cables spilling out like guilt. Our descendants will scoff at the tyranny of wires we suffered, the burden of dumb chords for connecting one thing to the other, Skull thought, staring at the tangles. Still staring he thought that perhaps on Friday he might pop along to the British Museum anyway, not for Uncle Daffy's lecture, but to see Jac, to say goodbye.

Jac had speculated that Jon's friend Deepak was key to the mystery, maybe even the other man in the video. Skull was not so sure, but he could acknowledge that, other than the text messages, it was the only lead there was to Jon. Tracking down Deepak shouldn't be too challenging, he decided.

The Internet is memory: it has its biases, its selective attention — all the imperfections of recall — but it is a record, perhaps even a chronicle. Every digital utterance, every micro-blogging word, each podcast opinion, each chat, snap, and instant message is indexed, tagged, catalogued, stored. Nothing deleted is ever removed, nothing destroyed, merely folded to alternate streams and carried off on counter currents. Currents, streams, clouds — a great exciting swirl of human dust, sucked up, spread about and left to settle slowly like ancient debris into layers — a sediment of decaying knowledge covered swiftly by the gentle silts of new old news. The archaeology of the Internet is performed with a click.

Skull had a first name (Deepak), and the month his wife was murdered (July). Less certain parameters were the location (somewhere in London), and the knowledge that Deepak had worked for a London based investment bank. It was a silken thread of information but such is the power of the Internet search that within an hour he had the details of the story as well as Deepak's address, his phone number, and the names and addresses of several of his relatives.

The murder had received a squall of media coverage across both national and local channels. It had been picked up by some of the foreign press and an eclectic range of blogs examining the Sikh community angle. According to the reports a single stab to the chest had stopped Dilpreet Singh's heart instantly, her body discovered in her own home by her mother-in-law later in the evening. There was little blood, no evidence of struggle, nothing of value stolen. It had, the papers reported with grave certainty, all the hallmarks of a robbery gone wrong. On the night of the attack Deepak had been out, attending a work-related function, with a number of witnesses able to place him in a sequence of bars over the course of that Thursday night.

Snippets of Dilpreet's background salted the story: a large, happy Birmingham family, a local school, a degree in Business Studies, marriage. She and Deepak had married nearly five years earlier and a photograph reproduced in the paper showed a serious couple in traditional Sikh wedding attire, self-consciously arranged in an affectionate, if formal pose. In one report two brothers and a male cousin glared menacingly from the pages. The family were devastated, neighbours shocked: they were such a happy couple ... they were so friendly ... who would have believed ... and in such a quiet community. The question was always, Who would kill such a beautiful young woman? And why?

Two men had been seen in the area earlier in the day. A shop-keeper described them as "shifty", another as "suspicious", "foreign looking"; grainy CCTV footage con-firmed two men boarding a local bus at around the time of the murder, but neither men nor murder weapon were ever traced.

The police looked to motivation: who would benefit from this murder? Exactly one year earlier, Deepak and Dilpreet had taken out level term mortgage life insurance on their house for half a million pounds.

*

Skull texted Jac: *Found Deepak.*

Clevr U r, she replied, and then after a significant delay while Skull puzzled the meaning of the first cryptic message she followed up with, *R U gng 2 C him?*

It was as if she was stuck in 1990s and had not progressed beyond the pioneering days of instant messaging; it was as if the new-fangled predictive text had not yet reached her, and had not freed her from the dark contortions, the mutant constrictions, of primitive SMS communications.

But he decided, on balance, that he valued the time and care she lavished crafting her texts for brevity and succinctness. He was charmed by it, he felt. He thought it quaint.

May B, he sent, wondering if she would appreciate his appreciation. The voice call followed almost instantly.

"Well done," she trilled. "How did you do it?"

"Internet search?" he said, surprised by her enthusiasm.

"Clever you." She seemed genuinely impressed.

"It was just a search," he said modestly, then quickly told her all he'd learnt about Deepak.

"So he might be a murderer after all," she said when he'd finished.

"He wasn't charged. He wasn't even there when it happened."

"All the same. Perhaps you shouldn't contact him. At least I don't think you should go and see him. I wouldn't feel comfortable. I don't think it's worth it."

The search for Deepak, the information, was a gift to her, like the visit to Anka, and the lift home to Churnwell. It was something he could do, something to pass the time and avoid attending to the more painful things in his life. Her gratitude pleased him but it really hadn't occurred to him that he might get more involved, that he might attempt to contact Deepak himself. Now he wondered: should he?

"How's your day been?" he asked.

"My day?" She sounded surprised, perhaps offended. "Oh. You know ..." Was that dismissal? A brush off? Skull couldn't be sure. Perhaps it was just surprise. "What about you?" she returned.

"Oh, you know ..."

She laughed, a gurgle. "Well we're both articulate today, aren't we? Great team communications — Team Skull," she gurgled again, rich, sweet, liquid. "Actually, to be honest, I slept in late. I couldn't sleep last night, and then this morning, of course, I couldn't wake up."

He saw her curled form in bed, un-sleeping, arm out-flung, the stubble of under-arm hair a dark vale below the rolling curves and mounds. He smelt the whiff of restless sheets, of re-plumped pillow, the sigh of stale thoughts exhaled. But she had not paused for his vision: "Now," she told him, "I'm passing the time until Berto calls so I can talk with Paolo. He frets when I'm not there."

"Berto?" Skull panicked. He'd forgotten who was who.

"Paolo," she giggled. "Although Berto does as well, I'm sure of it. It can be a long day getting Paolo ready and off to the centre; and then fetching him and getting him to bed. After a full day of work ..." The sentence seemed to fade with the effort it described.

Berto was the husband, of course; Paolo the boy. Jac continued, "But it settles Paolo if we talk. Well, I talk mostly. He likes to see my face on the screen. When he hears my voice it makes him laugh. And he nags me to bring him things from England."

"What sort of things?"

"Oh, the usual. A London bus; picture of the Queen. You know. A tube map. He's obsessed with trains at the moment. Anything to do with trains is a great hit."

Her voice was light and happy as she spoke of her son and the things he liked, what made him laugh, what he did to make her laugh, what he did to tease her. Just like a normal boy she seemed to be saying.

Skull listened, smiling politely, unseen. He found he was unable to re-conjure the figment of her sleeping form. He saw only the gurning boy drooling in a high chair, heard the slurred yowls, the smell of open bowels.

After a silence she said, "Your turn, Skull."

"You're a good mum," he said.

"No," she laughed. "Well. Maybe. But not such a good daughter, it seems." Now she whispered hoarsely, "I think the Prof's already irritated with me."

Skull laughed loud. He was tempted to suggest that he found it hard to believe she could irritate anyone but quickly said instead, "I went shopping. Food and essentials, since we're confessing. And I tidied up the kitchen a bit, you might be relieved to know. Although it's possibly even less sanitary now."

"Less?" she laughed. "Did you clean it with a toilet brush?"

"Ha, no. But I think there were possibly several new strains of penicillin I flushed away down the sink, alas now lost to science." It was a stupid, contrived joke but she rewarded him with her laugh anyway.

"But did you clean up all those crappy take-out menus in the lobby?" she asked. "I should think that would be your priority. In the name of good community relations."

"Indeed." He appreciated the levity but his voice became clipped with self-consciousness. "It's on the critical path," he said.

She asked him then about Mr Beavis and whether Mr Beavis lived alone; she asked him about the flat, how long he had lived there and what attractions and advantages the location had for him. He found talking to her was easy enough because she listened well. It seemed that not much news of his life had filtered down to her through Jon. When she ask him about Emily it seemed a natural component in the flow of their conversation so he told her that Emily had moved out a few weeks back.

"Can't blame her, really," he admitted.

Jac moved on deftly. "Anka rang," she said. "She's going to the flat tomorrow afternoon. The one in Docklands. She wants me to meet her there after her sandwich rounds to collect the post, but I can't do it."

"What post?"

"Oh, letters and bills, I think."

"Bills?"

"She seems to feel it's a family matter," said Jac. "She insisted I should have them. It is a bit odd, isn't it? Why should we pay the bills?"

"So are you coming up?" he asked, but thought it sounded eager, hopeful even, so he added quickly, "Although I doubt there'd be anything important."

"I promised to go with the Prof to a function at College."

"I'll go," Skull said, surprising himself with his own enthusiasm.

"With the Prof?"

"To the flat. If you like."

"Oh, the flat."

"If you like."

"I don't know, Skull ..." Maybe she didn't trust him, or didn't want to be obligated any further.

"I'm not overly busy at the moment," he added. "I could forward anything important down to Churnwell."

"Oh no," she said quickly. "The Prof wouldn't know what to do with it. It would simply —" She caught the inflection in her own voice, a sudden harshness. She continued after a pause: "That would be just great, Skull. If it's no trouble. If there is anything, hang on to it; I'm in town on Friday."

"The Uncle Daffy lecture," he said.

She laughed. "Have you changed your mind? Oh do change your mind, Skull. I'm sure he'll have forgiven you by now."

He knew she meant it lightly, ironically even, but forgiveness implied infraction on his part, and the day trip to Godwin Hill still rankled. "Indeed," he said tightly.

She laughed again. "But have you forgiven him?"

Photogrammetry

Jon and I were starving by the time we left the dig at Godwin Hill. As we drove slowly back along the rough track towards the macadam road I asked Betty to list all the local Sussex ales. The list was long.

Brighton Best, Rabbit's Wort, Downey Ale, The Flighty Monk...

"Just find the nearest pub," Jon said. He was grumpy.

Backter's Orchid, Ditchling Dizzer, Neanderthal...

"What's the point," I said cheerily, "in coming all the way out into the country and settling for a beer you can buy in Streatham?" Naturally, I was showing off, but also, I felt, trying to rescue the day.

Pale Dew, Snake and Sandpit...

"Neanderthal?" I could detect his ire rising. "Neanderthal! That sounds apt, don't you think? Betty! Find the nearest pub that sells Neanderthal beer."

Betty's navigation system instantly plotted a route to the *Robin Hood Inn* just outside Macclesfield in Cheshire with a journey time of around four and a half hours.

"Ah, Jesus Jonny, Skull. Can we just find a fucking pub? Who cares what beer it is as long as it's got some fucking alcohol in it? We passed a few on the way here."

I knew Jon had reached the stage where unless he had more alcohol to mellow him out, the alcohol he had already consumed was going to make him even more tetchy.

Turn around where possible, Betty suggested unhelpfully.

"Fuck. Sake."

"Fine," I said lightly, conscious that perhaps I was over-compensating with the positive cheeriness. "It's not perfect. Betty! Show local pubs." Over a dozen markers popped up on the display showing the location of more drinking holes in the Macclesfield area. I tried again, "Betty! List local Sussex pubs."

Duke of Sussex, Clarenden Road, Macclesfield, Betty chimed. *Joe's Off Licence, Sussex Avenue, Macclesfield...*

I pulled off the road then, and spent ten minutes trying to reset the instruction management interface. I tried explaining to Jon, "It's the command interface between the natural language interpreter and the —"

"Really-that's-so-interesting-I-don't-give-a-fuck," he said, and he swigged the last of his scotch, tossing the empty bottle onto the back seat. "Drive the car, Skull. Just drive the fucking car until we fucking find a fucking pub. I'm. Really. Hungry."

In the end I had to restart the entire navigation module and call the workshop to get the configuration settings, which I manually keyed in before the system was happy. By that stage Jon was comatose with anger. He wouldn't even look at me.

The inn, when we found one, was down a side road in a functional, rather than picture-postcard South Down village and, to be honest, was not your classic English country inn. In fact it put me in mind of a dreary Welsh chapel. Even the beer garden was laid out in mournful rows of wonky wooden benches much like tombstones in a graveyard. By now, anyway, the weather had changed to cloudy and the light spring breeze had sharpened to a spring nip. So we went inside.

"I'm buying," Jon said aggressively as we marched towards the bar. It took my best negotiation skills to persuade the publican to provide us with food because we had missed their lunch-time and the chef had already left. We ate stale sandwiches and cold pies in silence until our blood sugar levels were sufficiently restored to allow civil conversation.

"I heard voices," he said, avoiding my eye. "In the tunnel. I heard voices whispering, tittering. Very odd. I suppose I panicked. Ha."

Of course I laughed too. "You looked a bit pale when you came out," I said. "I thought it was the chalk."

"No," he said. "We shouldn't have gone in the tunnels."

*

Uncle Daffy had climbed down into the mine first. Jon was like a child, scrambling recklessly after him, whooping to see if he could get an echo. I peered over the edge, plucking up the courage to follow. It was a long way down. There was a young guy down at the bottom already — a student, I guessed. He waved cheerfully up at me. Uncle Daffy and Jon looked up too, so I waved back. They were all watching me now. I had to start the descent. By the time I got to the bottom they were deep into a tunnelling discussion, squatting low to peer into the dark narrow side tunnels just above floor level.

The young guy nodded at me and said, casually, "Yeah, I'm taking the snaps."

"Cool," I nodded back. Without further prompting he explained that he was using a highly specialist 3D modelling system with a thirty six mega-pixel sensor and a field of view in the seventy four vertical to fifty four horizontal degree range because his company were also the project co-sponsors selected for their expertise in photogrammetry and RTI techniques. "That's Reflectance Transformation Imaging," he said, adding patiently that in "the business" it was generally used for enhanced artefact visualisation.

The words tumbled from him like frozen chips from a packet, little nuggety acronyms and big lumps of jargon all welded together. Not my area, so there was little for me to chew on but I nodded politely which he took as encouragement. He ploughed into a description of the equipment's target reflectivity and the exciting temperature drift features, which I actually thought was tolerably interesting, but sadly he didn't get very far.

"Rob's our resident geek," Uncle Daffy interrupted, introducing him to Jon. "His firm's helping with the funding. Don't start yet," he said to Rob. "Let's get our audience seated."

Rob grinned, relieved to be put into context at last. He had this huge smile, a big, goofy lip curler that stretched across his face and made little creases around his eyes. A real smile, to which you could only respond in kind.

Uncle Daffy pointed at the side tunnel he'd come out of earlier, saying, "He's set up his wizzery in Gallery Five. Let's go and have a look-see. Lights on." We all turned on the little lights attached to our helmets, then he bent himself into the tunnel, wiggled about a bit and was gone. Once again Jon followed enthusiastically.

The tunnel entrance was roughly dome shaped and about two feet from the floor. There was nothing appealing about it. I had no intention of entering it. I tried engaging Rob in further technical discussion, asking about his research interests, hoping the conversation would broaden and we could parry skill-sets and jargon until Uncle Daffy forgot about me. Unfortunately Rob's work was inside the tunnel and he was eager to show me.

"It's quite cosy," he grinned, "but I'd leave the jacket out here."

Reluctantly I removed my jacket, transferring my phone and car key fob to my pant pockets as a natural reflex.

"I'd leave those too," he laughed. "Believe me, there's nothing more painful than a phone poking into your balls as you crawl through a tunnel. I learnt that the hard way. Literally, ha-ha. No signal anyway."

Condemned, I knelt before the tunnel entrance and lowered my head into the maw. The tunnel curved left so it was impossible to see how long it was. A faint glow seemed to soften the wall at the far end, but perhaps I imagined it because it was very dark, the sides were narrow, the floor hard and uneven. It smelled like a crypt, dank and earthy. I wriggled maybe fifteen feet or so emerging into a small gallery where Jon and Uncle David crouched in uncomfortable proximity, having a difficult chat about the Prof. My puffing, grunting entrance provided the excuse for them to bring their conversation to an abrupt end. Both looked relieved.

You couldn't stand in the gallery, you could barely crouch, and there were three more tight tunnels radiating away from it, although one was very short, more of a sepulchre. It was a tight fit for all of us.

"Well, there it is," said Uncle Daffy, indicating a grey metallic box mounted on a low tripod. A lens poked out front and a cable ran out back to a laptop. More wires ran from the laptop to a lighting rig and yet more cool looking metal boxes. We all nodded intelligently at the kit and the light from out helmets played across the squat tripods throwing these weird animated shadows on the cavern wall, like primitive dancing grotesques.

Hauling himself into the gallery, Rob curled up next to his equipment. Grinning his terrific grin, he switched on the floodlights, instantly killing the wall dancers, destroying with a click all the unwanted intimacy of the head-torch lighting.

"Well?" said Uncle Daffy raising his eyebrows, which was the cue for Rob to deliver a presentation on the imaging element of the project.

I don't know why it was important for Uncle Daffy to give us so much of his time, whether it was out of respect for the Prof or because we were a useful audience for him and Rob to practice on. All the same we found ourselves in one of those odd situations where no one quite understands the role they've been assigned but everyone continues to play their role in case all are revealed as frauds. So we were treated to this un-illustrated lecture on digital photogrammetry and RTI for Cultural Heritage Imaging, while sitting hunched uncomfortably thirty feet inside a hill in a subterranean void excavated five thousand years ago by men clothed in animal skins using antler picks and bone shovels.

I've sat through my fair share of technical presentations, and while none were quite as atmospheric, nor quite as cramped, Rob's was pretty typical. He started simply ("To take a good photograph you need good light"), before throwing us all into a thicket of technical detail.

Rob wasn't a natural communicator but I managed to follow some of what he told us. He was taking high definition photographs of the interior of a selection of the mines as they were excavated. He would then apply digital photogrammetry methods to build a three dimensional picture. Others in the team were going to use a range of geophysical techniques, like low frequency ground penetrating radar and seismic methods to construct an accurate mapping of all the shafts and tunnels across the whole of the hill. The data and textures from the photogrammetry could then be combined with the geophysical data to render a virtual reality model of the entire mine complex.

It seemed that everyone was sceptical of the geophysical aspects of the project due to the scale and depth of readings required. Even Uncle Daffy had said he doubted the archaeological value of the project; the hill had been mined sporadically, one shaft at a time, over a thousand years or so and, as such, it wasn't a coherent complex, even if many of the tunnels connected. But Rob didn't care because someone was paying for him to have fun with his kit. I liked Rob. He knew what he was talking about.

After the first couple of minutes Jon stopped listening. I could tell from his face he'd switched off. Within five minutes he and Uncle Daffy had started their own mumbling conversation with terms like "sherd analysis", and "contexts", and "artefact patterning" bandied about.

But Rob and I were all "X3D", "rendering engines", "Bezier curves", "hypergrids and splines". I felt my day had suddenly taken a turn for the better. I actually have a professional interest in real-time photogrammetry, so the exchange was somewhat optimal for us both. We were engrossed in a discussion of the massive potential in time-of-flight technologies so that we hardly noticed when Uncle Daffy and Jon slithered away down one of the tunnels at the other end of the gallery. We heard a few bellows and grunts echoing down the pipes but thought nothing of it, or at least it didn't penetrate our world.

A while later Uncle Daffy squeezed himself back into the gallery, entering from a different tunnel to the one he'd left by, favouring us with a triumphant look.

"Still at it?" he said. "Aren't you going to have a little look-see down some of the tunnels?"

Tight, dark spaces have no appeal to me so I said, "It's been a very interesting experience." Uncle Daffy nodded, Rob grinned. We sat in silence so I added a supplementary, "Would you say these new technologies provide many new insights into your work?"

"Sure," Uncle Daffy responded, looking sideways at me. "Sure. The technology is of course a great help. Visualisation and 3D is all the rage right now, see? But we've had radio carbon dating, satellite imaging, Geophys — and these are all very useful, there's no doubt about it. But, d'you know, it's not all about the technology. You can build your elegant computer models and your visual projections, but you still have to get your bum in the mud, and get the muck under your finger nails, and feel the grit in your teeth. You have to dig things up to look at them, hold them in your hand, touch them, feel them.

"Our knowledge advances in a series of little leaps and bounds, and so we start looking at things in different ways which makes us look for different things in different places. You can't get around it: you have to scratch at the past to make it reveal itself. Then we use our minds, our emotions, our human empathy. No technology can do that."

As he spoke he kept looking back into the tunnel he had crawled from. "Did Jon come out already?" he asked.

"Not out through here," said Rob.

"Oh, you have to come through here to get out there," said Uncle Daffy. "But does that answer your question, chap?" He glared at me. We were back to normal. "Here we are," he said, pointing at the photogrammetry kit, "here we are in the space age, the age of information, trying to understand the Neolithic mind. Is that really possible? I don't know. Is that even useful?" He shrugged. "Where is that boy?"

Leaning into the tunnel Uncle Daffy shouted. "Jon! Jon!" His voice had a hollow, flat sound as the darkness swallowed and killed it. We listened but heard nothing in response. "Oh, blast. I hope he hasn't got himself stuck. Jon!"

"Shall I go look?" Rob volunteered.

Uncle Daffy shook his head and we sat for a moment in silence before he continued: "On the other hand there's a theory that we've stopped evolving, that our brain has stopped evolving because, you know, it hasn't gotten any bigger. So we're not getting any smarter, see, but the pace of change gets faster, faster, faster. It's exponential." He illustrated the upward hook of an exponential graph with his arm. "Exponential, see. And us with our little Palaeolithic brain. Evolution can't work fast enough. So are we smart enough to keep up with our own inventions? I don't know, I don't know. Soon we might be bowing to our robotic masters, right?" We all laughed, and after a while he said, "But these little men down here — they didn't do so bad though, did they? Heh? Did they?"

Scraping and thumping signalled Jon's arrival long before his kicking legs slowly emerged from the same tunnel he'd left by. Rob reached out and pulled Jon backwards into the chamber. Jon sat up blinking madly at us. Sweat mingled with the blobs of chalk dust smeared on his face.

"What happened?" Uncle Daffy demanded cheerfully. "Get stuck, did you?"

"Something like that," Jon said.

Uncle Daffy nodded, said, "Right. That's it. I have to get back now. Shall we go?"

We left Godwin Hill soon after that, looking for a pub.

*

After I'd bought my round, I asked Jon what had really happened. He took a long slug of beer, shook his head, looked thoughtful, worked some food from a tooth with his tongue.

"I was a bit slow following Uncle Daffy down the tunnel," he said at last. "It's incredibly tough on the elbows and knees, crawling through those tunnels. He's a lithe little fellow is Uncle Daffy, and quite clearly he's aced the technique 'cause he shot ahead like a ferret down a rabbit hole. I followed him for bloody miles — well it felt like miles. Anyway, eventually I reached a tiny gallery where there were another couple of tunnels going off it and I didn't know which he'd gone down. Of course once you start you can't turn around. And it's dark, right. Those head lamp things are useless — the light just bounces about a bit and dies. I could hear him up ahead, but I couldn't tell which hole to choose. When I shouted, he shouted back, but it was all muffled and Welshy, impossible to tell the direction. Those little bastards followed the flint round and round so there're all these inter-connected tunnels down there. I picked the wrong one. Must have. I went on for hours before I realised I couldn't hear him anymore."

"You were only gone about ten minutes," I said.

"Really," he said. "Really? Felt like hours."

He swallowed more beer, squinting across the top of the beer glass at me to see if I was taking him seriously. I was. He carried on, "It's tough crawling along like that. Your shoulders ache, your neck aches, your head goes down, so you lie there and all you can see are the walls with the little scrapes and scratches, some of them so fresh, like they were made yesterday. Those little guys must have had the balls of a mammoth to go down there with just their sticks and candles. Anyway. I knew I was lost so I tried going back. Fuck me. That's worse than going forward.

"I have to say, there is a serious limitation in the human body which you only discover when you have to crawl backwards through a dark, narrow tunnel, by which time it's far too late to evolve a more suitable arrangement of limbs. Humans are not designed for backward crawling. You've got to —", here he silently demonstrated with both arms stretched up how he propelled himself backwards through the tunnel with a push and a little wiggle.

"So after about ten feet or so going backwards my shirt caught on a lump of flint or something. The tunnel's tight. You can't get your arms back to untangle it, can you. So I pulled forward. Push back. Stuck. Every time. The shirt hooked on some flint or chalk and rucked up. Couldn't dislodge it. Completely stuck. What d'you do?"

He chugged a bit more beer, worked the tooth, frowned thoughtfully. "Well you panic of course; you panic," he said, wiping his lips with the back of his hand. "I thought, I'm never getting out of here. Couldn't breathe; dark; air was stale — it's like a tomb. I could imagine my brown bones being discovered a thousand years hence. People did die down there, you know. There's these little rock falls you pass as you go along. You don't know what's behind the rocks. Anyhow, I lay there panicking and listening to the whispers — that's when I heard the whispers — people talking about me. You know how when people talk about you behind your back, you know it's about you, you just can't hear clearly what they're saying. It was like that. Just out of earshot behind the walls, just ahead in the dark. A low mumble — sort of a deep hum. Whispering."

His phone chuckled loudly in his pocket. He jumped a bit, swore, fumbled for the phone, squinted at the screen.

"Hey Nav!" he yelled chummily into his phone. "What is happening, bruv?"

He stood, edging edged away from our table as he spoke, then out into the beer garden where I saw him pacing up and down between the silent benches, the phone pressed to his ear, his spare arm waving. When he returned it was with a couple more pints of beer and a face like a sucked grape. He tossed his phone onto the table and set the beer down carefully beside it.

"Have you ever noticed," he said, "that when you're on the up, I'm on the down? And vice versa?"

"Can't say I have," I grunted. As far as I remembered, he was always on the up and I always down.

"Come-on? In Juniors, remember? You were a monitor and teacher's pet and I was always having to sit in the front. Then I got into St Eddies and you had to go to — the other place. Remember? I went up to Durham; you fucked up your A-levels and went to…where was it?"

"Kings." He never tired of rubbing it in.

"Kings? Jesus, Skull." He laughed, pleased. "You are a shocker. Kings? Is that what you tell people? I was at Kings-din, you know." He said it in a funny voice, but he didn't laugh, and neither did I. "Well who cares now, anyway," he said. "Look at you: successful entrepreneur, vanguard of the revolution, storm trooper of the new technocracy; and here I am with my fancy doctorate, hand cranking crap trades through the back office of a second rate investment bank; mortgage the size of a mansion on a flat the size of a rabbit hutch; last girlfriend sacked me, like all the others have. Can't even get another crap job. See? You're up, I'm down. Like a see-saw, we are."

"Ah, the phone call," I said. "This is about the phone call, isn't it?"

He knocked back the last half pint in the glass with a long gulp. I pushed my untouched pint towards him. "I'm driving," I told him.

I'm not so great with the confessional thing. A change of subject seemed in order so I picked his phone out of the beer slops on the table, wiped it on my sleeve and said, "This is a seriously offensive colour for a phone. What is it again?"

"Red," he said.

"The phone, fool."

"It's a phone, Skull."

"Girl's phone," I said. On the back, in black script, was written: The Lucy Phone. There was only one button on the side which I pressed but the screen stayed blank. He took the device from me.

"I think it's cool," he said caressing the smooth red casing. "One of the techies at work recommended it." He stared at the blank screen and gave the phone a little shake. "On," he said, and grinned with the pleasure of a boy on a new bicycle as the screen lit up. "See? It's got all the gubbins: face thingy, voice whatsisname. It's even got that pay-diddly-doody — functionality." (I got a sneer as he chewed on the word) "So now I can buy sandwiches at lunchtime without getting my hands filthy with filthy money."

"NFC," I said for his enlightenment. He glared at me so I expanded: "Near Field Communication."

"Of course," he said, "I am fondling the damned thing all the time so it must be covered in germs anyway. But at least they're my germs, right?"

"Well it's not so much the functionality as the platform," I said.

"Fuck off, Skull. It's got apps and everything. Look."

We shuftied around a bit so we could sit next to each other and he pointed out all the things he liked to do with his phone. There was nothing special. It was an ordinary smartphone running an obscure fork of a standard operating system, but he seemed happy with it and thrilled with the fact that it just did things without his intervention, like hooking into his wireless network and connecting to his TV to stream films. It came bundled with all the usual stuff, like an email reader and a range of social networking services. He showed me the music streaming service for which he had registered as well as a news aggregator, and the bargain shopping service he'd signed up to.

"'S all crap, isn't it?" he grinned diffidently. "I'm happy, though. Deepak thought it was the dog's tasty bits and he's a bit of a geek, like you. Only more handsome. Whatcha think, bruv?"

"Not too shabby," I said. He seemed to need the re-assurance because he'd got it through Deepak's cousin who owned a computer repair shop somewhere out in east London that among other things, sold phone contracts along with cheap mobile phones.

"It's a great little time waster," he said, "but it's not going to change my life. Apparently I'm not smart enough." He laughed. With a beer-wet finger he tapped on a poorly drawn icon of gold coins falling from the bottom of a to-do list. The label said: GOALD.

A dialogue box popped up on the screen: "Select Voice or Text".

"Let's try voice," he said, pressing the Voice button. "I did text last time. It was a bit confusing."

Hi Jon Fast, said a suitably tinny female voice. *Please provide voice cue. Click Q and speak.*

A fat green button labelled Q appeared, squatting across the screen like an ugly frog. The interface was dated, I thought, but Jon was delighted, thumbing the button: "Hi. My name ... is ... Werner Brandes," he said.

Voice cue not recognised. Please provide voice cue. Click Q and speak.

"It's rubbish, isn't it," he said.

"Yes. But it needs a short name, so you can talk to it," I explained. "Try Phone, or something. Just press the button and say Phone."

He held the phone gently, turning it in his hands, fondling the edges, caressing the curves thoughtfully before he pressed the Q button again. "Lucy," he said.

Voice cue is (then Jon's voice) *"Lucy." Please confirm.*

Jon clicked Yes and the button was replaced by an androgynous cartoon avatar with big eyes and a mobile mouth. When the phone spoke the avatar's mouth moved. In the silences and the pauses the eyes blinked.

Thank you Jon Fast. Set a goal.

"A goal. Yay! My goal is to be rich and —"

I cut in: "You need the cue word."

"The cue word? Oh right. The cue word. Lucy! My goal is to be rich and famous."

Thank you Jon Fast. Your goal must be SMART goal. Set a goal.

"See? Even my goals are dumb. I would like to — oh. Lucy! I would like unrestrained sexual intercourse with my boss. She's really fit," he explained to me. "She's got like these —"

Thank you Jon Fast. Your goal must be SMART goal. Set a goal.

We were starting to get nasty looks from an adjacent table, more I think for the annoying droid voice coming from the phone than for the puerile content of the conversation. Jon had a stilted delivery for his commands, calling out "Lucy!", then slowly and carefully enunciating each word.

"It needs a SMART goal," I said.

"Yeah I got that. So screwing the boss wouldn't be exactly smart, I get it. Lucy! My goal is to solve world hunger. That would be smart."

Thank you Jon Fast. Your goal must be SMART goal. Set a goal.

"That would be smart if I could do it, though, wouldn't it?"

"Yes it would," I agreed, "but that's not the kind of smart it means."

"How many kinds of smart are there?"

"Oh you wouldn't believe," I said.

"Your world, bruv." He shook his head sadly.

"You never heard of SMART goals?"

"Evidently not," said Jon with his hurt voice, as if he'd been left off a party invite. "I always thought a goal was merely a wish with a little reality smeared on it."

So I told him, SMART is an acronym. He gazed on me with the expression of one who has digested raw dough while I explained to him the concept of the SMART goal. Each goal, I said, should be specific, measurable, achievable, realistic and, timely. SMART. It's an acronym.

"Jesus, Skull. How do you know this stuff?"

"I once read the Internet," I explained.

"Ah, I should try it," he said. "So. Specific, manageable. Manageable?"

We went through it again a few times. "Usually," I said, "it's something like 'Our sales of product Y should increase by two percent in third quarter sales over second quarter sales'. Or even 'I want to lose ten pounds of body weight before Christmas'."

"Right, got it," he said. "Lucy! I want to solve world hunger using only two fish and — five loaves of bread."

"Timely," I said. "You need to set a time limit."

"In ten minutes," he added.

Thank you Jon Fast. Your goal must be SMART goal. Set a goal.

I said, "I think you may have failed in the realistic department."

"Ah, it's impossible." He drained the last of my beer. "Another?"

"I'm driving. We should go." I wanted to hit London at the peak of the rush hour so I could test how well the assisted urban driving module worked.

"One for the road," he said heading for the bar, returning with a packet of crisps and two double whiskeys. He poured the one whiskey into the other.

"OK, I've got it. I've got my SMART goal. Here it is. Lucy! My goal is to take one photograph of an empty packet of crisps every day from today until the end of the month, using my new smartphone."

Thank you Jon Fast, said Lucy. There was a pause, then: *SMART goal accepted.*

"Wey hey!" He sank the whiskey. "Looks like I am smart after all."

*

Jon was quiet on the drive back to London. He reclined the passenger seat until he was lying almost horizontal, his head back against the headrest, turned away from me. I thought he was sleeping but as we pulled up outside his flat he stirred, raising the seat to the normal position.

He asked me, "Do you have SMART goals?"

I said no and he, grabbing his jacket and rucksack from the back seat, replied: "That's because you are smart." He part-opened the door before he continued, "You know, everyone always said that of the two of us, I was the one most likely to succeed."

He made it sound as if we were some kind of couple. "Who's everyone?" I asked.

"Oh you know. Everyone we knew. Thing is," he went on, "you have the look of a victim, Skull. Sorry to say it, but you never seemed to have the qualities needed for success, whatever those are. But here you are now with your smart car and your smart gadgets — one of life's elites, a chieftain of the techno-warrior class. You are Homo Faber. You're making something special with your life and here's me with my stupid life, homo failure."

He sat a moment, and when I didn't know what to say to re-assure him he climbed out the car.

"Let's not do that again for a while," he suggested, slamming the door shut.

Tuesday

In the uneven mosaic of London, Docklands is the splinter of glass flaked from a cola bottle and pressed into the muddy gap between the cracked china tile of Greenwich and Southwark's worn pottery sherd. There is also the sense that while Docklands is in London, it is not of London, and much of its soul lies in another age, another country, even another continent.

Jon and Anka lived in a small apartment on the fifth floor of a block of flats, somewhere between Millwall Inner Dock and the River Thames. Neither of these landmarks were visible from any window of their apartment, nor from the feature balcony. It was a modern building, faced with light brown brick, and with cast iron balconies bolted around French windows suggesting a leisurely, continental lifestyle for the occupants. Ironically, the properties were affordable only by those living a frantic Anglo-American lifestyle.

Skull was delighted to find parking nearby after only a brief circuit of the area. A sharp wind came up off the river, funnelling through the concrete streets in sudden, cruel blasts. Docklands is windy, he remembered, wishing that he had brought a more robust jacket as he walked the short distance to the building's understated entrance.

Through the glass door he saw the lobby was empty, the concierge office closed. On the panel outside he pressed the number for the flat but there came no answering buzz from Anka.

Anka had told Jac she would be there late afternoon. Skull had tried calling Anka earlier to confirm but the call had gone straight through to voicemail. Now he tried again but with the same result; she might have been already, and gone.

On the point of returning to his car he noticed the numbers above the lift door counting down, a lift descending. He waited beside the front entrance making a great show of searching for his keys, patting his pockets, muttering curses while he watched the woman exit the lift. Quickly, as she left the building, he grabbed the door before it closed behind her, taking the lift to the fifth floor. He thought that if Anka wasn't there at least he could stay warm until she arrived.

The door to the flat was open.

"Hello," he called, knocking as he entered. "Hello? Anka?"

Had she not answered because it was him, Skull? Perhaps she had been vacuuming and hadn't heard his ringing. Perhaps Jon had returned.

The small entrance hall was empty but the shallow storage cupboards were opened, their contents spilling out. The toilet door on the left was also open, the room unoccupied. At the far end of the hall were three doors: left to the master bedroom, right to the living room and kitchen; straight ahead was the door to the second bedroom which Jon used as an office. This door was closed.

Skull stepped across the hall into the living room, glancing briefly left into the bedroom as he passed.

"Jon?" In the centre of the room was a thin man who smiled at Skull with big, meaty lips. "Jon Fast?" It sounded more like "Chon Fust".

"No," Skull said, smiling back before asking, "Is Anka here?"

"Anka? Sure, yes." The man wobbled his shaven head, a head on which all the features were too large, bullying each other for prominence at the front of a small, putty face: fleshy lips, bulbous nose, heavy, Homo Habilis eyebrows below which two brown, bleak eyes restlessly panned the room.

"Are you a friend of Anka?" Skull asked.

"Sure, sure. Anka." He wobbled his head again. Squished his lips into a new ghastly smile. More a sneer. It wasn't a smile after all. The man would not look at Skull. Wouldn't catch his eye.

"Where is she?"

Only now did Skull see the danger. This man didn't fit. He wasn't smiling, but then neither was Skull as he turned to leave.

The second man stood behind Skull, close, blocking the exit. This new man smelt sour, smelt of old steamed fish and boiled cabbage, of cheap smokes and all-day morning breath like a man on the move, like a man sleeping rough on a cold, filthy sofa. Short, thickset, his body spoke a simple language with a single word: menace. Chin, sloped eyes and a nose flattened by Tartar ancestry, or violence, or both, the round face was a natural home for ragged scars. Unlike Habilis his hair was cropped short, lying flat in oily streaks of grey-black which radiated away from a high impact crash site which marked yet another field of badly healed wounds.

Looking down on this head recalled suddenly to Skull an old photograph he'd once seen of the aftermath of the Tunguska event, a violent explosion high over the remote steppes of Russia at the beginning of the last century. Black and white photos taken twenty years later showed mile after mile of flattened forest trees, the black trunks lying in ranks like the corpses of fallen soldiers. That's what Skull thought as he tried to step around the man.

The man remained a block. No polite side-step, no diffident apology; just the minacious chin and the flat black eyes.

Everything moved slowly now. Skull, in a panic, tried pushing past the man; a mistake, because the man struck Skull in the solar plexus with two stubby fingers. While no expert in matters of violence, it nevertheless seemed to Skull — even as it was being done to him — that this was a highly competent, knowing action; it was an impassive response, a little piece of business rather than a matter of passion or anger. Skull doubled over, slowly, stepping away, jerkily, from the Tunguska Man. He felt the wind leave as his diaphragm curled, felt his legs go, hoped his bowels would hold. Unable to return the air to his lungs he continued backing away into the living room he had a moment before tried to leave.

The Tunguska Man followed Skull closely, reaching swiftly into his jacket and finding his wallet. Skull was as helpless as a two year old child.

The Tunguska Man said something guttural in a language Skull didn't understand and Habilis stepped forward with his foul fat smile, guiding Skull softly backwards to a dining chair where he sat heavily.

Skull bobbed slowly on choppy swells of nausea aware that all the sands of his courage were being carried away in this rip tide of agony. The two men seemed indifferent to his struggle for breath. The Tunguska Man flipped slowly through the wallet while Skull gasped like a landed fish.

The room combined a kitchen and dining area as well as a cosy, if cramped, sitting space at the far end. Skull had visited the flat only once before, attending a strange and awkward dinner party which Jon prepared in honour of Anka, with Skull and Emily as unwitting witnesses to his homage. Back then the room was neat, civil, constrained; now it was a mess. The kitchen was stripped of appliances leaving voids beneath the counter top, cupboard and drawers open and empty, contents strewn about. In the seating area a well-thumbed comfy chair faced a blank wall on which the dark outline showed where once a large TV screen had been affixed. Skull remembered the stash of furnishings in Anka's warehouse. If these guys were thieves they were clearly too late.

"What was that for?" It came out strained and rasping, more of a whine than the angry retort he might have hoped for. Relief from pain was slow in coming, his stomach clutching at his stomach in recursive spasms, chest clamped tight.

Habilis leaned in close. "You are Jon Fast?" (Chon Fust, again.)

"I'm not Jon. I already told you."

"What are you do here?" Habilis said slowly.

"What are you doing here?" Skull demanded. He was scared, not defiant. Pain and fear made him act more aggressively than he would have liked.

Habilis gave a curious tilt to his head, frowning. The Tunguska Man spoke again, a short, rapid-fire monologue like a man preparing to spit. Habilis answered in kind and then the Tunguska Man read slowly from a credit card he had extracted from Skull's wallet, masticating the words slowly: Muttchew Morrol. He passed the card to Habilis.

"You are Matthew Morrell?" Habilis asked holding the card out as evidence. "Where is Viktor? You know where is Viktor?" Skull was aware that they were both observing him closely.

"Who?" Skull addressed the Tunguska Man. Although Habilis seemed to be the English speaker of the pair, the Tunguska Man was clearly in charge.

"Vik-tor," the Tunguska Man repeated slowly, reaching into an inner pocket and extracting a folded paper which carefully he unfolded. "Viktor Petsch," he said, holding the paper up. It was a low resolution image of a man Skull had never seen.

Where's Anka? Skull thought. The front door had not been forced as far as he remembered. It occurred to him that she might have opened the door to these men, in which case she may be in more trouble than he was. Was she perhaps in another room? Were there more than just these two men?

"I don't know this man," Skull shook his head. "Viktor? Who's Viktor?"

The two men spoke briefly and contemptuously at each other again. Most European languages, when spoken by their natives, sounded to Skull like a series of mortal insults laced with threats of grievous violence. In the exchange he heard his name hawked and spit more than once, and thought he detected the mention of Anka.

"You know where is Jon Fast?" asked Habilis.

"No," Skull said. "No I don't. We want to find him too."

Habilis frowned and spoke again to Tunguska Man. They cursed each other back and forth until finally Habilis sneered at him: "We? Who is we?"

"We," Skull lied, "is council. I am a council official. Mr Fast is a tenant. This is council property. You understand? Property of the council. And you have just assaulted a council officer. Mr Fast owes rent on this property. The bailiffs will be here in a minute and then we'll call in the police too." He looked officiously at his watch, taking also the opportunity to stand up, hoping to recover a little dignity, perhaps even a little advantage. He extracted his phone, flicking the screen on. "Police. You understand?"

Habilis relayed this information to the Tunguska Man who shrugged indifferently, then called out "Hoi". As Skull looked up at him, he spun the wallet high so Skull had to reach up to catch it. The Tunguska Man stepped quickly forward and hit Skull again. He hit Skull in the same place he had hit him before only this time it felt harder and Skull instantly lost the use of his legs. He sat down abruptly. He thought his heart would stop.

Deftly the Tunguska Man prised the phone from Skull's failing fingers and, as once again Skull fought for breath, once again the man searched through his jacket pockets. This time he was more thorough, finding Skull's car key fob, which he examined briefly before tossing it across the room. Next he handled the phone, turning it on, holding it in front of Skull to see if access was by face recognition. He hesitated a moment, then plucked out the SIM card from the slot in the side, dropped the phone to the floor and kicked it across the room while Skull watched speechlessly. The SIM card he pocketed.

"You understan'," he said. The two men left.

*

For some time Skull sat upright on the dining room chair working to suck some air around the knot of pain just below his heart. After that he just sat, listening in the empty room for the sound of the men coming back. He was not entirely confident that he had actually heard them leave.

As he sat, gurning with discomfort, he wondered if he was altogether sure that he did "understan'" what the Tunguska Man had meant when he pocketed the SIM card. Was it that he would meet with more violence if he came across them again? Or were they going to make and receive premium rate phone calls on his SIM card?

It seemed a lot of effort for small reward. None of it made sense and after further reflection he concluded that on balance his first assumption was probably correct and, if so, their wishes happily coincided with his; he had no intention of meeting them again. Skull consoled himself with the discovery that as time passed he grew less inclined to vomit even though he still felt queasy.

He couldn't understand why things had taken this ugly turn; he regretted getting involved, resolved to leave well alone from now on, mind his own business, although he couldn't help speculating what the men were doing in Jon's flat. What did they want?

Ultimately it was a pointless question, he reflected, because he didn't want the answer. Nevertheless, attempting to suppress his curiosity only seemed to seed a further avalanche of questions. Were they Russians, for instance? And did it matter? Certainly they were east Europeans, but were they friends of Anka? Habilis seemed to recognise her name, and they clearly knew Jon's name but obviously not Jon since they assumed that he, Skull, might be Jon. Chon Fust. And where was Anka?

So who, then, was this Viktor Petsch? Another Russian, obviously. They had seemed much more interested in Viktor than in Jon, when he thought about it, but what had Jon to do with Viktor Petsch? And where was Anka?

The sudden horror that Anka may be lying dead or dying in one of the other rooms was enough get him out the chair and painfully, unsteadily, to the door. He peered tentatively into the hall, mercifully empty. He stepped across the hall to the main bedroom, entering reluctantly, entering slowly.

The bedroom, like the sitting room, was a mess: sheets strewn, clothes dumped, spilled pills, bottles, CDs, books and papers scattered over the bed, under the bed, drawers emptied and up-ended on the carpet like beached whales. No bodies.

The telephone was dead, ripped from the wall socket, the coloured wires a fist of mangled fingers sticking from the end of the cable.

Back in the hall Skull hovered outside the closed study door. All the other doors had been left open; why this one closed? What lay hidden behind it? He paused, steeling himself to enter. If they had killed her or raped her or tortured her they would hardly have left him alive, he reasoned. Logically he knew that the probability of shocking horrors waiting for him behind the door was low, but all the same he stood a while in the hall, his hand resting on the door handle, his resolve slouching against a wall of indecision.

Without his smartphone he felt disabled, as if a curtain had been drawn, a blanket thrown across his mind, dimming the luminance of any and all possible information. He felt lessened, diminished without access to the living breath of connectedness with the connected world. The phone linked him to a reality driven by logic, ordered by hierarchies, network layers, architectures, structured models, protocols. He was master in that world. Here, in the small space of this cramped flat, where the nonchalant violence, the gross barbarity of Tunguska Man and his Habilis side-kick was possible, here was a world unmediated, uncontrollable, unreal. Skull felt trapped, claustrophobic. He needed this connection to this outside world to prove to himself that while he'd been humiliated, he had not been disempowered.

There was another extension to the landline in the study. It became suddenly very important to establish whether or not it worked. He thought he should call the police.

The handle turned easily and the hinges squealed a gentle protest as he pushed open the door.

"Oh my God! What are you doing?"

Anka, behind him at the front door, scowled at the scene in the hall. Bulging shopping bags drooped from each arm, her face was red with effort, her shoulders round in a shapeless coat.

"What are you doing?" she wailed. "My God!"

"Thank God you're all right," Skull said, self-conscious suddenly, guilty. The study door whined like a complaining child before it clicked closed at his back. "Did you see the two guys leaving?"

"Two guys?" she asked, sceptical, suspicious. "What two guys?"

Skull explained quickly, badly, what had happened, following her as she walked through the flat tutting and hissing and picking at the odd item, muttering banes and dark curses in Bulgarian. The disruption of the bedroom upset her most.

When he told her of the assault, she stopped, looked him over. Her eyes lifted to his when she saw no sign of injury. Her mouth drew down with disbelief.

"Russians?" she asked.

"Sounded Russian. I wouldn't know. May I suggest that you don't touch anything, Anka. The police should see it as it is."

"Police?" she frowned at him. "What police?"

"We should call the police."

"For what?"

"For a crime. They broke into your flat. That's breaking and entering. You have to report it. Tell them what's missing. Is anything missing?"

"What could be missing? Some books? Some CDs?" She shook her head, pursing her brow. "No police."

"How d'you know they haven't stolen anything valuable?"

"Because I have taken it," she said dismissively.

"They broke in, though," Skull argued.

"You broke in. Maybe you make this mess."

She was right: nothing of value was taken except his dignity; nothing broken other than his pride. The police would only ask awkward questions.

"Who is Viktor?" Skull asked.

"I don't know," she shrugged distractedly, then clucked and sighed as she waved a despairing hand at the bed. "Fucking Russians," she said with venom.

Skull returned to the sitting room to retrieve his car keys and smartphone. The nausea lingered in his stomach, his chest hurt, his breathing felt tight. With unsteady fingers he switched on the phone, checking if it still worked after the kicking it had received. It booted up just fine, complaining momentarily about the lack of a SIM card, then reporting several nearby wireless networks before connecting automatically to Jon's network, which it remembered from the visit several months previously.

Once connected, a gentle buzz and ping drew his attention to new emails, texts and status updates he had missed since going offline. There were many, including an invitation from one of the Twydle twins to hang out with him on a group chat. He declined.

Back in the bedroom Anka was bent to the chore of folding items of Jon's clothing, placing them reverently back into the drawers from the dressing table.

He asked her, "Why did you want to meet me here, Anka?"

"Not you," she said. She still could not bring herself to look at him.

"Jacqueline couldn't get here on time. Was there something in the flat you wanted me to see? Or do?"

"You can take post."

"There may be bills, private letters ..."

"I can't pay bills," was all she said, her attention fixed on the gathering and the folding of scattered items of clothing.

Another vibrating ping called Skull back to his phone: Phillipa Miller had liked a comment Jamie Wood had made on LinkedIn about a funny cartoon involving spaghetti and meatballs; Razzi Amett had downloaded some MP3s from Amazon. A number of tech bloggers expressed dismay that the real Smartor code had been published and open-sourced. There were dozens more emails from a technical mailing list dissecting a bad solution to an obscure problem which could be solved by making the effort to read the documentation; some hate mail including one from Simon, and an email from Tom Twydle asking Skull to contact him "soonest". He had signed off "tt".

"Anka?" he asked. "Where's the wireless router?"

"It is safe. In my office," said Anka.

All Jon's gear had gone: the PC, the printer, the tablet and laptop, TV, hi-fi — she'd taken it all. The brief glance into the study had revealed a room denuded of everything except a scatter of files and books, the single desk pushed into the corner. Where was the router? If the phone had connected it meant the router was still working.

Anka looked at him. "You mean radio? Wireless radio?"

"No. Router. For wireless." Skull held up his phone. "For the phone?"

She frowned, lifting a pile of carefully folded underwear and tucked it into a gaping drawer. "Jon took his phone. I didn't find."

"Never mind," said Skull, muttering, "Not what I meant."

He poked among the kitchen cupboards and around the sitting room shelves, looking for wires, connections, wall sockets, anything that would indicate where the router might be concealed. Everything else had gone; why was the router still working? It was an anomaly. Worth investigating. Besides, he didn't want to leave yet. Anka, he reasoned, might not be safe here on her own.

He checked the walls and ceilings, closely examining the intercom near the door in the front hall before returning to Jon's office.

There were no electrical items in the office, no equipment other than the telephone handset which had been yanked from the wall socket and tossed to floor along with the spatter of magazines, books and manuals, ring binders, files swiped from the shelf; over it all floated a flotsam of old pens, pencils, a stapler, the two-hole punch, blocks of yellow sticky-back notes. The desk was similarly littered, although still visible beneath were the unfaded marks on the veneer where a desk-top computer had once sat.

Skull righted the chair which lay toppled on its side in the corner of the room, lowering himself onto the worn brown velvet cushion, leaning his elbows on the desk while he stared at the cheap whiteboard Jon had attached to the wall.

There was something odd about the board. It was not very big, but it was in an awkward place for a whiteboard. You had to stretch over the desk to access it and, as a result, there was little actual writing on it. It had found better employment as a magnetic pin-board. Wedged under bright, round magnets were the eclectic markers of Jon's life: cards for contacts, taxis, pizza; there were clippings, flyers, a fading Dilbert cartoon; prominent was a picture postcard of a standing ape with "Happy Birthday Aunt Lucy" scrawled over it; another postcard showed a tractor rusting in a bleak field. Over all these a weed-bed of yellow sticky notes was seeded with names, numbers, words.

Using his smartphone Skull took a few photos of the board, particularly of the yellow notes with their disconnected information. It was only while lining up for a long shot that he noticed the four larger magnets (blue, green, yellow and red) positioned an even distance from each corner of the board. Dark smears and scratches surrounded a fifth large magnet (black) half way down on the left, suggesting frequent handling. He reached across and pulled on the black magnet. The board swung open revealing a crude hole cut into the stud wall, hinged on the upright timber frame. The large magnets on the whiteboard were fake, fixed into position to cover the screw heads where the board was attached to the hinged door.

The wireless router stood upright on a narrow shelf inside the cavity, green LEDs winking spasmodically, three long, black plastic antennae poking up like silent sentinels. It looked out of place alongside the squat, wooden cigar box propped beside it.

The shelf itself was fixed between the two upright frames of the stud wall, extending the width of the wall cavity. Power and telephone cables snaked up from the skirting, threading through a hole in the shelf drilled specifically to allow the ingress of cables.

Why, Skull wondered? Why conceal a wireless router inside the wall cavity? Perhaps Jon had thought it would provide better access from all rooms in the flat. It was equally possible that Jon had decided that "wireless" should mean wireless and had therefore buried the router in the wall. Skull had long stopped trying to understand Jon's strange actions because whenever challenged Jon always implied a deeper purpose: his aims were subtle, he always insisted; his motives profound.

Carefully Skull lifted the cigar box from the hole and set it down on the desk to examine it.

A thick rubber band held the box lid closed. Stamped into the wood of the lid in a red serif font were the words "Double Claro". Below that, set in a fancy arced pattern was H.UPMAN and then HABANA. Some remnants of the tattered blue paper duty-stamps remained, and the small brass hinges looked worn and delicate. They may have been a later addition to the box. A film of ancient white dust had settled into the wood's thin grain, lifted only at the edges by the oil and grease of the fingers that had handed the box in and out of hiding over the years.

With the band removed, the lid yawned eagerly. The contents inside were carefully packed: on top, a stack of thick envelopes addressed, in a small neat hand, to "Master Jonathon Fast"; there was a brass fob watch, a plastic superhero figure, and an old family photo of Jon and Jac with their mother, all posing solemnly, standing, with muddy knees, in a sodden trench divided with white tape into regular squares. In the photo, all carried trowels, none looked happy. Also in the box, a highly polished flint axe-head. It had a familiar smoked-glass look to it. Skull wondered if Uncle Daffy had known all along that Jon had taken it.

Nestling in a corner of the box among the smaller stones, the shells, and slivers of worked flint, was another familiar tool. It was a grooved rectangle of browned metal, about an inch and half long. There was notch cut half-way along into the side of the tool, and just above the notch was a small, hooked folding blade on a crude hinge. A "compo" can opener. Skull recognised immediately the hint of rust around the hinge, the pattern of scratches, the corner bent by too much leverage — all the rhythms of wear which had followed the cadence of daily carry, of regular use. The tool had belonged to Skull; before that, to his father.

The can opener was standard army issue for boys suffering through national service in the late 1950s. A simple tool, it was designed to open composite ration tins, but Skull's dad had found new uses for it long after the army had forgotten all about him. Mr Morrell had attached the opener to his key ring where it was handy as a screwdriver, a letter opener, gouge, orange peeler — a simple, cheap multi-tool. The sheer utility of the thing became their joke when father and son together tackled some of the little chores around the house: *What we really need here son, is a mini hooking gouge — A mini hooking gouge, Dad? Where would we get one of those? — Well, son, would you believe it? I happen to have one right here on my key-ring.*

The tool was passed from father to son, and Skull felt profoundly honoured when he received "the compo". It was a coming-of-age gift, marking Skull's passage from boy to man, and his father's transition from man to dust, for Rodney Morrell passed on soon afterwards.

Skull had wept when "the compo" went missing, lost even before his father was buried. He had borne the guilt of that loss a long time, but now it neither surprised nor upset him to see it deposited here in Jon's box of private treasures and forget-me-nots. He picked up the tool, rubbing it gently between finger and thumb before setting it beside the open box on the desk. There was nothing else of value in the box.

The wall with its gaping cavity bothered Skull. A lot of effort had gone into first cutting and then concealing the space. There was thought and planning in the execution of it, as well as in delivering both power and connectivity to it; not something done on a whim as a joke. Skull leaned across the desk, pulling on the blinking router so he could see behind it, which is when he spotted the third cable feeding into the device which he had not previously noticed. The grey cable was plugged into a USB port on the router and had fed behind the box, the end disappearing out of sight behind the wall board. As he gently lifted the router from the shelf, the object on the end of the cable was dragged from the void. Slowly into view came a small black pad on which sat Jon's cardinal red smartphone. The USB cable was providing power to a wireless charging pad. The pad was keeping The Lucy Phone alive; the router kept it connected.

Skull lifted the phone from the pad. The screen was scratched and smeared with Jon's last strokes. On the back the text was worn. It read, *he Luc Phor*.

The Lucy Phone was overtly sexy with its seductive red satin casing and silken screen. The curves were voluptuous, the corners sensual and smooth. On the back, the camera lens and fingerprint sensor were housed in two small mounds thrust forward like breasts, while the bulge at the base had the profile of a woman's buttocks. You wanted to touch it, you wanted to cup it in the palm of your hand, and caress the sleekness of its body. It felt warm, as if alive.

In confirmation, the soft curves of the casing vibrated suddenly, briefly, in Skull's hand, an eager purr as the screen flickered on, splashing a monochrome image over the surface.

The photograph was of a couple, Jon and Anka, face-to-face in sharp profile, unsmiling, intense, drawn in towards each other by the edges of the image; behind them, an urban river (probably the Thames) stopped flowing, frozen solid in the moment like green ice. Over the picture hung the date and time, and a pulsing cursor demanding a secret before it would allow entry.

Almost no one writes down the pin or password for their phone because, in constant use, you don't easily forget it. However, Skull thought, you might jot it down the first time and stick it on a whiteboard. He made an easy connection. From the whiteboard he plucked out the postcard of the upright, waking ape. "Happy 34th Birthday Aunt Lucy 3/5/8" was written over the front in red marker pen.

He turned the card over.

Lucy, Australopithecus afarensis.
> *Lucy is the name given to the fossil hominid discovered in 1974 by Donald Johanson and Tom Gray in the Afar Depression of Ethiopia. Lucy lived around 3.2 million years ago. She was given the name "Lucy" after the Beatles song "Lucy in the Sky with Diamonds". It is thought that these hominids were among the first users of stone tools.*
Houston Museum of Natural Science

Well, thought Skull, here was a birthday date. Why not? For the password he keyed in 3-5-8.

The phone responded "Incorrect PIN", so he tried 3-5-0-8, then 3-4-3-5-8, with the same result.

Of course, he mentally slapped himself, the sequence 3, 5, 8, was the start of the classic Fibonacci sequence. Disguised as a date, and with the reference to Lucy, it must have some significance. Certain now that this knowledge was going to get the password, he opened a spreadsheet on his own smartphone, swiftly creating the first fifty points in the sequence, looking to see what patterns emerged.

The sequence works by adding two numbers to the sum of previous numbers in the list, so $1 + 1 = 2$, $1 + 2 = 3$, $2 + 3 = 5$, $5 + 3 = 8$, and so on. Interestingly, he noted, the number 34 ("Happy 34th Birthday") was the tenth item in the sequence so he entered 3-5-0-8-1-0, then tried 3-4-1-0, and similar variations. Then he noted that the thirty fourth number in the sequence yielded 3524578. It failed when keyed in. But starting the sequence with 3 and 5, rather than the usual 0 and 1, got him 24157817 for the thirty fourth result. That also failed.

It was an all-absorbing task which easily shouldered aside the dull ache in his stomach, the lingering flutters of fear.

In a browser on his phone he typed *f-i-b-o-n-a*, and was offered a list of completion phrases. There was a tempting reference to "Fibonacci coding", but he realised Jon would probably not have been familiar with the concept. There was however a link to an item on the golden ratio which caught his attention and he started to read it.

Anka stood in the room. He had not heard the handle turn on the door, nor the faint squeak of the hinges as she entered. Swiftly she stepped across to the desk and grabbed the Lucy phone from Skull's suppliant hands.

"It has password," she spat at him. "You can't spy."

She surveyed the room, the wall cavity, the open box, the upturned drawers. "You can go," she said, dropping the phone into the open cigar box, lifting the box off the desk.

He glanced inadvertently at the compo can opener, regretting instantly the action because she followed his eyes, then swiftly swept the tool off the desk into the open box, snapping shut the lid.

"That's mine," he said roupily. She clamped the box under an arm as if expecting to fight for it. He cleared his throat, repeating: "The can opener is mine."

Even at that moment he admired Anka for her simple dignity and the stubborn resolve to hold fast to what she believed was hers. She said nothing, but stood her ground without aggression, displaying an expression of infinite forbearance. Her eyes flicked towards the secret cupboard, her head inclining in a gesture of curiosity.

"I found the router in there," Skull tried conversationally.

"Go away," she said, eyes hooded.

Skull left.

*

Back in the car, back in the silent calm of Gabby, Skull's smartphone hooked instantly into the vehicle's wireless network and he placed a call to his mobile service provider using VObella, a Voice-over-IP service, to report the stolen SIM card. They were sympathetic but suggested he pay his phone bill which, they noted sourly, had remained unpaid despite numerous demands. It was unlikely, they advised, that a replacement SIM would be provided without the outstanding balance on the account being paid. He thumbed off.

Did he really need the SIM? It merely gave him one number on one network. His phone was a smartphone, a multi-function tool that could be adapted for many different uses. He had other networks, other contact points. Why should he limit himself?

Think of yourself, he thought, as a fat spider squatting at the centre of a well-positioned web, expecting the tiny shiver of a greenfly, hoping for the urgent tug of a house fly, but getting the violent twang of a transiting bluebottle. What are your options? As a fat spider?

Repair it, work around it, move on.

He couldn't move on: he had nowhere to move on to. And there was no chance of repairing his web back to the state it was before. So instead he re-set his smartphone to connect automatically with any open wireless access point. That way he could use the VObella smartphone app to make all his voice calls and dispense with the mobile phone service entirely. This was the work-around solution.

London is layered with the fabric of free and open access points — coffee shops, restaurants, fools and fraudsters dangling free flies for the desperate fly eater, and for the promiscuous fat spider. The VObella account was paid for by Smartor. It still had credit until someone noticed it and closed it down.

Remotely he reconfigured his answer phone to forward calls now to his VObella number. He hoped he hadn't already missed any calls from Emily, imagining her dialling, holding, hearing the ring. She would think he was ignoring her call. She would sigh, pout, maybe tear up a bit, frowning ...

He typed into the text application: "Hi Em. Please get in touch on this number. Missing you."

He looked at the message for a while, then deleted it and sent instead: "Please note new contact number."

Having successfully worked around this hole in his web he drove home, feeling satisfied that he was back in control, not seeing the battered red van that followed discretely behind him.

As he drove he returned the call from Tom Twydle. "Speak!" commanded Tom's answerphone. He spoke, but not as he really wanted to speak. Instead he said it was great to get Tom's call and he was sorry to have missed it and would call again later if Tom didn't call first which, if he did, he should do so on this new number, which Skull read out slowly.

The call from Jac (satisfying proof that the redirection of calls from the home landline was working adequately) came in as Skull was patrolling the streets near his flat, hunting down a parking space. A small tribe of cars circled the same streets like Red Indians around waggons, all intent on the same valuable parking prize.

"Are you alright?" she asked.

"Why?"

"Anka phoned. She said there were problems."

"I wasn't going to mention it." He was still processing the humiliations he had suffered. He hadn't thought it all through yet and so felt unable to talk about it.

"What happened?"

"Nothing. Nothing to worry about." He spotted a space which he judged big enough for Gabby and, pulling alongside, quickly engaged the active-parking control system.

"I'm not worried," she said evenly. "I'm simply glad that you're alright. Anka said something about Russians?"

"Couple of Russian thugs," he tried dismissively. It helped. It put them in perspective, although his stomach ached still and clenched a little each time he thought of them.

"My God, Skull. Russians? What did they want?"

The parking system confirmed the space was wide enough so he engaged reverse and the wheel above his lap spun under its own control. He was no longer disconcerted by the action — in fact he now found the whole process frustratingly slow. He felt he might have whipped the car into the space in half the time.

He said, "I don't think they wanted tea and biscuits."

"It's not funny," she laughed. "Did you call the police?"

The rear proximity sensor beeped so he engaged the forward gear. The wheel spun hard in the opposite direction as Gabby inched forward. The van that had followed him down the road now edged impatiently past, accelerating away like an angry bee.

As Gabby snuggled herself into the gap Skull described briefly what had happened in the flat, and the non-heroic role he had played.

"But what's any of that got to do with Jon?" Jac asked when he finished.

"I don't know," he said. "Viktor Petsch. There's a connection there somewhere."

"But Russians?"

It did sound odd, the way she put it, as if they had suddenly appeared with the snow still clinging to their boots.

He said, "Jon has developed a wide circle of business interests. He knows some strange people."

"But he wouldn't be involved in anything like that," Jac objected, adding uncertainly, "Would he?"

"Well," Skull said, "maybe through Anka. They might not have been Russian. Certainly Eastern Europe. Anka didn't seem too shocked, just put out. Maybe she knew something like this might happen."

"You mean, that's why she cleared out the flat?" Jac asked, and after a new thought, "And, of course, she didn't want to involve the police, did she?"

"She was right, though," Skull conceded. "The only damage done was to me."

"You should see a doctor," said Jac.

"I'll be fine." His brave voice sounded silly so he added, "It hurts only when I laugh, and there appears to be nothing especially funny in my life right now." She rewarded him again with her warm chocolatey laugh, and so encouraged, he went on to tell her how he had found the secret shelf in the wall of Jon's flat, about the Lucy phone, and the box of treasures containing the letters from their mother. He left out the discovery of the compo, but described how Anka had taken both the box and the phone, and had dismissed him with the post.

"So, despite all the other distractions," he concluded, "I managed to gather up all the letters and bills. Anka didn't want any of it. Are you sure you still want me to hang on to it?"

"So that would explain the texts, then," said Jac. "If the phone was still switched on, could it be stuck in some sort of loop?"

"No," Skull said. "The texts aren't coming from the phone. The texts are coming from an online text service. I don't understand why he left the phone on inside the wall — that's Jon. I wasn't able to access it."

He began describing in detail how he had attempted to enter the pin, but when he mentioned the Aunt Lucy postcard with the ape and the birthday message, Jac laughed.

"Aunt Lucy was a family joke," she said.

"Like Uncle Daffy?"

"More like your Werner Brandes," she said. "When he was a little boy, someone told Jon that Lucy was one of our ancestors. He naturally assumed she must be an aunt."

"There was a date on the card."

The date was still a puzzle to him and he went through his attempts to link the date information with a password for the phone, hoping Jac could add some vital knowledge. They thrashed the numbers around for a while but she had nothing of value to add, other than that it may be linked to the date of the discovery of Lucy, but even then she was doubtful. However she recalled, vaguely, receiving a postcard from Jon describing a natural history exhibition he attended in the United States when he visited in 2008.

"So why leave the phone on at all?" Jac asked when they had exhausted the password topic.

"Goald. I think he left it on for Goald. The Goald app became very big in his life."

Lunch at Spitalfields

After our day out on the South Downs, Jon and I avoided each other. We didn't meet up again for at least another six months. I mentioned before, I think, that the gaps between our meetings grew wider, but this was probably the longest break we'd had since university days.

That's not to say we weren't in touch. We regularly swapped emails, and I'd had a number of texts asking my opinion on particular tech stock (about which I knew nothing), and once a strange message recommending I rush out and buy a no-brand media streamer "with the gonads of a strutting bull and the sound of a milk-fed choir boy". He was making up on his promise to "buy gadgets".

I was regularly invited to follow, friend, like, link and add him on chats and blogs and social networks. He was very promiscuous. It became really quite annoying, at one stage, with all the comments and status updates. And all this from a man who a year before was still buying compact discs for his CD player, and updating all his appointments in a leather bound diary by hand.

Smartor was a demanding mistress at that time. The sales people were banging on the doors of every large corporate, trying to get a wedge into fleet management, while our programming teams were on two week sprint development cycles, releasing updates every four weeks. It was an aggressive delivery programme and we were spending money like water but without getting anything like the kind of media coverage we deserved. Simon joked that our business model was all torque and no traction, but I didn't think it was funny. I was dragging myself to investor parties, startup events, talks, piss-ups, out most nights of the week. It seemed like important work at the time. We were already in serious trouble, only none of us saw it.

Back then Jon was working at a firm in Docklands but he had contacted me to say he would be in the City area for a job interview, and why not let's get some lunch together when he'd finished. I suggested we meet at our new offices first and I'd show him around.

"So how's the LGBT scene in this part of town?" he asked loudly as we stepped into the quiet of the Smartor office.

A few of the guys looked up, offended at the disturbance itself rather than the content of it. An office full of developers can be quieter than a seminary on a Sunday. I have never been sure if he plans these moments or if they occur spontaneously. I'm easily embarrassed, which of course is his intention and his reward.

I grinned inanely, introducing him to a few of our people, and we screened our new marketing video which explained, with animation, how the TwoCAN worked, and all the cool things in your car it gave access to. I think Jon was impressed; he should have been because the thing blew a giant hole in our marketing budget. He asked a few intelligent questions and swore he wanted to buy one even though he didn't have a car.

"But why stop here?" he asked. "Why not take this idea into the home. Imagine the fridge connected up, or the toaster and the lighting all controlled from your smartphone, all talking to each other through something you could just plug into the wall. Oh I know — you could call it the tin can."

"Let's grab a quick coffee," I said. Not everyone gets Jon, and developers can sometimes take things quite literally.

I herded him into the break-out room. It sounds grand, a break-out room, but in fact it was no bigger that a large broom cupboard with a sink at one end. Along one wall was a narrow shelf on which we'd placed a small fridge and a coffee maker; below were a couple of bar stools. In the old days you would have called it the kitchen cupboard.

He asked me, "Did you give Emily the message?"

"What message?" I didn't know what he was talking about.

"The message you want to give her," he insisted.

"I don't want to give her a message."

"Well I'd give her one," he said, squinting sideways at me.

He was the very master. Caught me every time. I swore, he laughed, pleased with himself, but there was something different. He seemed happy, contented even. He was dressed in a dark blue suit with pink shirt and contrasting dark red tie, looking in better shape than when I'd last seen him. I thought he'd lost some weight. I asked him how his interview went.

"Oh, you know," he shrugged and changed the subject quickly.

"Not well?" I persisted, trying to sound light but sympathetic. Perhaps only the lightness came through.

"God, this place is a riot, Skull."

"Not what you expected?"

"Well," he said, "I see that you buy expensive cars and fancy coffee machines, but why can't you afford decent desks for your guys?"

He was referring of course to the rows of old tea crates with MDF board screwed on top. It was Simon's idea. The tea crates were modestly priced, but we had to sand them down to remove the splinters before strengthening them internally so they could support the multiple screen setups and all the other kit. Then one of the developers had objected to the fumes coming off the MDF boards, so we had to take a weekend varnishing them to seal in the toxic chemicals. We definitely couldn't afford the time. It would have been cheaper and simpler to buy proper desks, but that wasn't the story we told people.

When you're a startup, I explained to Jon, you've got to look like a startup. "It's the startup shed-look," I told him. "Impresses the hell out of our visitors, and our angels like it too. Shows we're not spending their notes on frivolities."

"Then how do you explain the fancy coffee machine?" Jon quipped.

"That's an essential," I told him. "If that ever broke down, productivity would be halved within the week." He laughed, even though it wasn't actually a joke.

We sat and drank our coffee, perching a buttock on the high bar stools.

"I thought there'd be more hot women," he said after a while.

"I thought you'd sorted yourself out in that department." During the course of some messaging exchange he had mentioned that there was a new woman in his life. His phone warbled gently before he could go into detail, and I left him in the room alone to talk with the agency that had set up the interview.

When I returned he was pinching and swiping his phone screen with all the dexterity of an adolescent girl texting her best friend.

"I say, Carruthers! Not still using that old girlie phone, are you?" He smiled but made no comment, so feeling a little stupid, I suggested we leave. We'd agreed lunch at wherever we could find a table in one of the food halls around the Old Spitalfields Market — nothing fancy, because I assumed he'd want to devote most of the effort on getting wasted in a wine bar.

"Hang on a sec," he said, all his attention on the little screen. "Just movin' the moola."

"Moola? You bank on your phone?"

"Don't you?"

"Absolutely not." I may be a little old-fashioned but it has always struck me as a particularly stupid thing to do.

"The future is now, buddy-mate. Move money, pay money, make money." He finished the task in hand and fixed me with a stern frown. "You should get yourself a Lucy Phone, Skull. It's incredibly brilliant. It will change your life. Changed mine."

I couldn't help laughing. "This sounds very much like the good news about Jesus Christ." I smirked.

"Yup." He held up his phone. "Near enough. Lucy saves." He was serious. "I'll show you."

A familiar cartoon avatar popped onto the phone's screen, smiling, blinking coquettishly. It looked so dated.

"Lucy," he commanded. "Give me a goal status summary."

Hi, Jon Fast, came the tinny voice, the avatar mouth opening and closing. *Status update, goal eight is, five-three point six-seven percent chance of success. Status update, goal three-one is, nine four point eight nine percent chance of success. Status update goal three-two is —*

"Lucy, stop. Give me a detailed status for goal three two. That's my job change goal," he added as aside to me.

Hi, Jon Fast. Status detail for goal three-two. Current success factor is eight-nine point eight-oh percent, rising from five-two point eight-two percent at oh nine hundred hours today. Current prediction is: Success.

The screen displayed a colourful graphic with about a dozen data points on an upward curve.

"Wa-hey," Jon said, pleased, thumbing the screen again so the graph flicked off and the avatar slid back into view. "Eighty nine percent! That's nearly a done deal."

The avatar blinked back. I wondered how it was working out the success factor. With two decimal places it seemed remarkably precise for an app, I told him.

"It's been pretty accurate so far," he agreed.

"This is that SMART goals app you showed me before, right?"

"Did I show you?" He seemed to have forgotten our session in the Sussex pub, because he went on to explain: "You set a goal, you see; give her a time band, some points to measure it all, and off she goes. She makes a bunch of suggestions and tells you how you're progressing, and how close you are to hitting your goal, or not."

"Thirty two goals. That's a lot of goals," I said.

"I'm a high achiever, Skull. Reaching for the juiciest berries on the higher branches requires a little stretching. Course, not all those goals are still active." He grinned smugly. "Some have already been achieved."

"You must spend your evenings keying in data," I told him, because I couldn't see how else it could measure progress.

"Oh, keep up, Matty boy," he sneered at me. "This is the modern age, remember? Lucy has access to all the data she needs. The more you give her, the better she likes it. Banking, social, CT, medical —"

"CT?" I interrupted. "What's CT?"

He pulled back his sleeve to reveal a slim maroon-grey wrist band, about a half-inch wide and a quarter in depth. It was an old-style fitness tracker. Most people I knew were getting smart watches now.

"It records all the physical events of my day," he said. "Walking, running, sleeping — basically it measures the pulse of my life." He pinched the band and a pattern of colourful LED lights pulsed briefly. "So as I go through my incredible day, it tracks my fabulous body. CT — Circadian Tracker. It tracks circadian rhythms. That's a body clock to you Skull. All my circadian markers are measured and stored. Then every now and then it sends all these interesting facts to Lucy who ponders on them and bakes me a big knowledge pie."

He tapped and swiped the screen on his phone a few times and flashed in front of me a graph. I knew exactly what it was. We were doing the same thing for cars at Smartor.

"It's better with pictures, isn't it? You can see what's trending in your own body. I found out I don't run on the normal twenty four hour clock," he confided. "I'm nearer twenty-five hours. Apparently that makes me a Martian."

"Doesn't surprise me," I laughed. "Always took you for an alien."

"Scoff away, my little tall friend. But I have re-aligned myself. I've already lost a stone in weight. Lucy suggested it. You should get one." He shook the band on his wrist at me. "You could add some flesh to your skeleton."

I think I nodded enthusiastically, but it worried me that he was getting these unqualified suggestions from a cheap smartphone. I asked him about it but he couldn't see the problem.

"She suggests stuff all the time, Skull. Cheapest groceries, clothes sales, savings accounts, investments. She's pretty good. Watch this. Lucy, give me some suggestions for goal eight."

Hi, Jon Fast. Premise: outlook for mining stock remains poor. Suggestion. Sell LSE RIO stock. And. Sell LSE BLT stock. Premise: Economic indicators suggest a fall in Chinese manufacturing output in Q 2. Suggestion: Consider spread bet on the Exchange Traded China 25 Tracker Fund of —

"Lucy, stop," he commanded, naturally at ease with the device now, no longer the self-conscious, slow delivery. To me he said. "There you go. Suggestions, advice, guidance — depending on the goal. So I wanted to lose some weight. You know, get fit. CT was one of her suggestions."

"Great," I said.

He seemed very pleased with himself so I felt now was probably not the time to raise the spectre of privacy and security. I don't know why it was that I felt just a little bit responsible. Of course I wish now that I'd been a bit more direct.

In the cab on the way to Spitalfields he gave me a catalogue of all his successes, listing his investments, his new fitness regime, his cultural life. Getting a new job was a goal he'd set a few months back and he and Lucy had been steadily working towards today. The job, if he got it, would pay better and hold more responsibility. It was a step up the ladder. Jon was pulling his life together.

"And I'm even getting a regular shag," he bellowed at me while I paid the cab driver. The cabbie leered at him through the open window, "Yeah — give 'er one for me, mate," he yelled as he pulled away from the curb, adding a couple of toots on his horn by way of a fanfare.

It was Friday lunchtime, and the new Old Spitalfields Market was as busy as usual. We queued a while for a table at a posh hamburger place. There was a satisfyingly fast turnover of tables populated either by small mixed groups of self-conscious co-workers enduring a Friday team outing, or tense smartphone-flicking couples who ate, diarised and left. Everyone seemed young, some of them were even happy, or at least they tried laughing.

As we sipped our drinks (cold lager for me, diet coke for Jon) and waited for our food (giant burger with fancy cheeses, falafel and feta salad) Jon told me how he had met his new friend, Anka, a few months back in his favourite sandwich shop. It wasn't her shop, but she ran some kind of catering business which regularly brought her into the outlet. It was in the isle between the cold pork pies and the reconstituted fresh orange-juice that their idle lunchtime flirting soon turned to something less idle, then more physical and, finally, more profound.

"She's got all the important ingredients, Skull" he confided frowningly, "although they don't necessarily blend in the traditional way."

I said I was intrigued, told him, "She seems different." It was an error: he related several of his favourite anecdotes illustrating the divine serendipity of their new found love. There were significant outings and soulful meals which they had shared together, a collection of you-had-to-be-there hilarious misunderstandings, and an astonishingly frank account of their first argument — a key marker, according to Jon, a major way-point, in any serious relationship.

Eventually — and you must have had this — eventually there comes a point in some conversations when a grin becomes a fixed grin, and where the enthusiasm for the story becomes anchored in a custard-skin mask. It's not just that I had grown accustomed to the spectacle of Jon's unsteady progress to self-destruction, but that I had learnt how to deal with it and understand it as the natural progression from the acerbic humour, the hollow cynicism, which he threw up as a defence.

This vivid new chapter in his life was a mid-life crisis heading in the wrong direction, in my view. Suddenly he wanted to be taken seriously. He had found sincerity. He had become earnest.

I finished lunch quickly and hurried back to the office on the pretext of an investor crisis. Later he texted me with news that he had had a job offer: *other guy broke a leg haha walkover for me.*

I texted back: *top hole carruthers.*

* * *

Mr Beavis was waiting for Skull. He had the frantic look of a man who has been trying not to cry.

"Ah, Matthew," he said, holding open the door to his flat, beckoning Skull to follow.

Skull stepped after him into a merged living space, similar in design to his own flat upstairs, but entirely different in character. Neighbours' homes are always intriguing but invariably, on inspection, less interesting than one has imagined them to be, and this was certainly true of the monochrome interior of Mr Beavis' Spartan dwelling. Everything was modern, everything clean and geometric, like a block of Lego. It occurred to Skull that this was how he might have liked his own flat to have looked had Emily's creative influences not dominated.

"Remember your mate with the baseball bat? Well he left these," Mr Beavis said, stepping aside and revealing three children sitting in a line like a row of muddy footprints on the polished wooden floor, watching television. "It didn't seem like the right thing, leaving them outside on the doorstep. When I asked, they asked for Matthew." Mr Beavis pulled a face. "That's you," he said, confirming Skull's worst fears.

The girl in the set, looked up at the mention of the name. She stared at Skull with open insolence, a rudeness allowed only by the very young and the very mad. She did not return Skull's tentative smile. Looking at her he was reminded of TV footage of child refugees in distant war-shredded places where all comfort and hope had been taken leaving only makeshift tents and corrugated huts for them to ply their childhood with their solemn faces. Sitting beside her the two smaller boys ignored him entirely. They were identical in looks, cloned from their father, indistinguishable one from the other even in their clothing.

"Are you Matthew?" the girl asked.

"Yes," said Skull. The girl continued to look him over without much warmth so he added, "I am Matthew."

"Simon says —" she glanced wearily down at her lap, the better to recall the sequence of words she had been tasked to deliver. "Simon says, you must look after us … if you won't … look after … Simon?" She frowned, not sure now if what she had said made any sense, shooting Skull a look to see if he was laughing at her, to make sure she hadn't made a fool of herself. He smiled, to reassure. She turned back to the television set, her thin shoulders drooping as the burden of duty was lifted, her thin body slumping as it was reabsorbed into the comforting flow of words and pictures.

Skull of course had seen the photograph on Simon's desk: a happy grinning group of children squinting into the sun, frozen in a pose around a pretty mother in a summer garden. The Bettersons at home, the photo seemed to say, along with the usual subtext of framed desk photos: this is why I'm here, this is what I fight for. But Skull didn't know where that home was, had never met his business partners' partners, knew nothing of their families.

"How long have they been here?" he asked Mr Beavis.

"Well. Your man started ringing the bell at about approximately twelve twenty-four," said Mr Beavis, "and he rang at the bell for about approximately ten minutes before he took himself away, but then he left without taking the children."

"I'm sorry it's been such a trouble, Mr Beavis."

"Oh no, it's been a trouble, alright. But there they were, on the street, like. They were getting a bit loud, a bit shouty, so I gave them a glass of cow's milk."

"That was thoughtful of you. Thank you."

"Are they allowed cow's milk? They do drink cow's milk don't they?"

"I believe it's a staple."

"Well, there was a wee accident."

"Wee?"

"Small. Small accident."

"I'm so sorry," Skull said, relieved.

"No, it was a bit of a trouble. But the couscous was a bad idea."

"Really?"

"In hindsight, in hindsight, yes," Mr Beavis mumbled. "This is not a house for the kiddies, Matthew. I'm not child-centred."

"What's your name?" Skull asked the girl.

"Dolly," she said. Once again, she stared big-eyed at him.

"Dolly? Really? That's a really nice name."

"It's a stupid name," she said, then pointed at each brother in turn: "His name is Rocky, and he's Rambo." Neither of the boys acknowledged the introductions.

"Excellent," said Skull. "Excellent. I think," he continued bravely, "I think maybe we should all go up the stairs to my flat. Shall we all go upstairs?" It sounded wrong somehow, the way it came out; like a molester. All the same the children remained welded to the floor.

"'Ave you got a big TV, Maffew?" asked Rocky, or Rambo, his voice gruff from lack of use or too much shouting. "'Cause this prick's jus' got this li'l shitty one."

"Now what did we say about potty-mouth?" Mr Beavis scolded sharply, but the children continued to stare inscrutably at the small screen. "There's been a lot of language," Mr Beavis complained to Skull. "A lot of language."

"Right! Come on," Skull tried breezily, but again there was no discernible movement.

Mr Beavis shook his head sadly, as one who has the advantage of experience. "Try food," he murmured out the side of his mouth.

"So who's hungry?" Skull called out.

"Meeey," the boys chanted back discordantly, though there was not much hunger in it.

"Perhaps if we turn the telly off?" Skull suggested desperately.

A cloud of abuse settled over Mr Beavis when he disconnected the television set and stood, back to the wall, holding the plug and cord; but now without the binding tug of sound and image streaming from the screen the children drifted away like balloons cut from a bunch. It required the additional lure of fast food as well as the promise of more channels on a bigger TV set, for Skull eventually to herd them upstairs to his own flat.

"Not the fucking news again," moaned Rambo, or Rocky, and there was a lot more language while a suitable channel was negotiated and agreed.

Skull ordered pizza from a flyer he found on his pile of post, paying with his precious hoard of cash when it was delivered. He then tried phoning Simon but the calls kept going to the answerphone. Finally he called the home telephone number which rang and rang before eventually it was answered.

"Oh," said Lauren Betterson after Skull explained the situation to her.

"So, can you collect them now?" he asked when no concern was expressed, no apology made, no explanation offered.

"Simon has the car." Lauren spoke with economy, slurring the words slowly and carefully, her voice as heavy as mist over a graveyard. "Who are you again?"

In the end Skull took the children home himself. It was the least he could do for Simon.

Wednesday

Over a small north eastern corner of London falls a shadow. Out beyond the noise and colour of Bethnal Green, past the civic discomfort of Poplar, through fresh-minted Bow, and leaving behind the irritable Olympic after-glow of Stratford, you enter the grim, grey suburban streets of Leyton slouching alongside the Hackney marshes. Boxed-in by trading parks and transport links, and lapped by successive waves of hard pressed immigrants, it is a place to dream of leaving.

Ajay's Techcare Ltd (PC Repairs & Games) was not hard to find where it shouldered into the space between Sonia's Hair Salon and JM Wireless, one small shop in a huddle of commerce straddling the trunk road.

The same chilled wind that had swept over the Isle of Dogs the day before now funnelled through the narrow streets as Skull made his way back to the cluster of shops from the distant parking space he had found outside a monotonous row of nineteen thirties terraced cottages. After the cosy warmth of the car his cheeks soon numbed, yet despite the cold he delayed, unsure of his mission.

Outside Ajay's, a large dark man bounced and swayed, nodding rhythmically into the window, broad shoulders hunched against the cold, hands in pocket, white woollen cap pulled deep over his ears. Skull crossed the road, aware that his stomach still ached stiffly where the Tunguska Man had hit him yesterday, a chronic reminder of his unsuitability for this kind of task. The man at the window lit a cigarette between cupped hands, sucked deep before spitting obliquely onto the pavement; he gave a final glare into the window before bobbing thoughtfully away down the road.

The Suleman Halal Butcher & Grocer shouldered onto the pavement with a display of vegetables and fruits in colourful plastic cartons. Skull took up position behind a box of bright bruised apples, staring uncertainly across the road at Ajay's. Long bags of potatoes and onions lay heaped behind him in neat piles; small bodies awaiting burial.

But what could possibly go wrong? If the worst came to the worst he could buy a Pay-As-You-Go SIM card for his mobile and leave.

He checked his phone. It was picking up a nearby open wireless connection. He was still connected. He was connected but felt out of place. In Clerkenwell the vibrant urban squalor had been a shock, at first, when he moved there. Gradually he had come to appreciate the cosmopolitan mix of money grubbing and grubbing along, of doing well and making do. Now he quite liked it. But out here, in this eastern suburb, there were no contrasts, no buzz of modernity, no transformative retail outlets or lifestyle coffee houses, just the grey, functional shops where you bought the stuff you needed: meat, vegetables, alcohol.

Inside the lace-curtained window of Sonia's Hair Salon alongside Ajay's, Sonia had taped photos of cheery young men and women sporting improbable hairdos of the sort that would surely invite common assault on anyone daring enough to wear such quiffs or dreads on the surrounding streets. The portraits were positioned at jaunty angles to suggest vitality and fun, but the colours had faded in the sun, the edges curled with age. In contrast JM Wireless, on the other side of Ajay's, had long since ushered out its last customer, leaving in the cavity of the shop the scattered bones of a gas stove still visible behind the browning windows.

Ajay's shop front was all glass. A blue steel frame in the centre fixed a glass door. Behind the glass windows the shelves were crowded with electrical goods positioned on glass pedestals. A LED Christmas light snaked around the display, winking a seasonal come-on. A large poster offered a free PC health check, and below that a dog-eared sticker advertised the Glad Heart Mobile service, boasting not only cheap international calls but easy top-ups and custom service as well. Or perhaps it was customer service — it was hard to read the wrinkled text. Either way, Skull felt, it was a strong selling point.

Above the shop the weathered signboard declared that Ajay's provided FAST INTERNET ACCESS, COMPUTER REPAIRS, adding below, Computer Parts & Accessories (wholesale and retail), along with Mobile Phones, Accessories and Unlocking. It was a list of good intentions, a promise of betterment, in the same way that the waxy polish on the boxed red apples in front of Skull, as he stood across the street, suggested health and the cheery fulfilment of nourishment.

"Dirty pee."

"What?" Skull had the impression the shopkeeper may have been watching him for some time. He had a face on which was engraved the ancient hostility of shopkeepers. Patches of white dotted the grey stubble, his strong nose pointed accusingly at Skull.

"What?"

"Upples." The shopkeeper's watchful eyes moved slowly to the apple Skull bounced in his hand. "Dirty pee itch."

"Right."

The man observed critically while Skull dug in his pocket for change, producing a fifty pence piece along with his best shark-like smile (it was the only smile he had). In return the man gave nothing, just the stare.

"Keep the change," said Skull. The man's eyes narrowed with suspicion. Skull quickly crossed the road to Ajay's, apple in hand.

The shop door was stiff to open and, as he shoved at it, he half expected a bell to ping his entrance. Three youths lounged around the counter at the far end of the shop, gossiping and giggling. A radio ground out a tune Skull almost recognised. The boys looked up, their smirking bonhomie fading. Skull nodded by way of greeting.

"Give it a push, mate," said the boy behind the counter. He was a dude, crisp and freshly pressed from the gym, slim and sharp, his strong, black hair shaved short over the ears and combed sleekly back over the top. He leaned on the counter with a broad, bright smile for his friends, perfect teeth.

"What?" Skull grinned, not understanding the joke.

"Door, man. Give. It. A push." He inclined his head towards the door. There was a soft snicker from the group at Skull's stupidity. The smiling had gone suddenly. It wasn't a joke after all.

Skull stepped back to the door and pushed it firmly closed so it banged up against the frame, juddering the window. When he turned back to the group they had resumed their conversation, subdued now but ignoring him, cutting him off.

"She's keepin' it hot for you, man," said the dude. The boys giggled again, but now a little self-consciously. "You got to make your move," he added and they all nodded.

The shop had a musty, damp smell, with a hint of ammonia suggesting something decaying slowly under the floorboards. Deep shelves pitched up against the long wall on the left bore cardboard boxes bent and dented and filled with cheap stock — keyboards, mice, headphones, speaker sets entombed in blister packs. A mixed box of colourful gel covers for mobile phones was labelled "£1" crossed out, and underneath written "50p". Cables hung in plastic packs from crude hooks: yellow patch cables, grey USB cables, Firewire, VGA, DVI, RCA, HDMI, all labelled. In the furthest corner a shelf of "Pre-Loved" computer games offered everything from Zombie Hell Redemption to Daisy Saw a Donkey.

To the right the shop counter, all glass, ran front to back. Here all the valuables — disks, memory, media players, streamers — were placed beyond the reach of fast fingers and quick hands. A special section was given to phones, smartphones, ultraphones, tablets. No-brand laptops and tablets stood on shelves behind the counter along with dusty motherboards in lurid blues and scarlet, graphic cards with bright orange and lime green cooling fans like funky, defrocked hovercraft.

At the very back, in front of the counter, a doorless door frame was hung with heavy plastic strips, colourful, clackety bunting, above which read a sign: Internet Cafe.

"I'm looking for Deepak. Is Deepak here?"

"Who are you?"

"Matt."

"Matt?" The boy sneered. "Does Deepak know you're coming, Matt?"

"I'm a friend." It was a risk because one of them might be Deepak, although Skull thought none were old enough.

"What you want with him?"

"Is he here?"

The youths looked Skull over in menacing silence. Skull stood his ground wondering whether now was the time to leave.

The plastic curtain swished, wet leaves blown across the churchyard. In the doorway stood an immensely tall man stooping forward, his long face mournfully scanning the room. He stopped scanning when he saw Skull.

Skull said quickly, "I'm a friend of Jon Fast. Are you Deepak?"

"You said you was Deep's friend." The dude was offended, wounded by Skull's dishonesty. "He said he was your friend, Deep."

"Shut up, Raj," Deepak spat back. He nodded at Skull before ducking back into the room behind. Skull followed.

*

In the long back room the smell of quiet rotting persisted. Formica catering tables lined up along the walls left and right. Each table hosted two screens, two keyboards, two mice, their cables seeping through purpose-cut holes down to computers below. Distributed around the room was a mix of battered folding chairs and stools. Bright neon strip lights illuminated the browning walls where yellowed posters provided multi-lingual instructions, admonishments and threats, along with cartoon warnings on the perils of the Internet. At the far end a steel lined door, padlocked and bolted top and bottom, let out to the back. A laminated notice said, Fire Exit.

The sole customer was an elderly man, grizzled, dressed in traditional tunic and baggy pants, a set of bulky headphones pulled over a white skull cap. He was watching cartoons on YouTube.

Deepak led Skull to the very end where a large table, pushed into the corner, served as both desk and workbench. The strip light immediately above had been removed, providing a leavening of gloom to the space. Around the table everything was precisely ordered. Two flat LCD screens were positioned centrally below the wall shelves, alongside them a keyboard, a mouse, a set of tools neatly arranged in a leather-look tool roll. Two cadaverous desktop computers were laid out, their outer casing removed, exposing dusty innards to the bright desk lamp positioned above them.

Beside the shelves cables, looped and tied, grew up towards the ceiling like ivy. Little boxes on narrow ledges winked their LED lights in red, green, orange, blue. On a deeper shelf was arranged an orderly row of practical manuals and ambitious guides: Cloud Computing for Dummies, Security Metrics Made Simple, Risk Management: An Introduction, An Idiot's Guide to Virtualization. On the upper shelves were plastic boxes: "Graphics Cards, faulty", "Network Cables < 2 Meters", "Power Supplies: 550W +", "Wipes & Sprays". The man was holding back chaos using only labels and colour-coding.

Deepak dragged a spare seat over, positioning it adjacent to his own — rather more substantial — office chair, into which he now folded himself. He kicked the heater around to blow some warmth in the guest seat's direction, waving an immensely long hand at the chair by way of invitation.

The once blue wavy fabric of the seat was now stained a permanent brown with a spatter of suspicious grey blooms.

"Thanks." Skull sat, carefully placing on the corner of the table the apple he still carried.

On noticing the apple Deepak asked with routine courtesy: "Coffee? Tea?" He nodded at the battered bedside table playing pedestal to a rusting tin tray on which stood the kettle, two half empty milk bottles, a brace of odd chipped mugs thickly encrusted with tannins, and a spray of plastic teaspoons. "There's tea bags in the — the thing," he added.

"I'm good," Skull smiled. "Thanks. Matt, by the way." They shook hands, half standing, awkwardly re-sitting. Deepak's hands were soft and cool, dry, like the outside of a leather glove. Skull said, "Jon and I are old friends. He may have mentioned me?"

Deepak lowered his head sadly; his gestures were weary, his limbs weighted seemingly by a dolorous liquid in his veins.

"Skull," Skull added. "Jon sometimes calls me Skull."

"Oh yeah, right. Right." Deepak nodded politely, pretending sudden recognition. Then he grinned, laddishly. "So how is my man Jon? Haven't seen him for a while."

"Well," Skull began. "He disappeared."

"Disappeared? You are shitting me. No way. When?"

"About a month ago. Maybe more."

"No way. Where? Where'd he go?"

"I was sort of hoping you might know."

"Nah, haven't seen him, man. Not for —" he stared bleakly down into the past, shaking his head minutely, "not since summer, right? Maybe five, six months?" He leaned back in his seat, his fingers absentmindedly curling around the lone pencil on his uncluttered desk. "Gone a month, hey? That's good, that's good."

"Good? How is it good?" Skull's laugh was forced, strained.

Despite the size of his body Deepak shrank into his chair, subsiding slowly like a deflating airbag. He glanced sideways at the old man on the nearby bench. The old fellow had clearly taken a position near Deepak's desk to share some comfort from the heater, which was also old and rattled terminally, stirring only a little dust as it exhaled a meagre breath of tepid air.

Deepak swallowed greasily, lubricating the passage of his thought. "A man should get away from things," he said at last.

"What things?" Skull asked.

Deepak toyed with the pencil in his pencil-like fingers, wobbling it between thumb and index, then between index and middle finger. "You know," he began, then had a sudden nasty thought: "Not a reporter are you? Newspapers? Press?"

"Just a friend of Jon's. A worried friend. I'm in IT," Skull added for reassurance.

"Yeah?" Deepak brightened. "Support?"

"Developer."

"City?"

"Startup."

Deepak seemed momentarily disappointed. "Royal Bank," he tapped his chest. "Before — you know. And before that JP." It was a battle roll, a listing of past glories that City techs on the contract circuit did. Skull knew the routine and allowed Deepak to enumerate his honours until he could conclude, "Now I run these services." He waggled the pencil at the room, squinted down its length as if aiming a Kalashnikov, mouth twisted into a lopsided grimace. "Thin clients, Linux Virtual Desktop. Awesome," he said mockingly.

It was the opening gambit to a technical discussion and for a while they sparred companionably over the state of operating systems, mulled the rise of virtualisation and cloud services, open source and the so called Internet of Things. Deepak had strident opinions on most subjects, but the conversation seemed to relax him.

"Know anything about overclocking?" He swung his chair to face the desk, standing to loom over the first of the computer shells lying exposed on the table.

"A little," Skull said, knowing well that the measure of technical expertise is a relative thing and that on questions of knowledge it is generally better to err on the side of modesty, since reticence is invariably interpreted as a sure sign of mastery in the topic.

"It's not so difficult nowadays, is it? Used to be difficult. Used to be."

"Is that what you do? Overclocking for gamers?"

"Not so much," Deepak said and there was a thread of regret in his voice before he went on, "Malwares. Most of the fixes on these old PCs are just cleaning up and taking out the malwares." He raised his shoulders in a gesture of despair but his smile was one of boundless forgiveness. "People like porn, innit. And free stuff. Games. Funny vids. What can you do, man. It would be the simple choice to re-install Windows, right. But ... they lose their holiday snaps, family videos. I wish I could work miracles, you know? I wish I could. Do you mind?" His long fingers were already reaching into the machine, tugging at cables, pulling connectors.

"When you saw Jon a few months ago," Skull said, "can I ask what you talked about?"

Deepak shifted the case on the desk to get a better view of the insides, his mouth a line of indecision. "Confidential, man."

"Indeed."

The old man surfing YouTube behind them grunted suddenly with displeasure, shaking and tapping the mouse, jabbing it across the table before clicking and settling back into his seat with a disgruntled tutting.

Skull decided he needed a more direct approach: "Jon thought his smartphone was trying to kill him," he said, surprised that it no longer felt odd saying it; Deepak didn't laugh either. In fact he barely reacted at all. Skull continued: "He bought the phone from you but he thought it was trying to kill him. Is that why he came to see you?"

Deepak continued to stare into the computer's internals but said nothing. Eventually Skull tried, "Where did the phones come from?"

"Shop," Deepak said, inclining his head towards the shop front. He pulled a sheet of paper, a form, across the desk, plucking a ballpoint from a quiver of pens in plastic pen-holder on the desk. The form was headed 'Your Ajay's Techcare Repair Report".

"I mean originally," Skull persisted. "Where did the phones come from originally?"

"Originally?" The repair report seemed quite detailed already with several lines of neat cursive writing recording the sins discovered, prescribing the salvation due. Deepak added another line of small neat text at the end of the list before he said, "Originally, I don't know. Is the answer. Suppliers send boxes, salesmen bring samples. I saw the phone, thought it looked cool so I bought it. Family discount." Again the grin.

"You bought Jon's phone?"

He pushed the form away and dropped the pen back into the pen holder. "Yeah, sure. Jon liked my phone. Said he wanted one. So I supplied him one."

"The Lucy Phone."

"Yeah. Lucy Phone."

"D'you know about Goald?" Skull asked but Deepak pretended not to have heard. After a while Skull added, "It's a sort of personal assistant app for setting and monitoring goals. It was a bundled app, I think. D'you know about it? Goald?"

"Yeah. Goald," Deepak conceded.

"Did he talk to you about that?"

"Yeah. We talked about it." The tall man's long hands drooped over the computer's innards, his shoulders slumped a little as he stared into the depths. He said, "Jon was worried. He wanted to know what happened to me."

After a while Skull prompted, "So, what happened to you?"

"You know what happened."

"Only from the papers. I'd like to hear what really happened," Skull said.

Deepak reached across to his tool set, selecting a long cross-drive screwdriver. "Money's not important, right?" he began, poking the tool carefully into the disk cage, lowering his head to get a better view. "I didn't want to be a rich bastard. I wanted … yeah … I wanted some respect. Money buys that. Money is success, man. Everybody likes success." Slowly he pulled the driver from the cage, carefully smearing the screw off the magnetic end, dropping it with a plunk onto a tin plate before returning the tool head into the bowels of the computer once more. He continued, "You can't make a goal for success in your community. How can you measure esteem, man? How do you measure admiration? When can you tell that you have a position of some importance in the minds of your friends?" He tossed another screw into the tin. "These things are what people want, but you can't make a task of it. It can't be your goal."

"You mean SMART goals?"

"Exac'ly." Deepak placed the screwdriver carefully back into the tool roll. "It was my wish to donate a … a large sum — a very large sum of money, to the new Gurdwara. That was my goal. It's not such a terrible thing, is it? I made it my goal to make that donation before Hola Mohalla."

His long fingers wiggled the rectangular disk drive free from the cage. He held it up for examination, passing the flat of his hand over the top, wiping away the dust of years before laying it carefully on the anti-static mat. "At first I was making good money. Working hard. Good investments. Property. The money was growing nicely. Assets, yeah?" He connected a ribbon cable from the second computer to the disk on the mat. "Then I lost the money on a silly gamble."

"Horses?" Skull asked, surprised.

"Worse," Deepak smiled. "Relatives." He gave his twisted, loopy grimace again as he connected a power cable to the disk. "So Goald proposed me to claim on the insurance money." Now he switched on the second computer. It clunked, clicked and buzzed, whined then purred as the power came up and the disk initialised. He flipped a switch on one of the little plastic boxes on the shelf and watched as the boot sequence started scrolling on the monitor. "See? Linux can clean out Windows viruses. I use Clam A.V. Have you used it?"

"No," Skull said. "No. I never have."

"You should try it."

"I will."

"Ah — but you are an Apple man, for sure."

It was said with such conviction that momentarily Skull felt he had been insulted. He experienced an instinctive flush of anger; he was being judged. In technology circles your choice of tooling defines you as much as the clothes you wear. Mentally, he prepared himself for engagement in a puerile platform war.

"I'm not," he objected.

Deepak pointed to the red apple on the corner of his table, and curled the briefest of smiles.

"Ha," Skull laughed, relieved. "Indeed. Although I'd prefer a Quince."

Deepak turned to watch his screen and the stream of scrolling text. "QPhone is overprice, man" he said dismissively. "All the Quince range is overpriced. In my view. Even the qTab. For a tablet, it's nothing special."

"They look good," Skull countered, but Deepak was adamant: "You're paying for the brand."

"So Goald," Skull quickly moved on, unwilling to get bogged down in a brand battle. "The Goald app suggested you claim on your property insurance?"

"Yes of course. That's the point, man. He told me — the app suggested me first to get into buy-to-let property, and then get insurance on the mortgage. Joint term insurance. It was in both names. We couldn't sell the property because we'd make a loss, right? To sell so soon. So he tells me her insurance payout will let me pay off the mortgage and realise the asset so I can reach this goal. He proposed Indi should reach term."

"Reach term?"

"Die, man. Terminate. Killed." He drew a piratical finger across his throat. "Reach term."

"Who is 'he'? You said 'he'. You mean the app?"

"Yeah, Goald."

"Goald told you to kill your wife?"

Deepak sat down heavily. "Suggest, man. Not tell. Suggest. Always suggest this, propose that. It's just an app, right? Ahm," he paused, waving his hands over the keyboard as if waving away a layer of thought, "ah — mount minus tee en, tee-en-eff-ess, er ... slash dev slash ..." he muttered slowly as he tapped the long string of letters and characters, prodding each key in turn before finally mashing the Enter key at the end.

It was an incantation of healing words, a benediction that would bring absolution to a disk infested with dirty images, malicious code, the bloat of years. The response was a chorus of cryptic diagnostic messages leaping joyously across the screen, answering the prayer in stuttering bursts of text. Skull sat quietly waiting for Deepak to continue his story.

"I tried," Deepak eventually went on, only slightly distracted, "I tried to contact the app developer, you know. Tell him: you sick fuck! What kind of sick fuck app is this? You —." He allowed the anger to die before he went on: "Couldn't get him.

There was an email address, no answer. Website, dead. Maybe somebody killed him. I hope so, man. I hope so. But I couldn't stop it, couldn't change the goals. Couldn't de-register from the app, couldn't remove it. Built in, right. Even after a factory reset, there it was. So I got rid of it. Dumped the phone. Chucked it, right?"

Slowly and carefully he copied onto the form a diagnostic message from the screen, copying it carefully, checking it, correcting, before continuing his story, saying, "Then it emailed me."

"Who?"

"App."

"The app emailed you?"

"Yeh. The app." Once again Deepak's eyes followed the flow of lines scrolling up the screen. "Sometimes text message. Mostly email. The app was still running. Somewhere. In the cloud."

"How did you get texts? You got rid of the phone."

"Kept the SIM, man." He pointed to the dark, wafer-slim device on the desk. "New phone."

Skull asked, "Where were the messages coming from? Did you trace them?"

"That's the thing," said Deepak. "Text was from different web-to-text services. Each time, different. The email was always from me but routed through different gateways — China, Australia, Ukraine ..."

"Ukraine?"

He shrugged: "Always different, man. Always different."

"What did the messages say?"

"It's goals — SMART goals, right? Status updates: you have eighty percent success factor for goal ten. I propose you do this, sell these stocks, short Roubles ... Well, you know the app, man. You can't change the goals after you put them in. Lucky was still giving me top investment advice."

"Lucky?"

"I called him Lucky. Yeah," he smiled bashfully. "Just a voice sim, innit. But you can choose a man or woman, like this funny, Chinese robot voice. It just an app, right? But even after I got rid of the phone I still thought of him as Lucky. Still sending the texts and emails. But what can an app do, yeah? That's what I thought. Except after ..."

Deepak's voice tightened, his throat constricted by the memory and he paused, fidgeting restlessly while he fought the emotion. He sat down suddenly, head bowed and said: "Couple of days after Indi was ... taken from me, he asks me — text asks me, confirm Indi is dead and —"

Deepak's face crumpled with the sudden memory of his loss and all the misery that had flowed from it. There was a gradual folding and creasing of the lugubrious face as he lost the battle for control, weeping silently into his hands at first before at last emitting a single loud sob. His body shook. Skull looked away, embarrassed, unsure whether to offer comfort or let him get on with it.

Raj stepped tentatively through the doorway, the rattle and hiss of the plastic curtain anticipating his entry.

"Alright, Deep?" He called down the room, glaring at Skull. "Deep! You OK?"

"Fuck off!" Deepak yelled. Perhaps he was angry more at himself than with Raj but the swift expression of rage allowed him to master his grief. Raj rapidly withdrew.

Inside the silence that followed, the glottal clatter of the blow heater swelled, providing a backdrop of brown noise. Skull rubbed his aching finger tips and pulled his jacket closer around him. At the table the old man snorted, annoyed at the noisy intrusion; he shuffled the mouse irritably again but his attention remained fixed on his cartoon.

"Sorry." Deepak swallowed hard, avoiding eye contact. "Sorry," he said again and glanced briefly at the screen which had frozen abruptly, as if unable to execute its logic without the sympathetic attention of an intelligent observer. "Continue (y/n)?" the screen asked. Deepak tapped the keyboard and the lines of text started rolling up the screen once more. The disk on the mat clicked and buzzed as if it held entrapped a maddened insect.

"Should've smashed Lucky with a bloody hammer," Deepak said. "That phone is evil, man."

"Did you warn Jon?"

"I warned him."

"What did you tell him?"

"Get rid of it. I told him to get rid of it. But he didn't. He said no. Said he was happy with it. I told him. I told him there's problems with privacy. I told him it might leak data to third parties or something. I did tell him."

"Is that what you think was really happening? Third party data leaks?" Skull asked.

Deepak was quiet again, watching the screen's diagnostic messages, watching without seeing, like a sailor watches waves, or a shepherd his flock. "Sure, why not?" he said at last.

Skull asked, "Did you ever get any demands for money, or ... or anything? From these third parties?"

"Nah. I had police, I had insurance, family — always family, right? What can you say? Phone killed wife? Who's going to believe that?"

"So you didn't tell Jon anything," Skull said.

Deepak was scribbling again, noting in careful script a nugget of information from the screen. Finally he said, "When Jon called me last time, it was too late. He was locked in. I said, run."

"Run? Run where?"

"Just run."

"Do you still get the messages?"

"For goals? Nah. Last message was, Goal Failed. Time was out, see. SMART goal has time-limits, and time was out. Insurance didn't pay out. Still hasn't. Goal failed, innit."

*

Back in the car, Skull adjusted the climate control, feeling the warmth from the heated seat rise deliciously though his numb buttocks and reach along the cold curve of his spine to his hunched shoulders. Slowly he thawed and when at last he could feel the tips of his fingers enough to use them, he checked his messages.

Jac had left a basket of texts. "Found vaseline" said one. Another read: "Man in video is vase. Call me so ones."

On balance he rather thought that he preferred the Cubist minimalism of her truncated-word texts to the psychedelic Surrealism of the phone's predictive text engine. He regretted now suggesting she try it out.

Before he called her back he checked all his other messages. The Werner Brandes texts had ceased but nothing else had changed. Emily was still silent on Twitter. Her last careful tweet, dated four weeks earlier, still stood accusingly, accompanied by a soft-focus selfie: *Learn from yesterday, live for today, hope for tomorrow. The important thing is not to stop questioning. #einstein #feelingsad*

"How d'you know it's Viktor?" Skull asked when Jac finally answered her phone.

"I've been working my way slowly through Jon's video store thing," she explained. "I started with the most recent and I've been working my way slowly back. It's very boring, but I suppose it's the right sort of approach for my training." She paused for Skull to register the joke.

An old woman emerged from the maisonette adjacent to Skull's parking spot. She banged her front door shut, locking it carefully with fingers slow from the cold and from swollen, arthritic knuckles.

Skull asked, "But how d'you know it's Viktor?"

The old woman placed the key carefully in her large handbag before pulling on her gloves. All her movements were careful and considered.

"Jon says his name. Viktor. It's on one of the clips."

"He could simply be talking about Viktor," said Skull.

"No. It's definitely Viktor. And he's almost certainly Russian. At least he's got some kind of accent. There are a few very odd photos of the occasion as well, but it's from the same sequence as the clip in the text message."

The old woman walked stiffly down the short, narrow path to the street pavement, pulling her wheeled case behind her. She looked neat, and respectable enough to be on her way to visit a sick friend or to tidy the weeds on her husband's grave. She was wrapped in a warm tweed coat. The faux-leather case matched the sensible flat, brown shoes.

Skull pulled up a browser on Gabby's internal display and navigated to the *rewindr* website, logging in to Jon's account.

"What do they talk about?" he asked.

"No idea. The clips are only a few seconds long. You'll have to watch them when you can. You might pick up more than I did — some of it sounds a bit technical. But Jon's obviously worried about something. Viktor seems mostly cross. I'm not sure how this helps, but at least it solves a mystery," she added.

Down the street, in the mirror, the old woman stopped then turned carefully to look back at Skull sitting alone in the car outside her home. He wondered if she would walk back, abandon her outing, but she must have decided he was harmless because she turned again and trudged on down the road.

"I've got it on the screen now," Skull said. "Where do I go?"

She gave him the date, and he watched the first clip in the day's sequence which was a blank wall (probably Jon's study), and a man's voice (Jon almost certainly), muffled and off camera; in a second clip a woman's voice says something short and emphatic, but it's not clear what she has said or where she is. The next is of Jon, at his desk, just the torso, the click of a mouse; the fourth is dark, a smudged, muted and rhythmic swishing — perhaps a pocket, or a bag. What triggered the camera to start up was still not clear — a change of light, certain volume threshold; maybe it was merely a random firing.

The fifth video was instantly recognisable. Here was the same dark grainy quality, the familiar low angle shot just like the clip from the text message, but now quite obviously the location is the interior of a car because Jon is driving, left arm in shot, reaching out to change gear. His expression is anxious. He says, "Shit, shit, shit...," glancing over his shoulder as he manoeuvres into or out of traffic. Jon was never a happy driver.

"— don't know what you mean by that," Jon says at the beginning of the next clip. The other man is now in shot in the passenger seat only you cannot see his face, just the shoulder, the neck, the ear. During the clip a brief pulse of light sweeps through the cab of the car as another vehicle passes by, and there's a flash of white cheek, a red tee-shirt beneath a dark jacket.

"Application is excellent demonstration of pieces." The man has a distinctive accent. "Pieces is Persistent Cloud Execution Services. If it was a possibility to terminate, it would not be considered persistent. Yes? There are multiple copies running — multiple servers, multiple clients, each running own environment. You cannot kill it."

"I hear the words you're saying, Viktor. It's just —"

"No names!" the man barks, shifting uneasily. "Fuck. I told you no names. Or I will go."

"Sorry, mate. Sorry." Jon holds up a placatory arm, pausing, gathering himself. "I don't understand, is all—" The clip stops abruptly.

"Shame we don't get a good look at him," Skull said.

"You do," Jac said. "Sort of. Later in the sequence."

Skull ran the next clip, the original. It seemed now less urgent, more ominous.

"Please help me."

"I cannot."

"I'll pay you."

He watched it all again through to the end: "What would my chances be?" Then Viktor's shrug: whatever.

The final clip. Viktor has shifted position a little so there is a little more of his face, although in the dark still largely unseen. He is partially facing Jon and speaking earnestly.

"— but if you tell the app you are dead it will of course seek confirmation indicators. It will continue to execute until all verification factors are satisfied. You understand this? This verification module is a very strong component of the system. The requirements for robust systems are —"

Viktor stops short, freezes, catching sight of the phone mounted low on the dashboard. He peers forward at the camera to confirm what he sees and his expression turns from incredulity to disgust.

"Fuck. Is that phone? You bring that phone? Fuck sake stupid fuck!" He raises a hand to block his face, but it's too late: dark hair, big dark eyes, wide lips. His jacket flaps open. The movements are blurred in the low light conditions as he curses richly but unintelligibly in his native tongue. The car door opens, the crescendo of expletives rising in intensity before cutting off abruptly as the door slams shut again. "Shit," Jon hisses as the sequence ends.

"It's not much to go on," Skull said doubtfully after running the final clip one more time.

"We know he's a real person, at least" she said brightly, then added: "And it ties in with your Russian friends." Skull quickly pointed out that he didn't really consider them friends. "You should have seen a doctor," she said. "Did you see the doctor this morning?"

Now that he thought about it he did feel a little sick, still the ache in his stomach where the man had hit him. On the other hand perhaps he was hungry. He wished now he hadn't left his apple with Deepak.

"I saw Deepak," he told her.

The man in the side mirror hesitated before choosing to cross the road, otherwise Skull probably would have missed him. Brown jacket, scarf, woolly hat. Why the indecision before crossing the road? Was that normal?

"I thought we agreed you wouldn't," she said. In the rear-view mirrors the man squeezed uncomfortably between a gap in the parked cars to cross to the other side of the road. "Was it alright? How did it go?"

"It went fine. Obviously we now know he's not the other man in the video."

"Is that good or bad for us?" she asked

The woolly hat bobbed along above the line of car roof tops on the opposite side.

"I don't know." He switched the display to a view from the rear cameras. The man had gone. Skull twisted painfully in his seat to look back the length of the road but the man had disappeared. A watcher, maybe? Ducking into his car? A local most likely, entering his own house. Skull would have seen him if he had walked past.

"I need to go," he said abruptly. "I have another meeting."

*

No one followed Skull as he extricated himself from Leyton, at least no one he could detect. He wove his way onto the North Circular Road, the ragged cable of highway that stitches the outer northern suburbs of London to its cosmopolitan heart. Jac listened quietly as he described his meeting with Deepak.

"It doesn't get us any closer, does it," she observed when he had finished.

The lunch-time traffic had at least the consistency of chilled vodka rather than the sluggish cold treacle of rush hour. Drivers snuggled smugly in the heated envelope of their vehicles, while out on the street only the foolish or the desperate braved the malicious gusts of icy wind.

Skull nosed Gabby into the outer stream of cars, tapped the accelerator to scoot around the battered van wandering the inside lane while the woolly-capped driver chattered on his mobile phone.

"He may have been lying," said Skull.

"Did he really do it? D'you think he is a murderer?" she asked.

"I'm no expert, but he's not a murderer. I think he knows more than he's saying, though. He said he got rid of the phone when he thought it might have something to do with his wife's murder, but I think he just sold it on to Jon."

"My God. Why would you sell a friend something like that?"

"Well, it is just a phone. But he said something about data leaks. Maybe there's some kind of extortion racket? I don't know, it didn't make much sense."

"How would that have anything to do with Jon?" she asked.

"Don't know. Blackmail?"

"My God, Skull. D'you think Deepak is blackmailing Jon?"

"Maybe," Skull said, but he was dubious. It sounded unlikely. "He's guilty about something."

For a while they mulled the notion of extortion, fraud, blackmail, but could make nothing of it. It sounded dramatic, too continental, and their ignorance of that world finally silenced them.

"What's your meeting's about?" Jac asked to cover the difficult pause.

"Debitage," said Skull. Jac would get the reference, he felt sure. She would understand what he meant, understand that he was picking over the discarded pieces of his world, looking for anything of any value remaining.

On the phone Tom Twydle had been laconic: they wanted to showcase their high-concept demo and it would be awesome for Skull to check it out and give them some input. They were keen to find synergies, eager for his word.

This strange fusion of urban management consultant street-speak, along with the arrogance and flattery, frightened Skull. At one point he thought that Tom had referred to him as an "old dog" but it may equally have been a reference to the performance of a misbehaving server or a warning about the family pet, because to see the demo it was necessary for Skull to attend them in the "code-forge" at their home in the suburbs of north London. Here, he was further warned, he would also encounter "the rents".

The suggestion had been that Skull "pop round our gaff after lunch sometime". It seemed odd, but there was of course a code. An invitation to lunch would have said quite obviously and quite crudely: we want something from you. Post-lunch meant, we're doing you a favour. But of course there are double-plays and reverse-double-plays. With the Twydle twins it wasn't so clear. It was entirely probable that the subtext was simply: we're free in the early afternoon and can't be bothered to come to yours.

Skull couldn't afford the Twydle twins. He needed cash more than the compliments and puffery they were rolling at him with such bad grace. Any involvement in their little enterprise would yield nothing for a very long time, if it yielded anything at all.

Perhaps it was denial. Perhaps he merely needed to keep believing that somehow he was still in the startup game, that all his endeavours had not just been ripped from his bleeding fingers and shredded in the winds of commerce. Everyone needs a failure, people kept telling him. You're not an entrepreneur until you've failed at least once. Twice is better. So why not three times, five times, to really secure your success?

What he needed was to keep his hand in. He needed to be seen, although the twins were not even on the fringes of the startup scene, but beyond the very outer rings, the asteroid belt of wannabees, the Oort cloud of me-too apps and vanity blogs suspended in an orbit of ego and hubris from which few would ever escape. He didn't need the Twydle twins, but everyone else was avoiding him.

Like many of his neighbours, Mr Twydle senior had converted the garage attached to his 1930s house into extra living space, providing a cool two story live-work-romp space for his twin sons. They slept upstairs in the down-time pad, but went down to the code-forge on the ground floor when they were up for a bit of coding. That's what the twins told Skull as they ushered him into their annex.

For decor they had gone for a minimalist approach. The walls were painted in shades of smoke-white and Cumberland greys, while the accessories were of the robust play-room style: big, yellow leather dude chairs, red zafu cushions, cobalt blue Swiss ball, an over-sized green foam dinosaur. A 24 hour news channel flickered quietly from a wall-mounted 52 inch TV, hooking them into world events as if they were on a trading floor or a newsroom.

Dad stood by, looking holiday-ish, proud and indulgent, hands in pocket, feet in house-slippers. Mummy hovered in the background threatening pots of tea and mince pies. These were "the rents", and also the twin's angels, their sole investors, Bob and Claire, socially obliged to support their offspring, genetically primed to believe in their boys.

Skull felt a sudden time dislocation — the 1930s houses, the 1950s parents — but the boys seemed only moderately sheepish about the situation. Skull thought that he was probably more embarrassed about it than they were.

All the same, their demonstration was surprisingly slick, technically impressive, even if their presentation was as hackneyed as the concept they were selling.

"We're all about social networking for the hard pressed urban car driver," Sam announced earnestly. Tom rubbed his nose while Claire smiled nervously at the audience (Skull). "We've unleashed the power of location-based services, and we've harnessed ad-hoc peer-to-peer networks to deliver a powerful tool that the urban dweller — the urban driver — can leverage in the ongoing battle to get on with her life." He paused, looking sideways to make sure Skull had gotten the sneaky gender fix.

Skull returned a zoned-out, glassy stare. "How are you handling cross-platform development?" he asked.

"It's a free download," Bob said quickly. They all nodded, so Skull nodded too.

The idea was to make a local parking market: anyone about to leave a parking spot would click a "seller" button which would notify nearby subscribers currently looking, that a slot was about to become free and they could bid for it up to their set limit. The incentive to publish your parking was that you "sold" your spot for ParkerPoints which you could use to buy another parking spot when you needed it. The twins made a profit on the spread, so if for instance the buyer payed twenty ParkerPoints (or pee-pees as Sam sniggered) the seller received 15pp while Tom and Sam got 5pp.

"We're monetising the concept right from the get-go," Tom pointed out. Bob nodded knowingly. "The bid-offer spread is adjustable depending on volume, or the location, or time of day. But we are taking a piece on each transaction. The pee-pee exchange rate is about 5 pence."

"Cool," said Skull, adding straight faced, "So five pee per pee-pee." Sam could barely contain himself.

"Knowsey Parker is making the problems of parking space the solution of cyberspace," sang Tom, concluding the presentation.

It wasn't an original idea (who ever had those these days) but it was reasonably well executed despite a few odd technical decisions.

"What about local authorities?" Skull asked. "You're making money from their services."

"They're selling knowledge, not real estate," Mr Twydle said with the quiet assurance of a man who has the right pension plan.

They moved then to the technical demo, with Tom and Sam playing buyer and seller using their mobiles in various simulated scenarios which played out on the big TV screen: Brent Cross, Shoreditch, somewhere in the West End. The demo was competent but quickly descended into a discussion of frameworks, grids, bridging tools and metrics processing. Mum and Dad drifted away.

This was always the heart of any meeting, the visceral core where you opened the toolbox and pulled out the tools one by one, thumbing the cutting edge, palming the haft, examining closely the nicks on the blade, the grease on the shafts, the oiled junctions, the teeth on the gears where the rust flaked. This is where you set aside your cap, unbuttoned your smock and walked naked through the room. The tools were everything and you could be yourself.

Skull pondered, as the discussions progressed, what he was doing there, and what was in it for the Twydle twins. In their position, he reasoned, what he would want from himself would be a roadmap for how they could future-proof their parking service against the flood of vehicle telematics protocols and car data service standards brimming over the horizon. Or were they simply aiming for some free consultancy?

"What d'you want from me?" Skull asked directly.

"Yeah, so what d'you think?" Tom quizzed him. Sam asked: "Should we pivot?"

*

Afterwards Mr Twydle, in his slippers and Christmas jumper, walked Skull out to his car. With his hands deep in his pant pockets, Mr Twydle jangled his small change rhythmically. Gabby buzzed gently and flashed as they approached, a greeting activated by the proximity detector.

"Nice car," Mr Twydle observed conversationally. "Yours?"

"Girlfriend's," Skull grunted.

"Ooh, do be careful with it," Mr Twydle advised solemnly. "You wouldn't want that to count against you too."

Skull opened the car's door. He felt it was far too cold to be standing around outside engaging in a surreal conversation about cars and girlfriends, but Mr Twydle seemed in no rush, politely holding the car door open.

"They're good boys," Mr Twydle said, allowing a twang of uncertainty in his voice. "Keen as mustard," he continued, "but then you have to be keen, don't you. You have to be completely focused, tunnel-visioned, eye fixed firmly on the future. Can't be worrying about the little things, fretting over the detail. Where's the rent coming from? How do I pay my bills? Basics. You can't worry about the basics. They say if you've done it once, twice, you get to know the ropes. Get to know the lay of the land."

"So they say." Skull slid behind the wheel, grateful, once again, for the warmth from the heated seat as it spread through his backside.

Mr Twydle continued to grasp onto the door, keeping it open. "So they say, so they say," he nodded. "And I suppose you know when the time is right to bury the silver and head for the hills, and where to go to dig it up again when it's all over. Or when simply to abandon the silverware and move on — let the Indians fight over the mustard pot, and the … the fish knives, and whatever." A hand came out of the pocket, fluttered at the futility of silly things before diving once more into the deep, dark warmth of the paternal pocket. "You can move on again, Matthew. It's in your power. Your choice."

Skull smiled bleakly up into Mr Twydle's bland face, wary of the unwanted sympathy erupting from this very odd, possibly mad, source. "I intend to," he said, adding, "Although I might just keep the mustard pots. The Indians can have the fish knives."

Skull tugged at the door but Mr Twydle was not yet willing to relinquish it. Skull pressed the window button. The window slid open quickly and quietly. Mr Twydle waited until the sigh of the electric motor had faded before speaking again.

"But you can't move on if you have nothing to move on with, Matthew. What you've done is really quite stupid, and very dangerous, and you need to put it right. And you should do that firstly by removing the software from all the web sites you published it on, and then assigning the intellectual property to BläsHög. And you should also return this vehicle to the company. As you know it's part of their settlement and I'm sure they will refund to your girlfriend whatever she paid, less any depreciation and damage. Now, if you do that, maybe she'll come back to you and you won't have to make that long journey all the way down to Maidstone."

Skull checked the mirrors, looking down the road, up the road. This was worse than Simon's sudden violence, more shocking even than the Tunguska Man's assault. He could hear the words the father was saying but his mind was re-calibrating the meeting with the twins, all his contact with them, the conversations they'd had before the meeting.

Parked across the road was a Honda Civic. A black Honda Civic.

"I can't believe you used your boys to get at me," Skull said, his voice pinched, his throat constricted with anger. Mr Twydle merely smiled.

Skull pulled the car door from Mr Twydle's hand, slamming it shut. Why hadn't he noticed the black car when he arrived?

"If you do all those things," Mr Twydle continued evenly, bending to the open window, "if you do all that, then BläsHög are still prepared to be generous, Matthew. Maybe not as generous as before, but still enough to make things right."

"Why are you following me?" Skull asked.

Mr Twydle smirked a bit. "Following you?"

Skull nodded at the black car and Mr Twydle swallowed hard, smirked. "To see where you go, of course." He patted Gabby. "This is my client's asset."

Skull said, "Gabby, Start!" and the engine rumbled quietly before settling into a satisfying purr.

"You've still got time to do the smart thing, Matthew," Mr Twydle called out over the gentle hum. "But if you don't, then terrible things could happen." He was hurrying now, speaking fast, loud, delivering the whole message. "Terrible things. Be wise. Do the smart thing, Matthew."

"Are you threatening me?" Skull asked.

"Oh, yes," Mr Twydle nodded. "Definitely."

"Are you a lawyer?"

"I am an accountant," he said with all humility, bowing gently. "Be smart, Matthew!" he yelled as Skull accelerated away.

*

"Is it possible to speak to Josh?"

The woman at the door frowned over the rim of her spectacles, salt-and-pepper hair gently tousled, not expecting visitors, not wanting visitors, she did not return Skull's friendly smile. Her eyes, a fading brown, were vaguely moist as if perhaps he'd caught her quietly grieving, or updating her Facebook page.

"Are you expected?" she asked.

"Of course," Skull grinned. He felt like a schoolboy asking, *Can Josh come and play?*

The woman hesitated, looking him over uncertainly, hoping he would go away. Out on the doorstep he felt exposed. He could hear a car turning at the end of the road. He stepped forward into the doorway, bullying the gentle woman into letting him in.

"I'm Matthew Morrell, by the way," he said cheerfully as she reluctantly closed the door behind him. He stood self-consciously on the shabby carpet in the shabby passage made narrow by an ancient hall-stand laden with shabby coats and shabby scarves. A staircase with wooden handrail ascended to the first floor on painted wooden steps, the paint now worn and chipped; piles of dusty books and fading magazines stacked up against the dusty, fading walls. This was not a home given over to the welcoming of guests.

"Wait here," she said, adding uncertainly, "Please," as she squeezed past him and disappeared down the dark passage like a badger passing into the night.

Skull now regretted the spur-of-the-moment decision to drop in on Josh. After leaving the Twydles he had taken a random route around the streets of north London checking always behind him to see if he was being followed.

I'm being paranoid, he told himself, but by the time he was sure there was no one tailing him, he was completely lost, and asked Gabby to plot a course for home. It was only because he was in the area that the mapping system, sensitive to the location of connections and contacts, flagged up Josh's address two blocks away from where he then was. Josh Hobbie (hawsehole69), it said.

Perhaps it was relief at encountering a familiar name, or a deep instinct to seek sanctuary in a hostile world that had brought him to this door without fully thinking through the consequences. Only now he remembered that Josh avoided all personal contact, preferred abrupt communications by chat or by email, insisted on being paid in crypto-currency. When he thought about it, no one he knew had ever met Josh face to face.

He was left waiting in the dismal hall for a very long time, and was about to let himself out when a short, round man appeared at the end of the passage.

"What the fuck d'you want, Matthew?" The man's hair was slicked over, short-back-and-sides, 1940s style; a tight fitting Oxford shirt contained a very large chest and it was tucked neatly into baggy trousers. The voice, though hard, was pitched high and round.

"Josh?"

"What d'you want?" He came down the passage on short quick steps. In the light of the hall, his face was soft and round, without the shadow of stubble.

"I need some help."

"So?"

"I need to trace someone."

"You need to fuck-off, is what you need to do. Nobody invited you here."

"I know. I'm sorry."

"Unacceptable. Fucking unacceptable. What's the problem with the usual channels, Matthew?"

"I was in the area. You came up on the map."

"Fuck off."

"Maybe it just matched your IP address or something."

"Don't be a prick. What IP address? You think you could track me with an IP address? That's an insult. I'm on your fuckin' contact list. You couriered me one of those stupid security tokens. Remember? I knew it was a fuckin' mistake at the time. You delete me from your contact list, OK? Or I'll fuck you up, and I'll fuck up all your contacts so you won't know your arse from your auntie. Is that clear enough for you?"

"Sure. Yes. It is."

"I mean it."

"I know you do." Skull filled the moment of uncomfortable silence reflecting on his immense surprise that Josh had turned out to be a mature woman and not the twenty two year old boy with bad skin and poor social skills that he had imagined. The gentle, weeping mother, however, was not a surprise.

"Well you're here now, you'd better tell me what you're after or it'll be a waste of everyone's fuckin' time."

They stepped into a living room decorated on the same design principles as the hallway. Skull sat warily on a grubby sofa and described in some detail his attempts to find Jon, explaining that the key may be in locating the mysterious Viktor Petsch. Josh was sceptical.

"No way. There's no way a phone app is going to develop some kind of spooky emergent intelligence. There's something incredibly dodgy behind it, for sure. Tell you what, I'll take a look at it for you Matthew, but I'm gonna charge double, OK? Shall I charge to the usual account?"

Skull nodded. Smartor could pay — the new directors would be deserving idiots if they defaulted on any of Josh's invoices.

"So, it shouldn't be too hard to track down this Viktor character," Josh said. "Everybody leaves some kind of a trace somewhere. Even me, it seems."

On his way out Skull apologised again for barging in. "And please give my apologies to your mum for disturbing her."

"That's no my mum, you prick. That's my wife."

*

Skull parked down a side street off Columbia Road stopping off at a corner shop to pick up a pint of milk and a ready meal on the walk home. It had become a habit, parking somewhere different each time. He had accumulated a ream of parking tickets for offences outside his parking zone, but he felt his paranoia was justified. On top of Simon's ambush, the un-settling conversation with Mr Twydle convinced him that he should take no more chances.

He paused at the corner of his street, looking towards his flat for strangers loitering, for parked cars with shadowy occupants. He felt vaguely ridiculous, less the hardened spy than the bullied schoolboy slinking to and from classes.

In the hall, Mr Beavis had gathered together all the junk mail and sorted it into piles: pizza, Indian, reliable gardening services. He had laid the piles alongside the small stack of legitimate, franked post. He had also left a note with a short list of builders' names and numbers: "darren — v.good brushman but v.busy", and "kosim (I think) reliable for a polack." At the bottom he had scrawled: "ps hope kiddies OK gasman been looking for you".

Skull shuffled all the paper piles together and carried them upstairs, dumping the lot on the small table just inside the flat's front door, adding to the increasingly unstable mound of unread post already scattered over the top. The flat was warm from the heating, and the light came on when he flicked the switch, so both gas and electric were flowing still. He opened the fridge door and dumped the groceries, still in their plastic bag, on an empty wire shelf.

He scrunched up the note from Mr Beavis and threw it into the brimming rubbish bin. Skull didn't want to think about Simon's kiddies; Simon's kiddies made him think about Simon; thinking about Simon was difficult. He blamed Simon for failing to produce winning sales for Smartor. If Simon had managed better sales they wouldn't have been so vulnerable to BläsHög, they might have attracted a more honest investor. Simon had never shared the vision. He had only ever wanted to know the value proposition, the bottom line, and the commission rate; everything else was camel crap, he said.

But Simon had refused the role of scapegoat, instead blaming Skull for not delivering a more compelling product: how could he, Simon, sell something so complicated that nobody could understand it? How could he, Simon, sell something that looked illegal and sounded dangerous? Simon hated him.

Picking up the TV remote he flicked the TV on, needing the comfort of voices, but no voices came, only the cold hiss of white noise. The screen displayed a terse message demanding that he contact the media company from whom he rented the service.

There was no broadband. The landline was dead too. The old answerphone was still showing the same 99 unread messages. In fact it had stopped at 99, as if it had given up counting, knowing he wasn't going to listen to any of the messages anyway.

Skull immediately reconfigured his router to piggy-back an unsecured wireless access point nearby, making sure he stayed connected. The link was slow, but the messages started coming again. Nothing from Emily. Nothing from Jac. There were a few thousand notifications and status updates. On LinkedIn Jamie Wood had endorsed Philippa Miller's Data Saucing skills; in return she had endorsed his Physical Engagement. Razzi Amett it seemed had stopped buying MP3s from Amazon but had sensibly invested in a high capacity disk. A blogger gave notice that she had published her article without quotes from Skull. All the tech bloggers now agreed that open-sourcing the Smartor code was a dumb idea. There were now messages from strangers that were abusive and threatening.

It was while reflecting on the unpaid bill and the ignored payment demands sitting somewhere in the mess on the side table, that it occurred to Skull there may be similar bills in the small collection of Jon's post that Anka had given him.

A paper bill was a rarity nowadays, and not all telephone bills itemise the numbers called, but it seemed that Jon was old-fashioned enough to insist on the assurance of hard copy. Jon's phone bill listed everything: text messages, numbers called, call duration, dates. It was clear that he had stopped making calls about six weeks earlier, around the time of the encounter with Viktor. There were numerous calls to a number that Skull confirmed (from his own contact list) was Anka's mobile phone number. Another frequently called number was Jon's place of work.

Only one other landline number stood out, a London number, to which several calls had been made in the days prior to the meeting with Viktor. A few of the calls had been quite short, no more than a minute, but there had been two that went on longer than ten minutes. When Skull ran a search in his browser it immediately identified the QStore at Covent Garden.

Jacqueline was not as pleased as he hoped she would be when he called her with his findings.

"Seems a long shot," she said morosely. Normally she was chatty, her conversation light and engaging. "Have you called them?"

"Yes. And there's no one called Viktor working there. They were quite sure about that."

"Well that's that then," she said. "Thanks, Skull" she added, but the tone of her voice seemed to be saying, Why are you bothering me with this?

Why indeed, Skull thought, but he said, "Viktor was quite secretive on the recording. He was upset when Jon said his name, remember. So I think it's possible that he's using a different name. Also, I've checked the video clip. When Viktor moves into shot his jacket opens. You can clearly see the yellow Quince logo on his shirt."

"But you can buy those, can't you?"

"You can."

"And Jon could simply have been calling the shop to book a repair to his computer."

"No. Not Jon. Not a fan. He thought Quince products were overpriced."

Jon had become surprisingly picky, surprisingly fast, about the kinds of technology gadgets he would or would not buy. Skull had been mildly amused at how easily his friend had developed the brand bigotry, the techno-evangelism, the fundamentalist passions of an enthusiast.

Jon rapidly grew religious. He scoffed volubly at the products he despised, sneering at the fools who endorsed them, disparaging their style, their intelligence, their social worth. He eulogised the things he admired.

Skull was his guru, at first. From time to time Jon would implore Skull to provide the unguent of his wisdom, the cool salve of reasoned advice. In this new role, Skull struggled. Too frequently he fell short in condoning or condemning a device; increasingly his expertise was found wanting sufficient insight. The calls for guidance became less frequent, the demands for his opinion faded.

All the same, by the time Skull and Emily dined with Jon and Anka in their new Docklands flat, that frantic phase in Jon's life had mostly passed. At the time of the Docklands dinner party, Skull told Jac, her brother had reached a disturbing new state of fanaticism.

The Quantified Self

Emily was nervous. Excited, but nervous. What should she wear? She used up a lot of worry cycles mulling the correct note to strike. In the past Jon's ladies were sophisticated, competitive, critical, so she fretted whether she should go formal, casual, or sloppy? Jeans or sweat pants? Dress or dungarees?

It was all my fault, of course. Jon had said, *Dinner, new flat, you and Em*, but I had failed to ask the relevant questions which might have given us all some clues as to how we should dress; I could've asked whether we should bring wine, beer, dessert; I should've asked if anyone else was going to be there.

In the end Emily decided on smart-informal and got it wrong. Anka was over-dressed, with makeup applied like render on a builder's garage. It was the first time either of us had met Anka, and frankly I thought she looked a little tarty.

Jon couldn't have been more chuffed with himself. He had decided to cook what he called "traditional Bulgarian", as a tribute to Anka. "She deals with food all week, so I'm cooking tonight," he said, stirring deeply through a large pot in which pale bodies floated on an oily broth.

In the living room Emily was being positive. "It feels so spacious," she said admiringly.

By this stage we'd already popped the bubbly and toasted the apartment, toasted the happy couple and their imminent marriage, toured the flat toasting the built-in cupboards, the plastic fittings in the en-suite bathroom, and raised our glasses at the river view (actually a distant point of light which Jon swore was a boat on the Thames). Em and Anka now sat awkwardly in the modern open plan seating area while I watched Jon patrolling the pots in the compact contemporary fitted kitchen.

"Yes. We are really lucky," said Anka.

Jon chopped a vegetable slowly and with care, leaning over the chopping board as he pressed down with a large knife. He looked healthy, fit and energetic.

"How's the car business?" He grinned at me. "When am I going to be able to buy the car that tells me where I need to go?"

Things were going fine, I told him.

This dinner party was an early celebration of Jon and Anka's registry office marriage. Emily and I could not attend because I was flying out to Sweden in a couple of days on business. I think they were as relieved as we were.

"This Stockholm thing sounds serious," Jon said seriously. The cut vegetable blocks were scraped into the pot where briefly they bobbed alongside the body parts before he stirred them down.

I had a series of meetings arranged in Stockholm with people who knew people with connections to serious players in the car manufacturing industry. I was going to demo our product and wow them with the new smartphone app we'd developed.

"Sounds serious," he said.

Well the thing about the car industry, I babbled — as much to re-assure myself as to impress Jon, is that the actual car-maker sits at the apex of a vast pyramid of component and parts manufacturers, technical services, research companies, consultancies and so on.

"Tip of the iceberg," he nodded busily, peering into the oven at a tray of what looked like short fat fish-fingers.

Well we'd solved most of the technical problems, I told him, and now just needed an injection of funding. We also needed a few "ins" to the top table. There was a consortium of makers who had let it be known that they may be interested in helping us if the conditions were right.

Jon seemed genuinely pleased. "That's fantastic," he said. He checked his watch then removed the thumbs of fish from the oven. They sizzled smugly on the tray, smelling garlicky.

Emily was saying, "I think the muted colours add to the sense of space."

"Yes," said Anka. "We are lucky." With a red napkin from the table she dabbed at her forehead while checking her phone with her free hand.

"I really wish I could get in on some of that action, mate," said Jon.

"Soon," I said. "Maybe. Maybe not for a while."

"Let me know. That app sounds intriguing. Tell me more."

I laughed. You could download the Smartor app from all the app-stores. It was a simple programme which, if you had the TwoCAN device, gave you more information about your car than you really wanted or really needed. The enhanced version we called SmartorPlus. This was a locked-down demonstration only, because with a few minor tweaks you could actually drive your car with it. We'd only ever used it on a simulator at that stage.

Jon said, "That's fantastic."

We gathered around the dining table, in the centre of which a dish of yellowing yogurt stood surrounded by burnt crusts on a bed of shredded green salad. Anka surveyed the table critically.

"Where is *kyopolou?*" she asked quietly.

Jon looked gut-shot for a moment. "Oops," he recovered with his best boyish grin, fetching from the fridge a sloppy brown dip, reeking of garlic.

We sat. Jon filled our glasses with a deep red Bulgarian wine the name of which escapes me but which happily was not entirely the vinegar I had expected. Jon drank hardly any of it.

He was the attentive host, the adoring partner, the modern man, playing the role with conviction; he leapt up between courses to clear plates, fill empty glasses, smooth the conversation. The conversation was light.

"Anka's leasing a new sandwich outlet," he announced. "It's a new venture."

"Oh that's super!" Emily enthused.

"Well done," I said.

"Yes!" Anka nodded.

"In Greenwich," Jon said.

"Oh, lovely."

"Ah!"

"Yes!" said Anka.

Jon said, "With the tourist trade there, she should clean up. It's a captive market, you see."

"Ooh."

"Absolutely."

"Yes!"

"I would just like to say," I said, tapping my glass with the edge of a spoon in the time honoured manner, "I'd just like to say that I'm really incredibly sorry we're not going to be at your wedding thing next week. I had always imagined that I would be the one who, you know, would drop the ring in the church, make a terribly filthy speech at your reception, get blind drunk and all that. But since it's not going to be that kind wedding anyway, I'll just say: Congratulations to you both. You deserve a long life of happiness together." I stood and raised my glass.

"Oh yes, absolutely," said Em. "To Jon and Anka." We all stood and clinked and then we all sat down again.

I don't know what made me do it, but I asked them, more or less, "Why the rush? Couldn't you wait and do it properly?" I smiled when I said it, but I never had the gift of the smile. Someone once told me that my smile reminded her of a gerbil just before it attacks. Jon has a great smile — you have it too — it's a family thing. Jon did it now, covered his annoyance quickly with a broad forgiving grin, but I'm afraid I persisted: "Not hurrying from necessity, are you?" I asked.

"Matty!" sang Emily, the hypocrite. It was she who had first suggested to me that poor family planning practises might be the root cause of these hasty arrangements.

But Jon said, "We love each other." He turned his smile, a different smile, on Anka. "What more is there?"

"Ah, bless," said Em.

"What more indeed," I said taking my queue from her. "Is the Prof staying over for the ceremony?"

"He — doesn't know about it. Yet," said Jon carefully. "We plan to make a visit in a week or so."

"I look forward," said Anka too loudly, too quickly, and glaring at me. Unlike Jon she was flushed with the wine and the *Rakija* shots she had been taking for her nerves when we arrived.

"Haven't you met the Professor yet?" Emily asked her.

"No. I look forward to it," said Anka again, this time with a sweeter delivery.

Emily has a naturally generous spirit but by now every time Anka spoke her shoulders would shake gently, and she would shoot me a goggle-eyed look full of scandal and the promise of gossip for the journey home.

After dinner we sat in the modern open plan seating area drinking coffee with liqueurs and admiring the massive flat screen TV set, the media streamer, the home cinema suite and, prominent on the storage rack, the new old-fashioned hi-fi system. A black vinyl record hovered as if on air, spinning slowly inside a glass dome, the discrete glass valves of the amplifier alongside glowing gently, like soft candles. A low warble flowed melodiously from the beautifully hand-crafted cherry wood speakers.

These were all new purchases to go with the new flat, all the best brands, the latest models with the highest specifications in wood, glass, brushed metals. Emily nodded sweetly while

Jon described this hoard. We had nothing new in our home, even our arguments were tired and worn. Smartor sucked everything.

"Yes, we're very lucky," Jon agreed, distracted suddenly by a low buzz from his wrist. He glanced down at the tiny screen, tapping it before reaching into a pocket for his phone.

Noticing the familiar cardinal red, the dated soft curves of his aged smartphone I said, "I say, Carruthers. Haven't you upgraded yet? You're not still using that old lady's phone."

"Lucy? Of course. Never get rid of her," he said, thumbing the screen with purpose. "Irreplaceable."

"Oh God!" Anka wailed. "That phone! It's so old style. It's embarrassing. It is like old Chinese wife: Jon Smart do this. Jon Smart do that. It's so embarrassing."

Jon grinned. "Irreplaceable," he said again.

"Quite right, Anka," I said. "You'd think by now he could afford a new one, wouldn't you."

"Yes, by now" she said, nodding energetically. Then suspecting an insult, she frowned. "We can afford it."

"Absolutely not a question of cost," Jon said quickly, but he relished the discussion because we'd caught him in an eccentricity. "Lucy's a one off," he said. "Unique. I think Lucy's beautiful."

"Loosee! Loosee! He's even give her a name," Anka cried joyfully, proud of Jon, proud of Lucy, proud of them all together. It was as if Lucy was a much loved member of the family, a characterful old dog, a salty aunt, rank and pungent among the fragrant charms of family life but cherished the more because of it.

"All this," Jon waived a hand around the room, "all this came from Lucy. If it wasn't for Lucy we wouldn't all be sitting here."

"Pah!" Anka laughed. "It's not Lucy. It's you. Clever man." She snuggled into him, presenting him her round faced, her soft eyes, her lips swollen for kisses. Emily and I looked away.

*

It was later that Jon showed me his graphs. He ushered me into the study and raised up on the computer screens the milestones and landmarks of his journey to self-improvement.

"I wish I'd started earlier," he said.

First was a web-based application which catalogued the basics: calories in, calories out, steps taken, daily weight with BMI and lean muscle ratio. I think he was looking for some kind of approval, because when I said it all looked OK he immediately showed me more websites with more charts which plotted his heart rate, his heart rate variability, respiratory rate, body temperature, blood pressure, blood oxygen levels, hydration levels; then charts of sleep cycles, with deep sleep and REM sleep set against nocturnal temperatures and breathing patterns.

The sites all had names like FitCast and LifeMover, FatSmashr, RunFunster, with pictures of bright, happy people running, swimming, jumping, laughing; there was punchy copy using punchy words: transforming, power, awesome, and of course social, smart, and connected.

"You're a bit obsessed with yourself," I told him.

"Yes." He was serious.

"Why?"

"It's interesting."

"For navel-gazing geeks pushing themselves up the OCD scales," I suggested.

"No, we need to know," he replied. "We know nothing. This is how we improve ourselves."

"I thought you were already perfect," I said, but he refused the bait. He had more to show.

His hand, a prehensile claw curled over the carefully styled mouse, jabbed the cursor over the monitor, plucking out the pages over which his data points were variously tracked in solid lines, in dotted lines, in fat columns, flat wedges, dark valleys and sharp mountains, swirls and blobs in red, black, green, rising, crossing, falling. "That's my life," he said. "It's like a work of art, isn't it."

He twitched his fingers over the keyboard, flipping onto the screen the metrics of the unmeasurable: a rage gauge, a dream map, a mood pie.

"I've got to go, mate" I said, thinking of Em, trapped in the modern open plan seating area with Anka. Earlier, when I had followed Jon into the study, she had shot me a glare, as if I had just taken for myself the last parachute on a doomed aeroplane plunging to earth in a mad death-spiral. I knew I would pay for it later.

"Check this out," Jon said as he slid open a deep desk drawer, revealing a neat arrangement of boxes containing more apparatus for measuring, monitoring and quantifying. He unpacked them one-by-one, handling them carefully, with reverence almost, describing to me the purpose of each, its function, use, options, limitations.

There were step counters and run trackers by the score, a few smart watches, a couple of sleep monitors. He showed me a small plastic box with a dark screen and a large button which measured his blood sugar levels, and another which had a small opening to accept a thin strip of paper onto which you dropped a pin-head of your blood so it would give you your cell count, your PH levels, and the state of your cholesterol, cortisol or triglycerides.

I was impressed. "Every man should have devices," I quipped.

"Absolutely," he countered without smiling. "A man without devices is a man without diversions. But the funny thing is," he continued, "no matter how much of yourself you measure, there's always something more. Something new to measure, something else you can measure it against, or a new refinement that gives you deeper insights."

"But the data's not information," I objected. "You can measure anything. You can measure the number of grains of sand in your shoe at the end of each day; and you can compare it with the number of steps you walked, but where's the value in that? All you know is the number of grains per step."

"Lucy tells me what the value is," he said. "She suggests things I can measure to improve myself, and then uses the data to help me. She tells me what to do. The more data I give her, the deeper her analysis and the better her suggestions are. She eats data like a fat bloke eats pie. Only difference is what comes out is information. She shits a pure, golden thread of knowledge."

That's what he said. And while talking of faeces, he went on to tell me that he was sending regular samples to a laboratory which had promised to provide him with a visualisation of the communities of bacteria that his gut hosted so that he could compare his gut with those of vegetarians, or old people; or even Californians.

"Wow, you really are getting to the bottom of this," I said but again he didn't pick up the cue. The same laboratory, he told me, accepted mouth swabs, armpit wipes and genital scrapes.

"It's not Lucy, you know," I said. "Lucy's just a smartphone. It's not the phone that's driving this demand for data."

"Oh I know that, Skull. I'm not totally stupid — there's the phone and the apps and all the data in the cloud and stuff, but she brings it all together, she assesses it, analyses, suggests new refinements. She gets me all this stuff. I don't know how it's done. Don't really care. I tell her what I want, point her at where the data is; she mulls it over, fires the suggestions at me. I'll never be a geek. Not like you. I'm not a toolmaker. But maybe I can be the other thing."

"A tool?" I suggested.

"No, the other thing. First we shape our tools and then our tools shape us? Who said that?"

"You did."

"It's a quote, fool."

"Lennon." I said emphatically, claiming two for the price of one. Whenever someone quotes something soulful, dumb or obscure it's usually John Lennon or Vladimir Lenin, in my experience.

"Anyway," he said. "That's me; I'm being shaped by the tools people like you are making. I am everyone else in five years' time. I'm telling you, in five years everyone will be like me, and if they aren't they should be."

"We should get back to the girls," I said, indicating the door. I wasn't ready to be held responsible for anything, particularly not in five years' time; next week was enough of a challenge.

"Haven't finished," he insisted.

He unpacked and waved at me one of the test strips that he dipped into the first piss of the day, and which, he said, measured a whole spectrum of markers that he recorded manually, along with a note of the volume, colour, smell. He wasn't sure why, but then again, why not? Since he had it, and it was measurable.

Then he lifted his shirt and showed me a strap around his lower back on which was attached a rectangular plastic plate with a button and a logo. It looked like a buckle but he said it tracked and corrected his posture by gently vibrating when he stood badly or sat slumped, or walked with a slouch or a drooping head. It kept him looking confident, he said, and by looking confident, he felt confident.

"Why are you showing me all this?" I asked. "It's interesting and I'm glad it works for you, but for me, I barely have the time to clean the fluff out my navel, let alone gaze at it."

"Yeah. You did the navel-gazing joke already, Skull. I'm showing you this as a friend. It's a journey of discovery which I think you should start. I'm sharing. It's all about self-knowledge, self-awareness. It's about improving yourself. It's also very democratic. For instance," he dangled a pair of socks in my face, "when I go for a little run, I wear smart socks. When I get back from the run, all the data is synced up to the app: how far I ran, how fast, of course; calories, step cadence, and also how efficiently I run; also tells me whether I have any pronation issues, poor footwork — all useful information. And then I upload it to the FitCast website and I can compare how well I'm doing with like-minded sock wearers all over the world. I can see that I'm better than some old granny in San Francisco, but not doing quite as well as the Gold Star Boys from Lagos, who I'm shadowing. And they can do the same with my data. Everybody shares. Sharing is the beautiful part of what it's all about: sharing so you can help others on the same journey; sharing so you can compare yourself with other people, compare yourself with yourself to see how far you've progressed. It's a real community."

"Cool," I said. It's the sort of thing he would have run a mile from before. In fact he wouldn't have run, he would have taken a bus. Now he was fitness shadowing a semi-professional football team in Lagos, he told me.

"But you hate football," I pointed out.

"It's not about the football."

The way it worked was that he would measure his fitness metrics against their team average, as an incentive to improve. Members of the team watched his data too and would send him upbeat encouragement or friendly admonishment, depending on his performance. The idea was that the team got some of the membership fee he paid and in return he got some interesting, if remote, workout buddies.

"Data privacy?" I asked. "Not a worry for you?"

"No." He was adamant. "Not a worry at all. All the babble about data privacy is pure journalistic claptrap. We should be sharing our information. It's an imperative. The more data we have the better we can understand our bodies. If we have that information we can make better decisions: better personal decisions, better medical decisions, better political decisions; defeat diseases, live longer, live more fulfilling lives, stuff like that. It's the simple logic of progress, and it's a civic duty, as I see it. Like voting and paying your taxes. Well, you know the arguments, I don't need to tell you what they are. There's a moral obligation, isn't there? And there's a political dimension too. Same as with your smarter car company. Am I right? I'm right, aren't I?"

I agreed with him; it was the line of least resistance but the truth was that at Smartor we mined our customers' data and showed them how they correlated with other customers, because that was the standard way to get people to surrender their information. It seems we can only understand ourselves in relation to others. At Smartor we may have started with the ideals of the democratisation of data, but we'd quickly reached the point where what we really wanted to do, what we really needed to do, was to use the data to sell tyres, spare parts, insurance. As I saw it our obligation was to our families, our duty was to our investors; forget the rest of the world. That was the simple logic of business.

"Talking about privacy," he said, "there's something I've been meaning to ask you. Can a phone —?"

Emily knocked. "Not interrupting anything am I?" she asked, poking her head into the room.

"Yes," said Jon. "You're interrupting me showing Skull the road to perfection. You might want to take notes, so you can advise him. Come and have a look."

"We should go, Matty," Emily said, smiling at me. Her eyes said 'bastard'.

"Where's Anka?" Jon asked.

"Oh," Emily said lightly, "she fell asleep, bless her."

"Yeah she does that," Jon said, returning to the beautifully graphed metrics on the screen. "It's the early starts."

"Ah, bless," said Emily. She was still working some furious eye messaging at me.

"We should go," I said.

"Not before Emily has a look at this," Jon said picking up the desk lamp and shining it into the back of his opened mouth.

"What am I looking for?" she asked squinting suspiciously into the moist hole.

He stuck a finger in his mouth, pointing. "Cunk yew thwhee dla cawa hee?"

"No. Oh!" She wrinkled her nose. "There's a massive hole in your back tooth. My God, Jon. It's enormous. You should get that seen to."

He sucked the spit from his finger as he removed it from his mouth, looking as pleased as a boy with a bogey. "Found a guy who will embed a tiny sensor in there. Costing me a small fortune. And it's only going to produce a few metrics — chews and bite strength, cadence, I think ... maybe some basic nutritional data — but a few firmware upgrades down the line should improve that, right? Fitting's next week. It's even got Bluetooth," he added proudly, "so I can get real time feeds into Lucy. How cool is that?"

Stupid cool I told him as Emily was herding me to the door. "A Bluetooth tooth?" I said. "Isn't that a blue tooth squared?"

He blanked me again, not even a smile so I tried taking him down a peg: "What are you going to do when it runs out of power?"

"Wireless charger," he said dismissively. "Battery lasts months, though."

He followed us into the long passage as we thanked him for the hospitality and marvelled, again, at the new flat. We peeped into the modern open plan seating area to wave goodbye to Anka, but she lay in a heap on the settee, head back, open-mouthed, snoring.

"I'll tell her you said goodbye," Jon said when we were standing grinning at the front door. "Oh yeah, that thing I was going to ask you. Quickly. Can a phone leak data?"

"Yes," I said. "Depends what you mean by leak. Why?"

"Mate who sold me the phone said I should get rid of it. It leaks data, he said. Is that even possible?"

Of course I know now what prompted the question, but at the time I was amused at the irony of a man who a moment ago was selling the morality of sharing personal data with the world, now worrying about the data leaking from his smartphone.

Emily pulled relentlessly at my sleeve.

"I doubt he means the phone itself," I said as I was towed gently towards the lifts. "More likely an operating system issue, or the apps."

"Can I stop it?" he called down the lobby.

"I wouldn't worry. Use an anti-virus app."

He waved, nodded (satisfied), shut the door. Emily and I went home.

Thursday

Viktor cantered heavily down the spiralling glass stair case of the QStore in Covent Garden, failing, despite the assistance of gravity, to emulate the gazelle-like skip of the boy going up.

There was a look. The lads in the store favoured the tousled appearance, as if they'd just this moment climbed from their bunk-beds and were thinking juice, coco-pops, chocolate spread. The older men looked lost and spare but the women, few in number, were round and bouncy and neat, attempting geeky without the stubble and bad breath, offering bubbly, positive personalities instead of laid-back zeal. There was an attitude too: youthful but not immature, earnest but not eager, clever but not intellectual, cool but not unspeakably so; you needed at least three of the attributes in that set to work in this place.

Viktor was trying to fit in. Skull, standing in the covered courtyard below, recognised him instantly from the video. Viktor wore an urgent scowl beneath a day-old beard. The yellow Quince logo shone luminous against the apple-red polo shirt. Around his neck a white lanyard looped down to a plastic case with yellow dots, tagging him as clergy, not congregation. Tucked into the back pocket of his jeans a yellow duster hung down, ready to hand for the wiping of holy relics where the faithful had touched, removing the common sweat and grease of ordinary fingers.

For this was a temple (perhaps more than a church, Skull reflected after walking through the store) where acolytes and priests moved among the believers with a ministry of show and tell. The relics (qPhone, qTab, and so on) were laid out on solid wooden tables, altar tables, for the brethren to touch and hold, while the clerics provided guidance.

Viktor quickly crossed the crowded courtyard, a sleek phone cupped reverently in his left hand, while in the other he clutched a pink form which flapped as he wove through the shuffling congregation to reach his supplicant, a middle aged man, well dressed, anxious, with spectacles. The two spoke at length, Viktor initially with regret, then contrition. The man tried an emotional appeal, his eyes sad, hurt, lips twisting like a hooked worm, but finally, despondently, he received into his own hands the phone, the pink form, defeat. He turned towards the exit, spiritless, stumbling out with short, baffled steps.

"More bad news, Viktor?" Skull asked.

Viktor froze only momentarily before smiling broadly into the distance as if summoned by a favoured aunt for some pleasant occupation. He side-stepped politely around Skull to make a quick escape across the busy floor.

"Where's Jon Fast?" Skull cut him off, raising his voice. "Remember Jon Fast, Viktor? You had a conversation with him a couple of months ago. In his van."

At last conceding Skull's presence Viktor paused, pointing at the staff card on the lanyard, and said: "You are making mistake. My name is Marcus." Below his picture the card said "Marcus".

"Indeed," said Skull. "But also Viktor Petsch. I am a friend." To re-assure, Skull smiled — an even set of small white teeth below the curled lip; classic dog.

"Not my friend." Viktor still refused eye contact. "I will call security guard if you do not leave now."

"Then I might have to disclose that your real name is Viktor Petsch." The man's shoulders hunched with uncertainty. "And also maybe show them this." Skull was ready with the video clip, holding his phone low in front of Viktor, clicking the play button. The sound was turned down low but the images were clear enough.

"I cannot help you," Viktor hissed. "Go away."

"Also I ran into some tough guys looking for you. Russians."

"Russians?"

"In Jon's flat. But they were looking for you."

"I told you, I don't know anyone called Jon. And I don't know any Russians. You have wrong man. Please. Leave. I am very busy with customers." His lips warped with misery.

"Everything alright, Markie?" The woman carried with her the tablet of authority and wore rimless glasses with broad red temples which poked into a thicket of dark red hair pulled back above her ears. The white lanyard of her staff key card tumbled over a large bosom and left the yellow card spinning helplessly below the red ledge like a stranded mountaineer. "Jo" the card read as it spun.

Jo smiled. Skull smiled. Viktor smiled. "Sure," said Viktor. "No issues. Business customer. I will take him upstairs. Please. Follow me." Jo smiled. Skull smiled. "Sir," Viktor added as a contemptuous afterthought.

Skull followed Viktor closely between the altar tables and through the milling clusters of worshippers to the square glass staircase at the back. Beside the stairs tourists queued for the glass lift which raised them grinning stupidly, to the next floor. Skull and Viktor climbed the stairs mounted between the bare London brick arches, and the old London brick walls blasted clean and lightly lacquered. It was like climbing through air, stepping on light cloud while ascending to heaven. Brick, steel, glass, wood: the four pillars of honest design, revealing nothing to hide, a sanctuary for purity, sincerity and truth.

This was not a shop, Skull realised, nor even a temple, after all. It was a museum. A museum of the future, a museum where time and value were pulled inside out. In this museum you could buy the artefacts. You could buy them now, immediately, while they were beautiful and classical and a priceless part of the human narrative. You could buy them now and you could take them home and make them ordinary, make them yours.

Just short of the mezzanine floor Viktor stopped, twisting around to look down on Skull. "Who were these tough guys?"

"Russians," Skull shrugged.

"How do you know they were Russians?"

"They sounded like you."

"I am from Estonia," Viktor said with disgust, shaking his head. "What did they want?"

"I'll tell you about them when you tell me about Jon."

"Are you police?" Viktor asked.

"No."

"This is really not a good time for me to talk."

"My friend is missing," Skull insisted.

They paused while a Chinese family, colourfully dressed and grinning with discomfort, sidled silently around them going down the stairs. Once passed, the family all began talking simultaneously.

"What do you want from me?" There was still a doubt in Viktor's voice, defiance, contempt.

"Jon is my friend."

"I can't help your friend. I already told him this."

"You may be the last person to have seen him. It's on the video. The police might be interested."

They climbed on up to the first floor, the business arena, entering a hushed and hallowed space and leaving behind the wide-eyed, bag carrying, only-browsing walk-ins, the callous-fingered, the sharp tongued, the pink, the wrinkled and the awestruck.

The receptionist was suitably huffy. She was surly with Viktor and insisted that Skull sign in, printing him a badge with his company name, proclaiming him VISITOR.

Viktor led Skull into a bright narrow room labelled the Briefing Room. Gone were the naked bricks and polished steel. Here the walls were painted stark white: serious, sober, business-like; on one side the wall was pierced by tall windows, at the far end a large screen presided over the long maple conference table.

The two men sat, one each side of the table, looking at their hands spread out flat before them.

Skull was direct, demanding: "Tell me about Goald."

Viktor winced, then paused while he stared at their dull reflection in the dead video screen. "If I tell you this, who will you tell?"

Skull shrugged. "I only want to help my friend."

"Dimitri Gorchakov," Viktor said at last. "You have heard this name? Famous. In Odessa he is famous. Famous for being dead. In many parts. Many pieces."

Skull shrugged. He had not heard of Dimitri Gorchakov.

Viktor and Dimitri were friends. Although they never met face to face, theirs was a beautiful, modern friendship forged in the spit and fire of the technical forums. For many months on specialist boards, on mailing lists and comment channels, *darkmoron* and *CapTBone* circled one another with complementary asides and chatty bonhomie, all the while probing the other's competencies, plumbing the depths of each other's knowledge of the obscure and the arcane, by lobbing technical pebbles into the social well and listening for the flat muddy plop echoing up from the bottom.

The shield of anonymity in their English online handles was a barrier. *CapTBone* was wary of *darkmoron*, *darkmoron* suspicious of *CapTBone*, neither able to make out anything of the other's background, his leanings or aspirations. But the clues were there, leaking slowly through the context of messages, the subtext in posts, comments and asides. Gradually their relationship warmed. They began to reach out to each other outside the forums using chat and emails, and were delighted to discover that, while born in different countries, they were both of Russian origin. They shared a common foundation of experience (singing wholesome Communist songs in primary school, then learning the true value of profit and loss as seniors after the Soviet bloc had crumbled). More to the point, there was a parallel trajectory of ambition, motivation, belief. They wanted to better themselves, they wanted to better their young countries using the power of their brains and the determination of their race.

Dimitri was already a legend in the Odessa technical community, Viktor a rising star, one to watch, among the so-called Estonian startup mafia. They agreed to work together on something meaningful, something that would make their mark on the wider world, seal their reputation, perhaps even make them a bit of money.

"Persistent Cloud Execution Service," Viktor told Skull gravely, prodding the table with a forefinger as strong and slender as a concert pianist's. "We would build a service that guaranteed execution. Robust virtual framework, massively distributed, dynamic service choreography, bomb-proof orchestration engine."

So they built a system that would guarantee to run any other programme, or application, no matter what happened. Once you started the process, you could not stop it; there was no pulling the plug. Execution was guaranteed because it ran multiple versions of itself in many locations, in numerous ways. A running system would shred itself into pods of independent threads that dispersed like spider's silk on cyber winds and wove themselves into the fabric of the infrastructure wherever they fell, secreting themselves in unlikely places on network hubs and nodes, on server farms, compute engines, devices and appliances, making copies that would lie dormant, inert and innocent (a harmless icon, an orphaned configuration module, a mute sound file), reforming, regrowing, responding only when the signal came. If a component was deleted, two more would re-spawn; if a process was blocked, another would step up into the circle and start cycling. The system was virtually undetectable, certainly indestructible. It was a massive technical feat. They called it Hydra, of course.

"Why?" Skull wanted to know. It seemed to him there were few legitimate reason to design and build such a system, but any number of nefarious and criminal purposes to which it could be applied. This was a worm on which to piggyback spyware, viruses, trojans, ransomware, botnets, carding scams, porn, spam ... and those were about all the bad things he knew about. The dark side of the Internet was not his strength. He knew enough to stay away from it. He knew also that while not all the bad things on the Internet came from the east there was enough of it to make Skull wary.

"What would you use it for?" he asked.

"It was a political act."

Skull hadn't thought of that.

Tyranny is never far from the door of a new democracy, Viktor observed, adding that technology can help the people bolt the doors and shutter the windows so the wolf cannot come back in. Tyranny will always try to stop the voices, stop the talking, stop the people organising.

"Look at the Arab spring," he said pointing at the window behind Skull. "Look at Georgia, look at Ukraine, the NSA." Skull nodded.

Someone in a brown suit stared in through the glass door, frowned at them and went away.

"We shouldn't be here. We must go," Viktor fretted.

"What has this to do with Jon? Adding a few personal goals into a smartphone app is not a political act."

"I'm explaining that I can't help your friend. I cannot stop the Hydra. Once it starts it runs to the end."

"But how would he be running Hydra? He's using a smartphone. And he's not even remotely technical."

"Goald. He used Goald. Goald runs on top of Hydra. Hydra is the service. Goald is the application."

They needed a demonstration, Viktor explained, a showcase for their work, something strong, non-political, maybe even a bit commercial: "We spent a lot of time designing and building Hydra. There are costs." Viktor gave a diffident twitch. "We ran out of money."

It was Dimi who thought up Goald. Dimi was a genius. "We didn't want to do just another to-do list," Viktor said. "Everyone is doing apps for mobile, all the market is in mobile apps. We knew we could make something so smart everyone would want it."

So Goald was born: a smartphone application that ran in the cloud, with guaranteed execution.

The man in the brown suit (there were more suits behind him) hesitated briefly at the glass door, before pushing it open and placing his head into the gap.

"Ah — sorry. Are you going to be much longer?"

"Go somewhere else," Skull told him curtly.

"Right." The man let the glass door close, standing stiffly behind it for a moment. Viktor smirked awkwardly, his eyes large with astonishment.

Skull said. "Tell me more about Goald."

"So, goal management is obvious smartphone app. We conceived it as a hybrid of to-do list and time management, combined with a virtual personal assistant. These are well known functional domains. Like Siri or Cortana, but with balls." He spread his hands in a gesture of modesty as if this was all so blindingly obvious only an idiot could have missed the conjunction. Integration, he moaned, was the main challenge.

Once they knew what they wanted to achieve, the design was trivial and came together quickly, and naturally. Building the application, they agreed, would just be a matter of pulling together libraries, modules, assemblies, and hooking into ready-made services.

Skull nodded. This is the way software development is done. It's like building a house. You don't start a house building project by knocking together a brick mould and fashioning a shovel; you buy the tools and order in supplies. More complex engineering constructions will deploy vast pre-fabricated frameworks or ready-made sections which are shipped and then assembled on-site. In much the same way software engineers build their fancies on well-tested frameworks, and libraries of lower-level code developed by other programmers in other places at other times. In this endeavour, progress is made not so much by standing on the shoulders of giants as it is crawling up a pyramid of dwarfs.

Skull understood all this well enough. The problem for Viktor and Dimi was that they needed a vast inventory of complex pieces to complete their demo: voice recognition processors, natural language interpreters, decision support tooling, machine learning algorithms, communications handlers — the list was long.

"We were a team of two, with no funding. It was big task, so we took components off the shelf where we could."

"Off-the-shelf components?"

"No. We took the components off the shelf. Some of the shelves were higher than others. Sometimes we had to reach a bit."

They would have preferred open source packages for everything of course but (and here Viktor shrugged again), the stability and "feature sets" of free software were not always what they required. They raided universities, research establishments, commercial software houses. "We ran out of time and took short-cut. It was a demo, we told ourselves. Not intended for commercial use."

"You built a worm," Skull said with disgust.

Viktor paused, then quietly he said, "We didn't see it like that. Smart agent. It is smart agent."

"Marcus, you have to go now." Behind the receptionist standing at the door, was the man in the brown suit, and behind him, his embarrassed guests. The woman refused to look at Skull. "Sam has booked this room."

"What if we haven't finished?" Skull said, his voice rising, the loudness delivered surprisingly on "finished".

Holding her own, the receptionist said unhappily, "The room is booked."

Viktor half stood up. "We should go," he said.

"Sit down," Skull pointed at Viktor. "We're not done here." Viktor sat abruptly. Skull now shook his finger at the receptionist, saying, "Do you want to lose the contract? Do you want that responsibility?"

"We have a room booking system —"

"I'm this close to taking my business to Dell. This close," Skull shouted.

The loud and the rude are also the mad and profane. No one met his eye because, as everyone knows, you should never stare at a madman. The receptionist withdrew behind the glass door, exchanging gestures with Sam who left soon afterwards with his visitors.

"Fuck. Fuck," Viktor clucked quietly. "Do you want me to lose my job?"

"What are you doing working as a sales wonk, anyway? With your skills?"

"It's a good job. For Marcus, it is a good job. Marcus has just the basic technical skills." He smiled. The smile was transforming and delightful. It brightened his face, arranging the depressed Slavic features suddenly into a beacon of jollity. Skull smiled back because, above all things, he could recognise and appreciate a good smile. "So with Marcus," Viktor went on, his glum returning naturally, fitting his face like a worn leather shoe, "with Marcus I can stay low. Off the radar."

"But why do you need to stay off the radar?" Skull asked.

The horrors of Goald were buried deep within the subterranean logic of borrowed processes and over-plumbed methods. Like a cracked sewer, they revealed themselves surely but subtly, first with odd, whiffy glitches, then light zephyrs sour with unwanted and unwished for results. It would take a while before the full, toxic storm blew up and blew them down.

"So how's it doing that? How does it cross the barrier from proposing goal solutions to actually dispatching hit men?"

Viktor winced. "You don't know that," he said. "You don't know."

"Oh, come on," said Skull. "Otherwise why would you tell Jon to disappear?"

"Pigey," Viktor said, conceding with a grimace. "Progressive Intervention with Guaranteed Execution."

"Really?" Skull was incredulous. "Pigey?"

"Our model was too simple," Viktor admitted. "We imagined our customers as people like us. Young people, startup people, Californians. Everyone is Californian nowadays, right? What do Californians want? Fun, sex, money, gorgeous bodies. So they say, I want to lose kilogram of body weight before holidays. This is their goal. Progressive intervention means, as you get near holidays, if you are not losing the pounds it blocks you from ordering pizza on your mobile phone, or buying six pack of beer from the off licence site. That was our model. Who knew you could actually order a hit man on the Internet? My God, imagine the buttons on that website: Add Killer to Basket."

Initial testing, alpha testing, they carried out themselves, of course; later they allowed a few friends and contacts into a restricted beta program, gradually widening out to friends of friends.

"So in summary," Skull observed, "your design model was narrow and limited, while your testing was shallow and constrained; you integrated complex libraries that you didn't fully understand and bolted it to the framework for Armageddon. What could possibly go wrong?"

"Most of our testers were like, 'meh'. Where are angry birds? I want more kittens — you know: where can I update my VK status (you know VK? VK is like a Russian Facebook)." Skull nodded: he didn't know that. "Some really liked it. Well. Maybe a few only."

One of the few who really liked it very much was Petro Panasuk, an Odessan businessman, self-made in the new global-businessman mould: unctuous, gregarious, connected. Nobody liked Petro Panasuk, not even Petro himself. All the same, he conceived himself as a man in the middle, an oleaginous, string-pulling, matchmaking, go-to guy for bright, hi-tech startups in Central and Eastern Europe. And he was connected. He was also quite persuasive.

He persuaded Dimi that Goald was ready for the market and the market was ready for Goald. But, and here's a thought, instead of playing Russian roulette with the apps market, why did they not load the gun in their favour by going into partnership with a phone manufacturer? Manufacturers were always looking to bundle new smart apps with their new smarter smartphones.

What they really needed, Petro told Dimi, was a business-to-business deal that was simple, direct, no fuss. What they didn't need, was to do their own marketing, and deal with the app stores, and the app customers, and app customer complaints, and app refunds, and customer lawyers. They certainly didn't need that. A licensing deal was exactly what they needed.

Now Petro just happened to be a friend of a friend of the marketing director of an electronics manufacturer, an old, established firm based in the Czech Republic, already well known in the security alarm business ("You know them. Everybody knows them. Their slogan is: Creating Alarms"). Well, Petro knew for a fact that they were preparing to launch a new, branded smartphone to be called the Lucky7. Let's make them an offer, Petro had said; let's do a deal.

"The deal was rubbish." Viktor flapped an arm. "I didn't like it. We made not much money. Nothing, in fact. After commissions and fees, sweeteners, the exchange rates, taxes — we made nothing."

Dimi packaged Goald for the Czech manufacturer and presented the arrangement to Viktor as a done-deal, so he had to accept it. The phones were made and assembled in South Korea and when, at the last minute, the Czech firm decided smartphones were a dumb direction for them, and they should stick to their core business, the stock was picked up cheap by an Australian distributor, re-branded and dumped in India. A few boxes of "The Lucy Phone" made it to the Netherlands, a few to the United Kingdom.

"Petro Panasuk was an idiot," Viktor said. "His only goal was to get rich, but he wanted also admirers, respect, beautiful girls — all the dumb things. Greed and stupidity is classic combination for a road crash. So he likes, a lot, what Goald can do for him, and he scores a few early successes with it so he thinks he has got magic beans in his pocket. He boasts to Dimi that he has set a target of doubling his business stake every eighteen months." Viktor shook his head sadly. "Anywhere in the world this is not possible to do with a legitimate business. In Odessa? Definitely no."

Petro very quickly ran into trouble with the local mafia. First they gave him a gentle warning, and after a while, a not so gentle warning. He swore blue that he had stopped all business activities, but the goals were still running and the mobsters wanted to know who was squeezing them on the alcohol supply to their clubs.

Petro ran to Dimi and begged him to delete the app, to destroy all the goals associated with him. Dimi explained why he couldn't do it (guaranteed execution), but in a call to Viktor he suggested that perhaps they should have an emergency kill routine. Their friendship already under strain, they argued. Viktor was against the idea because it undermined the entire philosophy of the system.

"But business is all about pragmatism," Viktor said. "The customer is always right, yes? So we began to sketch out a quick design for Hercules. In the story, it is Hercules who kills the Hydra. So, this is what we needed."

"But there must be some orchestration component," Skull said. "Some command and control function. Surely."

"What the fuck?" Viktor glared at Skull, angry, unbelieving. "You missed the point. Fuck. That was the clever thing. No command and control, guaranteed execution."

"It's madness," Skull said. "Please tell me you built Hercules." Viktor blinked, looked away. "Jesus," hissed Skull. "How far did you get?"

"Dimi was working on it. He lived in Odessa. He understood better than I did the danger we were in. Eventually the gangsters ran out of patience with Petro and ... well, they took him away to answer some questions. I think they didn't like his answers. For instance, they would not believe a mobile app was the cause of their unhappiness about the alcohol prices. Also rent on whore-houses, increased cost of money laundering on credit card scams and ransomwares. They knew Petro wasn't smart enough or dumb enough to run this himself, so they wanted to know who was Petro's boss. Well, of course before he died he gave some names.

"This I learnt only later. At the time I was planning my penthouse in Tallinn Old Town. I could not decide what colour for the sauna room I would build with money from the Lucky7 phone. Then I received one final message from Dimi. It said, Run." Viktor looked down at his restless hands twisting on the table. "I'm still running."

Outside the glass door a small crowd had gathered, including Jo-the-supervisor, and a large, smile-free man in a security guard suit. They were negotiating between themselves how to achieve the best positive outcome to the unbooked room situation.

"We're not going to have much longer here," Skull said. "Where can I contact you?"

"You cannot." Viktor was adamant. "Now your turn. Who are these Russians? You said you would tell me."

Skull quickly told him about his encounter with the Tunguska Man and Homo Habilis in Jon's flat. "But I don't know how they got hold of Jon's name," he concluded.

"Your friend must have drawn some attention to himself, maybe asking wrong questions in wrong places."

"So what do they want with you?" Skull asked.

Viktor shrugged. "To kill me, of course. These criminals have long memories and short tempers. Probably also, Petro's goals are still executing, making trouble for me." He shook his head. "That was a stupid man, that Petro."

"What will you do?" Skull asked.

"Run." He smiled sadly. "It's a shame. I was beginning to like Marcus."

Skull glanced at the door. There seemed to be a lot of gesturing going on behind it. "So how did Jon track you down in the end?" he asked Viktor. "Nobody else could."

Viktor smiled his bright smile. "He used Goald. How else? He set a SMART goal: Find Viktor."

Skull gave Viktor his business card, crossing out the printed contact numbers and writing the VObella number with his home address on the back. "That's my number," he told him. "Get in touch. If you can raise Hercules, he might solve your problems too."

Viktor looked at the card. "You are really Matt Morrell? Of Smartor? Smartor is dead, yes? It was a stupid idea. Really dangerous."

"Maybe," said Skull. "But maybe not as dangerous or as stupid as Hydra."

"Indeed," Viktor laughed as Jo pushed open the glass door, beaming managerially.

*

Across the greasy cobbled street a massive reindeer posed on a dais, bedecked front to back with spittle-strings of white light. Behind this festive topiary display stood the market, a glassy jewel of commerce, beckoning weary shoppers with hearty carols, seducing them with an abundance of warm golds, bright silvers, forest greens, berry reds.

Despite these joyous efforts Skull knew (like any Londoner) that Covent Garden is a summer venue, a spring platform for the pleasures of pavement peoples, a monument to the plump enjoyments of city raptures, the bellowing of buskers, of hawkers and truanting children; an opera of smells — fried sugar, old fruit, noisome London drains.

Sadly, not everybody knows this, for even the flinty shards of cold wind could not rid the square of its trudging tourists, those muffled beings meandering the stony piazza, stuffed grubbily into parkas and anoraks and clutching, in gloved fists, sprays of swinging brand-bags, stopping mercilessly to point at random things and share inscrutable observations before moving obliquely, once again, across the stuttering flow of peoples.

Leaving the store, Skull dialled Jac's number. He had promised to call her and she had said "call anytime" but the phone rang and rang. He was walking quickly now, phone cupped warmly inside his pocketed hand, a Bluetooth earpiece plugged firmly into his ear, crossing the open square, passing the entrance to the church, and heading south. He had already collided with a living statue ("thuck orth, noghead"), then had himself cursed a short-legged, slow moving Spanish woman and her companions — a small Armada moving erratically in line abreast under full retail sail. They had returned fire.

It was after this exchange he encountered the Tunguska Man again. Recognition was instant and mutual, the surprise was not, nor was there equal joy. The brutal hieroglyph etched raggedly to the side of his head with a bottle-end was now hidden, covered by a woolly hat rolled halfway over his ears, but the flat impenetrable face was recognisable anywhere: the hooded eyelids, the humourless horseman's eyes. Skull stopped instantly.

"Helloo," Professor Fast yelled down the line, the word carrying through the exchange, around the server farm, up through the registers and over the switches into the switching office then out the gateway through a series of bridges and hubs to a small wireless router halfway down Henrietta Street where it bounced down the road over the hardy cobblestones to the smartphone nestling in Skull's pocket, cascading rapidly up the Bluetooth protocol stack before beaming the short distance to the headset that snuggled in his cold, red ear.

The Tunguska Man bared some broken teeth in a fake smile, cocked his head, but did not turn away. He stood squarely in Skull's path, inviting acknowledgement.

"Helloo? Who is this? Hellooh!"

"Hello," Skull said, backing off, glancing behind, to the side, but seeing no sign of Habilis. The Tunguska Man held his ground, moving neither forwards nor backwards. What was the man doing here? It couldn't be coincidence. Had he been followed?

"Jon! Is that you, Jon, my boy?"

Under pressure Skull turned back. The two great covered halls of Covent Garden market are separated by the arched Central Avenue. On the lower side, the South Halls looked empty and unsafe from where he stood, but the Apple Market on the north side, beckoned with its bright, busy lights and apian cacophony. Here, far beneath the high steel arches and glass roof, there were happy shoppers fondling goods and gasping at prices; there were nodding, smiling shopkeepers calculating their narrow net profits, while stallholders companionably moaned over rents, reminiscing better days gone by. To Skull, suddenly, all these Other People herding together seemed welcoming.

"It's Matthew, Professor Fast." Somewhere in the market a choir began a jaunty rendition of "O Come All Ye Faithful."

"Matthew?" The Professor sounded confused. Skull began walking slowly (nonchalantly he hoped, just another happy shopper) on his failing knees. The knees wanted to run. The knees said, "Come on!" The happy shopper said: browsing speed only.

"Matthew?" the Professor pondered thoughtfully. "Matthew, Matthew who? I don't know a Matthew, do I?" That's what he did, that's what the Prof did. Jon had felt it, Jac had felt it. He denied you; you were nothing to him, nothing special. Each time you had to justify your place in his presence. Each time. And inside that tick of doubt, he drew his strength.

Skull said tightly, "I need to speak to Jacqueline."

The Tunguska Man was moving too now, twenty yards behind, moving leisurely, following. But had he seen Skull come out of the QStore? And if the Tunguska Man was here, where was Habilis?

"Oh," said the Professor. "Oh, that Matthew." He dropped the old-duffer tone, substituting the more familiar, the more comfortable, sneer. "I suppose you'll want to speak with Jacqueline. Haven't you found my son yet?"

"I'm still looking," Skull said, but all he could see ahead of him, behind the arched sign of the Apple Market, was a fat caterpillar of shoppers bent on the task of eating itself. From deep inside this heaving coil the odd shred of humanity emerged, a morsel ejected, flushed and dazed, onto the square, but then drawn slowly back by a fatal gravity to circulate once again within the colourful thorax below which a thousand pairs of legs wriggled and jostled. There would be no quick way through that crowd.

"Good, Matthew. Good. Keep on looking. I do wonder, however, where you are looking? Are you looking in the right places?"

Skull veered right, threading a path through the stone columns into Central Avenue. Where was Habilis?

"I'm looking in all the places I know," he said. A rod of cold air rolled over the stone tiles and clattered along the narrow corridor lifting coats and jackets. People didn't linger here. Progress suddenly seemed possible, but he could sense rather than see the Tunguska Man bearing down, closing the gap. Skull quickened his pace.

"All the places you know?" the Professor crowed. "All the places you know? That's quite ridiculous. You should be looking in all the places he knows. Any fool would see that."

"Indeed." Skull remembered as he walked down the avenue that the shops opened on both sides, providing the opportunity to move rapidly over to the South Hall, perhaps lose the dark presence following. He bullied through a small family obstructing a narrow door, stepping into a hot, cramped shop and stood, momentarily bewildered. It was an odditorium for girly fantasies in pastel polymers.

"If he's hiding, why would he be in any of the places you know?" the Professor persisted.

"Quite," Skull conceded.

Bright plastic parlour-ware lined the shelves: lavender hair brushes, lilac compacts, languorous salmon-pink cats. Pushing rudely around a clump of grandparents Skull reached the door on the opposite side, yelling down the phone, "But I only know the places I know."

The sour woman behind the till called out, "Thank you," the peculiarly English form of irony ringing like an empty till. Skull closed the door gently on the disapproving stares behind him.

The choir was noticeably louder out here in the South Hall as, from the lower gallery, they began to build their laudatory chorus: *O come let us adore him.*

"Did you speak to the Polish carthorse? She knows something. She's got something to do with — Good God. What is that frightful noise? Where are you? In a church?"

"Covent Garden." The whole place smelled of pies.

"The Opera?"

"Market."

"Oh," The Professor was disappointed. "Jacqueline with you?"

"I thought she was with you."

People were moving slowly through the South Hall, looking for food, looking for the choir, looking to see what everyone else was looking at. The hall was split over two floors with the lower level gallery bisected by a central bridge. The narrow walkway on the upper level was slow moving as the crowds were squeezed between the shops on the one side and the railings around the lower galleries on the other.

"I like the smell of this one down 'ere," a woman yelled cheerily in his face. She had deep brown eyes and although she look at him she didn't see him. "Or'reet," came from behind, a slow, rural delivery out of place in the bustle and shove of urban people.

Up here were movers and watchers. Below were the eaters. Skull fell in behind the woman who had joined the slow stream of movers edging left along the gallery walkway. Bent over the railings were the watchers, peering down on the seated eaters below.

A profusion of over-sized yuletide plumage hung weightily over the galleries, spinning gently on the sharp through-breeze. There were feathery lights constructed from leg-long neon tubes, massive snowdrops glistening with golden glitter, shiny red baubles the size of wrecking balls hanging low and reflecting a crowd of short fat people in a grotesque comic landscape.

"The possibilities," the professor declared, "the possibilities seem as infinite as your joy when they are born, you know. It's an instinctive thing. Universal."

Skull's instinct was to descend, to find a hole he could hide in like an animal. He tucked in closer to the cheery loud woman who was forcing a path across the shuffling flow of movers, down towards the stairs that dropped to the lower floor where the eaters sat among the pies.

"And for each child you have, you feel this, no matter how many times you've done it before. You feel they could do anything, be anyone. It's a wonderful feeling; a wonderful connection that runs across the generations, across all time. Your parents will have felt it. Your children will have it too, if you ever have children. Not a homo, are you, Matthew? You know there was always a question. Not a gay, are you?"

Skull pushed up against the woman and followed her down the square stairs to the lower gallery, weaving around the counter-flow of movers moving up. Her progress was steadily slow as she dropped heavily from one step to the next; the laboured breathing of the farm lad was audible behind even above the noise of crowd and choir.

"Where is Jac?" Skull asked, looking up. They had reached the mid-point landing on the staircase where it turned at right angles towards the lower gallery. He didn't see the Tunguska Man at first, giving him a flutter of hope, a beat of relief. Then way back, behind the watchers at the railing, he saw him pushing his way relentlessly to the front.

"But then they grow up and the possibilities seem to fall away in heaps like costumes from the dressing up box. Sailor, tailor, tinker, you know, dropping off, one by one as they run to catch the world, and the world walks away over the horizon. Then all you have is the child and the empty box, so you have to ask yourself, could I have done more? Should I have done more? Did I do enough? Did I miss an opportunity, perhaps, to make a difference? Did I do too much?"

"Was Jac coming up to London?"

By the time Skull reached the bottom of the steps, the Tunguska Man had elbowed his way to the railing and was now one of the watchers leaning over, looking down, watching. They exchanged an impassive stare, but Skull could read nothing in the look: the man looked at him; he looked at the man.

"Or was there too much meddling?" the Professor continued, his voice strong and argumentative. "Too much interference? Or perhaps it's something in me? Something in my genes? Maybe, something in the mother's genes? Oh yes."

Skull turned hard left then left again away from the watchers above, away from the watched pie eaters below, making for the dark passage that led under the bridge between the downstairs galleries.

"Give children in Africa a second chance!" The man tried rattling a plastic box at Skull but there was no room to shake it so he settled for guilt: "It's Christmas for fuck's sake!"

"You can see it, you know," confided the Professor. "The little vanities, the pride, cupidity. All the things you spend a lifetime suppressing, there they are, seeping through the DNA, spoiling all the good genes. Like mould in a fruit bowl, everything gets corrupted, eventually. Look at me, Daddy, I'm so pretty. Look at you, Daddy, you're so selfish and bitter."

The passage under the bridge was congested, the exit dark with watchers shuffling like penguins in an arctic storm. Skull pushed a crooked path slowly through the blockage.

"But in the end, you know, it's nothing you might have done or might not have done. No. It's nothing you can really blame yourself for. I think it's simply that we shrink. As men — as man, you understand. It's a human condition. We shrink, the more we know."

No one could follow behind, and there were no watchers looking down from the railings above as Skull emerged into the second lower gallery. Here the choir were formed in a tight arc around the steps on the left. In the centre of the gallery was an open cafe with tables and chairs, crowded and serviced by grim waiters.

"I don't mean anything as trite as the platitude that the more we learn, the less we seem to know. God, no. What I mean is that the more we know, the smaller we become — the more we discover ourselves, the less significant we seem to be. To ourselves."

"Joy to the world, the Lord is come," the choir began with festive vigour, mouthing flamboyantly at their audience and nodding earnestly to punctuate the jubilation of their simple message.

Skull worked his way towards the far end of the gallery where the signage above an arch read EXIT.

"We are diminished by our knowledge, Matthew. I mean, a fool will aspire to anything," the voice persisted in his ear. "Look at you. But Jon is so bright, so naturally smart. He'll work things out. He simply needs time. That's all he needs. Just time."

Skull passed quickly below the brightly lit arch and started up the stairs which he knew would deposit him back onto the piazza opposite the Jubilee Market. From there it was a quick trot to Chandos Place off the Strand where he had left Gabby. (Since he had decided not to pay for the parking he could not afford, nor to worry about the fines he was never going to pay, he now found parking in London quite satisfactory. There were always plenty of spaces.) Halfway up the stairs he looked to the top, to the exit; staring down, the Tunguska Man.

Quickly Skull twisted to run back down the steps, escape back into the crowds below, but behind him on the stairs with his loopy, stupid grin was Habilis. Skull turned again to meet the Tunguska Man now skipping down the steps towards him, his hand moving slowly inside his jacket. This is it, thought Skull, this is it. How dumb. Gunned down, knifed, bludgeoned in this cold stairwell. Like a stupid gangster.

"All good, Morrell," said the Tunguska Man. "All good." Out of the pocket, offered between two stubby fingers, was the tiny SIM card. He paused on the steps, nodding briskly at Skull. Warily Skull plucked the SIM from the hand, noting clipped finger-nails, manicured cuticles.

"SIM. Is SIM, yes? From phone," Habilis explained, bobbing his head. "Sorry," he added with a sad cock of his head, pressing his wormy lips in a grimace of apology, as if he really meant it.

*

"Why," Jac wondered, "would he want to give you back your old SIM card? Surely it has no value now."

"They want to be my new best friends."

The British Museum is busy at all times of the day but now, as the day drew down, the visitors were beginning to thin, particularly in the upper rooms. Skull stared into a cabinet of ancient urns arranged in a natural group on a fake earthen floor, but he was really watching Jac, reflected in the glass of the cabinet. "They know I'm looking for Jon and they want to help me find him," he continued. "They believe Jon knows where Viktor is, and they want to find Viktor really badly."

"Did they say why?"

She wore jeans and a simple white top beneath her open jacket. The glass stripped away the years, smudging off the extra pounds, smoothing the tired lines around her mouth and eyes, returning the youth of alabaster to her cheeks, her neck. He felt again the thrill of standing next to the girl hoping to catch a whiff of hair, perhaps a glancing touch of hands, feel the heat of her body as she leaned closely in.

"Apparently a wealthy relative left him some money."

"Really?"

"Apparently."

"Did you believe them?"

"That's what they told me."

"How lucky for Viktor."

"Well, there's a problem."

"Oh?"

"Time is running out. If he doesn't claim the money before the end of the year he'll lose the lot."

"Why didn't they tell you that the first time you met? At Jon's flat?"

"I doubt they'd thought of it then."

"Do you think that they think that you believed them?"

"No. I think they know that I think that they don't think it really matters." He caught the twitch of her smile in the glass. "We all know it was just a story."

"Oh," she said, disappointed. "So they don't really want to be your best friend?"

"They have never seemed especially convivial."

"What did you tell them?"

"I said I'd think about it."

"Did they see you leaving the QStore?" she asked.

Was she gazing at him in reflection too? The dark, ancient objects inside the cabinet absorbed all the detail; he wasn't sure. "I don't know," he said. "They must have followed me somehow. It's too much of a coincidence that they were in Covent Garden. But I don't think they can know where Viktor works, otherwise they wouldn't have bothered offering to be my friend. They'd have gone straight in to find him."

"Oh God. Have you warned him?"

"I left a message at the store. He wouldn't give me a contact number."

A woman with a child sidled up to the display and started reading aloud the information on the labels. She read slowly and with excessive wonderment: "Charred, remains, of the various food stuffs, found in the scullery! Look! That's wheat, Mimi! And that's lentils! You like lentils too, don't you?" The child nodded, pulling faces at herself, ephemeral selfies in the glass reflection.

Jac moved on to the next cabinet; Skull followed. "Oh I do wish Daffyd would hurry up," she said.

Uncle Daffy was in a meeting. He didn't work at the museum but he was giving the lecture tomorrow and today was taking the opportunity to discuss project collaborations, student placements, and explore any possibilities for funding. Jac had planned to attend the lecture tomorrow but, she told Skull, there had been a change of plans. She hinted there had been some fractiousness at Churnwell House, a few plain words spoken. She didn't elaborate. Tomorrow she was due to fly back to Florence, anyway, back to other burdens, other obligations, but tonight she wanted to be free. One night off. Was that so bad?

When Skull had called her earlier on her mobile she was meandering through the galleries. Busman's holiday, she quipped to Skull, adding: "Besides, I like to see what they've done with the old place. Why don't you join me? I'm in Mesopotamia."

Skull wished he hadn't come now. He felt uncomfortable among all the fragile ancient things dug up from tombs and ruined temples. When he looked at them he saw only what they were: dusty pots in a cabinet, grim totems carved in stone, grey naked figurines formed in clay or forged in bronze. They seemed gloomy. They gave him no insights, nothing he could connect with.

He wanted to tell her that what had previously seemed incredibly fanciful was, well, credible. Jon was right: his smartphone probably was trying to kill him, although he would most likely be alright if he could make it through the next few days to Christmas. But Skull didn't know how to tell her this. There was a new quality to her, something different.

They moved on to the next display, more cracked amphora, more jugs on a dark earth bank.

"That's my life," she said, staring into the cabinet. She was being serious. "It's just like that. Old clay pots pieced together from a hundred scattered sherds and a rough idea of what it probably should look like." She tapped on the pane of glass with a finger nail. "Experiences, memories, thoughts — exhumed from an old tomb and arranged into something resembling something you can put on display."

Embarrassed, Skull snorted. "What about the labels?" he asked, realising too late his error of literalism, laughing stiffly to cover up.

"Well ..." Jac came slowly to rescue him, "the labels in an exhibition tell you what, and where and when and sometimes they even take a stab at who, but they very rarely say why. And you see how it's all so out of reach, out there, behind the low reflection display glass." Again she tapped a rhythm against the glass. "The only way you can change the display is to move along." Now she laughed. She said, "Sorry. I've had a couple of bad days at home. It's made me philosophical."

On Wednesday she had worked her way methodically through Jon's archive on *rewindr*, she told Skull. At first it was compelling, watching the sequence of clips and images; she hoped somehow it might help her re-connect with her brother. But soon she realised there was no guiding narrative, no thread, no theme, to bind the assemblage into a whole. She was left feeling empty, like a voyeur, watching the short fragmented cuttings, the random bulletins with abrupt endings and contextless beginnings; it was a grotesque montage of a life already fractured, unhappy, obsessive. There were brief moments — intimate, vulnerable moments, captured covertly and with no reason — which brought recognition, recalling to her their shared childhood. "But it was like looking at a stranger's life, even though at times the small boy I knew seemed at least a little familiar. I remembered him; I remembered us; we were not the happiest of families. I exaggerate of course: we were all bloody miserable."

For a little while more, Skull and Jac looked unseeingly at the *Bab edh-Dhra* tomb pots, then sidled on along the row — a new display, a new millennium, same sort of brown pots.

"People made these." She stood next to him, close now, her hair smelling of apples. "People just like us, people with worries, difficult relationships, things they regretted, things they longed for."

He stared at the bowls.

"When you look at these things," she said after a while, "don't you try and imagine the people who made them? Who were the people who used them? Not what they looked like or how they dressed, but how they loved, who annoyed them, what they looked forward to, what they worried about when they stirred their broth." She pouted at his reflection. "Maybe those are only our things. Perhaps for them life was more basic, more routine. Maybe there was just duty and service without the anger, or the longing. That would be nice. That would be so nice. Take me to dinner, Skull."

He hesitated fatally, silently counting his remaining cash, knowing he couldn't afford dinner. She turned away, moving on again.

"Sure," he said, catching her up. "Let's have dinner."

"I should go home. Daddy will crow; I told him I wasn't coming back. What a disaster."

"Don't go home," Skull said to the back of her neck where it bent towards Ishtar, Goddess of the Night, revealed in stone relief.

"Jacqui!" It was Uncle Daffy. "Jacqui, I thought you said I would find you in the Mesopotamia." A few residual visitors turned their heads, stared at the small, vital man as he strode through the gallery with all the confidence of ownership.

"Well, time marches on, Daffyd," she said as he arrived and they hugged, touched cheeks. "Babylon lost its lustre and we found ourselves migrating to the Levant. You remember Skull."

Uncle Daffy had ignored Skull but now no longer could. "Not so much. Remind me again?"

"Jon's friend. You remember." There was curl on her lips. "You met before — at Churnwell. Godwin Hill?"

"Godwin Hill? Oh my gosh. Were you with Andrew on the BSR visit? No?" Uncle Daffy's grip was still a handful of sinew and callouses but now, instead of the shaggy academic hair he sported a short, no-nonsense City haircut. He wore a beige suit without the tie, as if he had just stepped off the steamer from Algiers. "Well nice to meet you again, chap. Are you at my lecture tomorrow?"

"I hadn't really planned ...," Skull dithered politely.

"You must. You must come. You may find it interesting. In fact you might actually learn something. A quiet word Jaqui, darling? Excuse us a moment will you, chap."

Uncle Daffy led Jac a short distance away. Not tall enough to put an arm around her shoulders, he steered her by the elbow.

Skull sidled up behind a large glass cabinet containing the stone likeness of Idrimi, exiled and restored King of all Alalakh, under whose millennial gaze he peered at Jac. Uncle Daffy, he observed, was apologetic but firm, his gestures humble, his face a perfect picture of contrition. From Jac's expressionless face he could read nothing until at last she smiled, a delicate wince, before she and Uncle Daffy touched cheeks again.

"So long, chap. Hope to see you tomorrow, right," Uncle Daffy bellowed, pointing briskly at Skull as he passed by on his way out of the gallery. Skull nodded his response but Uncle Daffy was already transiting through Anatolia and Urartu.

"He's become too successful," said Jac, suppressing a peculiar secret grin on her lips. "There was a time when Daffyd would have jumped at the chance of having me stay the night at his London flat. He says he's going to be here in the museum a couple more hours. I think he's had a better offer. Probably some little PhD research *puttana*. Oh don't look so shocked, Skull. I was never going to fuck him. I just wanted a nice meal and a place to sleep for the night. I'm going home tomorrow."

"I've got a place for you to sleep," he said. "Stay with me. I'll take you to dinner, too."

She arched her brows, her dark eyes never looked darker. "Same deal?" she asked.

"Maybe."

"Maybe?"

Skull knew of a Thai restaurant nearby where they served a passable Lobster Pad Kiew Wan and where the ambience was intimate and the service discrete. There he would tell her about the Gold Star Boys, and his argument with Jon.

The Gold Star Boys

When Jon said his phone would kill him I admit I laughed out loud. It was the funniest thing I had heard in a long time, although in my defence I was tired and somewhat under pressure.

I'm a professional. I know how hard it is to integrate components when you mean them to be integrated, so the idea of some rogue application operating intelligently on its own and actually interacting with the real world autonomously seemed ... well, fanciful, to say the least.

Wind back a little. Immediately after returning from Stockholm the outlook for Smartor had looked hopeful. Some people I'd been in touch with in London knew people in Stockholm who were well connected; so they connected me to the connected people and it turned out that the connected people were a consortium of manufacturers in the motor industry. Not actual car makers, you understand, but companies who depended on car makers, companies whose clients made cars. They were parts makers, designers, consultants, specialists. They called themselves BläsHög, and they loved my presentation, loved the demo, asked all the right challenging questions. We brainstormed, white-boarded, shared strategic thoughts, and after a few days I went home with a funding proposal, subject to the agreement of my partners and the approval of our lawyers.

Simon was all, "Fuck yeah! When will the cunts give us our fucking money?"

Our lawyer said, "Hang on a sec."

We couldn't hang on. We had been particularly stupid and had nothing to hang on to. Against all advice we'd thrown our own money into the company sink hole, our own assets, savings, debts, even our relationships. Our problem, of course, was cash flow — the crooked hand that choked a thousand startups. We were late paying our creditors.

One of the consortium was based in Stuttgart so over the next couple of months I flew a desperate triangle between London, Stockholm and Stuttgart but eventually we signed, as they knew we would. They released the first tranche of money immediately and we paid our priority bills — the web service, the rent, electricity. Next, BläsHög brought in their advisers, and with the second tranche we paid off most of our developers, our sales, our admin staff. It seems the death throttle was lifted just as the knife was slipped between our ribs.

So Jon and I hadn't been in touch since the dinner party in Docklands. Of course I'd followed his wedding updates on the social sites; I'd liked and shared the honeymoon pictures, but we'd both been busy and, as you know, our get-togethers were never a set thing. I was pretty much ignoring everyone at that time.

Anyway, one evening he calls me up at home to ask how he could easily set up data streaming from his connected tooth. He reported an odd tingling sensation in the tooth when it connected to the phone. He thought it might be the data streaming through his tooth. I told him he was imagining it.

"Well I'm getting the data into Lucy," he said, "but it's a hand job. There's an upload, and then it's a cut-and-paste to a spreadsheet for a gentle massage to something usable. What I really need is an app of some sort."

He wanted to know if that was something I could do for him. I laughed. I was working eighteen hour days and still not clearing my backlog.

"Thought so," he said. "Long shot. Just thought if I could get the best, screw the rest. Worth a try."

Now he wondered, should he have a go at it himself? And what did I think of his chances? Poor, I told him. Then maybe I knew someone who could do it for him? He said he didn't mind paying for it, in fact it might even make a nice little niche investment. He thought he might call it BlueTooth Squared, he said.

That's when I asked him for the money. I regret it now, but at the time it was one of those spur-of-the-moment things, the idea blowing into my mind like a sudden squall, the words spilling out, instantly regretting it. Not very clever.

"You always wanted to invest in Smartor," I said. "Now would be a good time."

Now was a really bad time. BläsHög had bought themselves onto the board and were pushing their agenda. They brought in their own consultants, hard-faced Danes and bearded Germans. They suggested a pivot. Simon took the bait. Pivoting is a big deal in the start-up world and he liked the idea, it sounded cool. They said scale down our ambitions. I said follow the vision, Simon said follow the money and Keith just followed whoever spoke to him last. BläsHög held the purse strings and by now I knew what they were really after, but I was playing for time and the sum I mentioned to Jon would give me only a few days, a week at best. My thinking was that if Jon was throwing cash about, why not toss a little in my direction? I regretted it immediately. He said he'd think about it. I quickly changed the subject.

"How's the fitness programme working out?" I asked him. "When are you going pro?"

He said, "Well, since the crash, I've been going a bit slower."

"What crash?" I asked, adding "Are you alright?"

"Not me," he said. "It was all over the news. Didn't you hear?"

There'd been a tragic accident. The Gold Star Boys, his Nigerian fitness-shadowing team were returning by air from a game in the north of the country when in the final approach to Lagos airport both engines shut down due to mechanical fault or pilot error or sabotage — the cause was yet to be determined. There were no survivors.

"All of them?" I asked.

"I thought you knew. I thought I'd told you."

It was news to me. Emily, during one of our many arguments, had accused me of logging out of our social life. This was evidence, I supposed, of the kind of thing she meant.

Before I rang off I gave him the names of a couple of the developers we had laid off who I thought might be interested in helping him with his tooth sensor project.

It was less than a week later he visited me in my office. I wasn't expecting him. Someone let him in downstairs and he found his way to my desk in the cavernous open space office we could no longer afford. It was early evening but I still had a day's work to finish. Earlier my database guy had walked out, and I had argued with Keith, which nobody ever did because he really was not argumentative. Simon and I were not speaking. Nobody at Smartor was happy. But any day was a bad day to catch me.

"Need some advice," he said. "Time for a swift pint?"

"No." I wanted him to go away. I very nearly said "go away", but I left it at "no" and let the uncomfortable silence spread.

"I think I might be in some kind of trouble," he said at last. He looked haggard, heavy, as if he wasn't sleeping well, not looking after himself.

"Is it Anka?" I asked, perhaps too eagerly.

"No." He seemed surprised. "Why would it be Anka?"

"Just asking." I shrugged. "So?"

Now that he had my attention he didn't seem able to speak. He looked around the office. Our numbers had thinned considerably since he was last there, but almost everyone still working for us had already left for the evening. A couple of desks away, my last remaining programmer was gazing impassively into his screens, hunting a pernicious bug I hoped, but probably updating his LinkedIn profile. On the other side of the room, Simon was folded over his elbows having a low, intimate telephone conversation, giggling stupidly from time to time; loud enough for me to hear.

Jon lowered himself into the chair of the desk next to mine. "You remember the football team I was shadowing?" he finally managed.

I nodded. "The Golden Boys."

"Gold Star Boys."

"Right. They were killed in an accident. You told me. Tragic."

"Right. Right. Well I was shadowing them through this web site —"

"You told me."

"And there's a bunch of metrics — some basic age-adjusted measures for fitness that the web app uses, like heart rate, blood pressure, body fat, VO2max." He looked at me, misunderstanding my irritable grimace, explaining: "VO2max is a measure of the amount of oxygen your body uses when you're going flat out. It's not important."

"Indeed. Stick with the important bits, then." Perhaps I raised my voice, because across the office Simon looked up, looked my way.

"So I was shadowing the Gold Star Boys' average ...," he paused in a significant way.

"I understand that bit. You told me that already. Since they're all dead, I presume you can no longer shadow them."

"Well, yes. That would seem to be blindingly obvious," he said. "The team average has now zeroed because it seems that even their injured players, who weren't even playing, went along to support the team. They were also — you know."

"Can you choose another team?" I asked, mastering my impatience. "I'd do that. There must be other teams to choose from. I don't understand why you didn't choose a pro team anyway. A cycling team would have been better, surely."

Simon swivelled his chair around so that he faced crotch-forward towards me, his light grey suit jacket open, breaking around his little pot belly. He was talking about me. I knew he was talking about me from the way he sneered.

I said, "Let's get a coffee," and Jon followed me to the break-out room.

"Of course there are other teams," Jon said while I rinsed a couple of mugs, filled the kettle and checked the fridge for any milk that still poured, "but none of them are professional European sports teams, because they don't need the money. The whole point of the programme was mutual benefit. Anyway, the point is, although I'm shadowing on the FitCast site, I also set a SMART goal through Lucy."

The expensive coffee maker had long ago packed up from over use and misuse. In any event the break-out room had never been the hub of creative interaction that was promised. Now it was simply yet another squalid place, a refuge for the disconsolate, a chapel for the miserable.

"D'you want milk?" I asked. The milk was off.

He ignored me, or didn't hear me. "I set a goal, Skull" he said, "I set a SMART goal. The goal was to match the mean fitness level of the Gold Star Boys by this Christmas." He gave me another look, the significance of which went right past me.

"Early Christmas for you then," I said. "They're dead. Even I would be fitter than they are."

"No. You're not getting it. I didn't set the goal to exceed their levels. If I had set the goal to exceed their fitness levels, I would be fine. What I locked in was a goal to match the average, to be equal to. So Lucy is telling me to match it."

I laughed; well it was funny. "What does she say? Die, bastard, die?"

"Not quite," he replied tightly. "But it amounts to the same thing." He pulled out his red phone and requested a status update on the fitness-shadowing goal.

Hi Jon Fast, came the familiar tinned voice. *Current success factor is one-two point eight-four percent, falling from one-six point two-two percent at Seventeen Fifty Three hours today. Current prediction is: Fail. Suggestion: Immediate Cessation.*

"A somewhat long-winded way of saying end the goal," I said. "Just delete it."

"You can't," he replied. "You can't delete a goal." He sat up on a bar stool, tentatively sipped at the hot, black coffee I'd placed on the shelf before him. "Isn't there any milk?" he asked. He pulled a face, put the coffee down, continued. "Once Lucy accepts a goal she keeps going until either the goal is achieved or the date has passed. It doesn't mean cessation of the goal, Skull. It means cessation of me."

"That's lame," I said. And that was the full extent of my professional assessment. It offended me that an application did not provide a function for the user to cancel or amend. "Two options then," I said. "One, ignore the suggestion. Two, un-install Goald. Or three, throw the phone away. Personally I think that's your best option. It's such an old phone now anyway."

He stared into his coffee as if deciding whether to drink it or spit in it. "I have a friend," he began, "whose wife was recently murdered."

Of course I realise now that he was telling me Deepak's story, but he never mentioned Deepak by name. I was only half listening anyway because at that moment Simon strolled into the break-out room.

Simon looked at me, looked at Jon, raised a satirical eyebrow, found a small satisfied smirk for his lips, sauntered over to the kettle. Jon paused briefly in his tale, looked at me, then carried on while Simon slowly went about brewing himself a mug of tea, pretending to pretend he was invisible.

Simon lifted the kettle, waggled it, popped open the lid and peeped inside. He added a little fresh water, switched the kettle on. He found a tea-stained mug on the draining board, bent to the sink, rinsed the mug slowly under running water, rubbing around the rim. He shook the drops off. He found a box of tea-bags, selected a bag with a paper tag attached on the end of a string, unwrapped the string, lowered the bag into the mug, leaving the tag hanging over the side. He stared into the maw of the mug, tapping a rhythm on the counter top with his two index fingers like drumsticks. The kettle boiled. He poured the hot water into the mug which pulled the tag over the side into the hot water. With a finger he hooked the tag and string from inside the mug, leaving the now sodden tag hanging over the side once again. He shuffled over to the fridge, brought the milk carton to the mug and poured. The milk came out in blobs, plopping into the brown water, splashing over the side. He returned the carton to the fridge. He loomed over his mug, dunking the bag on the string, one, two, three times among the floating curds. Carefully he deposited the bag in the sink. Then he left, bearing his mug before him like a vicar with a psalter.

Jon had long since finished his tale and sat in silence watching me watch Simon, waiting for my response. "So?" he asked.

"So what?" I said. "What do you want from me, Jon? Throw the phone away if it's worrying you. There's nothing I can do."

"I was hoping you could take a look at it for me," he said evenly.

"Like I've got the time," I said, picking up my mug of coffee and heading back to the office.

"I know you're busy with other things," Jon said when we regained my desk, sitting down back where we had started. Across the room, Simon was on the phone again, slowly swivelling from side to side in his chair like a shark moving through water. "But there must be a way of stopping it."

"You'd think," I said. In silence we each waited for the other to speak first, although I was also holding Simon in the corner of my eye.

"I can't throw Lucy away, Skull. She's the better part of me. Everything I have, everything that's important, has come from her. To her I confide my aspirations and she realises them for me, suggesting, advising, guiding and now, more and more, doing whatever is needed. She wakes me in the morning, she nudges me through the day, and soothes me to sleep at night; she books appointments and orders cabs to deliver me on time; she buys stock, sells stock, moves money. She anticipates every need I have, ensures my life runs like a Teutonic railway system. All the mundane things, all the boring chores, now taken care of, and I am freed up for the greater appreciation of higher things. I find I don't even need will power now. I have Lucy power. I do what she says and it all turns out well. I trust her and she holds me to my promises, keeps me on the track of all the things I should be doing. She's made an honest man of me, Skull."

Slowly Simon sat upright, pulling across a pad of paper, writing, nodding. He wasn't smiling now. He shot a glance in my direction; looked away.

"Thing is," Jon continued, "she won't undertake a project if there's a whiff of fantasy in it. You can have a desire but not a dream, you can have a want but not a wish. You can build a tower of fancies as high as the clouds but it must have that thick copper cable running down to the ground. A goal has to be SMART, remember; specific, measurable, achievable, relevant, timely."

Simon dropped the handset back on the cradle of the telephone, pondered briefly, scribbled a line on the pad. Then he laid down his pen, tore the top leaf from the pad and folded it carefully, sliding it into his jacket pocket.

"So now I don't dream," Jon said. "I don't make wishes. I plan only the things that can be named. I set targets. I have objectives for things that can be weighed, evaluated, counted, measured, timed. The things I want are the things I can define, things that are easily within my horizon of capabilities, things that fit inside a narrow cone of time. It's a solid, material reality, Skull, ruled by simple logic. Simple, relentless logic. But you know all this. It's your world, Skull. Our tools shape us, remember? Just as we shape them."

"Throw the phone away," I told him.

On the other side of the office Simon pushed his mouse and keyboard up flush with the base of the screen, reached across the desk and switched the screen off. He opened his briefcase and placed his writing pad and pens in it so that his desk was clear. Simon is surprising fastidious about his work space.

Jon said, "I don't want to get rid of Lucy, Skull. I don't want to sink back into what I was before. I didn't like the analogue me — it was messy and chaotic. I like myself better now. If I get rid of her I could lose everything. I could even lose Anka and I love Anka, Skull. Anka has no sides. What you see is what she is. That's why I love her."

Anka has no sides because she's round, I wanted to tell him, but instead I said, "Stop reporting your metrics. The phone is a tool. It will stop if it has no data."

"It's not about the data," Jon said. "It's about the logic, isn't it? I know you don't believe me, Skull, but just for a minute, please, acknowledge that it's possible."

"No," I said. "It's nonsense. There's a boundary: virtual, real; real, virtual."

"But what if there is a way for it to cross that boundary?"

"Then I'll look stupid," I said.

"And I'll be dead," he said. I shrugged. He looked at me a long time before he went on. "You know it's possible. You told me yourself. You've even got a driving app that can drive your car."

"It doesn't drive the car."

"You said it did."

"It provides access to the controls. A person still drives it. What you're talking about is an independent intelligence. Not possible. Not in a phone app. It's a trick, a slight of hand, to make you think it's smart."

Simon, as he left the office, cast a final look my way. He had found his superior smile again, adding a jaunty whistle as he pushed open the doors. I could hear the whistle echoing all the way up the stairwell as he descended.

"Please help me, Skull. You're the only person I know who's technical enough to help me."

"I'm not qualified to give you the kind of help you need," I told him.

If he registered the insult he didn't show it. "I've tried reaching Goald's creators," he said, "but they don't answer. I've left messages and contact details but they don't get back."

We sat in silence. Finally he said, "So you're not able to help me."

It wasn't a question but a statement. I read it as an accusation. "Why should I help you?" I said, "Why should I help you when you wouldn't help me?"

"What do you mean?" he frowned. "What do you mean I didn't help you?"

"For years you've been begging me for the opportunity to put money into Smartor. I gave you that chance, remember? Now suddenly you're all coy."

"That?" He waved his hand, a swatting motion. "I wanted to invest, Skull; but you're a bad risk. I can't do it. If it was just me, well ... I can't. You're a bad risk."

"It's short term. It's just short term. Anka doesn't understand how these things work," I said.

"It's not Anka," he said.

"She hates me."

"It's not Anka, it's Lucy, you idiot. I can't make her invest in you."

"It's your money," I sneered but he merely shrugged. "Our friendship means nothing?"

"It's a lot of money, Skull. It's business."

"Not to me," I told him, gesturing at the empty office. "I've put everything into this. Everything I have. Even everything I don't have."

"You're not living in a box yet. You've still got your flat," he pointed out.

"Fuck you."

It was a shoddy little scene, two grown men jousting profanities. My lonely developer a few desks down quickly un-ravelled his headphone, pushing them firmly over his head, poking the plug end into his laptop.

We had argued many times before, Jon and I, and our friendship had flexed with it. This was a fracture, a violent break. Oh, there was nothing more physical than a piercing glare and an air-stabbing finger, but it was a death match all the same. I suppose when you're so much a part of someone's life, you're already inside them. There are no defences in those circumstances, and so there is no quarter.

When there was nothing else to say he left and I watched him all the way to the door, his back as rigid as the MDF boards on our office desks. I left soon after.

Thursday Night

The flat was cold and dark with only a gaunt grey light from the street coming in through the far window. The light switch clicked dryly when Skull toggled it on, off, on.

"Not unexpected," Skull explained to Jac. "I haven't paid a bill in months."

He made his way across to the kitchen using his smartphone screen to throw a flat bubble of light ahead of him. In the kitchen he tested taps.

"Good news: water's still on," he said over the gentle gurgle of the drain. A sibilant hush from the stove told him that gas too, still flowed. He had water and gas, but without electricity to drive the pump there was no central heating, and no hot water. Jac stood quietly in the doorway.

"Hang on," he called, scrabbling through a kitchen drawer, finding an old box of safety matches. One by one he lit the gas rings on the stove, turning up the blue jets until orange flames flickered, licking his face in a warm primitive light and throwing his long, dark shadow onto the walls.

"Well that's something," he said staring into the flame. "Never say die. I'll drive you home. It's too late for a train."

"Why?" she said lightly, coming into the kitchen. "There's water and heat. What more do we need?"

Light, thought Skull, we need light. He dived below the counter into the long cupboard beneath, pulling out pots and bowls and plates until he found, mostly by touch, the forgotten box of tea-light candles Emily had bought when she still believed that romance was the natural gilding to love and came out in the same way that juices seep from a roasting joint.

Soon he had a large pot of water warming on the stove and bowls of tea lights dotted around the room like campfires on a hillside.

The knock on the front door rattled up the stairs.

"Ignore it," Skull said. "It'll be Simon again. There's nothing to say." Jac packed another cereal bowl with tea lights and Skull took it upstairs along with her suitcase. In the master bedroom he turned the valence sheet over on the bed and hung the car blanket over the window to block out the cold night light from the street. In the spare bedroom he made up a bed for himself using a heap of his clothes which he brought in armfuls from the main bedroom.

"Let's have tea," he suggested when he returned; it sounded so prosaic. "Or what about a bath?"

She laughed encouragingly so he filled more pots with water, putting them on the stove to boil. The room began to warm.

Jac made green tea and told him an anecdote about a power failure which had happened while she was in the basement archive of the museum where she worked. This was before the advent of smartphones, she said, and she had groped her way around boxes of mummies and shrunken heads, becoming hopelessly lost before the lights went on again. Nobody had thought to rescue her. Skull laughed but she told him she still had nightmares.

Skull began to carry pots of steaming water up the stairs pouring them into the large bath into which he also threw a handful of bath salts, making a steaming heap of bubbles.

"Your bedroom is ready," he told her. "And you're about three pots short of a decent bath." Jac went upstairs.

The knocking started again, this time louder, on the inner door.

Mr Beavis stood on the threshold wrapped in a short silk kimono with a dark swirling pattern; below the hemline spindle feet plugged into leather sandals.

"Did you not hear the knocking, Matthew?" On the narrow stairs behind and below Mr Beavis, Mr Twydle looked up, presenting a grave face. A large fleshy plaster straddled the bridge of his nose. A mottled maroon crescent hung like a bladder of poison below one eye, the other edged in a jaundiced yellow.

"It's late," Skull said.

"Is there something wrong with your doorbell?"

"Yes."

"We need to speak," Mr Twydle called, squinting up at Skull. There was room only for Mr Beavis on the landing.

"At this time?"

"May I come in?" he asked. He was struggling with his swollen nose, his ems and ens baffled by the blockage: *Bay I cub id*, is actually what came out.

"What happened to your nose?"

"Nose? What do you mean? Oh that." He touched his nose gently. "I got mugged." *Bugged* he said, which momentarily confused Skull.

"I'm sorry."

"Oh, it's OK," said Mr Twydle, "they didn't take anything. Mistaken identity. I need to come in."

"You are in," Skull said, standing his ground.

"Is there something wrong with your lights, Matthew?" Mr Beavis asked, peering past him into the room.

"Yes."

"I'm sorry about Simon," Mr Twydle said, his voice pinched as his neck strained upwards.

"What about Simon?"

"About the accident."

"What accident?"

"The car accident. Oh dear. You hadn't heard? Oh dear, I thought you would have heard."

"Heard what?"

"Oh dear. Perhaps I should come in."

"What's the news, Twydle?"

"There is some very bad news, I'm afraid. Very bad. You should know about it." Mr Twydle was uncomfortable, upset by the cramped intimacy of the dark stairwell, not wishing to unload his bad news without due ceremony. Eventually he said, "I am so very sorry to tell you."

"What? Tell me what?"

"Simon Betterson is dead."

"Oh no," murmured Mr Beavis. "Oh no. Oh dear."

Skull was struck by the very formality of the statement. Simon Betterson is dead. He heard the words, understood what they meant, but thought that he felt nothing — they were, after all, just words bluntly spoken, floating up from the well of the stairs, unable to penetrate far through the monotonous hiss of the gas stove's endless exhalation in the dark room behind him.

"I'm very, very sorry," Mr Twydle said again. "I should come in."

Is he very sorry that Simon is dead, or very sorry that he had to tell me about it? Skull thought. What did it mean? For sure it was one less thing for him to worry about. No more ambushes with a baseball bat, for a start. No more abusive phone calls. All the same it seemed improbable that such a loud, foul mouth might be stopped so suddenly, the rich flow of obscenities cease.

"Is that the man with the kiddies?" asked Mr Beavis. "Is Simon the one with the kiddies?"

"Kiddies?" said Mr Twydle.

"Yes," Skull answered Mr Beavis. "Those were Simon's children." There was a likable side to Simon that he couldn't now remember. It was a side few saw, and seldom saw. Simon's likable side was not his key strength. When you thought of Simon you remembered only the fuck-you glare and the fuck-me laugh, the flat slap of a word-stream rimmed with fucks and cunts.

"I didn't know," said Mr Twydle, his eyes wet from the strain of staring up at Skull through the remnants of the violence visited on his face. "I didn't know he had kiddies."

"How?" Skull asked.

"How? Oh, how. A car accident. Car crash."

"Yes — a car crash — you already said a car crash. But how?" Skull insisted.

"Drove off the road. Straight off the road. At some considerable speed, by all accounts. There was a fire. Terrible fire. Terrible. Apparently."

"And the kiddies?" said Mr Beavis.

"There was obviously some kind of malfunction," Mr Twydle added loudly.

"What about the kiddies?"

"What kiddies?"

"The man's kiddies." Mr Beavis was almost shouting. "He had children. Where are the children?"

Mr Twydle winced. "There was no mention of children," he said. "Simon was the only fatality, according to the information I have. This was yesterday. I really thought you'd know. It came in through the Smartor offices. Can I come in? I really should come in."

How typical of Simon to be loud and rude right to the end. Why not a quiet country lane, a little Amy Winehouse and a length of hose-pipe? Why use the car at all? Betty was invaluable, stuffed with advanced electronic sensors and a shockingly expensive sound system. Was he too good for a sudden leap from a suspension bridge, a swift blade in a motel bathtub? He was making a statement, of course. Sending a stupid message.

Mr Twydle was continuing: "The good thing is that he was probably killed outright. By the impact. He wouldn't have suffered in the fire at all. I mean that's not really a good thing, but you know what I mean. A comfort to know, although I understand Mrs Betterson has not taken the news at all well, by all accounts. Not well at all. Sad, sad news. We must talk, Matthew."

"Who's looking after the kiddies? Is anyone looking after the kiddies?" Mr Beavis asked, then "Jeezus!" he hissed, shaking his head when Mr Twydle only shrugged and shook his.

Mr Twydle continued, "The reason I know all this is because the police contacted Smartor. All the calls now are routed through my firm, you know. The car is still registered as a Smartor asset. We spoke about this. We need to manage this, Matthew. There will be an investigation. Naturally you must return all other vehicles so they can be examined by the proper authorities."

"What other vehicles?"

"Come now Matthew. Let me in. Let's talk this through. The vehicles you stole from Smartor. You must return them now. Before anyone else gets hurt."

"You can leave now before you get hurt. Again," Skull added.

"There are serious questions now about the safety of those vehicles on the road, Matthew."

"The only question that needs to be asked is whether the muppets you brought in when you stole my company have been pushing out bad code to the vehicle control systems."

"Oh come now. That's not even possible. Is it? Is that possible?" Mr Twydle blinked hard, dislodging a tear from his venomous eye which, skidding down his cheek, plunged into the dark fabric of his coat.

"Don't call here again," Skull said, swinging the door.

"Stop before you kill anyone else, Matthew," Mr Twydle shouted. "You are a danger to everyone."

Skull closed the door. Almost immediately there were a series of taps.

"It's only me," came from the other side. Skull opened the door again.

"Will the kiddies be alright?" Mr Beavis asked, his face a prune of worried frowns.

"I'm sure they'll be looked after."

Caught halfway down the stairs Mr Twydle turned sharply. "You're a danger to yourself and the public, Matthew."

"I couldn't bear to know," said Mr Beavis. "I couldn't bear it."

Skull closed the door once again, returning to the kitchen. Steam rose furiously from the pots on the stove, a thick mist coating the ceiling with fat droplets of condensation. He lifted off the largest pot and bore it carefully up the stairs, shouldering aside the half-open bathroom door.

"I was cold. I couldn't wait," she said from the bath tub. Her naked body was a formless mass wreathed in a froth of heavy golden bubbles, opaque below the foamy surface. Her black hair, loosely twisted and pinned in a choppy sea of curls heaped on her crown, exposed her pale neck as she lifted her face, her salmon lips, towards him. "Pour that in down there," she smiled, raising her knees from the waters, creating a space at the end of the bath.

The tide streamed out, the tide streamed in, an oily cascade first laying bare her breasts — two pale creatures stranded on a fragile shore — then, gently on the inward surge raising and flooding them with a soft and glittering crema quilt.

He emptied in the contents of his pot, misting his glasses as clouds billowed up from the bath.

"Oooh," she said. "That's lovely. What was all that about downstairs?"

"Nothing," he said.

"Is everything alright?"

"It's fine. I'll get the other pots."

He stumbled down the stairs and quickly poured the boiling water from the smaller pans into the larger pot until it brimmed and spilt over. When he returned she had rolled onto her belly, the lambent promontories of her broad buttocks glistening in the fickle candlelight, headlands on a semi-sunken island where the shallow waters slickly lipped on lower shores and through the darker valleys licked.

"This is the very heaven," she said. "You should try it."

He said, "I'll follow you."

"In my old water? Eeuw," she gurgled. "It's a big bath, Skull. Room for two."

She did not watch him as he swiftly, silently, removed his clothing, nor did she cede him space as carefully he stepped into the wide flat bath and slid down close behind her.

In the low light of many candles her body floated magically, borne below a bed of spume, a subtle undulation of skin and oil, sleek to touch, slow to yield, like caramel. They lay contentedly a while, moulding to each other's curves, fold on fold, their contours merging, pressing up for more warmth than the waters held. Their touching turned to stroking, to caressing, holding, cupping, guiding. In the warm lubricious lather love was easy, fluid, like runny toffee. No words no voice disturbed the urgent burble of rippling lapping slapping waves.

When the heat had gone and the bath grown cold, they dried each other quickly and slipped into the bed upstairs.

Friday

When Emily returned to the flat she let herself in with her own keys and, from habit, hung the bunch on the wall-hook adjacent to the inner door. It was not yet passed mid-morning; the winsome sun struggled with a leathery grey sky.

Below the hook, against the wall, she set down her sports holdall. Inside the holdall her gym kit, rolled up neatly in a plastic bag, was still damp and still warm from her spin class at the local gym where she was a member. The bag also housed a few overnight things — a toothbrush, some creams and potions, a nightie, a change of underwear — in case she encountered Skull, in case they talked things over, in case she decided to stay.

She frowned at the dispersal of crockery around the room, puzzled by the melted scraps of burnt-out tea-light candles. She tutted at the empty pots on the stove, the open cupboard doors below the sink, the near-empty box of candles on the draining board. Opening the fridge door she expected to register disgust but was all wide-eyed surprise when the light did not come on. She reached inside to feel but wasn't sure of the temperature because she herself was still warm from her workout, and the whole flat felt cold now she came to think of it. She crossed to the radiator, feeling the surface tentatively with the back of her hand before touching it with her fingers, pulling a funny face, raising her eyes to the ceiling. She flicked a light switch on and off a few times, watching the lifeless bulb.

"Oh Matty," she whispered, shaking the wisps of fine blond hair and pouting her plump red lips. She climbed the stairs, glancing in at the bathroom, noting with disappointment the tubful of cold scummy water, the discarded pot, the heap of clothing, the sodden bath mat.

When Emily pushed open the bedroom door she saw Jac who saw her too. In the momentary exchange of looks no data was transmitted but all the important information was passed, everything that should be known was shared and understood. It was difficult but not complicated: Skull lay belly-down beneath the plump duvet, his body half spread across Jac, blissfully abandoned to the stupidity of sleep, his face at rest towards her, eyes closed, lips a gentle curlicue.

No words were said. On her way out Emily paused at the door only to pick up her holdall.

*

Much later, Skull went out for breakfast.

He had woken when Jac rose from the bed to make a dash for the bathroom. Instantly he snuggled deeper into the wide, warm patch she had left, relishing her lingering heat, breathing deeply the hot perfume of her smell. When she returned she was already half dressed and he watched in silence as she continued the process.

"I'm sorry," she said.

"For what?"

"I have to go." She didn't look at him. "I'm sorry."

"Don't go then. Let's spend the day in bed and keep each other warm. We could tell each other all the things we told each other last night, all over again. We could make another bath, go out for dinner, lets —"

"It's cold." She continued to dress quickly.

"I have jerseys. Wear a jersey. Wear two jerseys."

With an ancient reflex built on habit he reached first for his spectacles on the platform beside the bed, then for his phone laid out on the charging pad. He clicked it on — nothing. Overnight the phone had died, the battery flattened, un-recharged. Without the flicker of light, without the haptic animus of a greeting buzz, it filled his hand as a mere rect-angular thing, a mute stone. I'm disconnected, he mused; no one can update me, no one knows my status.

The device was smeared with finger grease and thumb prints, lardy whorls against the dark screen. He wiped it on the duvet, cleansing it, staring at the shiny, silent, flat block, turn-ing it over, feeling the cold hard curves of plastic, metal, glass. As he looked, really looked, his own face sprang up, reflected inside the tough glass and framed in the void between the black bezel edges where the information flows through. He was surprised: I don't look unhappy.

"I don't do this," Jac said miserably.

"But I'm glad you did; I'm so glad we did." She was trembling as she dug in her suitcase for her vanity case, returning to the bathroom. "Jac."

He rose, dressed. "I'll get us breakfast," he shouted through the bathroom door. There was a cafe on the high road that brewed a tolerable coffee and made an egg-and-bacon butty that could keep you going all day. "Go downstairs. It'll be warmer downstairs. I'll be back in ten minutes with food."

Downstairs it was warmer than upstairs, but still cold. He felt energy bubbling through him like juice from a steak. He lit a match and switched on the gas stove, but after a short hiss it went quiet. The gas had gone too.

Leaving the flat, he forgot to check the road outside from the window, descending the steps rapidly, puzzled that he hadn't previously noticed Emily's keys on the key hook, then trying not to think about Emily.

"Do you not answer your door bell?" Viktor dropped into step beside him, hands buried deep inside his jacket pockets, hoodie pulled firmly over his head against the cold. Only now

Skull turned about, looking for the hidden ambusher, the silent watcher. "Also your phone — I tried calling a few times," Viktor added.

The street was clear.

"What are you doing here?"

"I had an idea."

"Strangely that doesn't fill me with joy," said Skull.

"I am serious," Viktor insisted. "I think it should be possible to kill connected instances of Hydra. I took a look last night in the codebase, and it seems Dimi had most of the problems solved. It's still pretty raw. Needs a few tweaks, but — where are we going?"

"I'm going for breakfast."

"Excellent! I'm starving."

*

Jac was gone when Skull returned to the flat with breakfast and with Viktor. Skull called out her name, then ran upstairs but she was definitely gone. A note on the bed read: *I am glad. J.* He folded the note, sliding it into his trouser pocket before returning to the living room where Viktor was already perched at the breakfast bar, eating breakfast.

"Is it cold or is it just me?" Viktor asked, biting into the overstuffed sandwich with the accomplishment of one whose skill comes from studied practice, a technique allowing him to gain the full benefit of the bursting egg yolk, dripping none of the yellow goodness. "This is really good butty," he said out the side of his mouth, adding, "I'm surprised you're not more fat."

"I have to go out again soon," Skull said.

Had he done something wrong? Said something? Or had he failed to say or do something that he should have? There had been nothing in their lovemaking to suggest anything other than pleasure, a mutual desire, the fulfilment of an old, shared longing.

"So what's your idea?" he asked Viktor as he sat down and began to attack his own breakfast.

"My idea," said Viktor, "is to run Hercules, kill the Hydra, go home."

"You said it was incomplete."

"I had a look last night. It needs some tweaking."

"Why's it taken you this long?"

"I've been off-radar. More than two years. No Facebook updates for Mom, no Snapchats for friends, no postcards to old girlfriends. No old life, nothing. I am Marcus: sales specialist from Czech Republic."

"I thought you said you were Lithuanian?"

"Estonia, actually. But my ID says Czech, so ..." He shrugged.

"So why aren't you a Quince Maven?" Skull asked, unable to prevent the sneer in his voice. Mavens were supposedly technical experts, helping Quince customers with their technical problems. "You could work shifts with all the other Mavens in the Maven Tavern?"

Viktor laughed. "It would be tempting to show off. But they're all nice guys. Really." He sucked his fingers with relish as he went on: "So I was too scared to revisit code-base before. I thought Dimi may have been forced to give logins, passwords ... I would've." He looked at his wet fingers. "They cut his off, you know. One by one." He curled his own fingers suddenly into a fist, pulling away from the image before going on. "Anyway, you don't know who might be monitoring the repository logs, so I stayed away from it. Listen: is your friend coming back? Are you going to eat that?" He pointed to Jac's bacon sandwich quietly seeping greases into the brown paper packet.

"She's not coming back," Skull said. She had left in a hurry to avoid him, of course. Why? He couldn't understand it. He felt the note in his pocket: *I am glad.* Perhaps it wasn't about him at all.

"Half each?" Viktor beamed as he tore open the packet. Skull poured the contents of Jac's coffee equally into both their paper coffee mugs. The steam plumed in ragged puffs.

"So I took a look last night. It seems Dimi did his best work during his last few days," Viktor continued, after a messy and noisy conclusion with the butty. "Of course he was inspired by the threats. He knew better than me what was coming, and I can see he was working with few breaks: the logs show it. He was committing updates to the repository very regular, in case things went bad. He was pulling the traditional all-nighter — but like three in a row — and the code is outstanding: minimal, balanced, perfect — the best I've seen. You know good code when you see it, right? There is nothing to add, and nothing to subtract. The man was on fire. He was writing at lightning speed but there is really good structure, short methods, precise comments. But, it turns out, not complete."

"What's left to do?"

"A few tweaks."

"So you keep saying. How long?"

"Mah — four, five days?" Viktor wobbled a greasy hand in the universal gesture of a rough estimate.

Skull nodded. Jon's deadline was Christmas, a mere few days away. Four or five days was not going to make any difference even if he was still alive. "There's a but?" he asked.

"There is always a but," Viktor agreed. "I need professional tools, dev tools."

"What do you have?"

"Nothing. I have nothing. I am Marcus, remember? I have qTab."

"But you work for Quince — they must have a ton of stuff available to you."

"Not for Marcus. Marcus can access stock lists, that's it." He frowned. "Fuck, it's cold here. Why don't you turn up the heating? Are you cheap, or what?"

"Not cheap, just broke," Skull said smiling.

"The heating is broken?"

"The electricity's gone. No power, no phone, no broadband."

"You shitting me." Viktor sat back. "You shitting me. What happened?"

"Nothing happened. I didn't pay my bills."

"Fuck!" He struck the table dramatically, open handed. "Idiot. There goes Plan B."

"Plan B? What happened to Plan A?"

"This is Plan A. Plan A is: Run. It's a good plan, but — OK. Stick with the plan. Keep running." Viktor drained the last of his coffee. "Fuck."

Skull wanted to look at the note again. He wanted to go back upstairs, sit on the bed; perhaps there were more clues to why she left. He said, "So what was Plan B? What was it that you wanted me to contribute?"

"Smartor. Smartor of course."

"Smartor is dead."

"For sure. But you still have infrastructure. The web service is running, yes? Yes. Because I checked."

Skull shook his head. "But I'm out. It's only running for existing customers until the new owners decide what they want to do with them. Nothing to do with me now."

"It is scalable compute service for high bandwidth application, yes?"

"I guess," Skull conceded.

"Perfect. That's exactly what we need. Hercules is a hunter-killer application. Very simple, not much integration. Once it detects a goal instance from Goald, it needs to kill all related threads simultaneously, before they re-spawn themselves. You set up the infrastructure yourself?"

"Mostly," said Skull.

"So you have a back door." It was a statement of fact. Skull smiled. Viktor continued with confidence: "Of course you have a back door into your own infrastructure. You would be massive idiot if you did not have at least one alternate way in."

"Ah," Skull smiled. "You thought I'd give you access to Smartor systems."

"Smartor is dead," Viktor pointed out. "Maybe your friend too, if we can't kill his goals first."

"So what's in it for you?" Skull asked, rising from the breakfast bar and crossing to the window. He stared down at the street below. Perhaps she would come back.

"For me? Nothing," Viktor said modestly, then after a pause, "Maybe, maybe if I can kill Petro's goals the gangsters will stop chasing me. Maybe."

A grocer's delivery van worked its way down the narrow one-way street, mounting the opposite pavement to avoid the parked cars. How quickly things change, Skull thought. Despite his gloom he couldn't rid himself of the sense of freedom, the contentment, he'd felt when he woke this morning. He didn't trust the feeling and wished it would go away. He felt safer with the containment that misery brought.

"Of all the people," Viktor was saying, "Of all the people I know, I thought you would have the tool set I need. My calculations did not take account of a lack of basic services. Who doesn't have electricity? Fuck."

"Indeed. Sorry about that," said Skull, and he was genuinely sorry. The solution was too late to help Jon, but he felt he would like to help Viktor. "On the other hand I have a few friends who I'm confident have, on a regular basis, paid their utility bills." He returned to the breakfast bar and leaned in towards Viktor. "Are you not working today?" he asked.

Viktor laughed. "You are kidding, right? After your visit yesterday at the store, the management have reached out to me and we believe that our futures do not lie on the same path."

Skull looked at his watch. Jac said she would be at the museum for Uncle Daffy's lecture this evening. There was time. He slid onto a bar stool. "So. Plan C," he said.

*

Josh stared out unblinkingly, a colourful but vigourless gaze, her mouth a pale blue ellipse stopped in the very act of a weary sigh. It wasn't the bulging eyes of violent red that caught Skull's attention, nor was it the livid scarlet bruising gouged with her own fingers below her chin. He saw only the dull grey network cable erupting like the body of a worm from the muddy purple folds of neck fat, saw only where it twisted hard behind her head, with each entwined end terminating in a grey-domed plug cover, two heads choking the life from a third.

"Fuck," Viktor hissed. "Fuck, fuck. This is not good."

Earlier, using the computer in Gabby, Skull had tried to reach Josh on her usual IRC channels but without response. He had tried a text, email, and eventually placed a voice call but there had been no answer by which time they were already settling into a parking bay on an adjacent street.

Josh had been the obvious choice for Plan C. She had the kit to help Viktor install and configure a running version of Hercules on the Smartor systems, with which she was also familiar; she also had the expertise to provide layers of cloaking where required, or at least advise on how Viktor could cover his tracks.

Skull had been surprised to find the front door ajar. Nobody answered the doorbell, no one responded to the knocking, nor the yelled "helloos". They stepped across the threshold into the hall. As they progressed meekly along the dark passage Viktor had quietly cursed; and in the homey kitchen that overlooked a small neat garden, he whispered both their fears: "Something is not right. Definitely, something is not right." Yet despite their uncertainty they followed the light down the steep steps to the basement office where they found Josh dead, discarded.

The stench was as violent as the scene itself, the morbid rankness overriding the dank of the basement, the musty flatness of somnolent dust disturbed. How long had she been there? Impossible to tell. She looked very dead, although degrees of deadness hardly seemed forensic in the determination of time of death. Death was binary in a way that life was not: you were dead or not dead, but life had qualities of aliveness which suddenly seemed well worth preserving.

Skull had only ever seen his dead father, all laid out and peaceful, a cadaver acceptable to the living, not so much dead as simply without life. In contrast, for Josh, the brutality of the moment that life ceased was frozen here in a grotesque tableau. Overturned in the corner, a tatty office chair; shelves pulled from the wall, equipment torn from its housing, files and their paper contents scattered everywhere; a shoe kicked into the far corner, the lace still tied.

"Fuck. Let's get out," said Viktor.

Apart from a vague background electric hum, the room was silent, no external sound able to penetrate into the basement.

"We should check if …," Skull pointed at the body. "Shouldn't we?"

"For what? He's dead."

"He's actually a woman," Skull noted, because suddenly precision was important.

"Fuck."

She had fought hard, kicking and pushing, tearing at her own throat to break the garrotte. How long before you lose consciousness? Skull wondered. He became keenly aware of how little he knew about life and how to keep it. Somewhere he had read that suffocation was considered a peaceful way to die. Nothing here looked peaceful.

At last he located the source of the hum — a power brick plugged into a wall socket above the desk. He reached out to feel if it was still warm.

"Don't touch," Viktor warned. "Fuck."

With his eyes Skull followed the cable from the power brick to where it ended in a plump round power plug. The plug might have powered a laptop, but that was gone. Now that he looked at it, the office was sparsely equipped: two large LED screens, a wired router or firewall of some sort, a pair of speakers, wired mouse and keyboard. There was no printer, no webcam, no racks of servers, no wireless router, no USB hubs or storage disks. Josh was a pro and ran a minimal setup in her own home. Slouched in her corner with the dead fish stare and the shoeless foot, she didn't look much like a pro now.

"Shsh," hissed Viktor.

"What?" All Skull could hear now was the thump of blood pumping through his neck.

After a moment Viktor shook his head, whispering, "What if they are still here?" Viktor had not entered far into the room but was now edging back towards the stairs. "I think I definitely heard something."

Quickly Skull followed Viktor back to the kitchen and cautiously back along the corridor to the front door. They stopped, unsure again.

"Someone might see us leaving," Skull whispered. From the floor above came a creak and a low thump.

"Fuck," said Viktor, reaching for the door, remembering for some reason, to pull his sleeve over his hand so he left no prints.

"Wait. She had a wife — a partner. She might be ..."

"It might be killers." Viktor pulled his hoodie over his head and peered out into the street from a gap in the doorway.

Skull raised the collar of his jacket and followed Viktor out the door, onto the street, feeling exposed and conspicuous.

Back in the car, Skull drove mechanically, shocked at what they'd seen, shocked at what they'd done, unsure what to do next. They hadn't broken into the house, but neither had they been invited; they hadn't witnessed the murder but neither had they reported it.

"We should call it in," Skull said.

"Call it in?"

"Phone the police."

"You are mad," Viktor said, matter of fact.

It would be madness indeed to report the murder. There'd be questions, investigation and he would spend the day talking to the police, perhaps the night too, helping them with their endless enquiries. He would miss Jac. He wouldn't get a last chance to talk to her before she left for Florence. He had to get to Uncle Daffy's lecture.

Skull was driving randomly again, steering down quiet streets, mirror checking, driving on. He never saw anyone following but he kept checking. Driving north they passed over a railway line then under the North Circular before getting trapped in a soulless residential area wedged between railway sidings and a river; the metal arc of Wembley stadium, like a giant eyelid, seemed to hover over the shoulder whichever way they turned.

"Who would do this?" Viktor said suddenly. "Was he criminal? Your friend? She. Was she mafia?"

"Far from it. A white hat, maybe a touch of the grey sometimes. But she did some consultancy for us, general security issues, advising on vulnerabilities, how to harden our systems and services, bit of penetration testing, that sort of thing. Standard stuff, mostly. Hawsehole. That was her handle. She was well known."

"Whore's hole? Jeez. I never heard of her."

"She was really good."

"So maybe she had enemies."

"Everyone has enemies, but they don't generally want to kill you," said Skull.

"Mine do," Viktor replied.

Do mine? Skull wondered, thinking of Mr Twydle, remembering Simon, reflecting that the possession of both a loud mouth and a foul mouth had brought Simon many detractors but no deadly enemies. In the end Simon's deadliest enemy had been himself.

But Josh had real deadly enemies. She must have had. People who play in the shadows have dark foes, perhaps even darker friends — everybody knows that — corporates, criminals and government spies, the evil triumvirate. It was well known, he consoled himself. It was well known and Josh would have understood the risks just as he himself understood the risks, and recognised his own limitations. Which is why he had asked her to try and find Viktor.

"I asked her to look for you," Skull confessed, braking sharply for a pedestrian crossing. The small group of adolescents waited impassively for Gabby to come to a complete halt.

"For me?"

Skull nodded. "Couple of days ago."

"Fuck."

"Before I found you at the Quince Store. I asked her to trace you."

The children sauntered slowly across the road, self-conscious in their moment of attention, relishing the sense of control.

"If she was a professional, she would cover her tracks," Viktor mused. "Wouldn't she? If she was professional, if she was good at her job, they couldn't locate her so quickly. Could they?"

"She was good," Skull said. Then, "But we need a Plan D."

*

The joy of a large shopping centre is that it is distinguished only by its location, and Brent Cross Shopping Centre, a premier retail gland for North London, exemplifies this no-nonsense tradition, straddling the North Circular road while also nudging up chummily against the mouth of the M1 motorway, just where it pours vehicles from the north into the London delta.

Skull chose it for its proximity and the flat, grey, anonymous car parks which surround the functional retail block. As the last Friday before Christmas however, the centre was enjoying brisk trade and the parks were full. Skull spiralled up the multi-story to find a space on the edge of the cold exposed roof top. Wireless connectivity, he reasoned, would be optimal up here.

Built into Gabby was a rack of computer systems all powered by a source independent of the electrical requirements of the vehicle itself. These systems were set up to monitor and control the car, gathering real-time data from the component sensors, running diagnostics, and generally recording car-related information before pumping it into the Smartor grid via a fast wireless service.

When he left the company, Skull had disabled the vehicle's up-links to the Smartor services. He didn't want anyone following his daily movements and activities. That was a few weeks back. Now he switched them all on again. Gigabytes of stored data were sucked, like the contents of a muddy pond, into the Smartor cloud. If anyone was watching — which he sincerely doubted, but if anyone was — they would be distracted by the sudden flood of data and perhaps not notice the quiet entry, through a discrete back door, into the Smartor compute grid.

Viktor would use Gabby's systems to complete the development of the Hercules code. Once complete he would install and run Hercules on the Smartor grid where it would find sufficient bandwidth and compute muscle to kill the multi-threaded Hydra. This was Plan D: vehicle-based development.

In the back of the car Viktor slouched over Skull's laptop which connected directly into Gabby's powerful systems through a wired link. Skull went through a basic orientation so that Viktor understood where everything was, how the vehicle's local systems were configured and how the Smartor cloud compute service worked. Viktor didn't need much instruction. What he didn't already know he learnt quickly, instinctively, and had soon set up and configured an environment he could work with, pulled the Hercules source from the repository and began dabbing away at the code, rapt in the abstract structures which were to him as manifest as bricks in a wall.

Skull sat quietly in the front seat, his phone plugged into Gabby, re-charging, while he flicked through emails, texts and messages. There were thousands. From time to time he fielded a technical question from Viktor. He calculated that in a little over an hour they would leave for the British Museum where he would meet Jac at the lecture.

It was already dark, the feeble winter sun giving up the day unnoticed behind the sullen Atlantic clouds. In the dark Skull checked the mirrors frequently, watching in reflection the flow of shoppers to and from their cars, steeled against the sharp wind that licked across the brightly lit rooftop.

There were no messages from Jac. There was nothing from Em either, but there it was again: *HI!My name is Werner Brandes*. Different messaging service, same message. Goald had found him again.

"Why am I still getting this?" he asked Viktor, showing him the message, explaining how he kept getting the same one.

"Ah," said Viktor. "That would be the social AI module. Find friends through friends. Goald is looking for your friend, so it sends out messages to his friends. You will probably keep getting until it finds him."

"That's lame," said Skull. "So why the video clip then? What's so special about this one?"

He screened again the video clip for Viktor who when it ended, shrugged, shook his head. "It's special because I'm in it. Joke. I think it's because your friend says 'help me'. It's probably a simple pattern match — a video of Jon saying 'help me'. Well, it got your attention," Viktor countered to Skull's sceptical sneer.

"Indeed."

Skull continued to prune his in-boxes. There was a voicemail message from Deepak.

"You are a bastard, man" it started, then went into the detailed provenance of this opinion: Raj had been beaten up, lost some teeth, broken a rib and a nose. The beautiful boy was broken. What had he done to deserve such ill treatment, and so forth. Two men — two scumbag-bastard foreigners — had come looking for Jon, just like Skull had come looking for Jon. They had walked into the shop and threatened Raj who was too young not to take offence. They didn't speak English well but one might have been called Vladimir, or maybe both were called Vladimir, or maybe they were also looking for someone called Vladimir. After they broke Raj and Raj was curled in a corner like a dead spider, they threatened Deepak himself who immediately told them everything he knew as well as some stuff they didn't ask about.

He told them about the phone, about the murder, about Jon, about Skull. The Vladimirs had not seemed satisfied with these answers so he had freely volunteered the contact card Skull had given him, although they hadn't even taken it.

"I told them that you know everything," Deepak said in the message. "I'm sorry, man." He had tried to reach Skull many times to warn him, and also to blame him, and hoped that Skull was OK. But, he added an addendum, he felt that Skull brought this on himself just as Skull had brought these men from hell into the shop.

Skull re-played the message. He knew now that the Tunguska Man and Habilis had somehow followed him to Covent Garden, arriving too late to find him leaving the QStore, but catching him cold in the piazza. He had thought that was a one-off, the consequence of lack of diligence on his part. Now it was obvious they had followed him everywhere. His instinct had been right, but he hadn't seen anyone.

If they had followed him to the meeting with Deepak at Ajay's PC store, they must have followed him to the Twydles too; the battered face of Mr Twydle who had been mugged but nothing stolen, spoke for that. In the circumstances Mr Twydle had escaped lightly considering that Josh had an Ethernet cable patched into her neck.

Why had the Russians killed Josh but spared Twydle? Twydle was a fool and knew nothing of Jon and Viktor. There would have been no need to kill him, but Josh knew nothing either. Not true: Josh knew Viktor's name and in fact by then may well have known a lot more than simply his name. How far had she got in her search for Viktor? Perhaps not far, but it wouldn't need much, a flick of recognition at the name, a glance at the laptop. They had taken the laptop. Good luck with hacking into that.

But why kill her? Did she know too much, perhaps? Even if she knew all about Viktor why take the risk of killing her? She would have put up a struggle, of course; not for pride like Raj, but perhaps for honour, reputation, loyalty maybe, even simply because it was in her Glaswegian blood, an instinctive refusal to be handled. Perhaps they just killed her because they didn't like her or her type.

Skull knew now that he had been stupid. He had led the thugs witlessly from victim to victim. They knew he was looking for Jon, because he had told them he was looking Jon. They knew Jon had been looking for Viktor because Jon had asked questions in the wrong places. They must have figured if they found Jon, they could use their primitive methods to persuade him into revealing the whereabouts of Viktor. It was a brutal if logical methodology.

He thought suddenly of Jac: what if they found Jac? What if they had been watching the flat, had seen Jac leave, followed her. Suddenly he needed to see her, make sure she was alright.

"Get down."

"What?" Viktor slid down in the back seat. "Fuck."

There was something about the movement of the man working against the steady stream of shoppers — head not down, arms not bearing parcels. In the mirror, in the harsh down-lighting of the car park, there was no detail; but the dark duffel coat, the bullish set of the shoulders, the round face, the woolly cap — almost certainly the Tunguska Man. Instinctively Skull slid lower in his seat too.

"It's them."

"Them?"

"Stay down."

"Fuck."

Hiding in the car is the wrong move, Skull thought: recognising the vehicle, and seeing it empty, the Tunguska Man walks across to take a look, immediately sees Skull skulking in the driver seat, sees Viktor crouching in the rear foot well, kills Viktor.

But sitting quietly is also the wrong move: the Tunguska Man sees Skull alone as if waiting for someone, so he strolls across for a leer and an unfriendly chat, notices Viktor crouching in the rear foot well, kills Viktor.

What should he then do?

Making a hurried getaway is also the wrong move: the Tunguska Man is alerted by the squeal of brakes, the whine of the over-revved engine, and is immediately suspicious, giving chase on foot and easily catching up in the stutteringly slow Christmas exit queues; notices Viktor crouching in the rear foot well, kills Viktor.

"Gabby! Start." The best move is to make a slow unhurried departure, pretend he hasn't seen the Tunguska Man and so give himself more time to think.

"Get right down on the floor," he hissed. Round-eyed with worry Viktor dropped uncomfortably to the floor. "Low as you can. Cover yourself with ... with whatever."

Slowly Skull backed out of the parking slot, acutely aware of each of his own movements: look back slowly when reversing, don't look too far back; turn and join the traffic queue; don't pause too long; don't look left or right, stare forward glumly, like all the other shoppers.

"What's happening?" Viktor sounded far away, a muffled, pale voice.

"It's all fine. Stay down." Don't move your lips when you talk, either.

Skull didn't watch the Tunguska Man but knew exactly what he was doing: he sees Gabby when she starts to back up; he stops, he observes, moving to the line of cars so that he's less conspicuous; he lifts his mobile to his ear; he starts towards the stairwell.

He's not suspicious but he's going to watch me down each level as we leave, thought Skull. And he's calling Habilis. I wish I could see what car he gets into. Then I'd know what to look for.

Back on the North Circular road Skull knew speed was not going to be his friend, not with the Friday-before-Christmas rush hour traffic. He would not be able to outrun his followers.

"What's happening?"

"Stay down."

The collision avoidance system saved him more than once as in the mirror he scanned the columns of cars crawling faithfully behind him. It was hopeless. They were all following him.

He left the North Circular early, returning to the residential roads around Wembley where he twisted through the streets and avenues, looping back, making sudden turns, illegal turns, U-turns. After ten minutes he knew there was no one following.

"How are they doing it? How are they following me?"

"How would you do it?" Viktor was now lying low on the back seat, his head below the window level, his fingers still flapping over the keyboard.

"Oh. Stupid." Skull pulled over, parked up. "Stupid, stupid" he said again, getting out the car.

The small GPS tracking device was easily accessible, easily found, attached by a couple of strong magnets to a retaining bracket behind the front bumper. About the size of a box of matches, the rigid black plastic box was covered by a protective plastic zip-bag. On one side were a couple of switches and a covered slot for a SIM card. "Basic Security, GPS Tracker" was stamped on it. He passed it back to Viktor.

"Ever seen anything like this?"

"Not my line of work," said Viktor without interest. "You should keep driving."

"Stupid," Skull said. It was beginning to sound like a chant. "Didn't occur to me. Trackers are built in nowadays so if your car's stolen, you can track it with GPS. You can buy these after-market add-ons for a few quid on the Internet. They didn't even have to watch me — it's got a motion sensor so they knew when I set off, where I went, when I stopped. Stupid."

"Maybe we should drop it on another car," Viktor suggested. "They can follow them."

It was a tempting thought, but these men were not good people. On the busy three lane Westway heading east, Skull tossed the tracker over the side somewhere near Wormwood Scrubs. Let them figure that one out.

*

He left Viktor with the car in Store Street, a short walk from the British Museum. Viktor barely acknowledged the new location, grunting an all-purpose monosyllable in response to Skull's instructions to get himself a coffee from the nearby cafe, and to message him if there were any problems.

Skull understood Viktor's reticence; Viktor's mind was stuffed with all the components of the Hercules software — their functions, dependencies, interactions, all mapped into an intricate but fragile internal model which could crumble if disturbed by conversation. Skull had been impressed at how quickly Viktor had adapted to his mobile development environment, working efficiently and without complaint in the cramped conditions at the back of the car. And Viktor had reported good progress: Dimi had, in fact, solved all the major problems; everything was in place, everything worked as expected. His estimate for completion of the work, he told Skull, was diminishing logarithmically. Already he was able to start configuring the grid ready for a test run.

Skull envied Viktor. He envied him the distraction. He envied him the clarity of purpose, the simple task, the clear objective where right and wrong were not bound to questions of good or bad, should or shouldn't, duty, obligation, loyalty. You got it right or you got it wrong, and the pure logic of the system told you which it was.

He also envied Viktor the coffee. He would kill for a good coffee.

It was past six and the crowds were already thinning when he walked through the entrance to the British Museum. A sweaty, uniformed man pointed him into the Great Court: "Turn sharp left or right, sir. The lecture theatre's down the stairs. You're welcome."

Outside the theatre entrance a lone attendant sat behind her trestle table staring at her lists. "You're too late," she said. "It's already started."

"I'll be very quiet," said Skull. "Promise." He grinned unsuccessfully. The woman frowned.

"That's hardly the point. You can't go in." She waved at a couple of large leather-covered benches where other late-comers sat disconsolately nursing their disappointment. Why were they waiting? Why not leave? Perhaps they weren't late-comers, merely lonely people enjoying a quiet public moment.

"OK. I'll just wait there."

"Yes. You do that." The woman turned back to her lists, dismissive in victory.

A few quick, long strides carried Skull to the theatre's double swing-door entrance. He heard a shocked "hey" as they flipped shut behind him but he was already opening the second set of doors into the darkened theatre.

Uncle Daffy stood stage centre dressed in a dark suit, his stocky body sharply delineated against the shiny red background. Beside him a range of artefacts were arranged on a table — stones, bones, a jug of water, a glass tumbler; projected onto the large screen behind him was a graph with a jagged line of red, crawling diagonally upwards, annotated at various points with drawings of stone tools. He spoke clearly, his voice strong and authoritative, his delivery mellifluous and with the surety of a man who relishes attention.

"So this slide," Uncle Daffy gestured behind him, "shows a simplification of the cycles of innovation getting tighter and tighter. We go from, down the bottom, from the Lomekwian and the Oldowan pebble choppers through to the widespread use of Acheulean hand axes in about two million years; and then there's this slow development to Levallois techniques, the Mousterian industries — another million years. Compare that," the slide changed, a blue ascendant annotated with telephones, "compare that innovation with modern communications technologies."

Uncle Daffy walked across the front of the screen.

"From fixed line telephone to mobile phone, ninety years. From mobile to smartphone, thirty years. From smartphone to wearables, fourteen years. With each iteration of technology, our brains must update their models faster, every innovation needs new thinking, new adaptations. But are our brains evolving as fast as our tools? How does our Palaeolithic brain manage all this in this age of the smart machine?"

The auditorium was arranged in an arc around the stage with access down each side; the tiered seating sloped gently down. Soft, corpse-grey leather-bound seats created an intimate if visceral atmosphere. The house was full, a few empty seats in the middle only.

Skull walked swiftly around the back, stooping below the projection room window, to find an inconspicuous place on the far steps. Uncle Daffy followed his progress without pausing the flow of his words.

"The mobile phone is the most ubiquitous human hand tool since the hand axe," Uncle Daffy was saying. It all sounded familiar and Skull was not listening. "There are now more active mobile phones on the planet than there are active humans. That's an awful lot of chatter." The audience tittered.

At first he couldn't see her. He scanned the rows of cabbage faces blankly receiving the illumination of Uncle Daffy's knowledge. He worried she might not be here; he worried she had already left; he worried she had been found and tortured, maimed, killed by the Tunguska Man. Slowly Skull edged down the steps, searching row by row.

"And it's everywhere, you can't escape it," Uncle Daffy declared. "Even on the highest mountains of the world you can receive a satellite signal. You have to descend into the deepest mines to get away from modern life where no light, and no sound, and no wireless messages can penetrate."

He saw her only because she turned her pale face towards him, her eyes dark seeds set in a halved pear. He thought he saw her give a quick smile but in the darkness of the theatre he couldn't be sure. He flashed his own teeth anyway, a puppy dog smile. He settled on a step to wait, paying no attention to the changing slides projected on the screen, to the drone of Uncle Daffy's voice.

"Perhaps," Uncle Daffy suddenly changed pace, changed the tone of his voice, lifting in one hand a large polished flint axe from the table, in the other a browning human skull, "perhaps the descendants of this stone artefact will come to regard the descendants of this object as merely a small step in their own evolutionary development." He held both axe and skull high over his head where they glowed against the blood-red Perspex backdrop.

Now Skull was listening. Not to the portentous predictions for the future of mankind, but listening for the echo of something Uncle Daffy had said earlier. What was it about signals on a mountain? It wasn't the mountain. It was the mines; it was the messages penetrating everywhere except the mines. Flint mines. Where else would you go if you were running from your smartphone?

Uncle Daffy had not yet finished. "We shape our tools and thereafter our tools shape us," he said, then he said it again, with emphatic pauses: "We shape our tools. And thereafter our tools shape us. Not my words. Marshal McLuhan. And in a different context but, I think, still apt in this one. For we are toolmakers to be sure, and the tools we have made have shaped our world as surely as they have shaped us, shaped the development of the human hand, the human voice, the human mind. But make no mistake, it is not the tools themselves that fashion or mould or shape us, for we are forged in the very act of shaping our tools. We are shaped by our own making because we become most human when we make, when we strive, when we strive together, and when we aspire to shape our world."

*

People started leaving even before the applause had died away, bolting up the stairs with time-pressed frowns. Others sat in clusters chatting and waiting for the slow shuffle of leavers along the rows and up the plodding stairs. On stage Uncle Daffy enjoyed the congratulations of a small coterie of colleagues and museum staff laughing and fingering the artefacts.

Skull pressed himself back against the wall allowing the treacle of people to flow slowly past him as he watched Jac. She remained unmoving in her seat. Once, she smiled at him then quickly looked away. He waited for a row (any row) to clear of people so he could make his way to her. He sidled self-consciously along the narrow spaces in front of upturned seats, clambering over back rests until he sat beside her.

"You made it," she smiled.

He smiled back. He didn't know what to say. His mind had focused on reaching her but now he was here, he was without words. Why did he have to say anything? Wasn't it enough that they sat together? He thought he could still smell on her the faint lavender of bath salts.

"Say something, Skull."

"I missed you this morning."

"Not that. It sounds so adolescent. Say something different." He thought she would cry.

"I missed you this afternoon," he told her.

"Did you like the lecture?" she asked.

"I liked the bit at the end. When he stopped talking," he said, and she laughed. Encouraged, he went on: "I like this bit." He saw Uncle Daffy looking across, caught his eye.

"Did you have to come?" she asked.

"I was invited."

"I hoped you wouldn't."

"I wanted to make sure you were OK."

"Well, I'm not OK."

"What can I do?"

"You can go away."

"I can't do that," he said. He showed her the note from his pocket. *I am glad, J.* She glanced at the crumpled paper, looked away. Up on stage Uncle Daffy was trying to shake off his hangers-on, frequently glancing over towards them.

"I can't leave until I know you're OK," Skull told her. "I understand why you left this morning."

"Do you?" Her voice was soaked with relief, but her face was a map of pain, as if a long needle had been stuck into her body.

He couldn't parse the frown with the voice and the eyes. He gave up. "You were glad. I was glad. Everything was perfect. Why wouldn't you leave?"

Her head drooped. "It was a mistake," she said.

"Leaving?"

"Staying."

He waved her note at her again: *I am glad.*

"Skull," she said. "There are whole lives wedged between us. We're twenty years too late; and I have to go home."

Finally free of his admirers, Uncle Daffy leapt off the stage, his movements vigorous, positive, his grin maniacal. Skull watched him make his way towards them thinking how promisingly the day had started out. He was having difficulty reconciling that elemental happiness with his current plunging gloom and the sense of pending disaster.

"What about Jon?" he asked Jac.

"What about him?"

"Godwin Hill," said Skull. "He's in the mine."

"Yes. It was rather obvious, really. Daffyd told me earlier."

"Jacqui!" Uncle Daffy side-stepped along the row in front. "Jacqui darling, there was a seat reserved for you up front."

"This was fine just here," said Jac.

Uncle Daffy knelt on a seat leaning against the backrest. "Well? Good? Bad? Indifferent?"

"It was great, Daffyd. A classic."

Uncle Daffy beamed. "So, there are a few drinks and nibbles in the green room," he said gesturing towards the stage exit. "Then after, are we doing dinner? "

"I must go," she said, standing. "I'm sorry, Daffyd."

"Me too," said Skull.

"Did I say something wrong?" Uncle Daffy quipped. "Do I smell?"

Jac smiled. "I have a flight. I need to go home. Thank you for everything, Daffyd." She reached forward and squeezed his hand.

"You can't go now, Jacqui," he objected. "We've got nibbles."

"Good luck with —" she shrugged, "with everything." She turned to Skull, hesitating. "Please don't follow me, Skull. Please."

Skull sat watching, bewildered, as she stepped carefully, head bowed, not looking back, to the end of the row. Stiffly she climbed the broad, shallow, steps and passed into the darkness below the green exit lamp.

Uncle Daffy sighed. "Must have been something you said, then." Skull said nothing but stood to leave. Uncle Daffy said, "She did ask you not to follow, chap." Skull sat again, and for a while Uncle Daffy observed him in silence. There was no eye contact.

"On mid-summer evenings," Uncle Daffy mused, "the fairies would dance in the moonlight over the old flint mines at Godwin Hill, according to the locals. They were places of great magic, you see, not of industry. They left, of course."

"The locals?"

"The fairies. The fairies left after the archaeologists began their digging, and their measuring, and recording of everything. Never more to be seen," he ended. Both men stared sadly at their hands. After a while Uncle Daffy spoke again. "Well I must attend to my hosts," he said. "There's a reception in the green room. You're most welcome ..."

Skull shook his head. "Thanks," he said.

"But you enjoyed the lecture?" Uncle Daffy asked as he stood.

"I missed the first bit," said Skull.

Uncle Daffy nodded, hesitating. He swallowed hard and said, "It was his idea, you know. I wasn't keen, myself, but he explained it all to me. I have to say that we both truly appreciated the glorious irony of using a Neolithic mine to escape the wrath of modern technology. He said he would be safe to leave after Christmas. Would that be right?"

"He'll be fine," said Skull. And then with great effort: "Thank you for believing him."

Friday Night

Under the windscreen wiper, when he returned to his car, Skull found a parking ticket. He tore it out and carried it into the nearby cafe where he knew he would find Viktor. Viktor had the laptop on the table and a line of empty coffee cups.

"I am done," Viktor said. "I need only now a unique I.D. for your friend's device — IMEI maybe, or MAC address."

"Not possible," said Skull. "I don't have the phone."

"OK. No problem. I can try something else. Maybe pattern matching on name. Takes longer but I found Petro's goal stream and now I'm already zapping them one by one. Personally I think Hercules works really well. Dimi would have been so proud. Oh. And you got a parking ticket, by the way," he added cheerfully.

Viktor had noticed the parking attendant printing out the ticket and placing it under the windscreen, but hadn't seen earlier the red van making a slow pass of Gabby before driving on.

Skull ate a hot pie while Viktor mulled aloud the various methods he could use to uniquely identify Jon's specific goal stream. Normally Skull would have followed the technical arguments closely but now he simply heard the words. The pie was dry, the filling claggy. He thought it the best pie he'd ever had. He nodded his agreement with Viktor's conclusions, licking the fatty flakes from his fingers, contemplating the merits of a second pie.

"I know where Jon is," he told Viktor. "And we're going to fetch him."

It wasn't an impulse decision — he had been mulling it while he ate his pie. Fetching Jon seemed like the right thing to do; it felt like closure. Everything else was gone, everything: the money, the flat, the lifestyle; even Emily had gone. Jac had other lives. Smartor: dead, like Simon, would never rise again because he had given away the goods, published the company secrets that nobody wanted to see. He was bankrupt. Gabby soon would be taken from him too. Collecting Jon from exile would draw a line, he felt. It would be like closing the door on the way out. After that, he thought, he might move on.

Uncle Daffy had given him a bunch of keys: "First there's the gate when you come off the road," he told Skull. "Then there's the lock on the outer fence, and then the shed itself has a bloody big padlock. Jon can bring the keys back when he returns all the camping gear he borrowed." Uncle Daffy had grinned at Skull then, a cockeyed rictus, the knurly twitch of a landed fish in the last throw of death. Skull, a connoisseur of smiles, noted the deformity with satisfaction.

Back on the road, heading south, Viktor monitored the progress of Hercules as the software tracked and slew the scattered fragments of Jon's goals wherever they lay hidden — lurking in memory banks, cache stores, unused registers — wherever they lay dormant waiting for the message, the signal, to resurrect themselves. Hercules sought them out one by one, hunted them down, killed them.

"Your friend Jon was very busy with goals," Viktor announced. "Of two hundred twenty four goal instances he created, two hundred and twenty one are flagged 'archive'. So they are already completed. Each goal has thousands of threads, so of remaining live goals, Hercules has killed two thousand three hundred seventy six threads for goal number 222, over a thousand for 223, and six hundred seventy two for goal 224. We are nearly finished. There is anomaly with the phone id and user id. Are there two users for this device?"

"Not now," Skull said. "Not anymore. There was a previous owner. Chap called Deepak. He was definitely using Goald before he sold the phone on to Jon."

"Really? Looks current."

"Maybe he has a few still running? Is that possible?"

"Anything is possible, my friend, anything is possible," Viktor said with confidence. "But I will investigate later. First we kill goal instances for Jon."

Viktor provided infrequent bulletins on progress as they worked south down the A24 towards Worthing. To fill the gaps between the bulletins Viktor asked Skull about Smartor. How, for instance, had he become aware of the problem for which Smartor represented the solution? What type of funding had he raised? Had he pivoted?

Skull extracted and dusted off his time-trusted set of responses which, like a favourite jacket, had provided good service at a hundred presentations, a hundred parties, a hundred talks and interviews: the age of the smart car is upon us and we deserve more than just diagnostics; making cars social is all about empowerment, wresting control from governments, corporates, the road lobby, and giving it back to drivers; it's all about efficiency and greener driving; putting the driver back in the driving seat.

"It's political?" Viktor asked.

"Of course it's political — it's your car, your data. But who owns the data now? The manufacturers do, the dealers, the marketers. And why do they want it? To keep control, to make more money. It's inefficient because they'll never share the data with their competitors or with government if it doesn't serve their own interests. They want the information so they can sell you more parts, more cars, services. Yes, of course it's political. Disrupt any vested interest and it very quickly becomes political. Why else would they want to destroy my company?"

Skull stopped for fuel at a service station outside Leatherhead. The cashier was suspicious when he paid in cash.

"You would have done it anyway," Viktor said once they had re-joined the traffic flowing south. The roads were thick with Christmas travellers and home-running commuters.

"Done what?"

"CAN bus. It's can of worms. I don't think you give a fuck about manufacturers, governments, even drivers in their driving seats. I think you saw a technical problem that nobody could solve and you solved it. You are a geek. That's why it all went to shit."

A thin soaking rain had added itself to the weather miseries. The windscreen wipers activated themselves automatically, adjusting the wipe rate for water volume and car speed. For a while they listened to the comforting rhythmic shushing.

"Maybe," Skull conceded.

Viktor was pleased. "We are not that different, you and me," he said. "I liked only the technical challenge too. Fuck the politics." But after while he said: "Dimi saw the politics. I miss Dimi."

*

The dirt road running over the Sussex hills was unsuited to an advanced car laden with delicate sensors. Skull switched off the headlights but in the black of the wet night he could see nothing ahead. What farmer is going to come out on a miserable Friday night like this, he thought. He put on the parking lights, and picked his way carefully along the flinty road. Finally he stopped where he had stopped before, on the saddle of the ridge where the road curved down to the valley and a rough farm track rose to the summit of Godwin Hill proper. He killed the engine, doused the light. The night rushed in, the darkness and the silence.

"Fuck," hissed Viktor. "I thought you said a mine."

"Up there." Skull nodded at the void ahead. "Inside the hill."

"Fuck." As he squinted out at the fine drizzle, Viktor's scowl looked like a grimace of pain in the low green glow from the laptop's screen. "Why are we here again?"

"I'm here to fetch my friend. You're here because it's all your fault."

"Ah, true. But how does he know we are here to fetch him?"

"He doesn't. We have to go and get him."

"We? No. You go. Your friend: you get. Anyway, I didn't bring a jacket."

Before he left the warmth of the car Skull asked Viktor: "Are you absolutely sure now, that there are no more goals running?"

"All dead," said Viktor. "All dead."

Skull knew the direction but it took twenty minutes of slipping and stumbling up the soggy path before his torch picked out the corrugated metal shed squatting over the open shaft of the mine. The metal cladding had been added since his last visit, as had the sturdy wire fence running all the way around; erected, no doubt, to keep out inquisitive animals — sheep, badgers, ramblers.

He fumbled the key into the gate's lock with stiff, shaking fingers. The cold wind cut easily through the fabric of his town jacket, sodden already from the soaking rain. His toes squelched in his loafers. Beyond the gate, the large plywood door giving access to the shed was bolted and padlocked on the outside; a crude hole had been cut into the wood below the bolt so the lock could be unfastened from inside if necessary.

Unlocked, the doors swung open of their own accord, exhaling the damp, chalky smells of the mine shaft along with a whiff of diesel and grease, old fumes, and a deeper note of something human. The light from the torch bounced around the metallic interior of the shed, revealing a framework of scaffolding pipes set above the shaft head. The scaffolding was much as Skull remembered it from the first visit, but the generator engine looked beefier than before, bigger and more battered, the orange paint flaking beneath a black grime. A plastic pipe pushed out from the generator through the metal wall to vent fumes, and cables sprouted from the side, up to a wall-mounted control box housing serious-looking switches and dials. Thumb-thick cables ran everywhere, while a black hose stuffed with more wires cascaded over the edge and disappeared into the dark void of the shaft. Below the wallboard was a rack holding four grimy batteries, and yet another cable ran up to a lamp bolted onto the ceiling. Skull found the switch and with rising hope flicked it on. There was a sharp click, but no light.

"Jon," he shouted. "Jon! It's me. Skull. Where are you?" He shone the flashlight over the edge but the feeble white light was easily defeated by the gloom of the hole. All he could make of the bottom were a few body-like forms.

"Jon! Jon Fast!" he shouted. He began the down climb into the pit, torch clamped firmly in his mouth.

The ladder dropped vertically to a narrow platform about halfway down from where a second ladder completed the descent to the base. At this staging platform he paused, bellowing for Jon again, looking over the edge once more. A shallow gallery, more of a shelf really, pierced the chalk wall starting just above the level of the platform. It extended only a couple of meters into the side, and a few white plastic builder's hats lay discarded inside it, abandoned by their owners as they left.

Peering over the edge again, he could see now that the floor of the pit was covered in wooden duck-boards and littered with black bin liners, the sullen, inert bodies he'd seen from the top. Against the wall a giant blue water butt rested on a table, alongside it a camping stove. Opposite was a forlorn camping toilet, hunkered up to the brown-stained chalk face, a yellow bucket on each side. Skull continued downward, the sour mix of chemical and nature smells rising to greet him.

"Gotta gun! Gotta gun!" A powerful beam drenched Skull with light.

Quickly Skull hooked his elbow over a rung on the ladder, trying not to panic as his wet shoes slipped a little on the wet metal rung. He clung on, removing the torch from his mouth. "Jon, it's me. Look!" he yelled, reversing the torch to illuminate his own face. "It's me. Skull."

"Skull?"

"I'm coming down. Don't shoot!"

It was a relief to feel the wooden boards under foot when he reached the floor.

"Have you really got a gun?"

"No," Jon said mildly. "It's a threat." He stood beside the entrance to the side tunnel, shining his torch directly at Skull.

"You're blinding me," Skull said, pushing Jon's arm aside and in turn shining his own at Jon.

In the sickly light Jon looked in bad shape. He was thin, unshaven, his lips dry and cracked; his eyes, squinting against the torch light, were rimmed in red, baggy and moist; the light-brown chalk mud matted his patchy beard and was caked onto his face and in the hair on his head. His clothes were filthy. Close up, Jon smelt bad.

"I've come to take you home, Carruthers," Skull said.

Jon nodded, scratching his rough chin with fingernails split and filthy. His hand shook a little, and he said, "Oh, OK. Is it time?"

"Yes. I think it's time," Skull said gently. "I think you've done enough."

Jon nodded. "Have we had, um, Christmas?"

"Not yet; but it's OK. I've fixed everything. You can have Christmas at home."

"Oh right," said Jon. "Right. So you fixed everything? That's very good."

"Indeed," said Skull.

"That's very good," Jon said again. "I thought you might. I thought you might fix everything, Skull."

"What happened to the lights?" Skull asked.

Jon frowned, looking startled. "What lights?"

"The electric lights. From the generator."

"Oh." Jon considered the question for a moment. "Oh that," he said, and winced. "I think it's broken?"

"How long have you been without light?"

"Um," Jon rubbed his head, pulled at his ear. "Um, I don't know. I don't know, I was sleeping."

"Come on. Let's get you home. Anka's missing you."

"Anka? What do you mean — Anka? No," Jon said, his voice a growl. "No, don't bring her in."

"Don't you want to see her?"

"Not here. She's not part of this ... all this. Why bring that up?"

"Let's go home, Jon."

But Jon insisted on returning down the tunnel, to the gallery where he lived and slept, so he could fetch his things.

"What things?" Skull asked.

"My goods."

Jon slipped easily into the hole, his legs disappearing with a few practised wiggles.

"Don't be long," Skull called after him.

Skull played the light of his torch over the walls of the mine shaft. From down here it all seemed narrower and more claustrophobic; it was smaller than he remembered it, but perhaps that was the effect of the torch light, he speculated. It brought the walls in closer.

The camping toilet was a crude container with a plastic seat and a lid. It was a comical, domestic detail. One of the yellow buckets beside it was overturned for use as a table, holding a few rolls of toilet paper and an assortment of paperbacks and magazines.

Emily had schooled Skull to the notion that bathroom reading matter was distasteful, even unhygienic. He wondered what she would make of this arrangement, and of the suspicious-looking staining on the floor around the toilet. He wondered what Jac would think of her brother in his current state.

On the other side of the shaft, the trestle table with the gas stove was laden with carrier bags and packets of food. A rubber tube connected the stove to a gas canister below. Pots were stacked up on each other, a couple of plates, a mug, a roll of kitchen towel. Next to the table another yellow bucket held tins of food, more pots, more carrier bags; on the other side, yet another bucket served as a garbage bin. There was much evidence of food fall, of spillage and waste; there were greasy blobs on the duck-board below the table; matter trodden into the gaps between the wooden batons. Skull thought about rats and decided that perhaps they would never survive the drop into the tunnel, although perhaps there were other ways in. Uncle Daffy had said that the tunnels connected up. What was taking him so long?

"Jon! Come on. Wasting time."

Skull couldn't imagine living in this hole with the infinite silence and the endless necessity of attending to practical matters: keeping clean, getting food in, getting water in, getting waste out, staying warm. Basics. You'd have to be desperate to think it might work; you'd have to be mad to actually make it work.

"Jon!" He bent to the tunnel entrance, shone the torch in, but the curve gave him only a view of the damp walls with their shiny smoothness. A grubby electric cable was just visible where it rose from below the boards and curved up into the tunnel mouth, partly embedded into the chalk.

"Jon! Are you there?" He listened, called again.

"Idiot," he said aloud, his voice flat and dead and stupid. He thought, Now I'm going to have to go in and fetch the fool.

Recalling his last visit, he moved both phone and wallet to his back trouser pocket. Once again torch in mouth, Skull slowly pulled himself forward through the chalk pipe into the gallery.

Long gone, of course, were the bright analytical floodlights, the photogrammetry equipment, the happy tangle of cables. Now in the narrow light of his LED torch everything in the gallery loomed threateningly. At the far end the entrance to the twin tunnels gaped like open eye sockets, sucking in all light that fell on them. In the shallower, crypt-like tunnel, large and tattered black plastic bags had been laid to rest, torn body-bags seeping out their contents over a sagging cardboard box: clothes, towelling, sheets.

Against the opposite wall lay Jon's body, curled between layers like a shrimp in a sandwich. Over him, a strata of grubby sleeping bags, unzipped and spread open as blankets; beneath, a caravan mattress oozed foam where the seams had burst; at bottom, a grounding of flattened cardboard boxes and a blue plastic tarpaulin sheet. Beside the makeshift bed an old desk lamp stood atop an upturned plastic storage box, both stained a dirty brown. Beside the box an electric heater plugged into a multi-point power adaptor. The lamp emitted no light, the heater no heat.

Jon's eyes were pinched closed, his greasy head resting on a greasy pillow. It felt warmer in the gallery but smelled worse.

Skull said gently, "Jon."

Jon raised up the sleeping bags layer, burying his head deeper beneath them.

"Jon. What's going on? We've got to go." Skull dragged himself up beside his friend, reaching over to pull back the sleeping bags. "Come on. We've got to go."

Jon's eyelids flickered closed, his features pulled into a tight knot as he shut out the torch light. Skull pointed the torch beam at the wall. "What's going on?" Skull asked again.

"Nothing," said Jon. "Nothing at all."

"I thought you were going to fetch your — your goods, and come back."

"That's right."

"Well you didn't come back," Skull said. "What's up, Jon? We've got to go."

"That's quite right," said Jon, emerging slowly from the covers. He shone his torch full in Skull's face again. "That's quite right," Jon repeated.

Skull tried his most re-assuring voice. "It's OK, Jon. We're going to go home."

"Really?"

"Really."

"Fine," said Jon. "Fine. I wasn't sure. Really. I knew you were there. I knew you were there, but when I came back I thought you might be ... you might be not really you. I thought you might —. When I came back here it didn't really seem real, really. I've had this dream before, you know." He wiggled himself upright until he was leaning against the wall. The light from his torch shook with his hand. "I think ... it's not the same dream. Not exactly the same dream. Nearly the same. Were you here before?"

"I am not a dream," Skull said loudly to emphasis his materiality. "D'you want me to pinch you?"

"Pinch you?"

"You know. Pinch you." Skull reached over and pinched Jon's arm.

"Pinch me? Pinch me," Jon giggled. "Pinch me." Once started, his giggling grew, grew louder, bordering on hysteria. Skull put out a hand toward his rancid friend, patting him kindly on the shoulder. He said, "It's OK. It's OK."

The plastic box beside the bed wobbled gently, its contents shaking while Jon's body shook. In addition to the lamp, the box supported a small stack of jacketless hardback books, the book boards faded, bent and curved with age. On top of the pile rested a head-torch, the elastic head-band drooping over the side; a grubby plastic water bottle, half filled, stood quivering alongside.

Slowly the convulsions subsided. Skull adjusted his body to find a more comfortable position, but scraped his head on an angular piece of chalk above him. The ceiling was ragged and damp; there were few places where it was possible to sit upright.

"It's good to see you Skull," Jon said at last. "It's really, really good. Is it Christmas yet?"

"Nearly," Skull said brightly. "But don't worry about it. I fixed everything, remember? It's all OK to go home. You don't need to stay here now."

"Right," Jon said, but seemed unsure. "You said that before, didn't you?"

"Let's go," said Skull and Jon nodded but still he dithered. What should he take? There was a lot to pack up. "We can come back," said Skull. "Just the essentials. There's plenty of time after Christmas. We'll come back, and clear everything up. I'll help you."

"I'm not sure about leaving, Skull." Jon pulled his knees up, hugging them to his body. "I really don't know. I'm not sure I can."

"Come on. Why not?"

"Well. I don't go out much now really. Not at all, in fact. I used to go out. Quite a lot. When I still had the courage. When, in fact, I had the strength to keep the voices out. I could still ignore them then. I used to climb out at night, when no one could see me. I could walk around the hill and listen to the night sounds, cattle calling, badgers, cars in the distance. Sometimes an aeroplane would go overhead. But they didn't like it. They hated that."

"Who? The farmer?"

"The tunnel people. The tunnel people; ancestors. I don't know. They're always here and it's always worse when I go out and come back. Whispering, gossiping, talking about me. If I stay busy I can keep them away; but it's when I stop, when I close my eyes, they start all over again. Whispering, always whispering stuff."

"Let's talk about that in the car," Skull suggested, but Jon seemed not to have heard him and went on: "Stupid swami son, they said. It's like an accusation, you see; they knew I could hear them. You weasel satellite. It's madness, isn't it? D'you think I'm going mad? Once they said, Try category stew. I thought it may have been, Tri-categories, do, but that's just drivel, isn't it."

Jon laughed briefly, harshly, then continued, "They're not always very clear, you see. Just out of range. You have to not be not listening to hear the words. And then they mock me. That school saucer assassin. Now, how would they know about that, Skull? I'd forgotten all about it. That school saucer assassin. But they bring it up, they keep bringing it up, so I've tried not to listen to them and that's why they come in dreams now. Actually, it's easier for us all when I sleep, but sometimes I'm not sure when I'm sleeping or not. If you dream you're dreaming, is that a dream? Or do they cancel out? I don't know."

"I think," said Skull, "you've been down here too long."

"Maybe I'm dreaming all this. Listen." Jon's mouth turned down, his eyes hooded over as the features on his face collapsed. "Hear that? I think they don't want me to go. Can you hear them?" Jon slid back down below his sleeping bags.

Skull experienced a momentary frisson, like an animal, a shiver running across his shoulders, his ears pricking at the faint muffled buzz rolling through the tunnel. The sound, he realised, had been there before but he hadn't registered it. Now he sat with Jon in frozen concentration, listening to the silence.

The sound came again, but louder, more distinct: "Aaay — waaay."

"That's not whispers," Skull said. "That's someone shouting. Actually shouting."

"Ah," said Jon, nodding. "That's what I thought. I thought that was it." He sat up again.

Now Skull heard solid sound: "Matthew! Matthew!" It could only be Viktor. Skull crawled back through the tunnel, Jon pushing at his heels.

Out in the open stage of the mine shaft, Viktor's panicked tones cascaded in a frothy stream from the mine head. "Matthew! Fuck! Hey! Where are you? Hey! Matthew!"

"That you, Viktor?" Skull called, shining his feeble light upwards. There was nothing to see except the scaffolding.

"They're coming!" Viktor hissed. He said something voluble in his own language, then, "Fuck. I'm coming down. Give me some light. I can't see."

Jon added his lamp's power to better illuminate the shaft. High above, Viktor's pale head could be seen staring. "Fuck," he said, pulling himself quickly over the ladder, starting down.

"Who's coming?" Skull called up. He didn't really need to ask who; the question really was, "How?"

"Van. Red van. Fuck." He was coming down fast, barely touching the rungs in a barely controlled drop. "They're already coming."

It would be stupid to be trapped in the mine shaft, Skull thought. There was no way out except up the ladder. "Stay up there," he called. "We'll come up."

Skull pulled Jon over to the ladder. "Up," he said, pushing him to start climbing.

Jon smiled seraphically. "Is it Uncle Daffy? Did he bring the van?"

"Just climb," said Skull.

"Too late," Viktor yelled from the platform half-way up. "It's too late. They are here nearly." Now he edged across to the second ladder. "Fuck. I need light. Give me fucking light." He started down the second ladder colliding near the bottom with Jon, reluctantly climbing up. Jon fell back onto Skull, Viktor followed. They all staggered, cursing and grunting with the effort of staying on their feet.

"We're trapped if we stay here," said Skull. "We need to get out."

"No time," Viktor said. "Fuck." Already there were new voices, a new bowl of light blossoming in the silver shed at the top of the shaft.

Jon studied Viktor. "I know you," he said pointing. "I've seen you before. Remember?" Viktor returned a mad stare but his reply was cut off.

"Hoi," came from the top. "Morrell! We come down, yes?" A bright new light flooded the shaft.

"What?" yelled Jon, shining his torch upwards as Skull and Viktor shuffled rapidly out of sight against the near wall, below the scaffolding. Skull grabbed Jon and pulled him over to the wall, pushing his torch down. "Who is that?" Jon asked Skull. "Who's up there?"

"Bad people," said Viktor. Viktor was wet and covered in mud. He was shivering uncontrollably.

"Bad people?" Jon asked. "Are they here to kill me?"

"Me," Viktor said miserably. "Me, I think. They want to kill me."

"How did they find us?" Skull asked. "Did you tell anyone we were coming here?"

"Did you?" Viktor responded. "Who would I tell?" he added.

"Gotta gun," Jon shouted suddenly, nodding knowingly at Skull. "I'm warning you. I'll shoot if you come down. I'll shoot."

The light above flickered, dimmed as it was pulled back from the edge. The mine shaft darkened again.

"I think that was a really bad idea," Skull said.

"Why? Worked on you."

The low voices above rumbled menacingly in private conversation, cut short by the slap of a single gunshot which rang down the narrow shaft with an odd percussive boom. A split second of silence followed before a lump of rock, dislodged from the shaft's wall, crashed onto the cooking table, knocking pots and plates in a clatter of loud protest, drowning the gentler patter of falling stones and the hushed whisper of sand slip. In the torchlight below a delicate curtain of dust drew softly down.

"Also gun," came from up top.

"Fuck," breathed Viktor. "Stupid, stupid."

"Tunnel," said Skull, but Jon had already dived into the hole ahead of him, disappearing quickly. As Skull scrambled into the gallery he could hear Viktor, very close behind, grunting each time he received a kick in the face.

"That was stupid," Skull growled at Jon, his voice low but angry. Scolding Jon suppressed his fear only momentarily. "Why did you do that?" he asked.

"It frightened you," Jon said.

"That's because I don't have a gun."

"Jeez," said Viktor, emerging from the narrow tunnel, looking around with wonder. "What is this?"

Jon said confidently, "They won't come down here now. Not if they think we also have a gun."

"If we'd actually had a gun," Skull hissed, "we'd have shot back at them. Now they know we don't have one."

"Fuck," said Viktor.

"Put your torch off," Skull whispered to Jon, killing his own light. They huddled up together, half crouching, half reclining in darkness as black as a hacker's hat. In this absence of light, signals from the lesser senses bloomed, and there was a comfort in each other's nearness, in each other's warmth, even in the pungent ripeness of Jon's unwashed bedding, his old clothes, his body.

"You live here?" Viktor asked.

"Yes."

"Like a tramp?"

"You told me to find a hole to hide in," said Jon. "This was the only one I could think of."

"It's really nice," Viktor whispered. "But I fixed your problems."

Skull half turned to Viktor. "Why didn't you warn us earlier?" he hissed from the side of his mouth. "We're trapped now."

"I thought to leave a nice voice-mail on your phone, right?" Viktor shrugged unseen in the dark. "They parked a van right up to the car. I had to run."

They fell silent again, shifting uncomfortably on the hard, uneven floor, listening for any indication of movement out in the main shaft, straining for any sliver of sound, any flick of light.

"What do they want anyway?" Jon asked suddenly, loudly.

"Shut up," Skull said, his voice a croak. "Viktor. They want Viktor."

Viktor said quickly, "I'm not. I'm not going out there."

"What are our options?" Skull asked.

"Are those more tunnels back there?" Viktor asked. "I thought I saw more tunnels."

"Yes," Skull whispered. "But it's like a maze."

"Let's go," said Viktor. "They could never find us then."

"Neither could we," said Skull. He thought he would rather face the Tunguska Man than get trapped and lost in a low, dark tunnel. "We'd get lost," he hissed. "Or stuck."

"Do we have a choice?"

"We could rush them," said Jon, seriously.

"Try to keep your voice down, Jon."

"There're three of us," Jon added.

"Seriously?" said Skull. "Rushing down the tunnel? With what? A couple of books as weapons?"

"Let's just wait. They may go," said Viktor, the hope clinging to the lift in his voice. "If we are quiet."

But a sharp clang, metal on metal, rolled up the tunnel towards them. It sounded close. They were at the base of the shaft.

"Fuck."

They all shrank a little further from the tunnel mouth. A light splashed around the curve of the tunnel sides, illuminating the gallery briefly with a warm, country cottage, hearth-side glow, sluicing the uneven walls with oily black cartoon shadows. A knot of voices floated down, unwelcome flotsam; Skull recognised immediately the tortured consonants, the contemptuous plosives of the Tunguska Man and Homo Habilis in conversation.

"Viktor, what are they saying?" he whispered.

Viktor paused, allowing a tick of disdain in his response: "It's not Russian. Serbian, maybe. Maybe Bosnian. I don't know what they're saying."

"Hoi!" Habilis again. The voice was close, intimate, inside the tunnel mouth. "Hoi. Morrell. You come now. OK? No shooting."

"Fuck."

"What do we do?" Skull felt his self-control sinking away through the gob of panic bubbling up. These men were killers; they would snuff his life as thoughtlessly as a boy stepping on a beetle, and here was the perfect killing place. Down here their bodies were already buried.

They wanted Viktor. He could give them Viktor, and he and Jon could leave, back to London, back to their old lives. But the brief moment of hope was soon swamped with reason: he couldn't give them Viktor, because if they killed Viktor they would have to kill them all.

"Hoi! You come now, Morrell."

But did they know there were three of them in here? They couldn't know that. If they thought Viktor was with them they would be calling for him. If he and Jon crawled out leaving Viktor in a tunnel perhaps they could talk their way out of it, pretend they were also trying to find Viktor. It was a risk. Skull shared his thinking ending, "So should I go out?"

"No," Viktor said. "They will cut your fingers off."

"What should we do then?" Skull was unable to hide the wave in his voice.

"We could try the side entrance," Jon suggested conversationally.

"What?" said Skull.

"We could try the side entrance."

"What side entrance?"

"The side entrance," Jon repeated as if everyone would know about it. "The tunnel which comes out on the side of the hill. That's where they usually started from when they were taking flint. It's where the rats come in."

"Fuck. Rats?"

"Morrell!"

Skull asked, "How d'you know about it?"

"They made a map last year. Uncle Daffy gave me a copy; in case I got lost."

"Where is it?" Skull asked.

"On the side of the hill."

"The map. Where's the map?"

"Oh, that. I lost it."

"Fuck."

"But I've been exploring."

"Exploring what?"

"Tunnels. I had a bit of time on my hands."

"D'you know the route?"

"I think so."

"You think so?" Jon's "Yeh" response, was more diffident than Skull would have liked. "Why didn't you tell us before?" Skull asked.

"Well ... it's a long way; and coming back is tricky. It's all up hill."

"We're not coming back."

"But what about my goods?"

"Shut up!" Viktor hissed.

The shot fired into the tunnel was sudden, shocking, violent, the sequence impossible to disentangle. Which came first? The quick white burst of light? Or the violent spatter of chalk shrapnel and dust scything around the gallery? Or was it the flat, drum-crack bang, a sound punch that ballooned over them, reverberating forever down the tunnels? Somewhere, someone bleated aloud; Skull wasn't sure that it wasn't him.

As the shattered chalk stones rolled to rest around them, and the pulsing echo ground out inside the hill, a deeper rumble rolled back. It had the quality of distant thunder.

"Ah. Rock fall," said Jon philosophically.

"Fuck."

Skull asked, "Is it safe? Can we still get out?"

"Oh yes," said Jon. "Happens all the time. It's quite dangerous."

"OK Morrell?" Habilis sounded cheerful, like a puppy asking to play. "You want again?"

Jon went first, Viktor followed with Jon's head torch tight around his forehead and with strict instruction to keep up with Jon. Skull brought up the rear, his thin LED torch light illuminating the soles of Viktor's shoes kicking away in front of him.

The relief of being active, of moving at last, soon gave way to anxiety. The tunnel from the gallery ran through the chalk where the seams of flint had been exploited, sometimes widening out, sometimes low and narrow. Jon lead them around chalk arches scored with the narrow chisel marks of ancient horn, over sharp flint and blocky chalk rubble, past modern metal scaffolding struts and wooden blocks propping up walls and ceilings. Sometimes they crawled — one behind the other — on hands and knees, sometimes crouching low, or lying flat and pulling with arms and knees outstretched. To Skull the direction seemed random but Jon seldom hesitated, picking his course deliberately.

For a while they could still hear the taunting calls, but they soon morphed into a distant bellowed invective bowling though the narrow passages, the words smudged, made indistinct, from bouncing; and once, the flat crack of another gunshot (or maybe two in quick succession) blasted over them, the sound cone felt as much as heard. They paused then, listening out for more rock falls, hearing only their quick, shallow breaths, and the rapid tapping of their own hearts. Quickly they moved on.

At last Jon stopped in a small chamber, smaller than the one he had lived in, but big enough for them all to sit upright together. The ceiling was robustly supported by a few wooden blocks resting on short stout beams.

"This is the bottom of another shaft," Jon said cheerily. "That's all backfill sitting above. It's probably the least safe place, but the going gets a bit tricky from here. There've been a few heavy falls since they cleared these tunnels for the photo projects. I'd lose the jacket if I were you," he said to Skull. "It gets quite narrow and drops down a bit. But we should be out soon after."

"Reminds me of basic training," said Viktor examining his shredded trouser legs and the bleeding knees beneath. "National service in the great army of Estonia was nearly as much fun, only more mud and less rocks."

Skull removed his jacket, folding it slowly before laying it aside. He wiped his glasses on a clean corner of his shirt.

"How far have we come, would you say?" he asked, playing for time, not wanting to move again.

Jon shrugged. "Miles. Ready?"

They moved on through the small chamber and soon it narrowed, the ceiling dropping sharply so that their low crawl became a cramped uncomfortable slither. It was not long before Skull's elbows were raw from scraping his body forward over sharp stones, his knees bruised and bloodied, his toes numb from lifting, thrusting, pushing; his back and shoulders ached, his neck drooped in the agony of holding his head upright, and his head hurt where it regularly clashed with the uneven lumps of chalk above and to the side. He wanted to stop but Viktor's legs kept worming forward. He knew he must keep them in sight.

At one time he thought he heard what might have been a yell, a cry of pain, but couldn't be sure because his own laboured panting filled his sound world along with the thump and scrape of Viktor's feet ahead of him. He wished they would stop.

The tunnel split; he followed the feet closely down the right-hand fork, squeezing over loose chalk blocks, around a jagged heap of flints, slithering down steep declines using both hands to stop himself from crashing into Viktor. The tunnel forked again, Viktor wriggling right and Skull allowed himself to worry that Viktor had lost touch with Jon and was now improvising. Were they going round in circles? What if they were going back to Jon's gallery? Or heading into a dead-end where they couldn't go back or turn around?

"Hold up!" Skull wept, but in the narrow tunnel blocked by bodies he doubted that his voice carried.

The pain was unbearable, time lost its beat. If he could pause a moment, if he could rest a second ... he redoubled his effort as Viktor's soles slid out of sight again. He focused on the narrow task of keeping a simple forward motion.

And then he was out — a sudden sweet chill, a cold damp breath, the musty smell of wet earth and rotting leaves, the muted rustle of sodden vegetation, creaking twigs, an open sound stage. Was that a distant bird cry? He allowed his head to droop onto the crook of his arm, closed his eyes as the muscles relaxed, his heavy head feeling suddenly light.

"Skull. You alright?" Jon shone his torch in Skull's face, swept it over a grimy Viktor blinking stupidly, then all around, illuminating a carpet of dead leaves and broken branches, mossy rocks and thin hardy trees.

Viktor said, "Shouldn't we switch our lights off?" but with all the torches off, they could see nothing. Skull put his on again.

They were in the scrubby wood clinging to the steep eastern side of Godwin Hill. There was no visible path, and the ground dropped away steeply, the trees and bushes thickening below them. The rain appeared to have stopped, although the stunted trees dripped steadily.

How long had it taken to exit the hill? Twenty minutes? Forty minutes? An hour? There was no way of knowing. His phone poked him uncomfortably in the bum but when he rose to extract it from his trouser pocket he became entangled in a low branch, slipped in his city shoes, made an ungainly recovery but dropped his torch and watched it briefly tumble down the slope and abruptly go dark.

"You'll never find that again," Viktor observed.

*

They made a slipping, stumbling progress around the side of the hill, keeping always within the cover of the wood. They used their torches sparingly, lacerating legs and feet on unseen sharp flints, fallen branches, sticks; while overhead, crooked-fingers from the stunted trees tore their heads and faces, threatening to pluck their eyes out.

At last they emerged from the tree-line where the hill folded into the saddle, and where the copse was divided from an open field by a wire fence. Skull argued that if anyone was waiting for them to return to their car, they would be looking towards the mine, not back down the road. So they scrambled over the fence and climbed to the top of the mound above the saddle, circling right until they intersected with the farm road on the far side. Here they turned left at last, moving towards where Gabby was parked.

Shortly after joining with the road Skull felt his phone vibrate, buzzing urgently some pointless notification in his trouser pocket. It came as a surprise until he realised that it meant they were close now, close enough for the phone to be picking up the wireless connection from Gabby.

They walked cautiously, keeping about twenty feet from the road as it crossed over the saddle. Every so often they paused to listen. Soon the ominous shape of the vehicles formed out of the dark, resolving into both car and van. Skull was disappointed. He had hoped the van would be gone.

A short distance off, not as close as a hundred feet but not much further, they squatted, studying the vehicles, shivering miserably. They were facing more or less side-on to Gabby; the van had been driven around the front so that the two vehicles faced each other at an oblique angle, which meant the van was pointing directly towards them where they hunched down in the field. There was a gap of maybe fifteen feet between the vehicles; both were dark, both silent.

"D'you think they're still up at the mine?" Skull whispered through chattering teeth. No one had an answer.

Jon stood up. He said, "Fuck it, I'm cold and I wanna go home." He walked down to the car, opened the front passenger door, climbed in, slammed the door shut.

"Fuck," said Viktor, but nothing happened. All Skull could think of was Jon's muddy, greasy clothes on the car's pristine upholstery.

"Maybe it's OK," Viktor said, his voice suffused with relief.

"Come on, then," said Skull. "We'd better hurry."

In the dark, as they started running towards the car, Skull slipped, rolled his foot on a wet stone, twisting his ankle painfully. He sprawled flat on his face. By the time he recovered, Viktor had made it all the way to the car, climbing quickly into the back seat, shutting the door.

Skull looked up cursing his luck. He watched the van lights flick on, the side doors open, and two figures step out. One, the Tunguska Man, waved a hand gun at Gabby's windscreen. The other, Habilis, jogged around the front to the passenger side, opened the rear door, reached in and dragged Viktor out.

Viktor protested loudly but Habilis man-handled him roughly towards the front, into the full glare of the van's headlights, kicking the back of his legs, pushing him down so he dropped to his knees. With the Tunguska Man waggling the gun at him, Jon opened the passenger door and climbed out, joining Viktor in the full wash of light from the van, kneeling down with his hands flat on his head.

Skull could hear the voices but couldn't understand the conversation. Viktor was doing most of the talking. Slowly Skull crawled backwards and sideways, staying low, gradually moving out of the direct beam of the van's headlights, although he doubted they would see him this far out.

Reaching into his coat, the Tunguska Man pulled out a scrap of paper, cardboard, perhaps a photograph. He studied the paper, showed it to Habilis who nodded, leering happily; he then held it out in front for Viktor to see. Viktor vigorously shook his head, arguing loudly again, talking quickly.

Skull wondered how long it would be before they figured out that he was missing and came looking for him; or before either Viktor or Jon revealed his presence. Once or twice he saw the Tunguska Man glancing out in the direction from which Jon and Viktor had come. Perhaps they wouldn't bother with him anyway. It was Viktor they wanted and now they had him.

At last outside the cone of light Skull rose slowly, leaning a little weight on his sprained right foot. He knew immediately that he would not be able to run very far very fast, putting a significant kink in the quick exit strategy he was formulating in which he ran for help.

Back at the van Jon, still kneeling obediently, suddenly lowered his arms, said something short and loud, and began to stand up. The Tunguska Man stepped forward and effortlessly kneed Jon in the head. Jon fell back like a tossed sack of sand. In that moment of distraction Viktor saw an opportunity and tried to make a run for it. He got as far as rising to one leg before the Tunguska Man side-swiped him on the head with the pistol butt, and Viktor fell sideways and forwards, then cowered with his hands over his head. Habilis, inspired perhaps by the blossoming of violence, casually kicked Jon as he lay on the ground, twice, shouting to rouse him. Jon's body shuddered with each kick, but otherwise did not respond.

It was a brutal theatre, hard to watch, the semi-mute action vivid in the bright spotlight that flooded the stage in front of the van, the monstrous shadows of the actors cast out onto the dark fields of Godwin Hill.

Skull extracted his smartphone from his back pocket, turning away from the drama in order to shield the screen light when he turned it on. He adjusted the brightness to a dull glow, bright enough to read but not so bright as to give his position away. He considered calling for help but doubted any would arrive in time.

Instead he opened up the SmartorPlus app, while at the same time he began a painful limp towards the farm track, staying outside the circle of light but inside the wireless range, keeping low, watching how the scene around the vehicles developed.

The Tunguska Man spat out a few harsh words and slowly Viktor rose from the ground, sat back on his knees. He raised his hands with effort, as if lifting a great weight, setting them flat on the top of his head once again, rubbing at his ear with his wrist. In the bright light even Skull could see the patch of blood on the side of Viktor's head. Viktor must have said something, perhaps raised some complaint, because the

Tunguska Man hit him again on the side of the head with the pistol butt. Viktor swung sideways again, falling forward onto his hands, crying out, but this time quickly returning to the kneeling position, hands raised up, head bent forward, eyes down.

The Tunguska Man spoke briefly to Habilis. Habilis shrugged, turning towards the mine, pointing at Gabby. The two men argued dispassionately, chewing their words like gristle. Were they discussing the practical details of execution or of torture? Skull was glad he couldn't understand.

As he hobbled in the dark across the track Skull saw that the app had now connected to the car and was reporting a status of "Ready". The app was never intended as a serious tool. It was a clever demo. He had only ever used it on the simulator, and once, briefly, on a test track.

Jon, on the ground, rolled slowly onto his front while Habilis continued prodding him with his foot, shouting at him. Jon raised himself to his knees once again, swaying wildly, head bowed.

In theory the SmartorPlus app had full access to all Gabby's drive functions. In theory he could drive the vehicle using the simple controls on the screen: buttons, slides and dials. In practice it was significantly more complicated because driving a vehicle traditionally uses four limbs plus in-vehicle eyes to give perspective, while a smartphone screen is only so big, the controls spread across a series of tabbed screens in addition to the problem of a static perspective, translating the turn of the wheel to the position of the car. Anyone who had ever driven a remote control buggy would understand the problem.

Skull's biggest problem were his fingers, numb with cold, and his hands, rigid with fear. Whatever he was going to do, digital subtlety with a dexterous touch was not going to be the key ingredient. Besides, he hadn't decided what he was going to do. He had the element of surprise, that was all. For now he was simply circling the action, working his way back down the farm track keeping out of view and trying not to sob loudly every time he put weight on his ankle.

The Tunguska Man held the pistol to Viktor's head. Viktor continued talking wildly. Skull knew he could wait no longer. On the SmartorPlus app he pressed the start button, heard the engine cough politely before settling into an expectant purr.

The Tunguska Man squatted quickly, a simple, automatic reflex, swinging the handgun two-handed towards Gabby. Habilis jumped with alarm before following the Tunguska Man's lead and dropping low. Both men cocked their heads to peer into the car's interior.

Problem was, Gabby was too close to the van. Skull couldn't power her forward to run the Tunguska Man down without also running over Jon and Viktor.

Skull flicked on the head lights to blind the mobsters so they couldn't see inside the car. On his feet he re-crossed the farm track so that he was on the same side of the track as the vehicles, fifty or so feet behind Gabby and the van. He had completed about 140 degrees of the circle around the vehicles.

The Tunguska Man rose like a cat now, moving sideways towards the driver's side, trying to see inside. He was cautious, circling left, gun straight out. He barked a few words at Habilis who ran around the back of Jon and Viktor, pushing them to the ground, standing menacingly over them.

Skull prodded his phone screen to select reverse gear, prodded again to apply a little acceleration. The electronic hand brake automatically disengaged and Gabby rolled back about five yards. This took the Tunguska Man by surprise. He stepped out in front, took three paces forward and fired two quick shots through the windscreen into the passenger side.

That seemed odd to Skull. Why not the driver's side? Perhaps the Tunguska Man was confused with right-hand English cars. Or perhaps he had seen no one in the driver seat and assumed the driver was controlling the car from the passenger seat.

It didn't matter now: the Tunguska Man was exactly where he wanted him, directly in front of Gabby. Skull's aching fingers fumbled the phone, selected Drive, mashed the accelerator slide bar again. Gabby leapt forward.

Not quick enough. The Tunguska Man threw himself to the right and Skull quickly applied the emergency brake before the car overran Jon. Habilis backed up quickly to the van, Viktor and Jon still on the ground crawled after him to get out the way. Skull rolled Gabby back to the earlier position.

The Tunguska Man recovered quickly. He was on the far side now, but back on his feet he stalked lightly towards the car again. Skull killed all lights before engaging reverse. He was close enough that he worried the reversing light would reveal him crouching a few feet in from the edge of the road.

As the Tunguska Man drew up to the car Skull reversed another five yards. The Tunguska Man advanced again, and again Skull reversed, this time adding a little spin on the wheel, turning Gabby gradually onto the road. This manoeuvre forced the Tunguska Man to run further around the outside in order to stay out of direct line. With each sporadic advance of the Tunguska Man, Skull reversed Gabby further, spinning the front wheels until at last she was on the road, backing down the track towards him.

He wasn't really sure what else he could do except bring Gabby to where he was on the side of the road. He thought that if he could get into the driver's seat he might be able to control the car with much greater finesse and run the man down. But the Tunguska Man was not going to fall for the same trick twice and made a quick dash across the front of the vehicle, too quick for Skull. Now they were both on the same side of the road.

Skull was not particularly confident of being able to reverse any great distance along the dirt road by remote control. The worst thing would be if the car left the road and got stuck in the field, so he reversed a little at a time, making micro adjustments and bringing Gabby towards him gradually. Inevitably it also brought the Tunguska Man nearer and Skull knew that soon the man would see him. Thirty feet, fifteen feet, five feet.

Skull flipped all lights on, headlights, emergency lights, interior lights. He thumbed down the car alarm switch, delivering a rimbombing cacophony to accompany the sudden illuminations. It was sufficient distraction for Skull to shuffle unseen, unheard, the short distance between him and the Tunguska Man.

For the Tunguska Man, curiosity beat caution and, after the sub-second surprise, he bent forward to peer into the bright interior of the car, puzzled still by who was in control of it.

From out of the dark, his hand a prehensile claw curled over the smooth casing of his smartphone, Skull smashed the edge of the phone down onto the side of the Tunguska Man's head. The phone came apart in Skull's fingers, and his fingers came apart from his hand as the force of the blow dislocated the middle and index fingers where they hooked over the stylishly thin bevelled edge of the phone. The Tunguska Man dropped where he stood, the gun slipping gently from his hand onto the muddy chalk-and-flint track.

Commanding Gabby to switch to voice control, Skull shut off the alarm, the flashing lights. He reached down and tried picking up the gun but his hand, numb and broken, failed to work, the knuckles grinding uselessly, painfully, as if grains of sand had worked into the joints. He lifted the gun in his left hand instead, holding it awkwardly forward, running back to the van to rescue Jon and Viktor.

There was no need for rescue. In the rampant light and noise of the self-driving car, Habilis had read defeat; perhaps he'd seen Skull's haggard form lurch from the shadows to brain the Tunguska Man from behind; perhaps he'd seen Skull bend and raise up the gun. Whatever his reasons, Habilis ran into the darkness.

Skull found Jon and Viktor huddled together beside the van, Jon slumped against the door staring out at the night. The fine, soaking rain had started again.

"I think I killed him," Skull said.

"Good," said Viktor distantly. He stood slowly, gathering himself.

Skull handed him the pistol. "You were in the army, weren't you?"

"Not by choice." Viktor held the gun like an unwanted baby, pushing it forward into the van headlights, noodling with the safety catch, forgetting which position was on or off. "Fuck," he said. Blood still oozed from the swollen cut over his ear where the Tunguska Man had hit him with the butt of the pistol, but when Skull tried to take a closer look he pushed him away: "It's fine" he said. "It's fine."

Skull held his own hand out, washing it with the light from the van. Now that he could see the deformed fingers properly he began to feel the urgency of the pain. The end bones of the middle finger lapped over the second knuckle, purple and lumpy, while the first knuckle of the index finger was already the size and colour of a small plum. He said, matter of fact, "I think my fingers are broken."

"Fuck," said Viktor squinting at the hand. "Dislocated, I think. You must pull it back into the right place."

Skull shook his head.

"Yes," Viktor insisted. "Before it gets really painful and stiff."

"It's really painful and stiff now," Skull insisted.

Viktor pushed the pistol into his jacket pocket and took hold of Skull's arm, pressing it firmly against his chest. He grasped the dislocated finger in his spare hand, pulling the middle finger as slowly and steadily as he could with his own wet, frozen fingers. Skull bellowed with the agony of it, but after the sensation of a soft plopping around the joint, the finger at least looked a little better, and Skull thought he could feel the pain easing slightly.

"You should bind it," Viktor said, picking up the gun again.

"We should go," Skull responded shakily. When he moved his fingers they hurt like hell but there was no more grinding in the joints.

They removed the keys from the van, which snuffed out the light, then stumbled over to where Gabby sat purring quietly on the road. Skull guided Jon gently into the passenger seat. That was when he noticed that the Tunguska Man no longer lay where he'd fallen on the side of the track.

"Fuck," said Viktor.

They left quickly.

*

In the car Jon was mute. Viktor wept quietly. Skull drove as fast as he dared, back up the dirt track onto the narrow country lane, joining the London road where he had left it only a few hours before; it seemed much longer than that.

Somewhere along the way they threw out the van keys and the dismantled parts of the pistol. Skull also paused briefly to tape, from the inside, the spider-web bullet holes in the windscreen, sealing the cab from a stream of cold air and rain but allowing the wiper blades to continue to function.

The traffic was light and fast now. He quickly settled into the rhythm of it, glad to have the distraction of driving, even if the swelling fingers of his right hand could not bend over the steering wheel, and his ankle sent sharp objections with each jab on the brake, each prod to the accelerator.

As the air con hushed and hummed boisterously, breathing out a sumptuous bone-warming heat, sucking away the steam that rose in tiny plumes from their muddy clothing, slowly their shivering subsided. Soon the smell became appalling. Gently roasting damp clothes, muddy clothes, old clothes, sweat, fear and Jon's homey body odours all contributed to the poisonous mix. The advanced dual-zone Climate Control System was entirely defeated and settled for merely stirring the toxic atmosphere, homogenising the several stinks into an old farty soup.

"How did they find us?" Skull asked, surprised by the sudden sound of his own voice.

"Heard us coming," Viktor said eventually.

After a long pause Skull tried again: "No, I mean, how did they track us? To the mine?"

"Oh. Two trackers," said Viktor. He spoke slowly, with gaps. "One front, one back. You only looked for one. The Kazakh told me. He thought it was a joke."

"Stupid," Skull said, then asked, "Which one was the Kazakh?"

"Genghis Khan. The man you killed. Or maybe didn't kill. He looked Kazakh to me. But ..." Viktor shrugged.

"I never met a Kazakh before," Jon piped up.

"What did they want?" Skull asked.

"Kill me, of course," Viktor said. "I told them there would be no more trouble but..." Again he shrugged. "They like the logic of violent death. It's not ambiguous."

Skull thought he would stop sometime soon to find and remove the second tracker, but he wanted a little more distance between himself and Godwin Hill. He had already decided to take Jon home to his father at Churnwell House rather than the empty flat in London. His own cold, dark home would not meet Jon's needs and he didn't know where Anka was staying and how to find her without his phone. All his personal numbers were on his phone. He could call using Gabby's connection but he couldn't remember any numbers.

"Jon, d'you know the Prof's number?" Skull asked, knowing they should call forward to warn the Professor they were coming. He wished he could call Jac, let her know that Jon was OK, that everything was going to be OK. That he was OK.

"Um," Jon considered. He recited a number which Skull tried, but it failed. "I think he changed it. I think he went ex-directory. New one's on Lucy."

"I found your phone, by the way," Skull told him.

"You found Lucy?"

"Why did you leave it in the wall? All charged and running. Very odd."

"Votive," said Jon. "A votive candle to the flame of progress. Did you bring her?"

"Anka took it. She took everything."

Jon nodded. He said, "She's lovely," adding wistfully, "I love her." Then with delight, "Oh! Oh, my tooth's tingling again." He shoved a grubby finger into his mouth.

"We'll get you to a dentist," said Skull. "Tomorrow. Bound to be an emergency dentist in Canterbury."

"No. No. My Bluetooth."

Viktor asked, "You have blue tooth?"

"I do. In my tooth," said Jon, pointing with his finger. "It's a Bluetooth tooth."

"Oh." Viktor was impressed. "You can eat with this blue tooth?"

"Absolutely. You can chew too with a blue two tooth," Jon said.

"Cool. I would like blue Bluetooth tooth."

"Then a blue two tooth to you too," giggled Jon.

It wasn't original, or even funny, but Skull began to chuckle because a chuckle erupted in his belly spontaneously and spread. Viktor joined, a low, guttural chortle. In the rear view mirror Skull could see Viktor's shoulders wobbling, his mouth valiantly suppressing his smile (his terrific, transforming smile) so that it would not stretch his painful, swollen face. For some reason this caused Skull to giggle all the more, which re-infected Jon with snickers, spreading once more to Viktor.

They were all laughing helplessly, a malodorous pocket of tittering madmen, as Gabby accelerated unexpectedly, swerved suddenly, skidded through the barrier, and tumbled down the embankment before a yew tree, ancient and solid, abruptly, fatally, halted the roll.

Spring

The library, facing south, was the warmest room in the house. Fat books, oak shelves and cracked leather chairs provided solid insulation from chilling draughts, and from the rustle of activity behind the oak door. The rest of the room was cosy but simple: a wooden mantle framed the stone hearth, a desk and chair posed beside a long sash window.

Beyond the library window the view resolved into a canvas of coloured shapes: a viridian triangle of trees; a trapezium meadow of yellows; a ploughed rhomboid of sienna, russet, ochre stripes; a crescent wood, jungle green and flecked with cinnabar, mint and myrtle, all held on the liver thread of a crooked road that wound through it. Above the land the shapes were less geometric, more random: a herd of grubby sheep washed away by a verdigris sea.

Dear Jacqueline, Skull wrote at the top of the page, the blue ink flowing smoothly from the fountain pen pinched stiffly between thumb and fingers, the nib rubbing over the heavy cream paper with an abrasive hiss. He looked down with distaste at the uneven scrawl, the jagged descender on the "q" of her name, the wobbling baseline. Something was missing, he felt. Old style hand-written correspondence needed more. He penned the date in the top right hand corner, and below that, *Churnwell House, Kent.* He looked again. Perhaps the address should come first. Whatever.

The view across the Downs is quite lovely at the moment, he wrote.

We await the imminent arrival of Anka. I'm dreading it. I don't know what to expect. It is only a flying visit since she is driving back home to Plovdiv in her new car, and is visiting us en-route to Dover. I doubt she'll be back in England for a while. I hope she will be able to post this to you, perhaps from the ferry. Otherwise it will have to wait until next week when the Prof goes to town.

In your last letter you asked if remembering things helped me at all, but I honestly don't remember much.

He remembered the sickening silence that followed the sigh of deflating airbags when his mind said something's-wrong-what's-wrong and his body said not-saying. He remembered the odd comfort from the warm smell of scorched engine oil.

Jon, staring at him, looked untroubled, his eyes wide, waiting for the question. Skull tried asking the question but his mouth refused and his tongue remained unvoiced. Jon didn't blink; his parted lips stayed parted, the riposte undelivered; his face, his head, unmoving, unaligned with his body.

I remember the lights. I remember the voices, but I passed out a lot. Even those early days in the hospital are mostly lost to me now. You buried Jon long before I knew he was dead. The thing I regret most is not remembering your visit. You said you sat at my bedside. Did you talk to me? I wish I knew what you said.

A second woman, he was told, had regularly sat with him, but she had also not returned when they raised him from his coma. Later there had been other visitors: a police man, a tax man, the insurance woman, someone from the Home Office, someone from the Smartor office. They all left with something — a statement, a signature, a fact; and when Skull had nothing left to give all the visits stopped. Except for the Professor, who brought with him grapes and hope.

The Prof continues to astonish with his kindness to me. He makes us meals, we play endless games of chess, watch TV together on the small set in the dining room. I can assure you that the sarcasms and snide comments are reserved for the doctors and nurses at the weekly clinic he drives me to. He is a bully when I forget to do my physio, and he nags me to take my medications. With summer almost upon us he is now threatening me with fresh vegetables from the garden, and long slow walks along the Downs. I am moving more now and manage short distances with the aid of a stout stick.

Skull had hobbled into the dining room just the other day and found the Professor's laptop open. He had quickly logged into Smartor using one of the hidden back-door accounts, rooted around the servers, found Gabby's logs, the diagnostic record of her final twenty four hours, the hours up to the crash.

Police investigators had accepted the version given by the new management at Smartor. They had testified that although registered to Smartor, the vehicle was not under their control or ownership at the time, had been illegally modified, and had clearly malfunctioned. They pointed to the evidence: the TwoCAN, the diagrams, the open-sourced algorithms, the smartphone app. The insurance company quickly concurred. Skull was liable. In the newspaper reports of the accident there were winks and nudges at the dumb irony of the accident: Not-So-Smart Car Crash, one headline had read.

But Skull knew all this was not true. His technology simply did not work in that way. There would need to be explicit instructions, direct interference to cause such an accident.

When he found the logs they were detailed and copious and, to process them properly, he would need a suite of tools he did not have. There was, however, a video recording from the smart airbag system installed in Gabby.

Ordinary dumb airbags killed passengers sometimes instead of saving them because the passenger was too small, too light or not in the right place when the bag explosively inflated. Gabby's smart airbag system provided an intelligent solution, using overhead mounted cameras and real-time image processing to continuously monitor the position of the vehicle's occupants. In an accident, a set of algorithms could instantly determine how the system should respond, deploying the correct airbags in the optimal way. A recording from that camera was dumped to disk.

Skull ran the monochrome recording several times, then sat quietly staring at the wall before running it once more in slow motion.

Here was the sudden acceleration of the vehicle, evident as everyone is pushed back into their seat. Except Jon's seat also slides forward, the backrest rising to tip him towards the dashboard. The small rear airbag deploys, pushing his head and body forward. The side bag deploys, pushing his head sideways. Very soon after that, the main dashboard airbag blooms, exploding against his head, the head that has been forced forward, the head that has been pushed to the side and now lies in the worst possible position to receive the expanding force of gasses.

Jon is already dead when the car hits the barrier. Skull's airbags open correctly. The video shows clearly that it is the long roll, the steering wheel, and the tree that deal him the damage he now suffers. In the back Viktor fares best, the side bags puffing out, his seatbelt holding him firm. Viktor is still in his seat when the car hits the tree, at which point the recording ends abruptly.

Jon's neck was broken before the car skidded sideways, before the other airbags blossomed. The smart airbag algorithms were designed to save lives, not end them, but the video shows Jon's life is deliberately ended: immediate cessation.

But that didn't make sense. Viktor had been adamant: all Jon's goals had been deleted, all the threads expired. There were no further threats to Jon. There was of course the anomaly of the other user of the Lucy Phone, but that could only have been Deepak, whose goals had expired. It didn't make sense.

I was thinking of that walk we once took through the pine forest, past the water tower and down to the field with the horses. You probably don't remember it, back when I stayed with you that summer. Jon had gone out for some reason (a music lesson, dentist appointment? I don't recall), and you wanted to go for a walk so we went.

While we stood on the gate watching the horses chewing you asked me what I thought was real. I knew it was a trick question but I answered you honestly. I said all the things you could touch and see and smell were real. You said give me an example and I wanted to say YOU, but I chickened out: I said trees, clouds, stones, stuff like that. You had the grace not to laugh at me but you told me that we make our own reality. You explained it all to me and I knew it was some deep philosophical thing but I didn't get it. Then you said, we make ourselves. I don't know why that struck such a chord with me, but I've always remembered that. We make ourselves.

I was thinking of it now because from here in the library I can see the path we took across to the forest. I remember I told you a joke and you didn't laugh because it was funny only to adolescent boys, you said. I tried so hard to make you smile. You have such a lovely smile. I know you don't want me to say that but you do.

When he re-read the last paragraph it seemed too much. If he crossed it out he would have to start the whole letter again and there would be no time to finish it so he let it stand.

He laid down the pen and slowly flexed the fingers of his right hand, relieving the ache only a little. He looked again across the Downs through the narrow window. The old panes were thicker at their base where the glass had flowed over the years. If he moved his head the entire landscape re-arranged itself, mixing up the palette, laying down new shapes.

I wish you would change your mind about visiting this summer. Other than the Prof, you are my only friend now, although Mr Beavis is steadily making his way onto my Christmas card list. He regularly intercepts my post at the old flat and forwards it on, including a wide selection of the local fast food menus. You should know that there is a particularly good deal on the 6 inch spicy Pizza (two for the price of one!) which is excellent value and, while not traditional Italian fare, I heartily recommend it next time you are in London.

Nobody knew about Viktor. He was not on the list of casualties from the accident, didn't seem to exist. When Skull asked, "What happened to the other man? What happened to Viktor?" the doctors had sent him for further brain scans. Skull had almost come to doubt Viktor's existence himself, but a couple of weeks ago, among the junk mail forwarded by Mr Beavis, was a postcard. The image was a monochrome photograph of a dramatic sculpture: "Hercules slaying the Hydra". On the back it said simply "Plan E." The postmark was Riga, Latvia.

Outside on the gravel driveway at the front of the house Skull heard a car drawing to a slow, crunchy halt. He heard a door slam, the doorbell and, after a short pause, voices.

Anka had not been among the visitors at the hospital, neither during nor after the coma. Skull had sent her a note long after: sorry for your loss, you were a beacon of hope for Jon, let us not lose touch. Eventually she replied, I don't want to see you, you killed my life, now I have nothing, hope you have some pain, words to that effect.

Anka has arrived so I had better finish off. Please give my regards to Berto and Paolo. By the way, I have now gathered all the pieces of Jon's wooden train set in a box. I will continue to nag the Prof until he takes it to the post office for Paolo.

Affectionately, Skull? With all my love? Yours?

Anka was the sole beneficiary of Jon's estate which included a modest life insurance policy, a well provisioned investment portfolio, some property, and, surprisingly, controlling ownership of a few catering firms. She sold the shares and the property, including the flat in Docklands. Then she rolled the catering companies in with her sandwich making business and sold that too, realising substantially more than the firms were individually worth. Now she was going back to Bulgaria, a very wealthy woman.

The voices bubbling outside the library door rose and fell, the low timbre of the Professor carrying more distinctly than Anka's breathy girl-tones. Skull folded up his letter listening for animosities, hearing none. He slid the letter into an envelope, addressed it and added a stamp from the stamp box. Finally the voices ceased, the door handle turned, the door hinge creaked.

"Skull?" She stood in the crack of the doorway, her brow a crease of uncertainty, her eye-paint smudged from dabbing tears. Skull smiled.

"Oh, Skull." Crossing on quick, short steps towards him, she said, "Don't stand up."

Skull raised himself effortfully, met her half way up, brushed cheeks. They sat side-by-side on the worn library sofa.

"You are walking. That is really good," she beamed. "Really good."

She carried the look, the accessories, and the fragrance of a woman with brands. It was lost on Skull for whom a swoosh, a chomped apple, and a pair of hanging quinces, comprised almost the full extent of his knowledge. He did note her hair though, styled and plump with vitality, just like the adverts. Her lips, a glossy bright red, offset the sparkle in her blue eyes, the blue stone around her neck, the delicate blue of the smart eye-wear. She had lost weight he thought, but perhaps it was simply that she had lost the weight of necessity, the burden of expedience and bustle. Anyway, she seemed somehow lighter.

He asked after her and she told him all the news that was now not news to him, but he listened with interest and interjected all the right noises in all the right places. Soon she relaxed and it was as if they were old friends. Softly they spoke of Jon, of things they missed, of future plans and prospects hoped for. There were no sides to Anka, he remembered.

"Professor says I cannot stay long. You will get tired."

"I'm fine. I'm very pleased to see you, Anka."

"But I am late for ferry." Their eyes met with genuine warmth. "Oh. I nearly forget. I have something for you." She opened her handbag (stamped Prada he noted, remembering, and adding the name to the set of "Brands I Know").

From the bag she drew a familiar red object. "I think Jon would like you to have it," she said, handing him the Lucy phone.

Of all the things.

"What happened to the box?" he asked. "Remember the box? The box in the wall? What happened to that?"

"Oh that," she laughed, her small white teeth flashing brightly in a way that reminded Skull of his own smile. "That was old rubbish, boy's things — stones, shells. I threw out. I gave letters to the Professor. They are lovely sad letters from Jon's mother."

"But the compo tin opener? The little can opener? You didn't throw that away, did you?" He was surprised at his own intensity, the urgency in his voice.

"Tin opener?" she frowned, alarmed.

"Yes. A little metal tin opener." He raised his hand, showing the approximate size of the tool between his thumb and bent index finger. "It was actually mine," he added.

"I don't remember," she laughed. "Why do you need this old tin can opener? Does Professor not feed you?"

Skull laughed back. "It's not important. I wondered what happened to it, is all."

"I will send you nice electric can opener when I get home," she patted him on the knee. "But you must use Lucy."

"I don't use a phone much these days," Skull said, adding, "No one to call. You keep it."

"I don't need it," she said, waving the elegant curved smart watch on her wrist, adjusting her smart eye-wear. She looked happy, satisfied, but then suddenly she frowned, puckering her eyebrows, looking grave. "I was very angry with you Skull. I didn't want to speak to you because —." Her eyes moistened at the memory of her anger.

After a moment to recompose herself she continued: "Remember you found Lucy in the wall, with the box. I thought maybe there was a message from Jon, or maybe a message how to find him on Lucy but I couldn't find the password. I pressed buttons, shouted, shook phone, and then she says, Make a wish, Anka. So. First I make a wish to find Jon. That was a good wish. And also for me, I make a wish to be millionaire; before I am thirty five — there is time limit, you know," she explained.

Skull nodded so she went on. "Both wishes come true. First, you found Jon, and then ... well. I thought you killed him with your stupid car. So. I was really angry. But now, after he is dead, now I am millionaire. My birthday is next week." She beamed, squeezing his arm before she added. "So my wish came true. I don't need Lucy now. It's yours. Make a wish, Skull. Jon would like that."

He didn't notice when she whispered "Goodbye Skull", kissed him lightly on the forehead, left. He sat a long time staring at the phone cupped comfortably in his hand, the deep voluptuous redness of it, the seductive curves, the sensual edges, the lubricious finish. He tapped it softly and it gave a suggestive shudder, buzzed a low contented sigh. The screen flashed briefly, flickered ...

Hi Matthew Morrell. Set a goal.

Author's Note

The Flint Mines of Sussex

The flint mines of Godwin Hill are entirely fictional, although readers steeped in the history of prehistoric flint mining in the UK may well recognise some archaeological as well as geographic similarities with Harrow Hill, Sussex. Such a comparison is well justified since I started with Harrow Hill before deciding that I needed more fictional leeway than it was reasonable to demand of the well-studied site at Harrow Hill.

A rich concentration of ancient flint mines lies along the South Downs of Sussex, stretching from the Cissbury Ring near Findon to East Horsley. Harrow Hill, on the western side of this cluster, boasts a possible 245 shafts and pits dug to exploit the seams of flint. Radiocarbon dating carried out in the 1980s on charcoal and antlers, indicate that mining activity was taking place around 3000 BC. At the top of the hill is a bronze age enclosure along with some evidence of Roman occupation.

Sneakers

Werner Brandes is, of course, the character played by Stephen Tobolowsky in the 1992 Universal Studios film *Sneakers*. The film included Robert Redford among an all-star cast, and floated the idea that the NSA might be interested in spying on American citizens.

Joel Mentmore

January 2016

London

www.ingramcontent.com/pod-product-compliance
Lightning Source LLC
Chambersburg PA
CBHW031213120726

47905CB00002B/318